"What the hell was that all about?" Theresa asked.

"Oh, the usual. Boss refuses to give you the tools you need to do the job, then leans on you to get the job done faster anyway."

Theresa sat down. "The magistrate denied the warrant?" Benson nodded. "Still think my theory about someone protecting him is crazy?"

Benson put his arms behind his head. "Interference from on high is looking more likely, but how does this help us find him?"

"Maybe we're not meant to."

Benson stood up. "Well, then they're going to be disappointed." He pushed past her on his way to the door.

"Going to go shoulder check the truth out of someone?"

"My job is a little more subtle these days."

"You're not a subtle man."

"I know," Benson shrugged. "It's a real problem."

PATRICK S TOMLINSON

THE ARK

ANGRY
ROBOT

ANGRY ROBOT
An imprint of Watkins Media Ltd

Lace Market House,
54-56 High Pavement,
Nottingham,
NG1 1HW
UK

angryrobotbooks.com
twitter.com/angryrobotbooks
Never go home again

An Angry Robot paperback original 2015

Cover by Larry Rostant
Set in Meridien by Epub Services

Distributed in the United States by Random House, Inc., New York.

ISBN 978 0 85766 484 6
Ebook ISBN 978 0 85766 485 3

Printed in the United States of America

9 8 7 6 5 4 3 2 1

*This novel is dedicated to Annabelle,
in the hopes she too finds her way home.*

CHAPTER ONE

The call came mere seconds before push-off of Game Four in the last Zero Finals ever played.

Bryan Benson took the call, not that he had much choice. The crew had command access over his implant, they could open the call without ringing. But over the generations, the benevolent autocrats had learned that little courtesies went a long way.

<This had better be good.>

<I'm sorry, detective. Am I interrupting?> It was First Officer Chao Feng's voice, or at least the voice he'd picked for plant conversations. Normally, the difference between a person's plant voice and their real voice could be chalked up to the slight difference between the voice they heard inside their head, and how they sounded speaking to everyone else. But that couldn't account for the difference between the mezzo-soprano of his real voice and the baritone Benson heard.

Detective Benson leaned back and crossed his arms, certain at least one of the stadium's cameras was watching. <You know you are. It's ten seconds to push-off.>

<Yes, I know. But your beloved Mustangs already forced Game Five.>

    <Spoken like a true Zero fan.>

    <Fans still have jobs, detective, which is why I called.
We have a situation that demands your immediate
attention.>

    <Yeah, what's that?>

    <We have a missing crewman.>

    Benson hoped the cameras caught his eyes rolling.
They certainly had the resolution for it. <I'm no tech, but
I'd suggest you ping his plant for a location. Case closed.>

    Each team floated into position at the far walls of the
Can while their captains shouted last-second formation
tweaks. The goalies swung out from their goal rings to
clear the way for the arrows waiting on the other side. The
crowd roared in anticipation of the whistle, while Benson
scrutinized the Mustangs' new umbrella formation,
only a season old. It was a ballsy way to start, but team
captain Sahni was no fool. His team was explosive, but
had trouble flying down the stretch. They needed to start
taking points off the board straight away. Zero wasn't
scored like old Earth sports. Each team started at forty
points. Whichever team reached zero first, won.

    Lau, the Yaoguais' captain, settled on a more
conservative formation called the "Great Wall." It
deserved the name. It made life hell for any fliers trying
to pierce the three staggered rows of five, four, and five.
But with the wingspan of an albatross and its endurance
to boot, those damned Kenyans at the corners were the
real problem. How that little community had managed to
avoid inbreeding markers over the last ten generations
was a matter of heated debate among Zero aficionados.

    <Detective? Did you hear me?> Feng said.

    Tuning out other people's conversations was one

thing, but ignoring voices in your head was a different skill entirely. After almost fifteen years on the beat with domestic disturbances, conservation violations, and even the occasional legitimate crime clogging up his inner monologue, Benson had learned.

<Sorry, Feng, they're forming up for the whistle.>

<Of course. I didn't mean to interrupt your sporting event with something as trivial as the fate of a human being.>

Benson gritted his teeth as the referee's whistle blew. The arrows leapt off toward the ball suspended in the middle of the Can.

<Repeat your last.> Benson managed not to mentally swear at the man on the other end of the link. Also a learned behavior.

<I *said*, we wouldn't be bothering you if we hadn't already pinged his plant. There was no response. He's off the grid.>

That got Bryan's attention. You couldn't just turn off your plant. It was a synthetic neural network blanketing the surface of the frontal lobe like a thin film of plastic wrap, eavesdropping on the brain's higher functions and linking to the ship's network. The brain's own bioelectrical impulses powered it, including its organic wireless transceiver.

<What's his name?>

<Edmond.>

<Edmond...> Benson waited.

<Laraby,> Feng answered after a pause. <Edmond Laraby. I'm sending over his file now. Short story is he works in the bio-labs. Director da Silva very much needs him back at his beakers.>

Laraby's name didn't ring any bells. But da Silva had been directing bio research for almost fifteen years. She was a powerful woman. Best to stay on her good side.

<How long's he been missing?>

<We lost his plant feed at 21.36 yesterday evening.>

Benson bristled. <That's almost twenty hours ago. Why are you only calling me now?>

The line paused. Benson stole a glance at the game. Vasquez, the Mustangs' arrow, reached the ball first, just as she'd done reliably all season. She snatched it up and passed it back to Lindqvist, their newest strong forward, but then the Mustangs' umbrella formation ran straight into the Great Wall and did as much damage as one would expect a fabric canopy to do against several thousand kilometers of masonry.

Officer Feng returned to the conversation. <The Loss-of-Signal alert glitched. No one noticed he was missing until he didn't show up for work.>

<Lots of things glitching lately.>

<Well, our grand old lady *is* coming up on two hundred and thirty. Anyway, Director da Silva tried to raise him, then called us. Now I'm calling you.>

<All right, I get it. It's nobody's fault.> *Or responsibility*, Benson thought. *Funny how often that happens*. <It's just better on my end to get started as soon as possible.>

<So you can have the case wrapped up before push-off tomorrow?>

<That's the plan.> Benson leaned back and watched as one of the Yaoguai miraculously stripped the ball from Lindqvist's vice grip for the game's first turnover, then hurtled it at the back wall for a five-point bouncer. Benson's guts tightened up as the ball bounced in for the

first score of the game, but the thrower misjudged the angle and sent it right into the Mustang goalie's gloves.

Oh, thank God.

<Detective?>

<Yes?>

<As you pointed out, time is of the essence if you're going to find Mr Laraby before we decelerate for Tau Ceti. It's very important he get back to work. The bio labs are already under a great deal of stress.>

That was polite floater-speak for, "Do your fucking job, already." Benson scowled as he unfastened his seatbelt. <Ten-Four, Benson out.> He cut the link, then glanced around the skybox at the other members of the Two-Eighteen PE Zero Champion Mustangs and gave an apologetic "giving up" shrug, then glided for the exit.

Detective Benson drifted through the lock that separated the stadium from his home module of Avalon and pushed the button for the lift. He called up the duty officer. Lieutenant Theresa Alexopoulos picked up the link. <If you're calling from your posh skybox to apologize for making me work during the game, you can forget it.>

Benson smirked. <We're in the same boat now, Esa. Got a case to open, a missing person.>

<A what?>

<You know, a person who can't be found?>

He could almost hear her eyes rolling through the plant link. <I *know* what a 'Missing Person' is, Bryan. It's how someone goes missing I'm having trouble with.>

<His plant is off the grid and he didn't show up for work. That's how.>

<Hmm. A Mad Hatter?>

<That's my guess. I'm sending you his file now. Put out

an APB and run a facial recognition search of the transit cameras and locks starting at 21.00 yesterday.>

<By your command, captain.>

Benson smiled. The honorific was an old one between them. The Ark PD didn't have captains, per se. The highest rank the police could achieve was chief constable, a title Benson shared with Chief Bahadur, his opposite in the Shangri-La module. Captain was a leftover from his days leading the Mustangs to their first championship in twenty-three years.

The lift doors opened and disgorged a dozen tardy, inebriated Zero fans donning Mustang jerseys and giant foam cheese wedges on their heads. No one could remember where that particular tradition had started, but it was as sacrosanct to Mustang fans, exactly none of whom had ever tasted real cheese, as halftime fireworks were to Yaoguai fans. The environmental system techs *hated* Yaoguai fans.

There'd been an uptick in the number of public intoxication incidents following the year-long countdown to the Flip. It made the crew nervous, but Benson had instructed his constables to show leniency. Humanity had been through a lot in the three centuries since the black hole they'd named Nibiru appeared at the edge of the solar system. Another fundamental shift approached in just two weeks. It was an exciting, stressful time. As coping strategies went, over-indulging in bathtub hooch was fairly harmless.

The group of Mustang backers greeted him in the usual game-day fashion, all cheering and poorly-aimed high-fives. Benson accepted their enthusiasm graciously and took the time to shake every hand while his plant flashed their profiles at the top right corner of his field of vision, peeking to see if any of them had outstanding fines or had fallen behind on community service hours.

Everyone checked out clean. It helped to maintain the image of beloved sport hero when it came time to start asking the hard questions. Indeed, he suspected it was a major reason he'd been offered the promotion to chief so soon after retiring from Zero.

Benson floated inside the empty lift. A perfectly round car spun gently around him, except for a flat panel that denoted the floor. Still weightless, he oriented himself and tucked his feet into a pair of straps. The back wall of the lift was a single, uninterrupted dome of glass, gracing its passengers with a grand view of the entire module. Benson had long ago become numb to the vista's grandeur. Instead, he hit the button for Spoke Fifteen and waited. The car rotated until it was lined up with the proper tracks, then lurched downward.

"Down" was a relative term inside a two kilometer long cylinder where centripetal force provided the gravity. As the car moved away from the center of the module, the apparent gravity increased. Benson felt weight begin to press against the soles of his feet, only a fraction at first, but it grew steadily.

Light exploded through the window. A pillar ran like an axle down the entire span of the Avalon module, as it did through Shangri-La, Avalon's twin on the other side of the stadium. More bulbs than could be counted ran the length of the pillar, bathing the entire habitat in artificial daylight for twelve hours before shutting down and sending the power to Shangri-La's pillar to do the same. Twenty people worked to replace the bulbs that burned out each day.

The lights of Avalon shone on twenty-five thousand people. Its blocky earth-tone buildings, snaking green parks, trellis hydroponic farms, and shimmering blue lake was home to fully half of humanity. But Benson's thoughts hovered around a single man. *Where have you run to, my little lamb?*

Odds were good that Laraby was still somewhere inside Avalon. Transfer points between the Ark's half-dozen modules made for natural bottlenecks. Anyone traveling between them would be picked up by the surveillance net. But the mystery of how he'd gone off grid in the first place remained. Only a few good ways to block a plant from the ship's wireless network existed. Over the decades, people had tried everything. Jammers and scramblers blocked data transmission, but their signals were easily triangulated.

One of the only effective ways happened to be the headgear of choice for the discerning crackpot for centuries. Enough layers of aluminum foil wrapped around a person's head would do the trick, although it made blending into a crowd problematic. Shiny side in or out didn't seem to make any difference. Constables called them "Mad Hatters," although it had been several years since he'd dealt with one.

One other way existed. A few meters of water was enough to block the signal. The memory of pulling a girl no more than six from the water sent a shiver through Benson's body.

<Esa. Let the rescue diver know we may need him.>

<You think our boy went skinnydipping?>

<I don't know, but there's only so many possibilities.>

<Understood.>

As the lift reached bottom, Benson's frame reached its

full weight of ninety-two kilos. Four more than when he'd hung up his jersey five years earlier, but nobody gave him guff about hoarding calories. He wore it along with a lot of lean muscle he maintained in the gym and with a morning run around the habitat. Some habits died hard.

<Esa, what was our boy's job?>

<You have his file, can't you look it up?>

<I'm walking, you know I won't.>

<Luddite,> she teased. <Give me a minute.>

Laraby's file was waiting for him in Benson's plant. He could have read it himself using the augmented reality interface plugged into his visual cortex, but Benson preferred reading things the old-fashioned way: on a proper tablet screen held in his hands. The fewer things cluttering up his head, the better. Walking through the habitat, passing by people staring blankly into the distance for awkwardly long stretches, he knew his was the minority position, but some battles were worth fighting to the bitter end.

Theresa returned. <OK. File says he was a bio-forming geneticist working on crop alterations and terraforming models for the colony.>

Benson's eyes widened. He'd assumed Laraby was an assistant or a lab tech, not a fully-fledged geneticist. The success or failure of the new colony literally rested on their efforts to adapt Earth plants to their new home. Now he understood why Feng and Director da Silva were in such a rush to get him back on the job.

<He's mission critical. What's he doing off the grid?>

<You're the detective. Figure it out.>

<Have you put yourself in for a demotion recently, Lt Alexopoulos?>

<When I'm next in line for your job?>

Benson smiled. He and Theresa had a healthy professional disrespect for each other, which made their time off the job all the more interesting.

<Dinner tomorrow?> Benson asked.

<Only if you spring for fish.>

His shoulders sagged. <Come on, you know I hate that small-plate stuff. It's expensive and I'm never full.>

<There's less than two weeks left before we Flip the ship. What else are you going to spend it on?>

<I think you're overestimating a detective's salary.>

<Do you really think I haven't seen your pay scale? Make the reservations, Zero Hero.>

Benson growled under his breath. <Fine, it's a date. Have you put out that APB yet?>

<Yes, and all the duty officers have acknowledged it already. Your Hatter isn't sneaking through a lock tonight.>

<Good. Send someone to cover his apartment for the rest of the day in case he doubles back. Tell them to be discreet.>

<Everyone is already upstairs covering the game.>

<So?> Benson said, with more than a little annoyance. <Nothing is going to be decided today. The fans will hold their fire until tomorrow at the earliest. What's the score, by the way?>

<Mustangs up by three.>

<Shit.>

CHAPTER TWO

Someone else was living in Laraby's apartment. The young lady said she'd moved in less than a month ago, but somehow the transfer hadn't updated in the housing records. She gave Laraby's forwarding address and wished him luck. The new address was a few minutes' walk, further from Avalon's rear bulkhead in the more exclusive suburbs. The buildings in the area were modeled after a small French hamlet. He updated Theresa back at the stationhouse and asked her to reroute whoever she'd sent as backup.

Benson met the constable he'd requested walking up to the second apartment's door. The young man stood in the doorway at parade ground attention, in full uniform. As discreet as a clown at a funeral. He threw a crisp salute.

"Good morning, detective."

Benson gave a half-hearted salute in reply. "What are you doing here, son?"

Confused, the constable stuttered an answer. "Well, I, um. Lt Alexopoulos asked me to come here and watch this apartment, sir."

Benson shook his head. "No, what are you doing *here*? You're supposed to be watching to see if he comes back, not standing here stiff as a statue where he can see you from a hundred meters away."

Recognition slowly dawned across the constable's face. "Oh. Oooh, right. Sorry, detective."

"Go change into plain clothes. Then hide in that grove of trees over there. Bring a pad with you. Try to look like you're reading or watching a vid. If anyone comes into or out of this place who isn't me, call it in immediately."

"Yes, sir!" The constable ran off. Benson rubbed his temples. It wasn't his fault, really. A whole new crop of recruits had just finished training not even a week before. With Tau Ceti G so close, the population was getting restless. Mostly, it was positive. People were energized, focused on the immense amount of preparation work to be done before the Flip. But with the end of the voyage in sight, many citizens were becoming pretty lax in their adherence to the Codes of Conservation that had kept the last sliver of mankind alive for nearly two and a half centuries.

The rash of drunk and disorderly incidents had been joined by a near riot over in Shangri-La as people brought home-made fishing poles to one of the hydroponics reclamation lakes. He'd even broken up one honest-to-goodness doomsday cult. Granted, it was a cult of three people, but still. The stress was taking its toll on law and order after more than two centuries living in a fishbowl.

Benson leaned over to the intercom next to Laraby's door and pressed the thumb scanner. "Detective Bryan Benson, declaring an emergency override."

The scanner beeped and the deadbolt whirred open. Benson twisted the door handle and swept into the apartment. The lights responded to his presence.

Benson whistled softly. The room was at least twice the size of his own, with spiral stairs off in the corner leading to another level. It had a full kitchen, complete with breakfast bar. The walls were adorned with artwork, much of it framed with what looked like genuine wood. It even had an antique reading chair over in one corner.

It wasn't an apartment, it was a proper house. The perks of being part of the crew.

"Mr Laraby?" Benson walked gently across the bamboo floor. The staircase was wrought iron, another piece of unexpected decadence. Eighteen steps later and he reached the bedroom. The lights came on as soon as his foot hit the carpet. Carpet! The most he'd ever had was a small area rug. Which was fine, because the area it covered wasn't much bigger. He fought the urge to take off his shoes and rub his bare feet against the luxury as he surveyed the room.

The queen-sized bed was empty, its silky sheets tucked into tight hospital corners. The entire apartment looked like a team of maids had spent the week scrubbing it down to the last square centimeter. A quick glance in the master bathroom revealed Edmond hadn't drowned himself in the claw-foot bathtub.

"Unbelievable," Benson muttered. He'd only gotten an apartment with a stand-up shower with his last promotion. The rest of the cattle had to make do with sonic showers and UV sterilizers.

Cattle. Although most citizens had never heard them say it, Benson's position as chief constable meant he dealt with crew members on a daily basis. He knew what they called the ninety-eight percent of humanity not fortunate enough to be one of them. Just cattle to be shipped twelve lightyears across space, valuable only for the genetic diversity and physical labor they'd provide to the Tau Ceti G colony. Never mind that every last person on board the Ark was a direct descendant of the fifty thousand smartest, strongest, healthiest people among the ten billion living on Earth when the end came.

Of course, everybody knew the cattle's name for their crew: floaters, because they spent most of their time in microgravity in the command and engineering modules, and because of the ever-annoying turd that was too full of fat to flush properly.

Between the two slurs, Benson always thought floater was the cleverer.

As he walked back to the stairs, he spotted a tablet and grabbed it. The bedroom light clicked off automatically, while the living room lights anticipated him. He crossed the living room and plopped into the reading chair. He ran a hand over the armrest, and, while he couldn't be sure without bringing in the museum curator, Benson bet it was genuine leather.

He logged into the tablet with a thumb, which brought up his familiar desktop screen, complete with the background of his Championship team picture taken just minutes after they came back to beat the Dervishes.

Emergency powers only went so far. He could enter Laraby's apartment to make sure he wasn't inside, but without a warrant, Benson wouldn't be reading any of Laraby's emails, journals, or other private files. That didn't stop him from reading the man's personnel file saved on his plant, however.

What he read was the story of a handsome, twenty-four year-old man who kept out of trouble by keeping to himself. He was well-liked by his superiors, competent, and respected by his coworkers. He'd not missed a day of work in more than three years, had never had a disciplinary mark against his record, and had been promoted several years faster than the usual career track.

In short, the opposite of someone you'd expect to go missing.

He moved on to Laraby's next-of-kin, of which there weren't any. He had no declared relationship, no siblings, and his parents had already been added to the Clock.

Benson stood to wander around the apartment again, trying to get a feel for the man. Just like the bedroom above, the living room and kitchen were spotless. Not just clean, but sterile. It looked like a display model, as if no one actually lived in it yet. Either Laraby was a compulsive cleaner, or someone came in after he went missing and wiped down the scene. Suddenly the twenty hour delay between Edmond dropping off the grid and Benson getting the call seemed less innocent.

One of the walls in the living room had the slight sheen of a painted OLED surface. Benson activated it, and watched as a loop of images scrolled past. They were stock images of the surface of Tau Ceti G, taken from the Pathfinder probe.

Pathfinder had entered orbit around Tau Ceti G nearly two years ago. It was an unmanned, scaled-down prototype for many of the Ark's systems, as well as a test-bed for the sorts of large-scale, orbital construction methods needed to build them both. Once her shakedown cruise was over, Pathfinder was refueled and loaded up with dozens of communications, mapping, and GPS satellites, as well as atmospheric probes, rovers, and drones.

Launched ahead of the Ark, Pathfinder spent two centuries acting as an early-warning platform mapping stellar debris and dust in the larger ship's course. But since reaching orbit, its mission changed to launching drones and rovers to study the surface in great detail, and set up a global communications network that would be in place the moment the first colonists touched down.

But most importantly, Pathfinder carried a spool of carbon-nanotube ribbon many tens of thousands of kilometers long. Once the Ark arrived and a small colony was established on the surface, the Ark would be moved out to geosynchronous orbit and become a space station for the planet's first space elevator, with Pathfinder some ten thousand kilometers further up the well acting as the counterweight.

New images of humanity's foster home taken from Pathfinder and her network of dirtside landers were uploaded almost daily to the net and ravenously consumed, studied, and debated by the public. If Zero had any competition as the Ark's favorite pastime, it had to be arguing over pictures of their soon-to-be-world.

It was no surprise Laraby would want to display the images in his home, considering he was part of the team working to adapt Earth crops to the new environment. If the loop of images held anything unusual, it was the number of orbital pictures of the Dark Continent, so-called because of a persistent cyclone storm that covered most of the landmass. One of Pathfinder's landers had been sent to get direct imaging, but an unlucky lightning strike had triggered its airfoil to deploy while it was still supersonic, shredding it like tissue paper. The lander and all of its drones and rovers augered into the ground at several hundred kilometer per hour.

As a result, almost nothing was known about Tau Ceti G's third largest landmass aside from what could be learned from orbital radar scans. It was an enticing mystery that had spawned endless speculation.

Benson turned the wall off and moved on. The art prints were largely reproductions of classical paintings, some religious in nature, some still lives, and a familiar looking painting of a pair of haystacks that, unlike the others, had its own spotlight. When he leaned in closer, Benson noticed the texture of fine brush strokes behind the glass.

"This isn't a reproduction?" He held up the tablet in his hands and snapped a picture, then ran a search. The results came back almost instantly:

Claude Monet. Haystack. End of the summer.
Morning. *Oil on canvas. 1891 ACE.*

Benson barely had time to take in the news when a new voice burst into his head.

<Detective Benson, where did you take that picture?>

Benson tensed, as if one of his old grade school teachers had just scolded him. The voice belonged to Mrs Devorah Feynman, a terror of a woman who had served as the Museum's curator for the last thirty-five years.

<Jesus, Devorah. Would it kill you to ring first? You scared the shit out of me.>

<Jumpy can't be a great quality in a police chief, I expect. And don't blaspheme.>

Benson ignored the rebuke. <How do you know about this painting already?>

<I have a program set up that watches for certain search parameters and image files and sends me an alert whenever it gets a hit.>

<That's a little invasive, don't you think?>

<I have a standing warrant for the search. We both have our jurisdictions, detective. Mine just happens to be the preservation of the cultural legacy of all mankind.>

God, she missed her calling. Should have been a drama coach, Benson thought off com. <And you could tell it's not a print just from the picture?>

<It piqued my interest enough to warrant a check. So you're sure it's not a reproduction?>

Benson shrugged. <I'm sure it's not a print, but that's as much as I know. It could still be a forgery.>

<Give me twenty minutes. Don't go anywhere, and don't let anyone else inside that apartment.>

Benson was a little taken aback by her tone. <Pardon? I'm not one of your security guards. I'm conducting an investigation here.>

The line paused. The equivalent of a stare-down. <I could call up the Council and make the order official, but I'd just as soon keep this as quiet as possible. So I'd consider it a favor if you would prevent any drunk Zero hooligans from stealing or otherwise defiling a lost relic of our shared past until I arrive. Is that fair enough?>

Benson forced himself to relax. Tomorrow's dinner with Theresa couldn't come fast enough. <I'd be happy to, Devorah.>

<Good. Do NOT touch it. I can't stress that enough.>

Benson snorted. <Don't worry. I won't smudge your little painting. Oh, and there's an old chair you might want to look at also.>

Seventeen minutes later, someone knocked on the door. Benson set down the tablet and got up from the sumptuous chair to answer it. A tiny woman, no more than a hundred and sixty centimeters tall and hunched with age, swept into the living room. She wore her silver hair in a bun so tight it seemed to quiver under the strain, held in place by a pair of wicked looking black lacquered chopsticks, doubtless far older than even the woman herself.

She ignored Benson completely as she spotted the painting on the far wall and stalked over to it.

"Good afternoon to you too, Devorah."

She looked back at him. "Hmm? Yes, yes. Bring me that stool, would you?"

Benson could only chuckle as he grabbed a stool from the breakfast bar and set it down in front of the painting. He offered the older woman a hand up, but she didn't even glance at it as she hopped onto the stool like a mountain goat. She leaned in close and murmured softly to herself.

"Whoever framed it used good glass, that's a plus. Wouldn't be surprised to see if I went back far enough in the museum stock room records that some display glass took a walk." She pulled a pair of pristine white gloves from a pocket and slipped them on her weathered hands, then removed the painting from the wall. She moved to the table and set it face down.

After a moment's study, she unlatched the backing plate and set it aside. Then she reached out and gently removed the painting from the frame with a careful reverence normally reserved for crying babies or ticking bombs.

She laid it face up in the open air for the first time in who knew how long. A large, antique magnifying glass appeared from somewhere on her tiny frame.

"The texturing lines up with the pigmentation, and the layering is obvious." She rubbed a gloved fingertip along the edge of the painting, a spot that had been hidden behind the frame. She licked her fingertip, then held it to her nose and inhaled deeply. "Traces of linseed oil."

"What does that tell you?"

She glanced up at Benson as though only just remembering he was in the room.

"Several things, detective. First, it means it's a real painting, not a print that's been doctored with layers of brush-stroked lacquer. Second, the only linseed plant aboard the Ark is stored in the Genome Archive, which means this is pre-launch."

Benson nodded along, not wanting to deflate her obvious excitement. "So, it's genuine?"

"It was genuinely painted on Earth, yes. But whether it was painted by Monet, or just an incredibly talented forger, I can't say yet. I need to take it back to the museum to run some spectrographic and radioactive decay tests."

Benson's left eyebrow inched up. "Aren't those destructive tests?"

The curator shrugged. "We need only milligrams of material. A few strands of canvas and a flake or two of paint from the margins will be enough. Then we'll know not only what time it came from, but where the paint was ground."

"You have records on *paint* that go back that far?"

"I have every record, from every museum, and every publication, current until one month before the launch, and stretching back at least four centuries. Surely law enforcement has similar resources?"

Benson could only laugh at that. "I'm sorry, Devorah, I don't mean to poke fun, but I think you'll find that the people of Earth spent a great deal more time committing crimes than creating art, and that many in the policing profession were not nearly so... clinical as you."

"I see," she said disapprovingly. Not in Benson, but in her expectation for the species at large. She busied herself placing the painting back inside its protective cocoon.

"How often does your search return a hit like this?"

"Not so often as in past years, but enough. We're still looking for pieces from the Heist. That's why I still have my warrant almost forty years later."

Benson nodded. The Heist had been the single most brazen crime ever committed onboard the Ark. Murders had happened, of course, and other crimes of passion or indifference, but nothing compared to the theft of over three hundred irreplaceable artifacts from mankind's last museum. It had meant the end of the previous curator's career, and Devorah's ascension. Both were well before Benson's time as chief. Indeed, before his birth.

"I thought everything had been recovered decades ago."

"That's what we told everyone, yes." She replaced the back cover. "I wanted the public to think we'd won, and for the vandals to think we'd given up the chase. I wanted them to get lazy and complacent. It worked too, up to a point. We quietly nabbed another fifty pieces in short order, but there's still about a dozen pieces outstanding."

"If that's true, why haven't you ordered a compartment-to-compartment search? We could have turned the ship inside out a hundred times by now."

"I ask in every session, but no council has ever given permission, that's why. They fear riots."

And they're probably right about that, Benson reflected. "Could this be one of your missing pieces?"

"Hmm? No, no. We never had this. It was reported lost in the looting of the Louvre in 2136. We never had *any* Monets."

Benson rubbed his chin. Nothing about this made sense. Laraby was certainly better off than most of the cattle, but among floaters, he was middle-management, at best. The painting, and frankly the house itself, seemed awfully extravagant.

"What will happen to it now, after your tests, I mean?"

"Well, if it's a forgery, I'd imagine it will be returned to whoever lives here."

"His name is Edmond Laraby," Benson added helpfully. "Although he's a bit difficult to reach at the moment."

She continued as though she hadn't heard him. "There's no law against private art collections, so long as the provenance can be traced. I've seen some pieces hung in the command crew's quarters that would make you weep." She looked up at Benson's hard face. "Well, maybe not you, detective."

"I'm a teddy bear."

"Sure you are. On the other hand, if it is genuine, then it was stolen from the Louvre two hundred and fifty years ago and no trail of provenance will protect it from confiscation." The tiny woman actually licked her lips. "I wouldn't even need to reframe it."

Devorah seemed to snap out of her daydream and picked up the painting, then headed for the door.

"I'll need an escort back to the museum. Come along, detective."

"Regrettably, I have more work here. But I have just the man for the job sitting outside." Benson eased by the woman, careful not to touch the frame as he passed, then opened the door. The rookie from before sat under the grove of trees in plain clothes, just as he'd been instructed. Yet he still managed to stick out like a shark fin prowling the waves at a crowded beach. He was hopeless.

"Constable!" Benson waved. "Come over here." The young man sprang up and trotted over double time. "What's your name, lad?"

"Constable Korolev, sir."

"A strong, Russian name, excellent. I assume you have your stun-stick in there somewhere?" Korolev nodded. The stun-stick was as close to a weapon as the constables got, but it was more than adequate. About the size of a pen, when pointed at a non-compliant suspect and activated, it triggered a short electrical spike in the suspect's plant, causing a grand-mal seizure. Every constable had one used on them during training, to instill the seriousness of having to push the button. Benson had used it only once in his years of service.

"Good. Constable Korolev, this is Madame Curator Feynman. I need you to escort her back to the museum. Make absolutely certain no harm comes to her."

"To hell with me," Devorah protested from behind him. "Guard the bloody painting!"

Benson looked at her, then back at Korolev with a somewhat pained expression. "Did you get that, constable?"

He threw another perfect salute. "Yes, detective.

Madame, if you'll accompany me, please."

Devorah stepped forward and sized up the young man with a withering glare. "What'd they carve you out of, boy?"

Korolev didn't miss a beat. "Determination, Madame Curator."

Devorah looked back at Benson and actually smirked. "He'll do."

Benson smiled back. "I thought he might. One last question?" Devorah nodded for him to continue. "If this thing is genuine, what's it worth?"

"An original Monet? Priceless. It would be one of the ten most important paintings in the collection."

Benson shook his head. You couldn't eat it, couldn't wear it, it didn't recycle air or water. What value could it really have?

"So, it's worth killing for, then?" he asked.

"To the right person, certainly. Why do you ask?"

Benson crossed his arms. "We both have our jurisdictions, Madame Curator."

Devorah regarded him for a long moment, but answered only with a shrug. As the two of them walked away, Benson realized Devorah had been too engrossed in the painting to even glance at the chair. He made the executive decision to finish reading Laraby's personnel file while sitting in it.

CHAPTER THREE

It was always a little too cool in the command module for Benson's liking. The crew had their reasons, of course. Command didn't have the huge banks of lights designed to mimic natural sunlight, including infrared. Nor did it have the population. With fifty thousand people busy metabolizing and radiating body heat into the environment, the habitats stayed very comfortable.

Floaters liked it cool. If you asked, they'd say the banks of computers and lab equipment worked optimally in a cooler environment. But Benson nursed the suspicion that they liked it because it made visiting cattle all the more eager to leave.

Benson glided through the central corridor on his way to the bio-lab module, where he'd been granted the courtesy of a ten minute audience with Ms Avelina Pereira da Silva. As the head of Environmental Development and Research, she was a very busy woman these days, which she was only too eager to explain to everyone, on the off chance they hadn't already heard it from the layers of subordinates one had to wade through to setup a meeting with her in the first place.

Benson found the correct lock and pushed the call

button. "Detective Benson to see Director da Silva, please."

A dark male face appeared on the monitor. "Have you showered, detective?"

Benson smiled courteously, "I always shower before calling on a lady."

The gatekeeper was not amused. "Director da Silva is expecting you, but this is a class three cleanroom. You will need to go through decontamination and put on scrubs before I let you enter."

"Sounds like fun."

"It isn't."

"You could have softened the blow."

"Not really my strong suit, detective." The lock's outer door slid open with a hiss. "Please step inside and disrobe, then put your clothes in a locker."

Fifteen minutes and a rather invasive cleansing later, Benson floated through the inner door wearing a thin microfiber suit that looked like the footie pajamas he wore when he was five, except lacking all of the warmth and comfort he remembered. Would it really have killed them to let him keep his clothes on underneath?

The same face from the monitor greeted him, if the word could be applied, inside the lab. "Good afternoon, detective. Director da Silva is in the sample garden, C5. She is waiting for you, but asked me to remind you that your appointment is limited to ten minutes."

"You're not the first to do so. Can we move along, please?"

"Very well. Follow me, and don't touch anything. I can't stress that enough."

"Not the first time I've heard that today, either."

"It's good advice."

Benson pushed down the sudden urge to "touch" his handler's scrawny little neck. Honestly, he hadn't heard "don't touch" this much since getting the pre-date rules from his first girlfriend's father.

Each floor of labs was labeled with a letter, while the individual labs were numbered, so C5 would be three rings in. For the average person, floating down, (up, through?) such a large, six-sided space with no defined ceiling, walls, or floor would have been tremendously disorienting, but that was one area where Benson was far from average. Zero players were second only to the crew in their familiarity with weightlessness.

One would expect floaters to fill the rosters of Zero teams, but the crewman culture viewed such pursuits as below their station. The unspoken reason was obvious as he looked at the other techs drifting around the department; most floaters lacked the muscle mass to be competitive at anything remotely athletic.

His handler opened the outer door to the sample garden and waved him inside.

"I'll return to help you through the exit procedure in ten minutes."

"Looking forward to it!" Benson gave the young man a big smile and slapped him on the shoulder hard enough to send him spinning. "Oh, sorry, son, I forget my own strength some days."

The tech grabbed a handhold and righted himself. "I'm sure. Ten minutes." The outer door snapped shut, leaving Benson alone in the lock for a few seconds as the seals completed their cycle.

The inner door opened onto a serene, if surreal

looking, garden as seen from above. Shelf after shelf of plants of all shapes and sizes grew in perfectly ordered rows, each carefully labeled and tagged by hand. The air in here was much warmer than the corridor, verging on hot, doubtless due to the racks of lights shining on the plants, casting the whole scene in a slightly orange glow.

Some of the samples were obviously doing better than others, but curiously, one trait they all shared was their pigment. Every plant in the garden was a varying shade of purple or lavender.

Coming up from the bottom of the lab, a striking woman rose up to meet him with a tablet in hand. Her raven hair sported several streaks of silver. Benson recognized her from some twenty-five years earlier, when his class had played host to a guest lecture on bio-forming from a grad student who had just started working in the command module. It had been very exciting for the young Benson, who had yet to see any part of the Ark beyond Avalon and the Zero stadium. It was like being visited by an explorer from an exotic land, even if that land was less than five kilometers away.

The woman floating up to meet him had advanced in years, but had lost none of the wonder in her eyes.

"Detective Benson, it's a pleasure to meet you," Avelina said, as she gently bumped into him and shook his hand.

"Actually, Director da Silva, we've met once before."

"Oh? I'm sorry, I don't recall."

"I'm not surprised. I think I asked you how crewmen poop in null gravity." She gave him a quizzical look. "I was around fifth grade at the time. You came to my school."

She laughed easily. "Ah, that explains it. Boys that age

have their own priorities, don't they? I hope my assistant didn't give you too much trouble on the way in?"

"Well, I'm certainly cleaner than I've been in a long time."

"A necessary precaution, I'm afraid. There's some very sensitive, very expensive equipment in here that we can't afford down time on, and many samples that can't handle contamination."

"I see that. How's it all going to handle the Flip?"

She shrugged. "No way to know until it happens. Which is just one reason we're rushing to finish as much as we can before the deceleration starts. Honestly, I haven't even started securing my quarters, we've just been too busy."

"Me either. My apartment will look like somebody flipped it on its side if I don't carve out some time to clean up and lash everything down."

"Some role models we make, hey?"

"Never was my strong suit, honestly." Benson glanced around at the purple plants once more. "Is something wrong with this batch? They look, er, wrong."

Avelina gave him a sideways grin. "I see the fifth grade Detective Benson had better things to do than listen to my boring lecture. No, everything in here is quite healthy, except the yams keep going sterile after a couple generations. They're purple because we're busy bioforming them for Tau Ceti G. As you know–"

Benson had always been amused at how the phrase "As you know" was immediately followed by an explanation assuming, in fact, that you didn't.

"–Tau Ceti's primary is only roughly analogous to Sol. It's a G-type star, but smaller, dimmer, and cooler than

Sol was. Those factors shift its spectral output deeper into the infrared. So we've been hard at work tweaking the chlorophyll and photosynthetic processes of every species in this room to absorb more of their energy from IR. They aren't as dependent on the visual part of the EM spectrum for their photosynthetic processes, so this is how they turn out."

Benson flashed his best "I follow you" face and nodded sagely. "Is that why it's so warm in here?"

"Yes, exactly. The bulbs in here emit more energy in IR. They're almost as bad as the very first incandescent bulbs Edison invented. The temperature is meant to mimic the average temp in Tau Ceti G's tropical regions. The color is only the most obvious change we're working on. Pathfinder has sent back a lot more than brochure pictures. We have spectrographic analysis of soil samples, atmospheric composition, even some insights into local insect-analogues and microbes. The staple crops need to be tweaked to tolerate all of these factors."

"Well, I doubt may people will complain about the heat, although purple salads will take some getting used to."

"Less than starvation would, I expect."

"True." Benson realized they were straying off topic. "Is this what Edmond was working on?"

A little of the excitement went out of Avelina's eyes at the mention of her missing man. "Yes. Poor Edmond. What do you need to know?"

Benson grabbed a rung to steady himself. "I want to get a feel for the man. He doesn't have any next of kin, and he doesn't have any registered partners, so that pretty much leaves coworkers. You've been his direct supervisor for almost five years. So here I am, chatting with you."

"I see. I mean no disrespect, detective, but wouldn't your time be better spent back in the habitats looking for him?"

Benson smiled. "I'm sure it would look that way from the outside, but I have all of my constables on the job. We're running a facial recognition search on all internal feeds and locks. We're already looking for him, but it's undirected. What I'm trying to do is narrow the search."

The director nodded. "I understand. It's just… it was so unexpected. Edmond was always so punctual. So focused. He loved his work, it was his whole life."

Well, maybe not his whole *life*, Benson thought. "You're talking about him in the past tense."

"I…" She swallowed hard. "I didn't realize I was doing that. But really, detective, be honest with me. He's been missing for over a day. What are the odds he'll turn up alive?"

"I don't know. This is already longer than any other missing person case I've dealt with. There's only so much internal volume to hide in, and our surveillance net is everywhere. Most of the time somebody wraps their head in aluminum foil. They're pretty easy to find. Was Edmond under an unusual amount of stress?"

Avelina snorted. "We all are, detective. But I didn't see any signs that he was about to snap, if that's what you mean."

"Can you show me what he was working on?"

"Sure, this way." She pushed off, back towards the floor of the room. Benson followed her gracefully through the open space.

"You fly like a crewman."

Benson smiled. "Thank you, but fifteen years playing Zero will give anyone space legs."

"Oh, yes, I'd heard something about that. You were a team captain, isn't that right?"

"Something like that. I take it you're not a fan?"

"Never found the time for it, I'm afraid. Here we are." She pulled out a tray of tiny lavender plants only a dozen centimeters tall. Their roots poked down through a clear gelatinous film and into a nutrient-rich hydroponic bath. It was all very similar to the multi-story aeroponic tower farms in the habitat modules, only much smaller. Benson knew those farms well. He'd worked in one for years. Zero saved him from that life.

"I know they don't look like much more than grass, but these are wheat seedlings, detective. Very special ones."

She pulled one free of the tray. "You see, we call these 'sliders'. Instead of pulling out and replacing the part of their genome needed to adapt them to Tau Ceti G, we've found a way to leave the original DNA intact, and add several more genetic profiles. Environmental triggers then determine which set of coding will work best and allow the plant to flip between them like a light switch. This strain has four distinct packets to choose from, each suited to a different environment."

Avelina's excitement was infectious, but Benson wasn't following anymore. "How does that help us? I thought you were bio-forming them for the new colony."

"The *first* colony, yes, but Tau Ceti G isn't the only candidate. Tau Ceti E and F were colonization targets even before G was discovered, although not nearly as ideal. The old Goldilocks issue, one too hot and the other too cold. But with this slider plant, one bag of seeds could grow in certain places on any of them. No more endless tinkering and tailoring for each new environment. It's damn near a universal plant."

Benson rubbed his chin. "And that's what Edmond was working on."

"Yes, exactly. It was his idea in the first place. He wrote his graduate dissertation on it. I was the only one in the department who didn't dismiss it as outright lunacy." She shook the seedling. "Now here it is in my hand."

"Careful. It wasn't that long ago people would storm your lab and accuse you of playing God. Some still might."

"I invite them to. I was raised Catholic, detective. I can quote chapter and verse, in Latin, with the best of them."

"And you don't have any compunctions about, you know, tinkering?"

She shrugged. "Necessity is the mother of invention, especially when it comes to biblical interpretation. No, I don't feel like we're playing God, but I do believe He left His toolbox unlocked when we needed it most."

"Now that we need a new place to live, after He wrecked the last one?"

"*We* wrecked the last place, detective, not Him. Earth was dying, Nibiru just moved things up by a century or two. We have to do better this time."

"You're a scientist," Benson said. "You're not one of those folks who believes Nibiru was God's punishment, are you?"

If the question upset her, da Silva didn't let it show. "I'm open to a better explanation, once science makes up its mind."

Benson paused to consider that. Nibiru was, by all accounts, an impossible object. It had been known for centuries that a star had to be several times the mass of Sol to go supernova and collapse into a black hole. But at only a third of Sol's mass, Nibiru was too small to form. It should not have existed at all. Physicists still pondered the question, some falling on the side of Nibiru being an ancient black hole, a relic from the earliest moments of the universe, formed immediately after the Big Bang when the laws of physics were more... fluid. Others insisted it was evidence of black holes splitting through some unknown mechanism, perhaps bisected by cosmic strings, or spinning so fast that they broke apart. Both possibilities were enthusiastically derided by those in the opposing camp as completely impossible, if not insane.

With science offering no coherent answers, it was easy to see why religion had stepped in to fill in the blanks for many. A significant minority of people aboard continued to see Nibiru as God's wrath, or anthropomorphize it entirely, giving it agency and motivations all its own.

Benson decided to table that line of inquiry. "We've done pretty well here over the generations. I think we're ready to take care of a new world."

"We've had to. People behave because the danger is always immediate. If we eat too much, or use too much, the shortages happen *to us*, not some vague concept of future generations. But what happens when all the limits and quotas are gone and people like you aren't enforcing the Conservation Codes? I'm afraid we're going to fall back into old habits. If we even live long enough."

"What do you mean?"

"I mean, we're one rogue prion or fungal infection

away from extinction. It's not just us, either. Even if nothing takes a liking to humans as hosts, all it will take is a blight to wipe out our staple crops and we'll be just as dead as the wheat."

"I thought our crops were bred for disease resistance?"

"*Earth* diseases, and that took many thousands of years of careful selective breeding and decades of genetic manipulation. We're about to touch down on an alien world with a completely unique ecology that we'll have to adapt to in months, years at the most. Who's to say the things that make a corn stalk resistant to Goss's Wilt wouldn't make it more susceptible to a Tau Ceti parasite of some kind? We're taking all the precautions we can, but, without direct samples to study, it's like trying to win a fist fight while looking through a straw. Honestly, we have no idea what's waiting for us, and there's no guarantee we'll be able to make adjustments fast enough."

"Setting us up for an 'I told you so'?"

Da Silva laughed, but Benson heard little humor in it. "Just trying to get someone to understand the shit taco I've been handed. Pardon my language."

"No worries, I can relate. Director, did Edmond have any enemies? Anyone who might want to hurt him?"

"Lord above, no. He was a sweet boy, always very polite. Remembered everyone's birthday here in the lab and always had a present for them."

Figures, Benson thought. "Any arguments lately? Jilted lovers, perhaps?"

"No, nothing like that. I don't think I ever saw him involved with a girl, he was kind of shy around them."

"I have to tell you, I was in Edmond's apartment this morning, just a routine check to make sure he wasn't there. I couldn't help but notice how... clean it was, almost sterile. I can't shake the feeling someone wiped the scene."

Avelina waved a hand dismissively at the thought. "Oh, no detective. He was a bit of a neat freak. Things always had to be 'just so', even here in the lab, sometimes even at other people's work stations. If he had one annoying trait, that was it, but it was sort of endearing, too."

The far door opened and spat out the tech from earlier. "Time's up, Detective Benson."

Avelina looked down at her tablet in surprise. "Ah, so it is! I really must be getting back to work, detective. We only have two weeks to go, and there're still plenty of bugs to work out. If you need anything else, we can arrange to talk through the coms."

"Of course. Thanks for your time, director. I have my own work to do, trying to bring home your missing man."

"I'd be eternally grateful if you did. Edmond is already missed around here."

Benson pushed off and headed back up to the lock. But as he reached it, he called back down to Avelina. "Oh, director, one last question. Did Edmond ever mention an interest in art to you, especially for pre-launch paintings?"

She shook her head. "Not that I remember. Why do you ask?"

"Just checking. Thanks for your help."

She waved it off. "God be with you."

CHAPTER FOUR

Benson poured himself another cup of sake and glanced up at the antique clock on the restaurant's wall. Then he realized he hadn't actually processed what the little hands said and looked again.

8.40… ish. Maybe. It was tough to be sure, because the damned clockmaker had only bothered with dots and hash-marks instead of legitimate numbers. Still, he was quite sure that Theresa was late, a very unnatural state for her.

Benson, on the other hand, had been early, which was a similarly notable departure from his modus operandi. The last two days trying to track down a missing person who seemed to have a vested interest in not being found, coupled with the Mustangs' loss of Game Four, had worn on him. A couple bottles of sake and a real meat dinner had sounded too good to delay any further. So he'd shown up a half hour early to "confirm" the reservation, then slid over to the bar to get a head start on his buzz.

In his youth, Benson had been known to overindulge on rare occasions such as celebrating a big win, or a particularly difficult loss, or on the weekends, or to mark the passing of another Thursday, or because it was dinner time.

But people had proven to be a little less accommodating of the chief constable than they had of the Zero Champion when it came to supplying him with copious amounts of free beer and liquor. Since then, budget constraints had done a decent job of keeping his bad habits in check. Still, days like today, he missed having the freedom to fill his stomach with hooch until the world went away. Of course, the real problem with chasing the world away with alcohol was how it always came roaring back in the morning.

A display on the far wall cycled through the day's Pathfinder cache. One of the drones was following a herd of the bipedal, filter-feeding herbivores everyone had taken to calling broom-heads as they started what appeared to be a massive, seasonal migration. Other guests "oohed" and "ahhed" at the new images, but Benson only thought of the wall in Laraby's apartment.

"Another carafe of sake, sir?"

"Hmm?" Benson realized the bartender was looking at him expectantly. "Oh, no thanks. I'm fine for now."

"OK, just let me know if you need anything."

"Thanks. Actually, Mitch? A glass of water, please."

Benson sipped on the water while his thoughts wandered back to the case. He found himself identifying with Edmond in ways he hadn't expected. They were both only children, for one thing. For another, their parents were already dead. In Laraby's case, his parents had kept deferring their child license until late in life, preferring to devote the time to their careers instead. Mr and Mrs Benson had been a different matter. They weren't even granted their child license until both were well into their fifties. Just another in a long line of insults his family had endured.

The first Bensons aboard the Ark were gene-cheats. They'd found a way to hack the selection filtering process with forged DNA samples. They'd gotten away with the forgery for years, until their first child came down with Addison's disease.

The disease was easy enough for the genetics boffins to pull out after the second generation and kick Addison's back into history's recycle bin. But the damage to the Benson name was done, and despite the fact no one beyond the original couple had been involved, society on the Ark had a long memory. The bloodline limped along stubbornly for eight generations, always among the last to get birth licenses, and usually only for a single child. The family toiled away in obscurity, never getting a member accepted to any of the crewmember training programs, much less through to graduation.

Benson's life started much the same way, working as nothing more glamorous than a farmhand in Avalon's aeroponics towers. A chance encounter with the Mustangs' coach while he and some friends were screwing off during open-gym changed the whole trajectory of his life. It had all the hallmarks of a movie script: humble beginnings, a chance at redemption, victory over adversity, fame, (although the traditional fortune part of that equation had gone out of fashion). He'd been turned into a symbol of the heights a working-class man could achieve, with the permission of their betters, of course.

He'd been rewarded for playing the part with status, fans, the affection of women, and finally a cushy job as a cop overseeing a generally cowed, docile population. Life was good, as long as he remembered his role. Benson poured the remains of his bottle into the porcelain cup and washed the bitter taste down.

"Mitch, I'll take the next carafe now."

A light breeze ran through his hair. Benson turned in his seat to take in the view the rooftop had to offer. He had to admit, it was impressive. The Koi Pond sat sixty-three stories above the deck, perched at the top of the Alexander Building, the most exclusive residential tower in Avalon, and tied with its twin in Shangri-La for tallest buildings on the Ark. Ironically, the Qin Shi Huang building had an American-style burger joint on top of it, although soy-burgers and Portobello mushrooms took the place of beef in the patties.

Like all structures above three stories, the Alexander Building was built as an outgrowth of the habitat's rear bulkhead. If it wasn't, deceleration would send it toppling when the ship flipped in twelve days. At just over two hundred meters tall, it was so much closer to the central hub that Benson, along with everyone else on the crowded roof, actually weighed a fifth less than at ground level.

This was the poorly guarded secret to the tower's exclusivity. Floaters who maintained apartments in the habitats found the lower gravity more comfortable higher up, setting a premium on the top floors. Even in the Ark's designed utopia, society had found ways to stratify itself.

The elevator at the far end of the bar chimed, bringing Benson's attention back to more practical matters. The doors opened, and Lieutenant Alexopoulos emerged from their embrace. Benson's jaw nearly hit the bar at the sight of her. She wore a blood red dress, the color of which set off her Mediterranean tone and features beautifully, while its low cut set off her other, more tangible assets just as successfully.

Theresa spotted him at the bar, and Benson stood up involuntarily as she approached. "Ah, um. Hi Esa," was the best he could do with so much blood suddenly rushing away from his brain.

Theresa smiled warmly. "Hi yourself."

"You're, um, a little late."

"I'm sorry, it took me longer than usual to get ready. It's not a problem, is it?" Her lower lip puffed out just a little bit at the end of the question.

"No, of course not. You cleaned up nice."

Theresa huffed. "Honestly, Bryan. I spend an hour pouring myself into this dress and wrestling with my hair, and you make it sound like I barely managed to throw on a clean shirt."

"No, that's not what I meant!" Theresa's glare bore into him expectantly. "I mean, you look–"

She put a hand on her hip. "Amazing, ravishing, stunning?"

"–like a fireplace on a cold night. Warm, inviting, and with a hint of danger."

She continued to glare at him for a long moment before her face softened. "All right, that was a good recovery. Is our table ready?"

"I'll let the host know you've arrived."

A few minutes later they sat next to the railing overlooking the entire length of Avalon. The view was spectacular. The lights above had finished cycling into night some twenty minutes ago, casting the scene in the dim twilight of streetlamps and windows that wrapped around them like constellations of stars. Or, Benson reflected, maybe more like a warm blanket. As massive as Avalon's habitat was, it was still a finite, comprehensible quantity.

He, along with everyone else born in the last two hundred and twenty odd years, had grown up knowing exactly how big the world was. Nothing lay "just over the horizon", because there *was* no horizon. What must it have been like for the countless generations of humans born before the Ark? What was it like to grow up beneath an infinite sky? Personally, Benson suspected it was the reason early man had sought the comfort of caves, and why people through the centuries had spent so extravagantly to construct artificial versions.

Theresa selected a pod from the bowl of edamame and pinched the beans into her mouth, then shared the view with him for a time.

"You're awfully quiet."

"Hmm?" Benson looked back from his introspection. "Sorry. It's been a long couple of days."

"Have you learned anything new about our missing man?"

"Oh, just that he was a model worker that everybody loved, despite no one really knowing anything about him, except that no one would ever dream of harming him."

"So, nothing useful."

Benson shook his head. "Not really, no."

"Any word on the painting? Is it real?"

"Devorah is still running her tests. She's supposed to call me as soon as she has an answer."

Their waiter reappeared with their orders and a fresh carafe of sake for the table. Bryan's plate was loaded down with perch, tench, and catfish rolls. Theresa had opted for bluegill and a veggie roll. Hardly "traditional" sushi fish, but due to the Ark's lack of saltwater oceans, chefs had adapted their recipes to the few species that were used in the hydroponic farms and water reclamation ponds.

Benson picked up his chopsticks and was about to dive in when a single piece of tempura sitting on a slice of ginger in the middle of his plate caught his eye. He glanced over and realized Theresa's plate had one as well.

"Excuse me, waiter?" Benson pointed at the golden fried lump. "But what is that?"

"That, sir, is a piece of white-meat chicken breast, marinated in a wasabi soy sauce, then dipped in an egg yolk tempura batter and deep fried."

They both looked at the waiter uncomprehendingly. Benson broke the moment of silence. "I'm sorry, did you say, 'chicken breast, and egg yolk'? Surely you meant tofu chicken?"

"No, sir. It is genuine chicken meat. It was a gift to the restaurant from the Genome Archive. This bird had been one of a small experimental batch to calibrate artificial wombs for different species ahead of Landing."

"And the egg yolks?"

The waiter smiled. "Two of the chickens survived to maturity and started laying eggs. Unfertilized, of course. The crew in the project saw no reason they should go to waste."

Benson nodded. Conservation at its finest. Nothing ever went to waste on the Ark. "That is quite a gift. Must be expensive."

"Really, Bryan," Theresa chided. "What else are you going to spend it on?"

The waiter held up a hand. "As these were a gift to us, they are a gift to you, compliments of Chef Takahashi, in honor of your Mustangs reaching the Championship."

"This isn't a bribe, is it? Is there a body in the freezer?"

Theresa slapped his hand. "Bryan, don't be rude."

"I'm kidding, of course. Tell Chef Takahashi that we are humbled by the honor."

The waiter bowed and left them to their meals. Theresa shook her head mockingly. "Zero Hero."

"Hey, I'll take it. Chief constable doesn't pull these kinds of perks. I doubt Chief Bahadur over in Shangri-La is eating a beef burger tonight."

"I doubt it too, considering Vikram is a Sikh."

Benson shook his head. "You're thinking of Hindus. They're the ones who venerate cows."

"Am I?" Theresa tilted her head as her eyes unfocused, consulting her plant. "Hmm, you're right. Although it hasn't been much of an issue for a while, since the last cow died two centuries ago."

"Not really, no." Benson picked at his catfish roll. "Still, the rest of the meal is going to set me back enough as it is."

"Hey, you splurged on the food, I splurged on the presentation." Theresa waved a hand over the dress. "Unless you think I pulled this off the rack."

"Well, I'd like to pull it off the rack."

"Ugh." Theresa threw a napkin at him. "Can you pretend not to be a boorish clod for just one meal?" She lowered her voice to a whisper. "Do you want us reported?"

She referred to the long-standing policy aboard the Ark of a couple's requirement to declare their relationship before intercourse. Officially, any two people, so long as they were unmarried and had reached the age of majority, could engage in any relationship they desired. In practice, however, social pressure had a habit of cropping up for couples who didn't have appropriate levels of genetic and personality compatibility.

The thing was, while Theresa didn't know it, she and Benson had already been reported twice before to other constables, who dutifully filed reports and submitted them directly to their chief, where the reports mysteriously got lost in the shuffle of paperwork.

"Sorry. I'll stop. But do you really think it's going to matter?"

"What do you mean, exactly?"

"I mean, in two weeks, we're going to start shuttling down to build a new world. All of the artificial limits we needed to survive in this fishbowl for the last two centuries will disappear." Benson poured himself another little cup of sake and held it up in a mock toast. "I'm about to be obsolete, my dear. Again."

"Can you stop that?"

"Stop what?"

"Stop looking backwards like all your best days are behind you. The most important moment in human history is about to happen and you're pouting about not playing Zero anymore. Isn't there anything you're looking forward to once we land?"

Benson could see where her train of thought was headed and tried to stop it before it built up steam. "No, that's not it at all."

"No?"

"No. Well, maybe a little. I've always felt like this job

was a sort of retirement gift. But really, Conservation Codes? Declared lovers? Licensed babies? The new world isn't going to need people like us enforcing any of that nonsense."

Theresa leaned back in her chair and hid an admiring smile behind a hand. "You really believe that, don't you? Even after dealing with people at their worst every day for years, you still believe in their fundamental decency. You're a strangely stubborn optimist, Bryan Benson."

"You disagree?"

"Of course. The old rules will become extinct, but a whole new set will have to take their place. People will run to find the new boundaries as fast as they can. Somebody is going to have to be ready to jerk their chains when they finally reach them." She held up her own little cup. "That's going to be us, sweetie."

"Funny, you're not the first person today to–"

<Detective Benson. Are you there?>

"Christ, Devorah. What did I say about ringing first?" Benson was startled enough that he both said it aloud and into his plant interface.

<What did I say about blasphemy?>

"Aren't you Jewish?"

<Yes, but your parents were Lutherans, and I doubt they would approve.>

"Really?" Theresa scolded. "Hang up, Bryan. We're having dinner."

Benson apologetically held up his hands. Theresa grabbed a segment of his perch roll with her chopsticks and angrily popped it into her mouth.

"I'm at dinner. A rather expensive one."

<It can wait two minutes. The tests are done. I carbon-

dated the canvas to the late nineteenth century, and the paint samples are not only contemporary, but the pigmentation is consistent with Monet's preferences and a comparison to our scan of the original came to within a half-millimeter of–>

<OK.> Benson switched back to just the plant. <So, you're telling me it's real.>

<I have a very high degree of confidence that it is.>

<Good enough. Thank you, Devorah. Oh, and there's still the matter of that chair.>

<What chair?>

<Never mind. I'll talk to you in the morning. I'm eating meat.>

<Whatever. Enjoy your fish.>

<Among other things.> Benson cut the link before she could inquire any further, then looked up at Theresa, who had moved on to his catfish roll.

"What's so important it can't wait until the end of our romantic dinner?" Theresa asked.

"Our dinner? You seem to be the only one eating."

"Lucky you. You know what they say about a girl with an appetite."

"That they're expensive dates?"

"I'm worth every red cent," Theresa said confidently.

"That you are." Benson admired her plunging neckline for a moment before he leaned in and pitched his voice lower. "The painting from Laraby's apartment is real."

Theresa put down her chopsticks and rested on her elbows with a strangely hungry look in her eyes. "What's it worth?"

"Incalculable."

"Well now, that's motive in my book."

Benson nodded. "Mine too, but for who? We don't have any suspects yet."

A sly smirk tugged at Theresa's lips. "The museum gets to keep the painting now that it's been confiscated, yes?"

"Yes, Devorah's quite excited about it, too."

"I bet she is."

Benson cocked an eyebrow. "Are you saying she's involved?"

Theresa shrugged. "She stands to benefit. And that woman has always struck me as more than a little cold."

Benson shook his head. "Why kill for it, though? If she knew about the painting before I found it, all she had to do was get a warrant to search the apartment, then she'd get to keep it anyway. No need to get her hands dirty."

"Maybe she couldn't get the warrant? I read your report, his home was way beyond the pay grade of a tech, even one at his level. Maybe someone has been keeping him in comfort, and protecting him to boot."

"A patron among the floaters?" Benson considered it for a long moment, but put it aside. "Devorah loves the chase. She's cunning, but as short-tempered as she can be, she's not malicious. I just don't see her being a murderer, even if I could see a tiny elderly woman disposing of a grown man cleanly. Besides, that assumes Laraby's dead in the first place."

"It's been two days. Aren't we assuming that at this point?"

Benson looked at her sternly. "It's our job not to."

Theresa looked as though she was about to take offense, but her face changed and she nodded instead. "Anyone else's DNA at his apartment?"

Benson shook his head. "Tests came back a couple

hours ago. No DNA at all. From anyone."

Theresa squared her shoulders. "That's not possible. I don't care how OCD somebody is, you can't live somewhere without leaving *some* evidence behind."

"There are ways to dissolve genetic material. The old Triads had aerosols that could do it."

"So a resurgent Chinese Triad broke into Laraby's home and wiped the scene clean to cover up a murder, only to leave a priceless French Impressionistic painting hanging on the wall?"

Benson perked up. "Well, you know what they say... More Monet, more problems."

Theresa visibly shuddered, then rubbed the side of her face. "You've been waiting all day to drop that bomb on some unsuspecting victim, haven't you?"

"Actually, I thought of it last night, right before bed. But you're right. As a theory, it lacks a certain... elegance."

Theresa took another pull from her sake and let the hot rice wine percolate through her stomach before continuing. "So, Laraby's apartment is clean?"

"Sterile."

"No evidence to contaminate?"

Benson's eyebrow cocked suspiciously. "No..."

"So, that perfect little bed with its silk sheets isn't being slept in? Seems like such a waste." She pinched her tempura chicken between her chopsticks, then held it between her full, pouting lips and bit the tip off.

Benson waved over their waiter.

"Check please."

CHAPTER FIVE

When he awoke the next morning, Benson felt like he'd been wrung dry. He reached an arm to the other side of the bed, but found it empty. He half-remembered Theresa sneaking out in the early morning hours. Her scent lingered on more than just the sheets.

The warm, sumptuous sheets called for him to pull them over his head and ignore the universe for a few more hours. Still, the evening had energized him. He'd been one of the first dozen or so people to eat real chicken meat in over two centuries, and as satisfying as that experience had been, it was only the first of his appetites to be satiated before the night was over.

With great effort, Benson extricated himself from the bed and dressed in yesterday's clothes. It was still twenty minutes before the morning lights warmed up, so he snuck around to the side of the apartment and off the main footpaths to avoid prying eyes. An easy job considering he knew where all the security cameras were, which ones were stuck pointing in one direction, and which ones were offline altogether.

The door opened on his small apartment. Benson sighed. "Back to reality," he mumbled. He glanced at the time stamp on his wall display. There was still time for his morning run around the module's circumference, if he pushed. But Benson wasn't in the mood to hurry. Besides, he'd gotten enough exercise the night before.

Instead, Benson jumped in the shower and quickly rinsed off the remaining evidence of the evening's... entertainments, then put on fresh clothes. The lights above flickered to life as he made his way to work.

Avalon's stationhouse was situated in the ground floor of one of the towers on the module's forward bulkhead, while a smaller outpost on the far end of the habitat served those residents. The layout was mirrored in Shangri-La, to give constables quick access to the lifts, if the two forces ever needed to come together for mutual support. So far, that hadn't been necessary, but Landing was in less than two weeks.

It was impossible to predict how people were going to react. Benson's counterpart, Chief Bahadur, had been gently suggesting a few joint crowd control exercises for weeks, an idea Benson was finally coming around to. They'd been adversaries once, playing for opposing teams. Their post-Zero careers had taken similar paths, and now instead of adversaries, they were close colleagues, even friends.

The stationhouses were an afterthought. Benson's was made up of just five rooms. A waiting area in front, Benson's closet of an office, two private debriefing rooms, and a storage area for equipment and the evidence locker. It lacked holding cells. Indeed, the ship had no jails of any kind.

The Ark Project had been suffused with almost delusional levels of optimism from its inception. The selection process that picked the first fifty thousand pioneers had many facets. Chief among them was physical fitness, disease resistance, and an absence of genetic defects. It was a chance to weed out the worst of the hereditary baggage mankind had accumulated over the last hundred thousand generations.

However, a parallel effort, not as well advertised, eliminated other troublesome traits. Criminal tendencies, antisocial behavior, and the predisposition towards violence were all factors that quietly moved candidates into the rejection pile, and moved criminality into the dustbin of history. The problem solved, the engineers hadn't bothered to waste precious space on jails that would stand empty for the entire trip anyway. At least, that had been the theory.

The program hadn't been without measurable successes. By and large, the population of the Ark was far less violent than the people who had lived on Earth, even eleven generations after launch. But some impulses were buried far too deeply in the software to be simply purged.

When someone did go off the script badly enough, sentences were simple by necessity. Minor infractions were dealt with through a combination of community service and house arrest. Serious crimes were a different matter. Since society couldn't afford to waste finite resources locking up someone who posed a danger to the ship, only one solution presented itself.

It kept recidivism down, at least.

Theresa saluted him as he walked into the stationhouse. He returned it jokingly, but the coy smile he'd expected to see on her face didn't materialize. Benson gave her a look that plainly said, "What's wrong?"

Her eyes darted to his office door, letting him know they weren't alone. Benson nodded almost imperceptibly, then entered his office.

"Officer Feng." Benson threw a salute, a real one this time. "I wasn't expecting you, sir."

Chao Feng returned his salute from Benson's own chair. "Unsurprising, as I only decided to come down here a half hour ago." He motioned towards the only other chair in the sparse room. "Please, detective, sit."

Benson did so. "You're here to tell me something I'm not going to like."

Feng laced his fingers. "So, we're skipping the small talk about the Mustangs' chances to keep the series going?"

"I know you're more of a bandwagon Yaoguai fan, sir. And I doubt you schlepped all the way down from Command to chat about Zero."

Feng smiled. "That's why you're the detective."

"I do try. What's the story?"

Feng sat up straighter and leaned over the desk. "The truth is, I came down here to tell you directly. Magistrate Boswell has reviewed your request to unlock crewman Edmond Laraby's personal files..."

Benson inhaled. He'd submitted the warrant request first thing upon getting back to his apartment in the morning.

"...and has declined to issue a warrant at this time."

Benson's shoulders slumped. "Is this a joke?"

Feng perked up at the question. "Not at all, detective. It was the magistrate's judgment that crewman Laraby's privacy must be respected."

"The man is missing! I'm supposed to find him before he becomes compost."

Feng opened his hands. "Which is why I strongly suggest you return to *looking* for him instead of going through his dirty laundry."

"Officer Feng…" Benson tried to calm himself before continuing. "The odds that Laraby's disappearance and that his priceless, stolen painting are unrelated are… well, an appropriately absurd metaphor doesn't jump to mind at the moment. Let's just say they're really low."

Feng shrugged. "It's the magistrate's call, detective, not mine. You know that, and I doubt your time would be any better spent arguing the point with him. Magistrate Boswell has made his decision for now, but he left the door open. Find crewman Laraby and you can question him about his taste in art all you like. But do it quickly, Director da Silva has been screaming at me for two days already about lost productivity. I suggest you go out and beat the bushes."

Benson felt a scathing comeback surging in his throat, but it would be futile.

"I'll be in need of my desk in that case, sir."

Feng stood up. He was rather more muscled than the average floater, but still leaner than people who spent most of their time in the habitats. They pirouetted in what little space was available and changed places. Benson threw a salute, then sat down as soon as Officer Feng had left. He was immediately replaced by Theresa.

"What the hell was that all about?" she asked.

"Oh, the usual. Boss refuses to give you the tools you need to do the job, then leans on you to get the job done faster anyway."

Theresa sat down. "The magistrate denied the warrant?" Benson nodded. "Still think my theory about someone protecting him is crazy?"

Benson put his arms behind his head. "Interference from on high is looking more likely, but how does this help us find him?"

"Maybe we're not meant to."

Benson stood up. "Well, then they're going to be disappointed." He pushed past her on his way to the door.

"Going to go shoulder check the truth out of someone?"

"My job is a little more subtle these days."

"You're not a subtle man."

"I know," Benson shrugged. "It's a real problem."

Benson pressed the call button to Apartment #168, on the bottom floor of the Mumbai Building, Shangri-La module. Nothing happened.

It wasn't that no one answered the door, but that literally nothing happened. The button itself didn't ring. He tried it again with identical results. Instead, Benson dug deep into his bag of detective tricks and simply knocked on the door the old-fashioned way. When that didn't get a response after a handful of seconds, he tried beating on it.

"Police! I know you're home, Mr Kite." Benson paused and listened for any movement, then knocked on the door again. "I can always just come to chat while you're at work."

That got a response. He could hear feet shuffling on the other side of the door, then the sound of a deadbolt sliding open. The door opened a crack, held in check by a chain. An angry eye glared through the slit.

"Mr Kite. I'm Detective Benson."

"I know who you are, detective," the dry voice said

impatiently. "Your jurisdiction ends at Avalon's lock. We're in Shangri-La. Unless you're stopping for directions?"

Benson shook his head. "It's not that kind of visit. You're not in any trouble. I just want some insight."

"Into what?"

"A young man is missing, and I think his hobbies have something to do with it. May I come in, please?"

The face peered out at him for a moment, but finally gave a curt nod. The door shut, the chain rattled, then it swung open again, revealing a gnarled man beaten down by the weight of a long life, yet standing as tall as his short frame would allow.

"Thank you, Mr Kite."

The older man shrugged. "Call me Sal. Everybody else does."

"OK, Sal. By the way, your call button is broken."

"It ain't broke, I disconnected it. I got tired of people askin' to hear the old war stories."

"Nobody thinks to knock?"

"You'd be surprised what nobody thinks to do." He motioned at a small plastic chair that looked like it had been scavenged from a kindergarten. "It's sturdier than it looks. Can I get you anything? Tea? Something stiffer?"

"Tea is fine. Just between you and me, I'm still nursing a bit of a hangover."

"Some honey with your tea, then." Sal disappeared around a corner into his kitchenette while Benson sat down. The apartment was... people trying to be polite would call it cozy and lived-in. In reality, it was a cramped dive. A strong scent of potpourri infused the air, trying to mask the undercurrents of something much fouler, but mostly failing.

The only bright spots in the otherwise dreary apartment were a pair of paintings hanging on the wall, right under a ceiling light in a place of honor. They were surrealist landscapes, one of ants and melting clocks, the other of a woman sitting on a shore with drawers in her chest.

Benson moved to inspect them more closely.

"You like my little collection, Detective?" Sal walked up behind him and offered him a plastic cup and saucer.

"They're certainly... different. Are they real?"

"You mean, did I somehow manage to hold onto some of my ill-begotten loot? No, detective, they're fakes. I paid for them to be printed fair and square." His watery eyes peered into Benson's when he didn't reply. "You don't recognize them, do you?" Benson shook his head. "I figured. An art aficionado would know the real *Persistence of Memory* is only as big as a sheet of paper. I had the printers enlarge it. But I did the brushstroke varnish myself," he said, with a trace of wistful pride.

"I was never one for art, I'm sorry to say." He pulled his tablet out of a jacket pocket, then brought up an image file of the Monet he'd found in Laraby's home. "But you, obviously, are. Can you tell me anything about this painting?"

Sal leaned in to get a better look. "Part of the Haystacks series. Monet painted a bunch of these things. The same haystack at different times of day. He was always experimenting with light and color. Obsessed with it, you could say." Sal's eyes seemed to go unfocused for a second, before zeroing back in on the image like a hawk. "Where was this taken?"

"Two days ago. In Avalon."

"And it's the real thing?" he asked breathlessly.

"Yes, Madam Curator confirmed it only last night."

A flicker of intense anger burned across his face. But it was gone in an instant, like a memory of hate. "So," Sal continued. "A Monet survived after all."

"It certainly seems that way. That's why I'm here, why I want to talk to you."

"Why? To warn me not to steal it?" His tone turned icy. "I'm a lonely old man. Why'd you come all the way over here to bother me?"

"Because the man who had this is the one who's missing, and I don't have much time to find him."

Some flicker of understanding passed between the two men. "This was in a private collection, then? Not hidden away in the museum's vaults?"

Benson nodded. "Yes, exactly."

"Of course it was," Sal smiled viciously. "Old Benny would have fingered a piece like that in a heartbeat. Never could've kept that hidden from him."

Benson sipped his tea and let the old criminal talk.

"We didn't do it for the money, you know. Not all of us, at least."

Benson set his cup down on a small table. "The Heist was before my time. I've read about it, seen the vids, but you're the only person directly involved I've ever talked to. On this side of the law, at least."

"Yeah, well, the Council made us hard to find, if you know what I mean."

Benson did. Every one of the Heist conspirators had been executed but Salvador Kite, and he'd only been saved because he'd been a few months shy of eighteen.

"I understand," Benson said. "You said you didn't do it for the money? Why *did* you do it, then?"

Sal took a deep, cleansing breath before answering. "Because people aren't supposed to live like this, are we? Two thousand calories a day, no more. Tell the government who you want to fuck. Get a license to make a baby." He laughed, almost giddily. "What's your birthday, Detective Benson?"

"January third."

"No, it isn't!" Kite snapped. "Because you weren't 'born' at all, were you? You, me, everybody came out of them gooey tanks." Sal ran a hand through his thinning hair, as if checking it for artificial amniotic fluid. "They says it's 'cause it's safer, but I say it's easier to control people. Back on Earth, nobody waited for the government to tell them they've been granted the privilege of parenthood, did they?"

"I suppose not," Benson allowed. "But Earth's resources were almost limitless. The Ark can only support fifty thousand at a time."

"Yeah, I know all the excuses. But what's stopping them from just saying 'First come, first serve,' answer me that? You can't, because you're their enforcer, aren't you? How many kids you got already, young man?"

"I…" The question caught Benson off-guard. "I haven't found the right woman yet." He hoped the answer would deflect the growing diatribe, but it only seemed to fuel Kite's anger.

"The right girl? You're a Zero Hero. You've probably bedded more right women than I've ever locked lips with in fifty-three years, son. And a police chief? The floaters would sign off on any kid you wanted to shit out."

An unexpected surge of anger threatened to boil over, but Benson beat it back. "I think we're veering off-topic."

"Damned right we are." Sal took a long pull from a tumbler in his left hand, then saluted to Benson. "Hope you don't mind if I indulge a little, detective. You're missing out on choice stuff. Genuine whiskey made the old way by a friend of mine down in the ponds. Has a still hidden in the pipes that your boys've never found."

Benson sensed an opportunity. He held out his hand for the tumbler. Kite regarded him coolly, but handed him the glass after a moment's reflection.

Benson took the tumbler and sniffed the amber liquid, letting the smoky, oaken flavors dance through his nose before taking a generous sip. A decade of nights spent drinking, cavorting, and taking liberal advantage of the ship's mandatory birth-control regimen came flooding back. Too many nights, and too many mornings wasted.

"I didn't think you were allowed to drink on duty."

"We're not. I guess that means you have some leverage on me." The two men locked eyes until Sal nodded his understanding. "My compliments to your friend," Benson said. "Although I'd love to know where he got the wood to age it."

"You'd be surprised how crafty people can be down in the ponds, detective."

"Not really. I spent ten years working an aeroponics farm myself. Some of the boys made white lightning that burned all the way down to your toenails." Benson handed the glass back to its rightful owner. "I'm not here to bust illegal stills, Sal. It doesn't matter much at this point anyway. You still didn't tell me why you did it."

Sal took his own sip from the tumbler, then savored the delicate aftertaste before answering. "I couldn't tell you, exactly. I guess most of us, the younger ones at least, wanted to send a message. That all this," he held out his hands, motioning to his small gallery, "belongs to everybody, not some self-appointed, nepotistic overlords. This is our history, our legacy as human beings. It's all we've got left besides our genes, and they control those too. Well, mostly."

"That's a bit jaded, isn't it? Anyone can apply for a berth among the crew if their marks are good enough."

"And who votes on what's 'good enough,' eh? Remember what happened to that rabble-rouser Kimura when he tried to use the Council to leverage the selection process away from them? How long before he had a 'heart attack'?"

Benson did remember, even though David Kimura had died several years before he'd been born. Kimura was a firebrand from Shangri-La. He was one of only a handful of crewmembers to ever resign their post, and instead took up politics running on a platform of greater transparency for the crew and privacy for citizens. A staunch opponent of implants in children, he'd been elected to a seat on the Council with a mandate to transfer the crew selection process to the civilian authority. His bill died with him less than a year into his first term.

"How many cattle kids make it through?" Sal continued. "Just enough to give us plebs hope, but never enough to actually change the culture. Shit, I'll bet they know exactly what that number is, too. Probably have an algorithm all figured out for it." He waved an angry hand in the air. "Bah, you don't want to listen to an old crook rant. They won a long time ago. Now, I just work in the shit pits and try to keep my head down."

Benson sat back down in the little chair. "You're a

passionate man, Mr Kite, and there's a lot more depth to you than I expected. But if you're serious about the Heist being about liberating our legacy, then how do you explain the fact that most of the pieces disappeared for years? About a dozen are *still* missing."

Sal's angry expression turned sour. "Because not all of us were in it for the right reasons. Maybe most of us weren't and I was blinded by youthful idealism, I don't know anymore. But almost as soon as we got back to the hide-out, everyone started fighting about who to sell them to. We were getting bids on stuff through back channels and plant messages every ten seconds."

"From who?" Benson jumped from his seat. "That's what I need to know. Your accomplices are all dead, I understand that, but your buyers aren't. We've caught a lot of them, but a lot of pieces were turned in anonymously. If I know who the players were, then maybe I can apply some pressure and figure out not only how this kid came to have a Monet hanging in his home, but why he went missing."

"Sorry, detective," Sal shook his head, "but I can't help you."

"Why not?"

"Because powerful people are on that list. As low as I've been knocked down here, they can still hurt me. No, I'm going to hunker down until I'm strapped into my shuttle seat down to the surface, then take my chances."

Benson leaned back. "I'm confused. You talk like you're being persecuted, but you think you're going to be given a spot in the colony?"

Sal smiled. "I like you, detective. You're still young enough to buy into the whole idea of 'justice'. But I'll bet you dollars to donuts that I'm on the second shuttle down. The first will be loaded with debutants. The second will be loaded with us disposables, the people who'll be hacking down the trees or whatever, shoveling the ditches and pouring the concrete. The people taking all the real risks, the ones they won't mind losing when a tree falls the wrong way, or some wild animal gets past the fence. Nobody relies on me, they made sure of that. I got no family left, never got approved for kids, and now I'm too old to start. What do you think that makes me?"

Benson smiled. "I think my father was fifty-seven when I was bor... when he had me, and that the whole reproductive selection process probably isn't going to survive Landing. But that's not anything I can guarantee. Instead, I have something else you might be interested in."

Sal looked skeptical, to say the least, but nodded for him to continue.

"I know you've been banned for life from the museum. What if I could get you private time, after hours? No one to disturb you."

A hearty laugh erupted from deep in Sal's belly. "Why don't you head outside and part the reclamation lake while you're at it?"

"Laugh all you like, but Madame Feynman and I are on very good terms. In fact, she owes me a favor."

"She owes *you* a favor. Me, she'd just as soon see 'recycled' as spit on me."

"Maybe so, but if any of the names you coughed up meant even one more piece of her lost collection was returned to her loving care, I guarantee she'd carry you piggyback through a guided tour."

Sal regarded him coolly, but Benson thought he saw a flickering spark of optimism, too.

"C'mon Sal, what do you say? Is it worth taking a little risk for a real look at some old flames? I hear the *Birth of Venus* is coming out of storage for a viewing this week. You haven't seen her in a while, have you?"

"That's not fighting fair, son. Did you cheat this bad in the Zero can, too?"

Benson bristled at the accusation. "I never cheated, Mr Kite. Maybe they did write a few new rules as a direct response to some of my more brilliant formation building, but that was after the fact."

The old man smirked, recognizing a kindred spirit when he saw one. "One last chance to stick my thumb in their eye, eh?"

Benson nodded.

"Tour first. If that doesn't happen, I ain't saying nothing."

"Naturally. I'll speak to Feynman as soon as I leave here. You'll have an answer before your next shift starts."

"Maybe my last shift, too." Sal's eyes fixed on the bottom of his glass. He swirled the whiskey around a couple times, turning the idea over in his head, giving it a taste. Then he swallowed the rest of the illicit booze in one mighty gulp.

"We have a deal, detective."

CHAPTER SIX

The call came at a bad time. Benson decided that, if during a Zero Championship game was bad, three o'clock in the morning was definitely worse.

"Accept call," he said to the dark room. A chime rang, letting him know the call had connected.

"Hello, detective." It was First Officer Feng's plant voice again, so different from the one Benson had sat through in his office only that morning. "I hope I'm not interrupting."

"Feng, anything I could be doing at 03.00, you'd be interrupting."

"Sorry, but this can't wait. We've found something."

Benson's stomach sank. "What did you find?"

"Probably better if you just come to Command, detective."

"Do I have time for a cup of tea?"

"We'll have a bag waiting for you."

Benson shook head. "Right. Give me twenty."

"Hurry, detective."

Five locks and two retina scans later, Benson floated through the door into Command. It was only the third time in his life he'd been a guest inside the sphere that was the epicenter of all the Ark's operations.

Command was a gleaming beacon, awash in the light of computer screens, holographic displays, and work stations covering every square meter of its inside surface. It was cool here, just as it had been in the labs, but around two hundred people, nearly a fifth of the crew's complement, busied themselves overseeing every aspect of the Ark's myriad of automated systems, sensors, and life support systems. It was all slightly overwhelming, even for someone who'd spent as many hours in microgravity as Benson had.

Hovering at the geometric center of the maelstrom, perched in a sort of cradle, First Officer Feng noticed Benson floating near the entrance and waved him up. No guards stood watch here. None were necessary with only one door. If the crew didn't trust someone to be in Command, they would never have entered in the first place. David Kimura had been right; this was where the real power was concentrated on the Ark. Most people would never set foot in Command, much less have any real say in the decisions made here.

"Good evening, detective," Feng called over his shoulder as Benson drifted closer. "Or I suppose good morning, in your case."

"Either could apply. Where's the captain?"

"Sleeping, I expect. Not her watch."

Benson reflected that sleep hadn't stopped Feng from disturbing him, but let it pass without comment. "So, what did you find?"

"Here, let me show you what we've got." Feng waved a hand, scrolling through a series of menus until he found the icon he wanted. A velvety black hologram coalesced in the air in front of them both. At its center, a faint grey smudge marred the otherwise endless black. Feng held out his hands and made an enlarging gesture with his thumbs and index fingers. The smudge grew and resolved into a slightly more coherent blur tumbling slowly through space. It took a few rotations before Benson's mind worked out the pattern. A central mass with four extremities.

"A body," Benson sighed heavily. "Our missing man."

"As I said, we don't know yet, but I wanted you to be the first to see."

"Well, what else could it be? Unless you're suggesting a meteor just happened to fall into formation with us at five percent lightspeed."

"Certainly not, but it may still be a piece of the Ark herself. Some insulation foam, or a chunk of ablative plating from the shield. We entered Tau Ceti's Oort cloud almost a year ago, after all. We've had quite a few impacts in that time. No telling what may have gotten knocked loose."

"Then why is this only turning up now?"

"We only spotted it now. There isn't usually any reason to look anywhere but straight ahead. We don't know how long it's been there."

"Can you resolve the image?"

"No. There's very little ambient light to begin with, and our ten-meter optical telescope in the bow can't get an angle. This isn't even a real image. It's a render based off an old collision avoidance radar leftover from construction that just happened to be pointed in the right direction."

Benson frowned. "OK, how far out is it?"

"Twenty-seven hundred meters and increasing by a few meters per minute."

"Growing?" Benson said. "Shouldn't the ship's gravity be pulling it back in?"

Feng shrugged. "It may have been, but we made a small course correction to avoid a comet fragment a couple hours ago. That probably broke it free of our gravity well."

"How long before our recovery window closes?"

"Ninety minutes."

"Then we need to go now."

Feng nodded agreement. "We're prepping an EVA pod now. I'll link us into the live feed."

"No, I'm going out," Benson said firmly, surprising even himself.

"Out there?" Feng said carefully. "You'll be outside of the Ark's meteor shield. We could probably spare a couple of nav lasers to clear anything bigger than a millimeter or so from your path, but smaller than that is below our radar's detection threshold. The shield soaks up everything too small to spot, but an EVA pod doesn't have the armor for it. A grain of sand or speck of dust would go straight through it. And you."

Benson already knew all of that, although maybe not in such stark terms, but held his ground regardless. "I know you're holding out hope that this thing isn't a body, but I have to proceed assuming it is. As of right now, I'm declaring that object to be part of a crime scene and potential evidence in an ongoing investigation. Which means I have to go investigate it."

Feng eyed him apprehensively. "Are you sure you want to do this?"

"Nope," Benson shook his head. "Not at all."

"Good, that means you're not suicidal at least." Feng's eyes went gently out of focus, a telltale sign he'd started a plant call. Benson waited patiently for the conversation to run its course.

"I've just spoken with Engineering Director Hekekia. He's about as thrilled with the idea as I am, but he's prepping an EVA pod. He'll be waiting for you in the portside hanger."

"It'll take me a half hour to get all the way back to the engineering module."

"Preflight checks will take about that long. Be quick, detective. And don't take any unnecessary risks. If that's our missing man, then we've already lost enough."

Benson nodded, then pushed back towards the exit.

In fact, it was almost forty-five minutes by the time Benson finally entered the port maintenance bay. This did not impress the dark, thick Samoan waiting for him near the door. Hekekia was, by any measure, the sturdiest crewmember on the ship. A man who spent so much time in micro had no business looking like a keg with arms.

"You're late," Director Hekekia reprimanded.

"Not my fault," Benson said. "One of the locks between Shangri-La and Avalon was closed for maintenance."

"Is that a joke?"

Benson shook his head innocently. "Only on a cosmic level."

Hekekia squinted at him, but let it lie. "The pod is ready for you. Follow me and we'll get you in a suit."

"I thought the EVA pods were shirt-sleeve environments."

"They are. But my people don't insist on taking them past the shield umbrella and out into a shooting gallery. If you have a hull breach and lose atmosphere, the suit will give you time to come back home."

"And what are the odds of that happening?"

He shrugged. "Who knows? The shield gets hit between eighteen and fifty times per day. My advice? Be quick."

Even with help, it took him another ten minutes to get buttoned up inside the vac-suit. It wasn't a true spacesuit; their life-support systems were too bulky to fit inside the maintenance pod's hatch, but it would keep his blood from boiling and held enough air for about a half hour, so if anything went wrong he would have plenty of time to think about how stupid the idea had been.

"OK," Hekekia tucked the last zipper into its flap. "Remember, we're going to pilot the pod from here. You're just a passenger, so don't touch anything. I can't stress that enough."

Benson sighed. "Seriously, did you all take training on tape or something?"

He ignored him and continued. "We'll have a real-time video feed, so if you need something done, just ask and we'll handle it."

He guided him in his squishy vac-suit to the EVA pod's hatch. The "hangar" wasn't exactly what one would expect. No shuttles or pods cluttered the deck like forgotten children's toys. Instead, each pod butted up directly against the exterior hull like blisters, with small locks and tunnels providing pilot access. The director opened an inner hatch and waved Benson through.

"Be careful, detective."

Benson smirked. "Was that a trace of concern I heard?"

"Of course. I can't afford to lose the pod. We're overscheduled with prep and inspections as it is."

"Gee, thanks."

"You asked. Good luck."

Benson smiled back at him sarcastically as the hatch closed and locked. He pushed off and floated the rest of the way down the narrow tube, past the emergency pressure doors and grabbed the handle of the outer hatch. It swung inward, revealing the interior of the pod itself.

The pod's hull was a flawless acrylic sphere more than two meters across and five centimeters thick, intended to maximize visibility. Everything else, including the life support pack, maneuvering thrusters, and hydraulic manipulator arms were bolted to the back and outside of the crystal orb. It reminded Benson of the sort of small submarines built for deep sea exploration back on Earth. Like most people on the Ark, he'd gone through a phase watching every documentary about Earth life he could find in the database, if only to feel a deeper connection to the homeworld no one would ever see again. Benson had always liked the deep sea vids, if only because the weightlessness of being suspended in water seemed so familiar to him, and the creatures so alien. He'd often dreamed about exploring the Tau Ceti G oceans in one of those little subs.

Now, faced with the cramped confines and the endless, infinite black of deep space without the warm blanket of the Ark surrounding him, a chill ran down the length of his spine, then turned right around and made a lap of it.

"What the hell were you thinking, Bryan?" he chastised himself.

"What was that?" Hekekia said through the com built

into his helmet. "I didn't copy."

"Nothing. Closing the hatch." He pulled the door shut behind him and spun the manual locks into place.

"Strap in tight, detective. Wouldn't want you to bump your head."

Benson arranged himself in the pilot's seat and fumbled through the thick gloves until he'd managed to click the five-point harness into place. "Ready."

"OK, launching now."

Benson heard the metallic snap as the docking clamps released the pod. For a moment, nothing happened as he drifted gently away from the Ark. Then the thrusters kicked in, sending a shudder through the pod and gently pressing Benson back into his seat. The outer hull fell away.

For the first time in his life, Benson left the Ark. His eyes adjusted quickly to the total black of space, revealing it to be anything but total. A billion points of light stared back at him like eyes in a dark forest.

It wasn't anything like the deep sea vids. Those were closed in, claustrophobic, extending only so far as the submersible's lights could claw their way through the dark. He entirely forgot about the close confines of the pod as his consciousness ran in every direction trying to fill the immense void. Primal fear grabbed his heart in its cold embrace and squeezed like a vice.

He grabbed the control sticks and cranked on them in a desperate bid to turn the pod around, but nothing happened. Then the infinite abyss sucked Benson's mind into its depth.

"Detective," said a tinny voice in his ear. "Your vitals just spiked. Are you OK?"

"Too…" He gasped for breath. "Too big."

"You're having a panic attack, detective," Hekekia said. "Listen to me. This isn't unusual. Focus on something in the cockpit, anything. Look at your hand if you have to."

He ignored him and strained against his harness in a panicked attempt to get to the hatch.

"Detective Benson!" Hekekia shouted. "If you can't get a hold of yourself, I will have to abort and return the pod to the ship."

A significant portion of Benson's fragile psyche thought that sounded just lovely. However, enough of him remained that he managed to listen to Hekekia's commands and fixated on his own palm. For a long, long moment, Benson forced himself to be very interested in the stitching on the inside of his glove.

"Detective, be advised, we're going to spin the pod around a hundred and eighty degrees. Keep your focus on the Ark herself. This will give you a point of reference. Just avoid looking at the stars for now."

"OK," he said weakly. Cold sweat beaded on his forehead. A thruster fired and the pod gently spun around on its central axis. The Ark drifted into view in all its glory, starting with the enormous, ablative orange cone at the front that was the meteor shield. Very quickly, the command module came into view, with the Operations sphere right at the front, followed by the myriad of cylindrical towers and wart-like projections that held the labs.

Next, the two gigantic cans of Shangri-La and Avalon rotated into view. From this angle, Benson couldn't even see the module that housed the Zero stadium nestled between them. It was too narrow. Barely visible in the dark, the flags of every nation of Earth had been painted on the ribbed hulls of the habitats, over two hundred in total. Some were larger than others, a none-too-subtle reminder of which countries had contributed the most to the project. A final boast to ensure their legacy far into the future.

Benson didn't recognize more than a handful of them.

The engineering section drifted into view. Compared to the simple, almost organic aesthetic of Command and the habitat modules, it was a jumbled mess of pipes, conduits, and sharp angles. Benson saw a half dozen of the fleet of atmospheric shuttles stuck to the hull like remoras. Soon, they would begin to ferry people down to the surface of Tau Ceti G. Each one could hold almost five hundred passengers. They were all individually bigger than any airplane mankind had ever built, but were still dwarfed by the Ark herself.

Beyond engineering, thirty-two stupendous two-stage shock absorbers stretched backwards over two kilometers until they joined with the aft shield dish. For over two centuries, the shock-absorbers and aft disk had waited patiently for their second and final spot in the limelight.

And sitting right in the middle of it all, a repository of almost inconceivable destructive power sat waiting for someone to light the fuse. During a short time in the twentieth century, what propelled the Ark had been the single greatest threat the continued survival of mankind had ever faced. Hidden away deep inside the engineering section, literally tens of thousands of thermonuclear bombs sat at the ready. But instead of being put to use destroying entire continents, they had, somewhat ironically, been harnessed to ensure the salvation of the entire species.

The Ark was Project Orion taken to proportions never dreamed of by the men who had first proposed its brilliant insanity. Benson had once heard the ship's propulsion described in the crudest of terms: a sixteen kilometer long pogo-stick that shits atomic bombs. Crude, but entirely accurate. Bombs were thrown out the back, then detonated. The aft dish absorbed the immense shockwave from all the violence and converted it into forward momentum. The kilometers-long shock absorbers helped to even out the concussion enough that the force didn't convert everyone inside into red pudding.

Repeated thousands of times, the bombs had accelerated the Ark to her current velocity of fifteen thousand kilometers per second, carrying her almost a dozen lightyears away from the star of her birth. And in less than two weeks, a torrent of nuclear bombs that had once threatened Armageddon would slow the Ark back down and deliver mankind to the Promised Land.

Benson's little pod finally drifted far enough that he could fit the entire Ark into his peripheral vision. The surrounding stars provided dim illumination, and Tau Ceti itself was still so far away as to only be the brightest among them. But in the absence of any other lights to pollute his eyes, he could still see the ship clearly. For over two centuries, every human life had taken place inside this enormous, ungainly, beautiful girl. Every birth, every death. Every intimate moment, every argument. Every crime, and every act of charity.

A tiny blob intruded into his view. It took him a moment to realize what it was. It was a tear, suspended by microgravity into a perfect sphere. He was crying.

"Detective, are you all right?"

Benson wiped his eyes. "Yes, I'm better. I think I have a handle on it. Sorry."

"As I said, it's not unusual your first time out." Hekekia's sarcastic voice had softened. It sounded almost paternal. "I should tell you, you're the first person in a hundred years to be so far out. You weaseled your way into a heck of a view."

"That I did," he agreed solemnly.

"You're almost on top of the object. We need to spin the pod back around. Are you ready to proceed?"

"Yes, I think so."

"OK. We're keeping a close watch on your vitals. If you start to feel the attack return, try to focus on the arm of the galaxy to keep yourself oriented."

Benson took a deep breath and stole one more look at the Ark. As huge as it was, weighed against infinity, it seemed tiny, fragile. Vulnerable.

"Roger that," he said finally. "Go ahead and get me back in position."

The pod shuttered once more as the thruster pack fired. Slowly, the Ark fell back out of view, replaced by a great milky band of stars that was the galaxy seen edge on. It looked like a single grand stroke of a mad painter's brush. Suspended right in the middle of it, like an ink stain, a shadow moved against the stars.

"I've spotted the target," Benson said. "Can we get a light on it?"

The black smudge turned white a heartbeat later.

"We're about to decelerate the pod to bring you to a zero/zero intercept. Ready?"

Benson clenched his stomach and grabbed his shoulder straps. "Do it."

The pod shook as he was thrown forward into his harness. A fog formed ahead of the pod as escaping propellant gasses hit the floodlights. A few seconds later, the shaking stopped abruptly and the fog disappeared, replaced by a gently tumbling form drifting dead ahead.

Emphasis on dead.

Benson let out a long, ragged sigh. "I've reached the target. It's a body all right. One more for the Clock."

"Is it the man you're looking for?"

"I can't see his face yet, but the list of candidates isn't very long. Standby." Benson leaned forward, as if the extra couple centimeters would help, and waited for the body to spin back around to face him. He'd seen bodies before, of course, but always at memorial services just before they were recycled. After they'd been cleaned up, and usually well into their golden years. Benson tried to brace himself for what he was about to see.

He was completely unprepared for the explosion.

CHAPTER SEVEN

The starboard manipulator arm disintegrated into a violent swarm of tiny projectiles pinging off the acrylic sphere like a shotgun blast, leaving a dozen chips in the glass and sending the pod spinning out of control.

"Mayday!" Benson shouted into the com as the Ark tumbled into and out of his view. "Mayday! I'm hit!"

Only years spinning around in the Zero ring kept him from blacking out or throwing up. Warning lights blinked angrily all around him, while an alarm screamed throughout the tiny cabin loud enough to ring in his ears until his visor snapped shut, silencing them.

"Mayday, does anyone copy?" Bursts of static filled his ears. "Mayday. I'm calling from inside the EVA pod."

Agonizing seconds ticked by while Benson waited for a response. The pod's gyrations continued unabated. The com was his only hope, he was way outside of the range of his plant's wireless connection.

Memories of his rookie season came flooding back unexpectedly, when he'd first been strapped into the "Gyrotron." Ostensibly, it was a training tool meant to acclimatize rookies to the disorientation of microgravity. In practice, it was a way to knock cocky newbies down a peg by making them puke in front of their teammates. He'd been put in it four times his first season before the lesson finally sank in.

An eternity later, a message finally came through, albeit in text form projected on the inside of the canopy glass.

—This is Command. Your main coms appear to be out. Connection limited to emergency backup. What is your status?—

Benson touched an icon to switch his transmissions to voice-to-text. "I've been hit by a meteor. Starboard arm is gone. Hangar's control has been lost and I'm spinning like a piñata. I need local control restored. Send."

Vertigo set in. No matter how much training or experience, no one could fend it off forever in such a chaotic spin.

—Hangar reports it cannot restore control. There's a manual override in the cabin.—

"What does it look like? Send."

—It is a small amber light that started blinking after the connection was cut.—

"They're ALL fucking blinking! Send!" He immediately regretted shouting as bile rose in his throat.

—Standby…—

"Really, an ellipsis?" Benson laughed at the punctuation, if only to keep his growing panic at bay for a few seconds longer.

—Amber light. Control panel by your right shoulder.—

He craned his head around inside the helmet and spotted the light. With the gyrations throwing off his aim, it took three tries, but Benson finally landed a thumb on it. Half of the blinking lights switched off immediately, while a new holographic HUD and systems interface overlaid themselves on the inside of the cracked canopy glass. The twin joysticks built into his chair's armrests also seemed to stiffen.

"Got it. Send."

—Your joysticks are feedback sensitive. Push in the direction of the most resistance to slow the spin.—

Benson wiggled the sticks around until he found where they seemed to be pushing back the hardest, then cranked down on them as hard as he could. The pod groaned and shook as the thrusters fired at full strength. A cloud of gas shot out in every direction, enveloping the pod like a ninja's smoke bomb and completely obscuring any outside point of reference Benson had. He had to fall back on the artificial horizon on the HUD.

Gradually, glacially, the pod's chaotic spin slowed, but the attitude and angle kept drifting. Benson had to make constant adjustments to the joysticks to keep up. A new warning flashed crimson across the HUD: THRUSTER PROPELLANT 30%.

He was burning though propellant too fast. Unless he stopped soon, he wouldn't have enough left to turn around and return to the Ark. He'd just have to tap into the emergency reserve. There was always an emergency reserve. Right?

By the time Benson brought the pod to heel, scarcely ten percent of the propellant remained. The cloud of spent gas dissipated as quickly as it had formed, leaving him alone with the galaxy once more. He caught a glimpse of the Ark's aft plate off to port. For quite a long time, he just sat soaked through with cold sweat, breathing heavily, and waiting for the fluid in his inner ears to stop spinning.

Still disoriented, Benson went to wipe the sweat of his face, but his hand bounced off glass. It was a moment before the enormity of the crisis sunk in. If his helmet had sealed, that meant...

He looked up at the array of tiny pockmarks in the glass dome. One of them was significantly bigger than the others. Big enough to go straight through the acrylic. The puncture was deceptively small, no more than a half centimeter across. It was enough. The cabin was entirely out of air. The vac-suit had saved his life, after all.

—Detective Benson. What is your status?—

He couldn't help but chuckle. "I'm swell. How about you? Send."

—Have you regained control of the pod?—

"Yes. But the cabin's been punctured. There's no more internal air, and I'm down to ten percent propellant. Figure I have about half an hour to wrap this up. Send."

—Recovery is aborted. Return to the portside hangar immediately.—

Oh, like hell it is, Benson thought. "Didn't copy that last. You're breaking up. Send."

He cut the connection before Command had a chance to respond and turned his attention back to the space outside his little bubble. If the ass end of the Ark was to port, then the body would be to starboard, provided it hadn't been hit by debris from the pod and knocked clear.

With one eye glued on the propellant status, Benson goosed the pod around ninety degrees to try to spot the body again. He didn't have the benefit of the radar telemetry from the Ark, and half of the pod's floodlights had been lost with the starboard manipulator arm.

With his blood still drenched with adrenaline and

another panic attack threatening to grab hold of him, Benson stopped everything long enough to bring his breathing back under control. He'd already gone through the propellant too quickly, no sense burning up the oxygen just as recklessly. The short break took the edge off his nerves and gave his sense of balance time to center itself as well.

After some trial and error with the control interface, Benson figured out which toggle controlled the remaining spotlight, and even managed to synch it up to track his eye movements. He slowly, deliberately scanned the field in a grid pattern. His excitement rose when the beam returned a bright reflection, but a closer look revealed it was the remains of the severed manipulator arm.

Benson spared a thought for the meteor that had come so close to killing him. How big had it been? At their relative velocities, it could have been as small as an eyelash. $E=MC^2$ was a harsh mistress. But really, it had been a fluke. What were the odds he'd run afoul of another one?

Growing by the second, said the analytical part of his brain uninterested in bullshitting itself. Thankfully, a familiar ink blot floated into his peripheral vision. A small ranging laser built into the spotlight module put the body at just over a hundred meters away.

Benson knew enough about microgravity maneuvering to know that for every percent of propellant he used up getting to the body, he'd need to use three more to slow back down, turn around, speed back up, and then slow back down again once he reached the Ark, and he would need something left in the tank for last minute maneuvering to the nearest lock.

So, from a fuel standpoint, slower was better. But from a not-suffocating-to-death and not-getting-exploded-by-space-dust perspective, speed was king. Catch-22.

Benson decided it would be best to burn the thrusters down a point-and-a-half to reach the body, but no more. The pod swayed gently as the thrust built up. By the time he cut the throttle, he was only doing three meters per second relative to the Ark. The trip was the longest thirty-seven seconds of his life. Benson was careful to angle the pod ever so slightly away from the body before hitting the thrusters to avoid pushing it further away.

The body slowly span in space, rigid as a statue. The moment came that Benson finally had to look into the face of the victim. Despite being desiccated and discolored, it obviously matched Edmond Laraby's pictures, twisted into a frozen, primal scream. His bulging eyes had pushed themselves out from behind their lids.

Benson did his best to avoid the corpse's gaze and keyed up the manipulator arm controls, but that led to yet another warning, this time about a loss of hydraulic pressure. Debris must have punctured the line. He'd have one grab, maybe two, before the system ran dry.

"Does anything on this boat *not* have a hole in it?" Benson shouted to the heavens. He wondered, not for the first time, which of the pantheon of deities mankind still worshiped that he had upset.

Fortunately, the pod's controls had proven to be surprisingly intuitive. The arm was no different. Benson found a brief tutorial on how to use it inside the command interface. Once activated, the arm simply mimicked the operator's own arm movement. He reached out for the late Mr Laraby's ankle. A cone of finely atomized hydraulic fluid shot out the side of the arm. In his haste to grab Laraby before the fluid all bled out, Benson misjudged the distance and hit the body in the calf, sending it tumbling away and out of reach.

Benson swallowed a curse and nudged the pod forward just enough to close the gap once more, but burned up another few tenths of a percent of the remaining propellant to do so. Benson reached out again, more gingerly this time, trying to match his movements to the body's rotation. The last of the fluid squirted out into the vacuum like a new constellation.

With a last frantic grasp, Benson reached out and snagged himself an ankle. Fortunately, the claw was run off electric actuators instead of hydraulic pressure, so he didn't have to worry about Laraby's remains drifting off again. As soon as Benson had the body secured, he spun the pod back around to face the Ark, then burned for home, using as much of the remaining propellant as he dared. It earned him a meager two meters per second relative speed. Considering he was over three kilometers out, it was going to be a long trip back, maybe too long.

With the imminent threat of oxygen starvation chewing at his nerves, Benson passed the time going over the body in great detail, trying to reconstruct the last few terrible minutes of Laraby's life. The man was underdressed for a spacewalk, in the same scrubs Benson had seen the other environmental techs wear. No pressure suit, no helmet, missing a shoe. He had probably dressed for work the same way every day for months.

The exposed skin on his face and hands was too discolored to get any sense of bruising or signs of a struggle. Hopefully, an autopsy would be able to tell vacuum damage from other injuries, if any. The trouble was, with almost everyone dying of old age, the two doctors who served double duty as coroners had about as much experience examining potential murder victims as Benson himself did.

The other option, of course, was Laraby had simply decided to go for a swim without his trunks for his own reasons. Suicides were not unheard of, but still rare for several reasons. First, the most effective methods, guns and drugs, were nonexistent in the case of the former, and tightly controlled in the case of the latter. Coupled with the fact the seed population for the Ark had been screened for psychological disorders just as thoroughly as they had been for disease and genetic defects meant their great-great-great grandchildren were still largely free of depression and anxiety, at least as chronic conditions.

So what would convince a young man, respected for the work he was doing, and living in an enviable home, to off himself in just about the most violent and terrifying way possible? A few people over the years had taken a long step off the top of one of the residential towers, but to Benson's recollection, no one had ever voluntarily blown themselves out of an airlock.

As a method of suicide, it didn't make much sense. As a way to get rid of an inconvenient body, on the other hand, it was very convenient indeed. A decomposing body would be very difficult to hide anywhere onboard. The smell alone would be nearly impossible to contain. And the best way to get rid of a body, through the recycling process, would leave genetic material all over the place even after it had been dissolved, and that was assuming you could convince the reclamation techs to process a body "off the books" in the first place.

Benson thought back to Laraby's absolutely sterile house. If his instinct was right and it had been scrubbed intentionally, then the hypothetical killer wasn't one to take those kinds of chances. Shoving someone out of an airlock left no body behind to confirm a murder had even taken place.

But that scenario had problems of its own. First, locks were all under camera observation. Second, and more perplexing at the moment, was why Laraby's body was still here at all. As massive as the Ark was, its native gravity field was still extremely weak compared to Earth normal. Someone standing on the surface of the hull could achieve escape velocity with an overly-enthusiastic hop. Somebody who went to all this trouble surely would have known that and given Laraby's body a healthy enough shove to ensure he floated clear. So why hadn't they?

And how did the Monet fit into all of this, and what about the extremely convenient plant system glitch that had let Laraby's disappearing act go unnoticed for hours? Discovering the body hadn't really done anything but confirm what Benson had already known in the back of his mind. Instead of answering the hows and whys, Laraby's body only opened up more vexing questions.

None of which would be answered if Benson didn't bring his attention back to the sixteen kilometer ship growing in the canopy at an unsettling rate.

He glanced down at range and speed indicators. The pod's speed had grown from two meters per second, to nearly five. He hadn't hit the thrusters again, yet even as he watched the number trickled up. He was falling towards the Ark. Weak or not, its gravity was pulling him in.

"Stupid!" Benson actually hit himself on the side of the helmet. The low oxygen was affecting his brain. He hadn't factored in the extra speed now piling on from the Ark's gravity. Did he have enough propellant left to avoid a collision? How much more punishment could the pod take? The next few minutes were about to get very interesting.

He reopened the link back to Command. "This is Benson. I've completed recovery operations, but I'm low on O_2, almost out of propellant and am in danger of crashing into the Ark. Please advise. Send."

The response came quickly. —Ah, detective, we're glad to see your communication system has miraculously healed itself.—

"Hilarious, Feng. I'm in a bit of a jam out here. Send."

The Ark swelled beyond his field of vision, yet still it grew. Benson and the pod were being pulled ever so gently towards its center of mass, which happened to be the giant habitat modules spinning at hundreds of kilometers per hour. They were the absolute last place he wanted to crash into, except maybe the nuclear bomb vaults back in engineering.

Stars traced little paths through his field of vision. Benson grew dizzy and gulped for air.

"This is serious! Send!"

—Hangar informs us that there's a small emergency reserve of propellant aboard, but you shouldn't be so low in the first place. One or more propellant tanks must have been punctured in the accident. Without telemetry from the pod, we can't know if the reserve is still intact.—

Benson's stomach dropped to his feet, which was a curious sensation in microgravity. It came down to a roll of the dice. He goosed the joystick to angle the pod back towards the area of the hangars and away from the habitats, then began terminal maneuvers with the dwindling hope that the label wouldn't prove prescient.

The pod passed back inside the protective umbrella of the Ark's forward shield. At the very least, he had survived the shooting gallery, not that the realization gave him much comfort as the engineering section loomed. His speed had grown to seven and a half meters per second. The distance dropped to one hundred meters.

"Showtime."

He opened the taps on the thrusters. Harsh deceleration threw him forward into the harness and squeezed his chest. Already struggling for breath, Benson shook his heavy head and clung to consciousness. The propellant gauge counted down alarmingly fast as many dozens of cubic meters of gas escaped into the void between stars. In a handful of seconds, it reached zero. Benson's heart froze in his chest just as solidly as the corpse outside.

The thrusters continued to fire as the display turned red and the digits went into the negatives, eating up the emergency reserve. The pod's speed fell back below four meters per second, then below three as the distance continued to drop away. His vision shrank at the edges, as though he was looking into a tunnel.

Then, with forty meters left, the thrusters ran dry.

"Thrusters are spent. Impact with the hull in, uh, some seconds. If you could have someone come and get me that would be great. Send."

The hull was only meters away, but his sight was too cloudy to make out any detail. Then the tunnel closed in around him. As Benson plunged into blackness, the last thing he saw was the canopy silently shatter against the hull.

CHAPTER EIGHT

When Benson woke, it was not floating on a cloud before a set of gates, or even falling into a lake of fire. It was on a bed, in a small room, with an uncomfortably large plastic tube shoved down his throat.

He coughed violently as his eyes tried to adjust to the harsh white lights. The choking sensation became too much and he yanked at the tube sticking from his mouth. As soon as he did, alarms started to sound. The tube fought him all the way out, triggering his gag reflex twice before he finally pulled it free with a decisive jerk.

Benson's vision cleared just as the first person entered the room. It was a woman he didn't recognize, but her long coat shouted "Doctor". The second person, on the other hand, he knew quite well. Which is why it didn't come as any surprise when Theresa waltzed right up and slapped him across the face.

"What the fuck were you thinking?" she demanded before the doctor intervened.

"Constable, that's not helping." The doctor put herself between Theresa and her patient.

"The idiot has a death wish," Theresa shouted. "I can help him with that."

"I'll have to ask you to wait outside, ma'am."

Theresa's glare burned through the fuzziness still clinging to Benson's consciousness. "Gladly. See you back at the office, *detective*." She span around on a heel and stormed out of the small room like a tornado exiting a closet.

The doctor looked back and put a hand on Benson's shoulder. "Lovely lady."

"We're just coworkers," he said weakly.

"Uh huh. Because a 'coworker' would have rushed down here and refused to leave until you woke up again."

Benson sat up and tried to shake out the cobwebs. "That obvious, huh?"

"Don't worry," she smiled warmly. "I won't tell anyone. Doctor/patient confidentiality and all that."

A terrible thought went through Benson's mind. "How long have I been out?" He sounded a little more demanding than he meant to.

"It's OK. It's–" she consulted her pad "–almost 19.00. You were only out for a couple hours. You'll probably be discharged in time for the game."

"Game?"

"Game Five. The Zero Championships?" She grabbed a penlight out of her pocket and shone it in his eyes. "Are you feeling all right? Dizzy?"

"No," Benson waved her off. "I'm fine. Just have a lot of other things on my mind besides Zero, for once."

"Well, I'm sure a near-death experience would do that for anyone, even you, Captain Benson."

Something about her inflection set off alarm bells. "I'm sorry, have we met?"

"You don't remember me, do you?" she asked pensively.

Benson tried to focus on her face, but her voice registered first.

"I was an intern a few years ago, working extra hours doing sports medicine for the–"

"Mustangs," Benson finished for her. Her hair had been a lot shorter then, and most of her freckles had faded. "Jasmine?"

"Jeanine," she corrected. "Although most people call me Dr Russell these days."

It all came back to him. "After the Championship win in Eighteen, didn't we get drunk and, ah…"

She chuckled. "Yes, we did, and then you neglected to call."

Benson put up a hand in defense. "Sorry, I meant to, but–"

"Sorry for what? I knew what I wanted, Zero Hero. I've hardly been wasting away pining after you." She looked down at his naked torso. "Although I'd be lying if I said it wasn't nice to see you with your shirt off again. But you're underdressed. Your 'coworker' wasn't the only person waiting for you."

A sense of dread welled up into Benson's stomach. "Who's out there?"

"Oh, you've attracted quite a following. Captain Mahama arrived twenty minutes ago, and someone from engineering just brought in the body you recovered."

"Both of them?"

"Yes, and they seem very excited to see you." Jeanine paused with a mischievous smirk. "Maybe 'excited' isn't the right word."

"Tell them I'm in an irreversible coma."

She leaned out of the door and called down the hall.

"He'll be out as soon as he gets dressed."

Benson grit his teeth. "Thanks a lot. I suppose I deserved that."

Jeanine smiled. "I suppose you did. Your vitals are all in the green. I'll want to see you again for a checkup tomorrow, but frankly I think you're probably in the clear. You lost consciousness from hypoxia, but they got you back inside before your heart stopped. No signs of edema, either. You've kept yourself in remarkably good shape."

"Thanks. Where are my clothes?"

"We had to cut them off." Jeanine nodded towards a chair sitting by the back wall. "Your coworker brought you some fresh ones to change into."

"Thank you."

She turned to leave, but Benson called out to her. "Jeanine, I mean, doctor? Who will be performing the autopsy on Mr Laraby?"

She thumbed towards another room. "The body you brought back? I will, but it's going to be a while yet."

Benson shook his head. "I need you to start right away. While everything's still fresh."

"Fresh isn't going to be a problem, detective. The man is frozen solid. I can't start until he thaws out. Unless you want me to use a hammer and chisel?"

"Can't you just heat him up?"

"Sure, I could cut him up into pizza-sized slices and use an oven. Or maybe engineering would let me stick him inside the fusion reactor chamber for a few seconds."

"All right," Benson put up his hands in surrender. "That sounded less stupid in my head. How long, do you think?"

"Honestly, I don't know. I don't have much experience defrosting a seventy kilo steak. I don't think anyone does, really. Two days? Three?"

Benson tried not to let his frustration show. "OK, I understand. When you do get started, I need you to pay extra attention for signs of struggle. Bruising, abrasions, fractures. Any sort of defensive wounds."

Jeanine looked slightly lost for a moment. "You think he was fighting back against someone?"

He nodded. "I strongly suspect so, yes."

"I don't understand. He's a suicide."

Benson's eyes narrowed at the last word. "Who told you that?"

"The captain did when the body came in. Said he threw himself out an airlock."

"Did she now?" Benson filed that interesting little tidbit away. "Never mind what you heard. I just want you to look at the body with fresh eyes and see whatever there is to see. OK?"

Jeanine seemed to know she was missing some important context, but moved on. "Fine, but the body's a mess. It's going to be tough to single out bruises or any other minor injuries from all the damage the dermis suffered from vacuum and flash-freezing. Not to mention the arm."

"What's wrong with the arm?" Benson asked suspiciously.

"Well, aside from being missing, I expect it's in the same shoddy condition as the rest of him."

"Missing?" Benson said. "Who cut off his arm?"

"You did when you crushed the body between the ship and your EVA pod. Although the correct word would probably be closer to 'snapped' off. The crash didn't do the body any favors."

Benson scratched his head. "Yeah, well, any landing you can walk away from."

"You were carried in on a stretcher."

"Close enough. Now, if I could ask you to step outside so I can get dressed?"

Jeanine smirked devilishly. "Not even a peek for old time's sake?"

"Not after you sold me out to the buzzards outside. Shoo."

"That's fine. How do you think you got into that gown, detective?" She winked. "I'll schedule a follow-up appointment for tomorrow. See you then." Jeanine closed the door behind her. Benson listened to her steps fade down the hallway, then stood up, somewhat unsteadily, and put on his clothes.

As much as he loved microgravity, some things were just plain easier when you could stand up. Putting on pants was one such thing. Careful his shirt was tucked in presentably, Benson left the recovery room and walked down the hall. Not being a man with much remaining shame, he propped a hand against the wall, embellishing his condition in the hope it might elicit some small measure of sympathy from the people waiting to tear a strip off his hide.

He should have known better. Captain Mahama stood up just as soon as she noticed Benson coming down the hall, but Director Hekekia beat her off the line.

"What the hell were you thinking?" he shouted. Benson resigned himself to hearing a similar refrain several more times today. Although no matter who else said it, Theresa's rage would probably remain the most intimidating.

"Actually, I thought I did rather well, considering the circumstances."

"Oh, you do, do you? Hear that everybody? The shaved ape thinks he's earned a peanut!" He pointed a finger at Benson's face. "I told you I couldn't afford to lose the pod."

"You didn't lose it. I brought it back."

"Yeah, with more holes than a pasta strainer, a shattered canopy, and a body tangled up in its arm. Its *remaining* arm."

"You'll have to take that up with the meteorite. I wasn't entirely thrilled about it myself, I'll have you know. Besides, if you'd have sent it out by remote like you'd planned, you really would have lost it. I'm the one who piloted it back. Without any training, I might add."

This took most of the steam out of Hekekia's brewing rant, even if his expression showed he didn't find the argument entirely persuasive.

"Yeah, well, I had to pull my entire team off their assignments to clean up after your little stunt. And prying that meat-popsicle out of the wreck? Three of my guys have already asked for trauma counseling."

Benson briefly wondered what had been the more traumatic sight for the techies: the body with a missing arm, or the pod with a missing arm. He left this thought unspoken, however.

"I'm sorry I've made more work for you. But someone's been making more work for me, too."

"Yeah, well, just let the professionals handle space from now on. OK?"

Benson chuckled. "Don't worry, it's all yours."

Seemingly satisfied, Hekekia strutted out of the waiting area without another word, leaving Benson to deal with the captain.

Mahama was a tall, thin woman with tightly curled hair slowly giving way to silver. Her skin was a caramel hue common among the Ark's citizens after eleven generations of interbreeding, but her sharp jawline, dark eyes, and wide nose revealed a proud ancestry tracing its roots back to Zimbabwe. The blue-over-green uniform that usually made the too-skinny crewmembers look like kids playing dress up, she wore with distinction. Benson wondered who her tailor was.

"Detective, may we speak in private?"

Benson held his hand towards the door. "As 'private' as anything ever gets on this ship. Let's take a walk."

Mahama looked him over for a moment. "Are you sure you're up for that?"

"Sure I am. As long as you don't mind walking slowly. I'm still the tiniest bit wobbly."

"Not at all." The captain leaned in and pitched her voice low for privacy. "Just between us, I'm not exactly a sprinter myself in gravity."

Benson chuckled politely. They walked together into Avalon's evening air. Everyone called it Sickbay, but it was easily the size of a hospital, with a campus laid out in a similar fashion. Unlike many of the other large structures inside the habitats, the two identical Sickbays were built in the middle of the modules so that transit times from the residential centers at each end were roughly equal.

The day grew short. Only another hour before the lights would dim, an hour after that and Game Five would start. People scurried about in all directions, either in a hurry to finish their work, or to make game day preparations. All were too busy to pay much attention to the two of them strolling down the wooded path. Most had never seen the captain in person before anyway.

The apple trees here had been grown thick and pruned short, like oversized bonsai. Any tree much over five meters would topple over during the deceleration phase after the Flip. Workmen were busy anchoring the larger trees to the ground with wire.

"So, what can I do for my captain today?"

Mahama took in a deep breath through her nose before starting. "You present me with a unique set of problems, Detective Benson. I wonder if you appreciate that."

"I think I might," Benson said carefully. "And thank you for not starting this out with 'What the hell were you thinking?'"

Mahama sighed. "Don't worry, that's coming." She spotted a bench and pointed at it. They sat down. Once comfortable, the captain reached out and picked an apple blossom. "Do you know why these trees were planted, detective? What their purpose is?"

Benson wasn't sure where this was leading, but played along anyway. "Of course. They make oxygen and food. Can't have apple pie without apples."

"That is the common belief, yes. Would you like to know the truth?"

"That's my job, isn't it?"

"I suppose that's one way of seeing it. The truth about the trees is they make almost no net oxygen when all is said and done. And what little surplus they do make is entirely outweighed by the havoc their pollen wreaks on the air filtration system each 'spring.' They require huge amounts of fresh water, placing additional stress on the systems. They're completely dead weight when it comes to life support."

Benson sat and considered this for a moment while Mahama smelled the blossom. "You're waiting for me to ask why we keep them, then."

"An excellent question. Have you studied much about the Ark's development?"

Benson shrugged. "About as much as the average person, I expect."

Mahama nodded. "Did you know these were not the first habitats?" When Benson shook his head, she continued, "The first habitat was actually built on the Earth's surface. While obviously not a cylinder, it was built with the same acreage and completely self-contained, right down to a ceiling of lights. It was an experiment, you see. Even as the Ark's keel was being laid in orbit and Nibiru tore through the Kuiper belt, twenty five thousand people were living their lives inside the fake habitat. The experiment ran for almost thirty years, and everything they learned was incorporated into the designs of Avalon and Shangri-La in real time. Do you know what they learned?"

"No," Benson said honestly.

"That people need trees. Or at least we need to know they exist. People need to believe there's an inside where we work and sleep, but also an outside where we can visit, play, exercise, and all the rest. Otherwise, given enough time, we go crazy. Cabin fever, it used to be called. We plant the trees to give the appearance of an outside.. Appearances are often even more important than the reality behind them. They have to be maintained, just as our air scrubbers or water purifiers do."

Here it comes, Benson thought sourly.

"Which is why you pose a unique challenge for me, detective, and the rest of the crew. You see, we're sprinting the last hundred meters of a marathon we've been running for two hundred and thirty years. We need everyone, crewmembers and citizens alike, focused on the task at hand; preparing this ship for the Flip and then the Landing. You may not know this, but your, let's say, 'mission' today has become big news, and it's causing unnecessary distractions."

"So," Benson interrupted her. "For the sake of *appearances*, you want me to declare Edmond Laraby's death a suicide and bury the investigation."

"Goodness, no," Mahama blanched. "Whatever gave you that idea?"

"Well, you already told the doctor performing the autopsy that he was a suicide, which could cause her to prejudge the situation and overlook clues."

Mahama waved her hand. "A slip of the tongue, I assure you. But if she did, it wouldn't be the only thing 'overlooked' lately."

Benson's eyes narrowed. "What's that supposed to mean?"

Mahama looked around conspiratorially. Satisfied that no cattle were within earshot, she leaned closer to Benson's face. "Please understand, I'm not supposed to be sharing this with you, because it's internal crew deliberations. But we know full well that your comlink back to Command didn't magically fail the moment you were ordered to abort. Several people, including my first officer, argued quite strenuously to have you punished for insubordination."

Finally goaded past his tolerance, Benson sat up. "With all due respect, ma'am, I don't answer to the crew. Not even to you. My charter makes it quite clear that I have independence and broad discretion while in pursuit of my duties as detective, or chief constable, for that matter."

Mahama leaned back and waved her hand, palm down, in the universal "keep it down" gesture. "Within your *jurisdiction*, yes. No one disputes that. But, Bryan, it would do well for you to remember that your jurisdiction is Avalon Module, and by tradition the Zero stadium. I'm sure I don't have to tell you, but you weren't in Avalon when you were ordered to return. The only reason you were allowed in the pod was as a courtesy. You were in crew equipment, operating in Ark airspace. We hold authority over ship operations. You know that. I'm not even sure why Officer Feng let you get in the pod in the first place. I wouldn't have approved it had I known. Not to play Captain Hindsight, but the risks were too great."

Benson readied a sharp retort, but held his tongue. The trouble was, Mahama was technically right. Even if a magistrate might eventually approve of Benson's actions after a charter fight, the regulations at that moment were untested and unambiguous.

When she didn't see a reply brewing, Mahama continued, "Anyway. I decided that you are simply an extremely dedicated constable, and that punishing a man for risking his own life in the line of duty would send entirely the wrong message less than two weeks before so many others may be called to do the same thing for the survival of the species."

"Thanks," Benson said sarcastically.

If Mahama picked up on his tone, she didn't let it show. "Don't mention it. Now, you're the detective who faced down a meteor shower to bring a disturbed man home to be laid to rest. The Zero Hero who refused to leave a man behind. Surely you can see how valuable that appearance is to our little family?"

Benson crossed his arms and leaned back on the bench. "Is that an order, sir?"

Mahama laughed. "Heavens, no. As you already said, you don't answer to the crew. I couldn't give you an order if I wanted to. We're just two professionals comparing notes. I'm sure you understand."

"Oh, I'm pretty sure I do."

"Excellent." Mahama stood up. "I'm glad we found common ground. And on behalf of the crew, I'm relieved to see you made it out unscathed. You're a respected and valuable man, Detective Benson. We wouldn't want anything to happen to you."

Mahama stood, placed the apple blossom on the bench where she'd been sitting, then turned and walked off in the general direction of the lifts.

Benson watched her leave without comment. This was the second time a crew bigwig had spoken to him in person in as many days.

Something smelled funny, and it wasn't the fertilizer they were using on the apple trees.

CHAPTER NINE

After his encounter with Mahama, Benson made his way back to the office as quickly as his feet would carry him. He had a hunch, and he wanted to put it to the test.

Along the way, he had to shake hands with several admiring Zero fans already several drinks deep into pre-game preparations. A small but growing part of him was glad only three games remained. Probably one, if the Mustangs didn't find some way to breach the Yaoguais' Great Wall formation like so many Mongols.

He reached the stationhouse quickly. It was empty, except for Lieutenant Alexopoulos sitting at the shift supervisor's desk. Everyone else was out patrolling the footpaths or setting up for Game Five. Theresa looked up at the sound of the sliding doors, then jumped out of her chair and ran at Benson. He put up his forearms, ready to deflect a renewed assault, but instead of another slap, she threw her arms around his waist and squeezed him tight.

"I'm sorry," she said.

"Whoa, lady." Benson returned the hug. "Pick an emotion and run with it, maybe?"

Theresa sighed and shook her head. "Men. Like it's

healthy to limit the feelings you display to 'hungry' and 'horny'."

"What a coincidence, I'm both."

That earned him another slap, although it lacked the conviction of the one she'd delivered in the recovery room.

"I listened to the whole thing, you know? I thought you'd died when the explosion happened, and then your coms were down, and..."

"Shhhh." Benson returned her hug. "It's OK, Esa. I'm here."

"Don't ever do that to me again," she said firmly. "It was terrifying."

Benson stroked her soft hair and kissed her forehead. "Trust me, it wasn't a picnic on my end either. C'mon, we have work to do." They held hands as he walked her back behind her desk. "I just had a very enlightening conversation with Captain Mahama."

"I saw her in the waiting room. So, she didn't come by to express relief at your miraculous survival?"

"Not in so many words." Benson sat down. "Or in any words, for that matter. Instead, she seemed very eager for us to declare Laraby's death a suicide and forget the whole thing ever happened. Oh, and I get to be canonized a hero in the process."

"And you're not taking her up on it? I'd have thought that would appeal to your ego."

Benson scoffed. "My ego is already well cared for, thank you. And there's just the tiny problem that I continue to believe Laraby was killed. I'm going to need the video files from all of the locks, starting from when Laraby's plant went off the grid, until he was reported missing."

"I already did," Theresa said.

"No, not just the internal locks. I need all of the *external* airlocks, too."

Theresa rolled her eyes. "I heard you, Bryan. I already ran that search. I figured it would be the first thing you asked for, so I went looking. Nothing."

Benson scowled. "What do you mean, 'nothing'?"

"I mean, the video files from the security cams in and around the external airlocks are all gone."

"Someone deleted them? Who? There has to be an ID fingerprint on the command history."

Theresa shook her head. "The memory cluster glitched. At least that's what the tech I spoke to said."

"Glitched, huh?" Benson smirked. "Seems to be a lot of that going around."

Theresa nodded. "The tech said, and I quote, 'Let's see how good your memory is when you're two hundred years old.'"

"I swear they all take a condescension class before they're allowed to talk to us." Benson leaned forward and put his elbows on Theresa's desk. "But that confirms it. Someone killed Edmond Laraby, someone with deep access to the ship's computer networks. Unless we're really expected to believe he deleted the videos *after* he threw himself out an airlock."

"That would be an impressive trick," Theresa agreed. "The kind of network access you're talking about screams crewmember. Even our permissions don't come close to letting us pull it off. I told you from the beginning we should be looking at crew."

Benson's shoulders slumped. "Yeah, you've earned that 'I told you so.' Before I thought maybe somebody was protecting him. But now? Someone is trying to cover up a murder."

"Maybe more than one someone," Theresa added quietly.

Benson's head tilted. "Explain."

"Well, think about the timeline. Laraby slips off the grid at the same time he's shoved out into the black. Laraby wasn't very big, but he was still an adult male. It couldn't be easy to cram him into an airlock and push the button, while manipulating the plant network and security cameras. I don't even know if you could do all that remotely."

"Maybe Laraby was drugged," Benson countered.

"Which doctor provided the drugs?" Theresa responded. "I still think this would require more than one person to pull it off."

Benson wasn't entirely persuaded, but he had to admit that it could be true. The thought of trying to take down one floater was scary enough, but a *conspiracy* of them? Being a fake hero held more appeal than being a genuine corpse.

"What are we going to do?" Theresa asked, bringing his attention back to the here and now.

"I don't know," he admitted. "This whole thing is getting out of hand."

"You're not seriously considering going along with this, are you?"

Benson sighed. "No, just bidding goodbye to my career and personal safety."

Theresa shrugged. "Those were screwed as soon as we landed anyway. But we still need a case. Suspects, motive, little things like that. Why go to all this trouble to kill a competent, well liked geneticist doing important work?"

Benson laced his fingers. "I think Laraby knew something dangerous. Something that could damage whatever member of the crew killed him. I think the big house and the painting tried to buy his silence. When it looked like that wouldn't work, he was silenced permanently."

"And you want to know what he knew?"

"Knowledge is power, they say. And maybe leverage. We need to get into Laraby's private files. It was strange enough to block us the first time, but now that we know he's dead under mysterious circumstances? They can't fall back on the 'privacy' of a dead man anymore."

Benson stood up from the chair to pace the floor. "We have to keep this front and center among the cattle. If they manage to bury the news, it'll be that much easier to bury us, too. Figuratively or literally. We need to publicly announce that we're launching a murder investigation. Then any move against us will obviously be part of a larger cover up."

Theresa watched him wear a rut into the floor as he paced. "You want to announce a murder investigation before the autopsy is finished? Are you sure you're not jumping the gun?"

Benson stopped in his tracks. It was a valid point. Any announcement ahead of the autopsy could be spun as grandstanding.

"You're right. But we can't wait on the warrant in case another 'glitch' gets to his private files, too. Draft it up and send it over to the magistrate. Even if you're right and we're dealing with a conspiracy, it still has to be a small one. Right?"

Theresa looked up at him doubtfully. "How do you figure?"

"Well, if all the floaters were in on it, then they'd never have reported him missing in the first place, would they? And they really wouldn't have let us know about the body. Whoever this is has enough power to muddy the water, but not enough to actually keep it buried."

Theresa considered this for a moment before answering. "But the captain's leaning on you. How much more powerful can you get than that?"

Benson sucked air through his teeth. "I don't think she's in on it. I get the feeling she's just trying to keep it from blowing up."

"But you're not sure."

"Does it matter? If I'm wrong we're dead in the water, no matter what we do."

Theresa gazed off into the distance in deep contemplation. "Or just plain dead."

"I guess that's possible. You OK?"

She took a deep, cleansing breath. "Yeah, I think so. Just... never walked into the crosshairs before."

Benson smiled warmly and came around to hug her. "It grows on you."

"Not the most reassuring thing I've heard. I'll draft up the new warrant, then?"

"Draft it, send it. I'll call over to the doc and make sure she pays close attention to the tox screen."

"Make sure that's all she pays 'close attention' to."

Benson reeled back. "Really? You're picking a time like this to be jealous?"

"Who's being jealous?"

Benson leaned down and kissed Theresa on the cheek.

"Don't worry, lieutenant. You are the sexiest thing on this boat. And the scariest."

"Don't give me a reason to give you another reminder of the latter."

"Wouldn't dream of it." He stood up and headed for the door.

"Where are you going?"

"To the Mustang game," Benson called back, as the doors slid closed behind him. "There are appearances to maintain."

"Bryan, wait!" Theresa shouted after him. Benson stopped in his tracks and thrust a hand back into the doors to stop them.

"Just…" she sighed. "Keep your stun-stick handy."

Benson patted his pocket where the pen-sized device had spent the last ten years. "You too."

The lights above darkened as he walked to the lift.

Against all odds, and to the jubilation of the Mustang faithful, Sahni got the better of Lau's fliers early with a rather brilliant unorthodox formation. Really, it was a complete lack of formation that finally punched a hole in the Great Wall. From the first push-off, Sahni's fliers came at the Yaoguai without any apparent coordination or plan whatsoever. It was like fighting an angry drunk; pure chaos with no tactics to adapt to.

By the time Lau made the necessary adjustments, the Mustangs were already down to twenty-three points. The spread was too much for the Yaoguai to close. Game Six would happen after all.

The Mustang fans were a little rowdier than normal, so Benson stuck around the stadium to help his constables clear the crowd. By the time the last stragglers were packed into the lifts for the walk of shame back to their apartments, it was nearly 02.00 Avalon Time.

Exhaustion threatened to overtake him as he said goodnight to his men. The lift doors opened onto an empty car, leaving him alone with his thoughts. All in all, it had been a fairly shitty day. Nearly dying, uncovering a conspiracy, and being politely threatened by the most powerful woman alive all competed for the honor of being the worst part of it. Thank goodness the Mustangs had pulled out a win, or Benson may have just thrown in the towel and called it a life.

As the lift car descended to the deck, the artificial gravity began to pile onto Benson's eyelids, pulling them down with the inevitability of the setting sun. He fought against it, jerking awake twice as his knees nearly buckled under the growing weight of his body. By the time he reached the bottom, Benson staggered out of the lift like a shambling horror from the movies, but instead of brains, he craved only the warmth of his soft bed.

He'd spend the night alone, as Theresa had pulled the third shift supervisor slot for the evening, not that he had enough energy left to make the time worthwhile for either of them. Still, he couldn't help but feel a little guilty about her late night. Usually, Theresa would have slept through the day to be rested for the graveyard shift, but instead, she'd been waiting for Benson to recover from the pod crash. It wasn't exactly his fault, but she–

The bushes on the path ahead to his left moved unnaturally, which, considering they were bushes, meant moving at all. The light breeze running around the habitat wasn't enough to push around the thin, tightly trimmed juniper leaves. The tremor was so slight Benson almost didn't catch it, but years chasing down a fast moving ball while trying not to get smeared by defenders had made his eyes keen to movement. Benson assumed he was dealing with an overindulgent Mustang fan either relieving themselves behind the shrubbery, or excavating their stomach contents. Strangely, his plant wasn't feeding him an ID.

"Hey, buddy. You OK?" he asked.

Instead of an answering groan, the bush exploded in a shower of leaves as a dark figure leaped out from hiding. Benson braced his stocky frame for the impact, but at the last moment his eyes caught the glint of a knife.

The equation changed dramatically. With no time to think, Benson acted on reflex alone, pushing off from the ground exactly as he would to avoid an incoming flier. The artificial gravity quickly brought him back down to the deck again, but it had been enough to throw off the attacker's aim. Instead of Benson's heart, the blade found only a tail of his jacket. Sloppy, but it worked.

Benson heard fabric tear as he spun around and clamped a meaty hand down on the back of the assailant's neck. Whoever it was wasn't very big. Benson thought for a horrible moment that his assailant might be a teen.

A quick spin, followed by a deep slice against his forearm purged any blossoming guilt he may have felt about beating up a belligerent adolescent. His coat sleeve took the brunt of the cut, but the assailant pulled their arm back and reset for a decisive stab against Benson's vital organs.

Panicked, Benson again fell back on instinct and kicked the figure in the chest, not to inflict damage, but to put distance between them. It was something he'd done a thousand times playing Zero. In Avalon's gravity, however, it sent them both flailing off-balance. Being smaller, his assailant took the brunt of the force, exactly as Newton would predict, but his assailant found their feet again even as Benson fell flat on his backside.

Standing against the background of Avalon's night, the figure flipped the knife into an icepick grip and came at him again. Benson crab-walked backwards while he dug through his jacket pocket in a desperate search for his stun-stick. His fingertips fixed on the small cylinder and pointed it, still in his pocket, and pushed the button.

Nothing happened.

Benson found himself tempted to push the button again, but a more immediate concern presented itself in the form of the fifteen centimeter length of steel coming for his heart. Benson put up his legs in a defensive posture that had been beaten into him during the best three weeks of law enforcement training available. The attacker tried to get inside for a mortal strike, but Benson kicked him back several times, getting slashed on his shins twice for his trouble.

With adrenaline surging through his veins, Benson landed a heel squarely at the base of the assailant's jaw, snapping it shut with a painful *click*. The blow knocked them back far enough that Benson could retreat out of range.

Clearly dazed from the kick, the assailant turned and staggered back into the shadows.

Burning with testosterone and rising fury, Benson jumped to his feet. Knife be damned, no one was going to get away with attempted murder of a constable on Benson's watch. Especially when *he* was the officer in question. Exhaustion forgotten, Benson ran straight after the retreating footsteps. He opened a link through his plant. <Command. This is Chief Benson in pursuit of a suspect. I need ID on the individual running twenty meters ahead of me.>

Benson barely cleared a hedge while he waited. The suspect was quick, and he lost sight of him twice while he waited for the ID.

<Chief Benson, this is Command. What is the charge pending against the suspect?>

<Are you kidding? They just tried to carve me up like a fucking Halloween pumpkin. Is that good enough?>

<Standby.>

He lost sight of the suspect again. Even the sounds of their footsteps were starting to fade.

<I'm losing them. Which direction are they going?>

Benson tried to get a bearing on the footsteps, but echoes off nearby buildings and the forward bulkhead itself made it an impossible task. <Now would be good!>

<I'm sorry, chief, but there isn't anyone near you.>

<Repeat your last,> Benson said incredulously.

<There's no one near you, chief. No one is running in any direction.>

<I can *hear* them running!>

<I'm sorry, but we just don't have any plant regist–> Benson tuned out the man's excuses. A mad-hatter, he thought. But he'd seen the knife, how would an aluminum-foil hat escape his attention?

<Turn on the lights,> Benson said.

<But it's past nightfall.>

Benson's patience was at an end. <Turn on the fucking lights!>

It took a few seconds, but far above him, the axle that ran through the center of Avalon started to glow. Several minutes would pass before the bulbs would reach their full brightness, but already enough light reached Benson, giving him pause.

The surge of adrenaline had masked the pain, but the streaks of angry crimson along his forearm and lower legs told the story. Benson had been cut, and cut deep. He was losing quite a lot of blood, especially from his arm..

Gingerly, Benson flexed his hand to make sure all of his fingers still worked. Fortunately, the assailant had failed to slice through the tendons, but the damage was enough. Benson clamped his left hand down hard on the wound to slow the bleeding, then bent over to get a look at his legs. Unlike the thick fibers of his jacket and shirt, the thin fabric of his pants had done little to slow the blade. The two slashes to his shins had cut straight to the bone.

Still fuming, it took an act of will to convince his enraged lizard brain that he was too tired and wounded to continue. Benson abandoned the pursuit and instead used the growing light to try and trace the suspect's steps. He managed to follow a short trail of disturbed grass, but the footprints quickly ran back to the walking path, leaving no further trace.

All around him, confused citizens started leaning out of windows and opening doors to look up at the unexpected light. Frustrated, Benson sat down in the middle of the path where no one could sneak up on him and waited for backup to arrive.

CHAPTER TEN

The rest of Benson's night passed in a blur of statements, a quick jaunt off to Sickbay to get his wounds stitched up, a bucketful of admonishment from Dr Jeanine for forcing her out of bed to attend to his wounds, and again from Theresa for winding up in Sickbay twice in one day.

Despite fighting for his life, Benson gained almost nothing from the encounter. He had no useful description, other than average height and weight. He didn't even know the suspect's gender! At least his wounds proved that he hadn't hallucinated the whole encounter.

It was well past five in the morning Avalon Time before his head finally met his pillow. It was barely two hours before his alarm went off. But, being a plant alarm, he couldn't just smash it and throw it out the nearest window.

"Not cool!" he shouted as the chimes gently, but firmly, continued to ring through his brain. He couldn't turn it off. The alarm knew if he was still in bed or not, based on his locator. It couldn't be tricked, and it was relentless. It was, in the opinion of many, the single most inhumanly evil piece of software ever written.

Benson had once tried simply rolling out of bed and lying on the floor, but apparently the soulless coder responsible for the abomination had anticipated the move and the alarm resumed several seconds later when it realized he was still prone.

Instead of fighting it, he simply got up and moved to the shower. He didn't need to disrobe. Benson slept naked, never grasping the point of wearing pajamas to bed when the only people who might see him were the ones he intended to get naked with anyway. It was one less thing to buy, and one less thing to wash.

He stepped into the stand-up shower, his aching muscles and joints longing for the luxury of hot water. But instead, the dressings on his injuries meant he had to settle for ultrasonic pulses and a burst of UV.

"Just like the good old days," Benson lamented.

The sound waves were well above the threshold of his hearing, but it never failed to make his skin crawl as though he was swimming in one of the fingerling tanks. A fog of dirt and dead skin cells floated off his body before getting sucked away by the shower's air circulation system. In minutes, it would be carried through a series of collection ducts and deposited in a cistern of waste water, urine, feces, and inedible organics leftover from food processing. Next, an insatiable army of trillions of bacteria specially bred for the task would break the revolting mix down into a soupy slurry. Then, the slurry's components would be separated out through a series of centrifuges, chemical strippers, magnetic eddy currents, and filter screens. Finally, vital ingredients like iron and salt would be purified back into raw material, while the rest processed into fertilizer for the farms.

Nothing went to waste on the Ark. Except maybe Benson's time.

Someone was fixed on keeping him from solving the Laraby case. He'd been ambushed, plain and simple. Punishment for pressing on with the murder investigation, even if he hadn't announced it yet. His attacker had been no random Zero hooligan. The only thing that saved Benson's life was spotting the slight rustling in the bushes. If his attacker had snuck up from behind, it would have been a small matter to slash his throat and watch him bleed out before any help could arrive.

For the dozenth time, Benson struggled to remember anything useful about the attacker. Average height and build for a male from the habitats, although he wasn't about to discount a stocky female, either. Several girls in the Zero league were a match in size and strength for any of the boys they played against. Benson never forgot the lesson Madison Atwood had taught him in the 221 PE season opener. He missed four games after *that* hit dislocated his shoulder. She worked for Chief Bahadur as a constable in Shangri-La now.

Still, he could safely cross floaters off the list of suspects. Whoever had attacked him had been quick, agile, and strong. Not as strong as Benson himself, but certainly a beat faster. That sort of conditioning wasn't something one developed in microgravity sixteen hours a day, while sleeping the other eight.

Why the hell hadn't his stun-stick worked? And why hadn't Command been able to track their plant? And how had someone even known he was pressing ahead with the investigation in the first place? On Theresa's suggestion, he'd held off on any public announcements of his intention to slap the *murder* label on the investigation before the autopsy was done. No one should even know.

Theresa.

For a terrible moment, Benson weighed her prospects as a suspect. She was the only one who knew his intentions for the case. She knew nearly everything about him: his schedule, routines, everything. If anyone was in a position to plan an ambush for him, it was her. And she was the obvious choice to replace him as chief should anything happen.

Benson shook off the thought as he cooked in the UV. The ultraviolet light was intense enough to kill off nearly every last bacterium clinging to his skin, but brief enough to keep ambitious cancer cells in his dermis from getting any funny ideas.

Theresa was many things, but indirect was not one of them. If she wanted him dead, she'd do it herself. He'd certainly given her cause to over the last year. Unsanctioned as it was, their relationship was stuck in its adolescence. They couldn't come clean with their friends, couldn't move in together, and couldn't even think about starting a family. And that unfortunate situation had no chance of changing unless one of them switched jobs and got out of the other's chain of command. Something neither of them had expressed any interest in doing.

Besides, either his attacker had found a new way to block their plant signal, or someone else was jamming it for them. Both possibilities were beyond anything he or Theresa were capable of. It smacked of more interference from someone in the crew.

The lights timed out and Benson got out of the shower, taking a moment to towel off the thin, powdery layer of detritus that the fans hadn't managed to dislodge. He rubbed down with a squirt of moisturizer, then used mouth rinse. His teeth didn't need brushing. A colony of genetically-tailored bacteria lived inside his mouth, breaking up plaque and eating the acid that would have caused cavities and tooth decay in centuries past. The rinse was filled with the little buggers, along with special nutrients to supplement their unique diet.

It also tasted like burnt spaghetti sauce and stale peppermint, but for a life lived without dentists, most people chose not to nitpick.

Benson threw on some clothes and toasted a bagel, then spread a generous layer of peanut butter once it was good and hot. Hans at the bakery wouldn't like that. "I already baked it once," his wounded voice would say. Being one of only three rabbis left in existence, Hans was a traditionalist. He insisted on running a kosher kitchen, which, considering the Ark's limited supply of ingredients, must have presented interesting challenges.

Cleaned, fed, and clothed, Benson stood favoring his right leg, taking care not to put too much strain on his stitches. He was met at the door by the tall, uncertain back of Constable Korolev.

"Jeez, Pavel," Benson said with a start. "You surprised me. What are you doing here?"

"Standing watch, sir."

"Over my apartment?"

"Yes sir. Lieutenant Alexopoulos asked me to guard you against further attacks."

"Of course she did," Benson said. "Thank you, job well done. You may go now."

Korolev shuffled his feet nervously. "I would sir, it's just that–"

"That Alexopoulos told you to follow me around like a

lost puppy for the rest of the day."

"Not in so many words, chief."

"Ugh! You do understand I outrank her, yes?"

"Yes, but if I listen to her, you're mad at me. However, if I listen to you, she's mad at both of us."

Benson nearly ordered him away, but the math made an odd sort of sense. "Do you always approach the chain of command so pragmatically, constable?"

"I'm Russian, sir."

Benson couldn't help but snort at that. "Come along, comrade. We have errands to run."

Twenty minutes later, the two of them floated down the central corridor towards the bio-lab module. The microgravity took all of the strain off his injured legs. It felt good.

Korolev drifted just behind him, silent as a tomb. Benson looked back at the younger man. "Never been outside of the habitats, have you, constable?"

"First time, chief."

"Well, don't be nervous. Crewmembers are people just like the rest of us."

"I'm not nervous, sir."

"Yeah? It's maybe fifteen degrees in here and your forehead's sweating." The lock for the bio-lab came up on the right. "OK, wait here. Trust me, you don't want to go through the 'decontamination procedure.' I won't tell the lieutenant."

"Sounds good to me, chief."

Benson nodded, then brought up his plant menu and found Director da Silva's entry. Of everyone on the crew, da Silva had the best reasons to help him find Laraby, so Benson had the least reason to suspect her involvement.

He had questions only a crewman could answer and she was the one to ask.

<Director da Silva,> he said, once the call went through. <It's Detective Benson. Can you spare a moment?>

<Oh, hello detective. Yes, I suppose I can take a short break while this retro-virus sequences. How can I help?>

<I'd like to have a word face to face if I might.>

<OK... I'm sure we can schedule something for tomorrow morning–>

<Actually, I'm outside your lock right now. And since that retro-virus is sequestering...>

<Sequencing,> she corrected. <I thought we talked about doing this over the plants from now on, detective.>

<I know, but I'd prefer to keep this conversation off the network.>

<I really don't have time. We're short-staffed and running out of daylight.>

<I'll just be a minute, and it could really help me with Edmond's case.>

The line fell uncomfortably silent.

<All right, I'll come get you.>

After being cleaned off for a second, and even more thorough time that morning, Avelina da Silva met him at the door.

"Hello again, detective. I'm sorry to be short with you, but you need to be quick."

Benson glanced around at all the techs straining to pretend they weren't listening. He didn't have many reasons to be here outside of Laraby's investigation, and they were all interested in any news.

"Actually, director, is there somewhere noisier we could talk?"

She looked around and saw the same thing Benson did. "Don't you all have projects to work on?" Avelina shook her head and nudged Benson towards one of the labs in the second ring. Inside, he was surrounded by centrifuges; some no bigger than a teapot, others as long as he was tall with row after row of seedlings spinning away. The electric hum filled the background.

"Better?" Avelina asked.

"Yes. What are all these for?" Benson asked.

"The small units are just separators. The larger ones are incubators. Seeds need gravity to develop properly. Now, what 'secret squirrel' stuff brought you up here?"

"Well, I'm sure you've heard by now, but I wanted to extend my condolences for Laraby's loss. I know he was a valuable member of your team."

She took a moment to compose herself. "Thank you. I heard while you were in Sickbay. I'm actually glad you came. I wanted to thank you for bringing Edmond back home. We can have a proper ceremony for him now. I know it wasn't an easy thing."

Benson smiled. "That's a bit of an understatement, but it's the least I could do for him. I'm curious, though, did Edmond keep any logs at work? Notes about his projects, maybe?"

"Of course. We all keep detailed records. Why, are you looking for a suicide note hidden in them?"

Benson sighed. So that really was the "official" story. Amazing how quickly it made the rounds. "I haven't determined cause of death yet. I'd like a look at his work records, just to be sure I haven't missed anything."

"Erm, that's fine, but I don't know if you're going to be able to make much sense of them."

"I might surprise you."

"OK…" da Silvia sounded dubious. "I doubt they're going to do us much good anyway. We're over-committed as it is. With Edmond gone, I don't have enough manpower to actually finish his projects. I'll upload his work files to your plant as soon as I break for lunch."

Benson nodded. "That'll be fine, but it's only half of the reason I came."

Da Silva cocked any eyebrow quizzically. "And the other half?"

"You're one of the best scientists alive."

"Well," da Silva blushed at the compliment. "There's a couple of grad students bucking for my job who might disagree with that assessment, but I'm pretty good."

Benson made a mental note to look into which of Laraby's coworkers would have been in a similar position. Professional jealousy could be a powerful motive.

"That'll do. You may not have heard, but I was attacked after the game last night by someone whose plant was immune to my stun-stick and couldn't be tracked by Command. Is there any way to reprogram a plant to be invisible like that?"

Avclina considered the question. "Implants are like solid-state wetware. They *can* be reprogramed, but it's not something you can upload. It's a physical change that'd require surgery, which would mean somebody both writing the new program, and someone else doing the cutting. I don't think that's the sort of thing you could keep quiet."

The creases in Benson's forehead deepened. "What if it wasn't reprogramed? What if the original unit was made differently?"

"You mean when it was implanted? Awfully long term planning, don't you think?"

Benson sighed. Putting a modified plant in a baby hoping they'd grow up to be a killer was an unlikely scenario, to say the least.

"OK, I see your point. Thanks, and please keep that bit between us, will you? It's not public knowledge yet, and I don't want it getting out."

She crossed her arms. "You think a crewmember killed Edmond and attacked you? That's why you wanted to talk in person and avoid the network. You think someone's watching you."

Benson put up his hands. "I'm just trying to be careful."

"And yet you trust me?"

"Gotta trust somebody. And you're the only person who really seemed to care after Laraby went missing. I'm betting you want me to find out what happened more than anyone on this ship."

Avelina bit her lip. "God knows Edmond deserved so much better than what happened. Don't worry, detective, I'll keep your killer ghost theory between us."

Benson smirked at that. "Thanks, and I'll look forward to reading those files."

"I'll put them on a pad and drop it off at the stationhouse after the shift change. It'll take a little longer, but that will keep it off the network."

"With Edmond gone, do you have enough time? I mean, to finish your assignments before Landing?"

"That's the million dollar question, isn't it?" da Silva shook her head. "God willing, but it's going to be close."

Benson thanked her, then returned to the lock and met up with Korolev in the central corridor.

"One down, two more to go." Benson glided past the younger man and back towards the habitats.

Korolev spun around and pushed off the wall to follow him. "Where to now, chief?"

"Back to Avalon, constable. We're off to see a magistrate."

CHAPTER ELEVEN

Magistrate Jindal, and a few others within the cattle's government with the perverse desire to do their jobs properly, was suspicious and resentful of the way crewmembers always seemed to, well, float above the fray, delicately tugging a string here, applying pressure there, a nice little reward for agreeable behavior where no one could see it.

After hearing of the previous night's attack and the odd pattern of interference, Jindal approved the warrant for Laraby's personal files. Several hours later, Korolev was finally let off the hook as they crossed the door into the stationhouse.

"Thank you for babysitting me, constable, but I think you should go home and get some sleep."

"Delighted to, chief." He snapped a salute and span right back around and out the door again.

"Package for you, chief," the duty officer, Hernandez, said. "I put it in your office."

Benson nodded, walked into his office and shut the door. He wasn't trying to be rude, but in truth, he really didn't have much to say. Hernandez and he had never quite hit it off. The man was a hothead, a little too quick to pull his stun-stick, and a little too slow to think about repercussions. Despite his seniority, Benson had passed him over for promotion twice, the last time giving Theresa the spot. Hernandez had made several not-so-private accusations about favoritism in the ranks, which hadn't really helped his career prospects either.

A tablet sat on his desk with a little red ribbon tied around it. That made him chuckle. So Avelina had come through with Edmond's work files. Benson had another pad tucked under his arm, filled with everything the man was doing and thinking during the other half of his waking hours.

He set the two pads next to each other and opened their files. Sixteen terabytes of data, arranged in dozens of cascading folders and directories exploded from the work tablet, while two more terabytes filled the other.

"Holy shit..." Benson mumbled. "You were a busy little bee, Edmond."

The pile of data was... daunting. Going through it blind would take months, maybe a year. Needless to say, it was time he didn't have.

What am I even doing? he thought bitterly. The truth of his existence was starting to come into stark relief. He was no police detective. He was a figurehead, a public relations move by the crew to appease the cattle.

Feng had tried to remind him, and so had the captain in her gentle way. The next reminder had arrived with a little more bite. Benson flexed the muscles in his forearm, feeling the sting of his stitches. *They want me to roll over. They* expect *me to roll over.*

Benson nearly spat at the thought. He'd certainly not been shy about enjoying the rewards bestowed on him through playing Zero, but he'd earned them by working his ass off and becoming great at his job.

His first day training with the Mustangs seemed like an insurmountable mountain to climb, too. But coach always told him to ignore the mountain. Take everything one small step at a time. Enough small steps would climb any mountain, cross any desert.

Solve any crime?

OK, small steps. Little bites. Or bytes, in this case. What's the first step? Show it wasn't suicide.

Benson opened his plant and linked it to both files, then opened the search menu. "Search all files and documents for terms suicide, kill, ah… and depressed."

New bubbles appeared on the tablets. Several seconds passed as even the immensely powerful computers took their time to search such large data caches. The hits rolled in, but not where Benson expected. Laraby's work files returned forty-nine uses of the word *suicide*, over a hundred for *kill*, and three for *depressed*. Meanwhile, his personal files held none, nadda.

"Display results for 'suicide' in reverse chronological order."

— Sample #8472 *suicided* three days after gestation. Severe deformation of the vascular system observed.

— Sample #8435 *suicided* five days after gestation cycle started. Root growth failed after 14 millimeters.

— Sample #8426 *suicided* seventeen days after the start of the gestational cycle. Leaves failed to unfurl properly.

"OK, I can see where this is headed. Display results for 'kill' in reverse chronological order."

— Sample #8469 *killed* thirty days after gestation. Failed to meet revised absorption goals.

— Sample #8461 *killed* sixty-three days after gestation. Failed to branch properly.

— Sample #8448 *killed* fifteen days after gestation cycle began. Chlorophyll reverted to Earth norm.

The list went on, with each incidence of the searched words relating directly to a failed experiment or new plant strain. Even where *depressed* was used, it was talking about "depressed levels of photon transference." Benson was no psychologist, but he was pretty sure it had more to do with photosynthesis than suicide.

It was the complete dearth of hits in Laraby's personal files that really struck Benson as strange, however. The table contained not only Laraby's private journal entries, of which he had been a prodigious writer, but transcripts of all of his plant conversations, and web correspondence since he'd turned eighteen. It was as close to a complete record of all his thoughts and actions as anyone but a psychic medium was going to get.

Benson hadn't expected anything as grandiose as a video recording of Edmond reading his suicide note, but the odds that someone wouldn't say *kill* over the course of years had to be staggering. Who didn't say "Let's go kill a couple beers," or "Ben's really killing it on the drums," or "Work almost killed me today" at some point in their life?

Laraby was either some sort of superstitious, word-avoiding eccentric, or someone had gone through and cleaned up the files using the same mental checklist Benson was going through now. His suspicion growing, Benson opened Edmond's last journal entry from less than a day before he went missing and checked the revision history.

Last Edited on 15/04/233PE 17:49. Edited by Laraby, Edmond, ID #C47-74205

Less than four hours before he'd disappeared. Benson tried to call up the prior version, but, to no great surprise, it wasn't available. He checked the next three older entries with similar results. How hard would it be to alter a time/date stamp and User ID? Probably not very, if you had the right permissions and knew your way around the Ark's coding architecture. Covering up all of your digital tracks would be harder, but not impossible. Benson ran a few more searches that came to mind, but with identical disappointment.

The only alternative was to read through each entry and transcript individually looking for whatever crumbs hadn't been vacuumed up. It was an unappealing prospect, and he didn't have enough time left anyway. It was exactly what Benson had feared. The delay gave whoever wanted the investigation stopped the time they needed to clean up their tracks. He wasn't meant to find anything here.

Benson threw the tablet at his desk in a fit of frustration. It caught a corner, sending spider-web cracks racing through the glass in an instant. He picked it up gingerly, gently tapping the screen, but the fractured, flickering image told him the tablet was beyond salvage.

Benson sighed. In his anger, he'd just committed a crime. To be specific, a violation of Conservation Code Forty-Seven: The Negligent Destruction of an Asset Prior to the End of its Projected Design Lifetime. For an asset like a tablet, the fine was nearly a week's pay at his compensation, and an equal length of time spent wasting his nights doing community service.

Benson tucked the shattered pad under his arm and left the stationhouse. He had bigger crimes to solve than the mystery of who broke the tablet, and he wasn't out of leads just yet.

CHAPTER TWELVE

"I want him strip-searched." Devorah's arms crossed her chest tighter than steel barrel hoops. She was not a happy little woman. Her dour expression was matched only by the look of childlike delight playing across Salvador Kite's face. He clearly enjoyed watching his old nemesis contort with disgust.

"Devorah," Benson chided, "he's our guest. You want to know what he knows just as badly as I do. We'll both be able to keep an eye on him, there are cameras everywhere, and we're locking the doors behind us. Now, be a good host and let's get started."

"Give me your stun-stick, then."

Benson shook his head. "Not gonna happen."

Devorah tilted her head up and shook a bony finger at the smiling ex-con. "You try anything and I'll chew your kneecaps off."

"I believe you," Sal said in a crooning voice.

Madame Curator scowled, but waved a hand to unlock the museum's grand entrance. It had been three in the afternoon when Benson crossed over from Avalon, immediately flipping him twelve hours to three in the morning Shangri-La Time.

The three of them were the only people on the museum grounds, on account of Devorah demanding complete control over the situation without any distractions or risk of accomplices hidden in the crowds. A very private tour indeed.

The silent darkness of night in Shangri-La made the three-story building loom that much higher. Its edifice had been designed with the great museums of the old world firmly in mind. Great marble columns in the Roman tradition, more than two meters across, "held" the massive stone roof and trio of domes aloft. Of course, the marble steps, columns, and giant quarried blocks that made up the museum's walls were imitations, cleverly textured and painted stucco over lightweight composites and alloys, much like the rest of the Ark's structure. Real marble carried far too great a weight penalty. Still, it was a masterful illusion, executed by the best, and last, set builders of Hollywood. Like the majority of workers who had built the Ark but hadn't made the passenger list, it had been their final job before returning to Earth to await their fate.

The show must go on.

There was nothing illusionary about the museum's contents, however. Every piece of art, every document, every artifact had a trail of documentation proving its provenance beyond all doubt. Every museum, gallery, and private collection on Earth had been scoured for the priceless treasures that filled the building.

Benson marveled at the sights in the central atrium as the doors closed and locked behind the trio. In a place of honor at the center, Michelangelo's *David* stood in his resolute magnificence, separated from viewers by the sort of barriers that once kept rampaging polar bears safely away from delicious children. The sculpture was, by weight, the largest object in the museum to have made the journey, and looking up at him, it wasn't difficult to see why.

The inventory held no collections. Only the very best examples of each artist, sculptor, and inventor had been preserved. It would be impossible to fit anything resembling a complete accounting of the accomplishments of the entire species into a single building otherwise.

Benson forgot about Sal and Devorah as a familiar display caught his eye. Not far from *David*, on a small slope of artificial red sand, sat one of only a handful of contributions from the Mars Colony. The early twenty-first century NASA rover, *Spirit*, stared back at him through its binocular cameras. It had undergone a complete restoration more than a century ago by that year's class of engineering students. Even now, it looked as new as the day it had left Earth.

"Hey," Devorah came alongside him. "Aren't you supposed to be watching Kite so he doesn't stuff my Rembrandt down his pants?"

Benson rolled his eyes. "That was more than thirty years ago. How long are you going to hold that grudge?"

"I'm Jewish, detective. We have long memories."

"Touché." Benson looked back at the rover. "It's beautiful, in its own way, don't you think?"

She nodded. "Ruggedness has its own beauty. Do you know how it got here?"

He shrugged. "I know the Mars colony sent a ship to rendezvous with the Ark on its way out and transferred some artifacts."

Devorah put a thin hand on the railing surrounding the exhibit. "This little critter had a hard life. Back when it was launched, it was designed to last for three months. It lasted more than six years on Mars before the poor thing got stuck and froze to death. It sat for another fifty before the Mars colonists launched their first archeological expedition to go dig it out. They were too busy trying to get the colony running to do much more than dust it off and put it on display.

"But when Nibiru turned up, Mars was cut off. All Earth's resources were put to building the Ark. The Xanadu colony was barely self-sustaining, but they managed to strap enough ion drives onto one of their Earth return taxis and make it fast enough to match up with us and transfer cargo. Seventeen artifacts. The legacy of an entire world."

"And three people," Benson added. "The 'Children of Ares'."

Devorah snorted. "And where are they now? Their culture lost and their bloodlines diluted until all that's left is a single surname. People die, society forgets. But these..." Her hands swept through the entire hall. "These artifacts, pieces of art, letters, remain frozen in time. They don't forget, and they don't lie."

A shrill alarm went out through the hall, followed by a flat, recorded voice announcing: "We regret to inform you that this is not an interactive exhibit. Please wait until a museum attendant arrives to answer any questions."

Benson and Devorah span around to see Sal standing next to the Brough Superior SS100 motorcycle Lawrence of Arabia was riding when he died.

"And they don't try to get their sticky fingers on

everything!" Devorah stalked over to where Kite stood with his hands held up.

"I just leaned over to look at it! What do you think I was going to do, tuck it under my shirt?"

"He has a point, Devorah." Benson sidled up next to her. "And I doubt he's got any petrol to ride it out of here."

"He could be trying to take a souvenir."

"I don't see a wrench in his hand." Benson pointed a finger at the ex-con. "But you're not making this any easier on me either, Sal. Behave, or the deal's off and we walk out of here right now."

Kite shrugged his understanding, then looked back down at the incensed curator. "I thought this was going to be a private tour. Aren't you going to teach me things?"

"Like how to beat the security systems?" she quipped. "Indulge me."

Devorah did nothing to hide her annoyance as her wedges clomped against the granite floor, beckoning the two men to follow her. Once everyone was in position, she began the most exasperated and sarcastic guided tour ever given in the museum's long history.

The odd trio started in the central atrium where the largest displays sat, passing by *David*; the Spirit Rover; Armstrong's boots from Apollo 11; a meter long section of the Eiffel Tower; a terracotta warrior from the tomb of Qin Shi Huang; Ramesses II in the flesh, or what remained of it; a Devatas relief taken from Angkor Wat; and what the Japanese-Korean Alignment assured the museum project to be the true Honjo Masamune katana.

Political considerations heavily influenced the

selection process for what constituted important historical artifacts. The United States, China, the Japanese-Korean Alignment, India, Brazil, and the European Union, the largest financial and technical contributors to the Ark project, had the greatest pull in the selection process, and each did their best to stack the deck of future history.

What those centuries-dead politicos hadn't realized was the very process of stuffing fifty thousand people onto a single ship and shooting it out among the stars meant that in a very short time, all their petty squabbles were forgotten. Within a generation, the people born on the Ark had much more in common with each other than with any race, religion, or government left behind on the dead Earth. Old grudges were set aside as basic survival took priority. By the time everyone found the right balance, it was two generations later and no one cared about their grandparents' squabbles.

Benson sympathized with Devorah's love of history, but maybe some things were better left in the past.

They moved on from the central atrium to the museum's documents wing. Here, protected behind bullet-proof glass designed for guns that no longer existed, nestled inside gentle atmospheres of inert gasses, sat shelf after shelf of letters, journals, first edition books, poetry, and the founding documents of a dozen nations. The original US Constitution was here, although the Declaration of Independence had finally succumbed to the ravages of time. The Chinese Constitution of 2047 sat immediately next to it, printed on a traditional rolling scroll of silk nearly three meters long, and handwritten in stunning calligraphy.

Sal pushed a button in the frame and watched the scroll wind slowly by as Devorah spoke of the populist uprisings that finally ended Communist rule. Not far from them was the Mars Compact, granting self-rule to the Xanadu colony and mineral resource rights to the asteroid miners based there, much to the chagrin of the Earth-based corporations that had sent them there.

However the largest and most impressive display was reserved for the most important document aboard: the Ark Treaty itself. Written just five months after mapping the course of the black hole they'd named Nibiru, it defined the entire Ark program. It was the only pact in the history of the old world signed by each and every nation state. The leaders of every country on Earth were present at the signing ceremony, along with representatives from the Lunar Polar bases and Mars. It was the one time everyone agreed on anything, and certainly the fastest treaty ever ratified.

They passed by floor to ceiling shelves of first editions from all of the greatest authors and the collected works of brilliant poets dating back centuries. Devorah stopped at a display and thumbed through a series of menus until she found what she wanted. From behind the protective glass, a robotic arm set on clever tracks built into the shelves ran down their length before shooting up three stories. It slowed, then very gingerly reached out and grabbed a book. Its target secured, the arm ran back down to where the trio stood and opened the book, holding it to the glass for everyone to see.

Devorah leaned in and read from the page with a calm, even voice:

"Some say the world will end in fire,
Some say in ice.
From what I've tasted of desire
I hold with those who favor fire.
But if it had to perish twice,
I think I know enough of hate
To say that for destruction ice
Is also great
And would suffice."

"Robert Frost," Sal said. "'Fire and Ice.'"

"Very good, Mr Kite. Got it in one."

"Why that one?" Benson asked.

"I always read that poem on the tour. Chalk it up to my dark sense of humor."

That was an understatement. As precise as the astrophysicists of old Earth had become, the gravitational interactions of a sun, a stellar-mass black hole, and eight planets proved too chaotic to model accurately. By the time the end came, the Ark was already many lightweeks away. All of its telescopes were pointed for Tau Ceti. After a contentious debate, the survivors voted to look forward, not back. To this day, no one knew if Earth had been devoured in the fires of Nibiru's event horizon, or thrown clear of its orbit to forever roam the frozen spaces between the stars.

After all this time, Robert Frost's question remained unanswered. Benson struggled to see the humor in it, but it took all kinds. Devorah hit the return button on the display. The book shut, then sped back towards its home.

The tour continued into the east wing, which held paintings and sculptures. There probably weren't two

people alive more intimately familiar with this part of
the museum than Devorah and Salvador, albeit for very
different reasons. Sal's jovial demeanor melted away as
soon as he stepped into the wing, replaced by something
indistinguishable from reverence.

The change didn't go unnoticed. Devorah eyed him
suspiciously for a long moment, but if he had any devious
intent, she couldn't spot it. Neither could Benson. If
anything, his face had the conflicted look of a man who
had stepped into a church he hadn't seen in years, where
he wasn't even sure he was welcome.

They walked through centuries of art, from the muted,
two-dimensional iconography of the early religious
painters, flowing into the expanded palette of the early
Renaissance. Da Vinci was here, one of the few artists
with multiple pieces in the collection. The *Mona Lisa*
smirked back at them from behind glass.

Baroque art with its sweeping sense of movement
came next, while the Neoclassicists harkened back to the
glories of the past. Romanticism reached out to the far
corners of the Earth searching for the exotic, and then
the Realists pulled right back to inspect what had been in
front of them the whole time.

Impressionism followed, trying to capture the essence
of action, light, and life by rejecting a devotion to minute
details. The Monet would soon find a home among them.

They entered the age of cubists and surrealism, leaving
the real world behind entirely. It was here that Sal really
lit up, showing a command of the subjects that matched
Devorah herself. She was less than enthused.

"You should remember this piece, Mr Kite. *Starry Night*
by Vincent van Gogh. I believe you were caught with it

rolled into a backpack, if memory serves."

Sal nodded. "That and the Picasso."

"That you slashed out of its frame!" Devorah stamped her feet, her fury as fresh as the morning the Heist had been discovered. "We lost almost three centimeters reframing it. A common vandal would have taken more care."

"I didn't cut it out, all right? I just carried it. I wanted to do it right and disassemble the frame, but Turner said it would take too much time. And you already got your revenge on him, sure enough."

"Is that supposed to exonerate you?"

"I was a kid, lady! Just the mule for them, but I knew more about this stuff," his arms swept to encompass the entire hall, "than any of them. They didn't listen, OK? They recruited me because I could pick out the best stuff and run it around without drawing attention. That's all they wanted me for."

"And you were only too eager to help them do it, Mr Kite."

Sal looked away, shame filling his voice. "I was naïve."

Benson stepped in. "Yes, you were. But he's served his sentence, Devorah, and he's here because he volunteered to help us. Now, may we finish?"

"Fine, it's way past my bedtime as it is." Devorah moved on with the tour, explaining the significance of a print of a large can of soup before leaving the modernists behind and entering the new millennium.

She spent a lot of time explaining an evening gown woven from old-fashioned magnetic data tapes by an American artist named Timothy Westbrook, the leader of the Reclamation Movement. After his death in 2059, his work rose to prominence as a rejection of consumerism and the entire corporate mentality of planned obsolescence, a message that held obvious appeal for the people of the Ark. For his part, Benson thought the dress would look rather fetching hanging on Theresa's lithe frame.

They wove their way through the rest of the twenty-first century before reaching the *pièce de résistance*: the Kilimanjaro collection. Kilimanjaro was the only name anyone had ever known her as. Some stories said she'd grown up in Johannesburg. Others that she was from the slums of Cairo. The only thing the legends agreed on was she was from Africa, and she was the last Master of Earth.

Her work was simultaneously heart-wrenching and inspirational. They paused in front of Kilimanjaro's seminal work, *Last Launch*, which was nothing more than a selfie of the artist standing among a sea of people, their faces lit in a bright yellow against the night by the fires of the last rocket launched to supply the Ark itself. Alone in their despair and rage, her face was lit with hope. A week earlier, she'd declined an invitation to join the ranks of survivors. "You have my work, the future has no need of my body. Give my seat to a scientist," she'd said.

The Ark launched two days later.

With her well-rehearsed tour exhausted, Devorah turned and faced Sal, toe-to-toe.

"That was my half of the bargain, Mr Kite. Now tell me where my missing pieces are!"

To his credit, Sal had the sense to step back before answering the tiny crazy woman. "There's one more thing I would like to see."

"What?" she demanded.

Sal squared his shoulders. "I would like to see the Monet."

Like a steam train switching tracks at full speed, Devorah's piercing gaze swept over to Benson and bored into him. "You told him about the Monet?"

Benson put up his hands. "Honey for the flies, Devorah."

"No one's seen it yet, and you want me to give this petty criminal the honor?"

"Watch who you're calling 'petty' lady," Sal injected. Devorah looked like she might throw a punch, but Benson put a hand on her shoulder, arresting her momentum.

"It's just one more viewing. It'll take five minutes. That's worth it, isn't it?"

She threw his hand off her shoulder and crossed her arms. "No. It isn't."

"Well, maybe I can sweeten the deal." Sal reached into a pocket, but before he could pull back out again, Benson grabbed his wrist. Hard.

"Drop it." Benson's other hand grabbed his stun-stick and trained it on Sal's left eye to emphasize the point.

"I can't," Sal winced. "It's fragile."

"What is 'it'?"

"It's not a weapon, if that's what you're asking."

Benson relaxed his grip, but kept the stun-stick in place. Devorah looked like an angry rabbit unsure about which way to jump.

"Pull it out, slowly."

Sal gently removed his hand from the pocket, holding a small rectangular silver case not much bigger than a deck of playing cards. He presented it to Devorah.

"I would like to make a donation to the museum, from my private collection."

Devorah eyed the case with suspicion, but curiosity won out as she donned a pair of white gloves that seemed to appear from thin air. She opened the lid with a tiny *click*. When no explosion or puff of poison gas followed, Benson finally relaxed.

Inside was a small manila envelope. She opened it and dropped the contents into her palm. "It's movie film." Devorah ran over to the nearest light source and held one of the small strips up to it. "Thirty-five millimeters. The old-fashioned celluloid, but not the nitrate stuff." She leaned in and brought the frames right up to her face, almost touching her eyeball. "I don't recognize the film, and my plant isn't showing any matches from the database."

Sal chuckled. "Nor could it. I had them deleted."

"You what?" Benson and Devorah said in unison. The admission got both of their attention.

Sal leaned against a column. "We knew you had automated searches running, Madam Curator. You weren't the first one to come up with that trick. The only way to keep some of these pieces out of your view was to create a blind spot."

"OK," Benson said slowly. "But how did you delete them?"

Sal shrugged. "Some of our customers had the permissions and figured they owed us some small favors. What you're holding is forty-three frames from Salvador Dali's movie–"

"*Destino*," Devorah finished for him. She looked down at the frames as though she might faint. "Made in partnership with Walt Disney."

"Very good, Madam Curator. Got it in one."

"But... these should have turned to sludge centuries ago."

"Yes, they should've, but a very studious collector had them treated with stabilizers and kept them safe. For my part, I've kept them away from light and in a humidor chilled to five degrees."

"Where?" Benson asked incredulously. "Your apartment's been searched a dozen times."

"You would be surprised what a ship this large can keep hidden, detective."

"But how did *you* get it?" Devorah asked.

"Let's just say 'Salvador' is a family name. Now, I've shown you a piece of art that no one else has seen in generations. Is that worth a ticket to the Monet?"

"Yes." Devorah slipped the filmstrip back into the case and snapped the lid closed, then stalked off towards a recess in the wall. "It most certainly is." She waved a hand and a secret door sprang open. "Well, are you coming or what?"

CHAPTER THIRTEEN

"These are the archives," Devorah said, as the trio walked down the stairs to the museum's basement. "All our restoration, preservation, and long-term storage happens down here. Only around fifteen percent of the collection is on display at any given time. We rotate the exhibits to limit their light exposure and risk. That and…" They reached the landing at the bottom of the stairs. The overhead lights sensed their arrival and flickered to life, casting a gentle white glow onto row after row of shelves, stretching back far enough that the curvature of the habitat's hull was apparent in the floor. "…We don't have the display space."

Benson and Kite stood gobsmacked at the enormity of the room and its contents. She wasn't kidding; enough shelves, crates, and boxes filled the space to provide for another half dozen museums just as big as the one above them. Benson leaned over and whispered to Sal so Devorah couldn't hear.

"Did you know about this place?"

"Yeah, but we never found out how to get in."

Devorah beckoned for them to follow as she hurried deeper into the archives. She stopped at a table just long enough to slap an RFID tag on Sal's donation and scan it into the computer, then opened a door set into the far wall. A gentle fog rolled out, followed by a cool breeze. The inside of the room was refrigerated. Racks of warehoused exhibits sat in foam cases stacked high to the ceiling. Devorah stuck the small case on a shelf and scanned in its location.

"There, it'll keep until I can get it in a proper mounting. Now, where were we?"

"Good question," Sal said, still bewildered by the mass of artifacts around him. "I knew this room existed, I just didn't know it was so..."

"Full?" Devorah finished for him. "We've had to keep the exhibits fresh and exciting for over two centuries. Where did you think all of that was kept? I'm just relieved your gang never got in here."

"So am I," Sal said quietly. The admission surprised Devorah. Her face softened ever so slightly as she looked at him, her assumptions about the man toppling one by one.

"I'm glad we agree. This way." She sprang off in a new direction. Benson was amazed at her stamina. It was closing in on four in the morning Shangri-La Time, yet she hadn't lost a step, despite her years. The curator stopped short at what seemed like a random stack and scampered up a ladder.

"Here, detective, this piece might interest you." She pulled out a nondescript white foam box sealed with clear tape. A small knife clicked open in her hand, also apparently out of nowhere, and made short work of the seal.

When she pulled back the lid, Benson gasped. Even

though he'd never seen one in person, the artifact in front of him was unmistakable.

"That's a gun," he said.

Devorah smiled patronizingly. "Indeed it is, detective, but it's not just any gun. This is the weapon that killed Archduke Ferdinand of Austria and launched the First World War." She took the small black handgun from the box and held it out. "An FN Model 1910 Automatic in 9mm Kurz. Those seven bullets," she nodded down to the tiny brass cylinders arranged in a line next to a box magazine, "are the only ones in existence."

"Are they still live?" Benson asked.

Devorah shrugged. "Who knows? They're almost three hundred years old, and the gun itself hasn't been fired in at least that long."

"I didn't know any guns made it onto the Ark. They were contraband."

"As Mr Kite said, you'd be surprised what remains hidden."

"Is it dangerous?"

"Are you kidding? The last time some idiot got his hands on it, sixteen million people died. Then they did it all over again a couple decades later and thirty million people died. This gun shaped world affairs for an entire century."

"Can I hold it?" Benson asked.

"Don't push your luck, detective." She put the gun back in its case and resealed it, then put it back in its place on the shelf. "The Monet is over here."

They followed her over to a table used to prep displays. She pulled back a cloth lying on the table, and Sal gasped. *Haystacks in Summer* lay there, not even a meter away from his face. No glass, no protective barriers, no elaborate security systems, just a simple canvas covered in a sea of vibrant color.

Sal set down the stave and reached out to run his fingers over the brushstrokes, but stopped himself short before Devorah had to say anything.

"It's beautiful. The archival images don't come close to matching the hues."

"They never do," Devorah said softly, the edge of distrust gone from her voice for the first time since starting the tour.

"Thank you. And…" Tears welled up in his eyes. "…and I'm sorry."

"For what?" Devorah asked.

"For being a young, idealistic idiot. I thought by robbing you, I was returning art to the people, whoever the hell they are. I thought the museum represented tyranny. Total government control over our heritage. But they used my passion, and then the pieces I helped 'liberate' got sucked down an even deeper hole where only the true tyrants could see them. I was such a fucking fool!

"And what's worse, for thirty-five years I've been too much of a coward to do anything about it. Kept my head down. Stayed off the radar. Too afraid of the tyrants who used me to get their pretty things, then turned around and killed my mates who'd done their dirty work. Everyday praying that they'd forget about that stupid kid I used to be."

Benson put a hand on his shoulder. "That's a lot of regret to carry around for a whole lifetime."

"Sure is." The ex-con wiped tears from his cheeks. "I

should go to bed. I have to work in four hours. I'll show myself out." Sal took one more look at the Monet, then headed back to the stairs. He set foot on the first stair, then looked back with a chuckle. "One more thing, you might want to take another look at that film case." Then he left.

Devorah and Benson almost tripped over each other in the scramble to get back to the cool room. Being the faster of the two, Benson got there first, but being a gentleman, he held the door for the lady.

Devorah snatched the silver case off the shelf and snapped it open, inspecting every face of it for clues. She pulled out the envelope and dumped out the film, then ran back out again and laid them out on a light table. As she poured over the film frame by frame, Benson picked up the envelope. It was real paper, worn around the edges, maybe as old as the film itself, but a quick sniff hinted at fresh glue.

Benson squeezed the sides of the envelope to get a peek inside. He saw writing.

"Devorah, give me your knife."

She whipped the small blade out from wherever it was kept without looking up from the film. With two quick slices, Benson opened the envelope and read what had been hidden inside.

"Ah, Devorah?" He put a hand on the table to steady himself. "You can stop now."

She looked up from the light table to see Benson holding out the exposed titles of twelve pieces of stolen art written in a column on the left, the entire cache still missing from the Museum's inventory, and four names written in a column on the right, with brackets drawn to show who had acquired what: Alfonz Lorenzo, Darius Krupt, Celine DiMaggio, and Chao Feng, Senior. The deceased father of First Officer Chao Feng, Junior, the first person in line to inherit his father's stolen art.

"Gotcha, you son of a bitch," Benson whispered.

Devorah inspected the list and let out a long, low whistle. "That's going to rock the boat."

"We'll capsize it if we have to."

"It's not that simple." Devorah shook her head. "This will upset a lot of important people if we're not delicate about it."

"Since when have you been delicate with anyone? You have a standing warrant to track down this stuff. Use it."

"This info is thirty years out of date. Three of these people are already dead. We have no way to know where their collections went. Celine is the only one still alive, and she's got late stage Alzheimer's."

Benson was incensed. "It's a lead, which is more than you've had in decades. You're seriously not going to follow it up?"

"It's a bunch of names scrawled by an ex-con. You really expect me to bust down the door to a woman on her deathbed and ransack her closet on evidence that flimsy?"

"Honestly, I'm more interested in Feng."

"Feng?" Devorah was surprised. "Why? This isn't still about the boy that went missing, is it?"

"He's not missing, he's dead. I pulled his body back inside with an EVA pod. Almost died in the process. Didn't you hear?"

She shrugged.

"Really, Devorah, you need to get out more."

She sighed. "You're determined to make trouble, aren't you? Why are you interested in Feng?"

Benson rubbed at his injured forearm. "I have my reasons."

"Fine, I'll serve the warrant on him first, so he doesn't get any warning. I'll wait on Celine until last, give her family a chance to come forward on their own."

"Works for me."

"I'll want a couple of constables along with me when I execute the searches."

"I'm only too happy to help. Just give me an hour's notice and I'll get a couple of people together."

Devorah led him out, back up into the atrium and towards the main entrance. They both paused at the archway. Hung above them was the Tribute to Lost Pioneers, but everyone simply called it the Clock. In bright red digits, it tallied every life lost aboard the Ark since launch and would only stop counting once they landed on Tau Ceti G. It stood at just over half a million people. Ten generations had lived their entire lives inside this fishbowl. The deaths had slowed down in the last few months. Like grandma holding out until after Christmas, nobody wanted to miss the big show.

The number at the very end belonged to Edmond Laraby. If someone had gotten their way, Benson would have been added to the tally last night. That wouldn't go unpunished.

Ten hours later, Benson, Theresa, Chief Vikram Bahadur, and Devorah stacked up outside the first officer's penthouse at the top of the Qin Shi Huang building. Strictly speaking, Benson and Theresa weren't supposed to be there. Their authority ended at Avalon's lock. But Vikram had as much patience for assaults on constables as anyone else on the force, which was to say none at all. Bahadur had "invited" Benson along on the raid as a courtesy, and Theresa had sort of invited herself as soon as she heard about it.

Bahadur took a moment to adjust the dastar expertly wrapped around his head. Then he pulled out his stunstick to check its charge.

"You're not nervous, are you, Vikram?" Benson asked.

The Sikh stroked his beard. "It would be a lie to deny it."

"Don't worry, I've got your back."

"It's not that, my friend. I've never gone after someone of such… prominence before."

Benson nodded. "Crewmembers put their pants on one leg at a time just like the rest of us."

"Actually," Devorah piped up, "they usually shove both feet through at once when they're in micrograv."

"Not really helping, Devorah." Benson stole a peek around the corner hallway. It was empty. Not surprising at this time of day. Both Feng and his wife were on duty, and their son was in daycare. Standard procedure would have them ping Command to check plant locations and see if anyone was inside the residence before entering, but Bahadur couldn't do that without alerting Feng to the fact his penthouse was about to be raided.

"OK, we're set. Theresa, you–"

"If you say 'hang back', 'watch the door', or some other protective macho bullshit, I'll kick you right in the stitches on your shin."

Benson swallowed the rest of his sentence and pulled

out his own stun-stick.

Bahadur gave the device a sideways look and tugged at his curly, yet perfectly trimmed beard. "What if your ghost is inside, Bryan? These sticks won't do us much good."

Benson pointed at the ornate curved dagger tucked into Bahadur's belt. "Then I hope that kanga isn't just for ceremony."

"It's a kirpan, and no, it's not."

Benson scratched his head. "What's a kanga, then?"

"My comb. Maybe I'll let you use it if things get rough. You could groom him into submission."

"All right, we go on three, two, one!"

"Busting down the door" was somewhat more exciting in the movies, where a big, burly man would swing a twenty kilo battering ram through the lock. Or a shotgun would be put to the door's hinges, reducing them to dust. In this case, Devorah just pushed her thumb up to the door plate and punched in an override code. That was the beauty of bringing her along; Devorah's standing warrant meant she didn't have to go to the local magistrate to get permission to enter, so no notices popped up on the network until she'd already opened the door. Of course, the people who had given her that unprecedented power probably never dreamed she would have the unmitigated gall to break into the first officer's home.

Something told Benson that her unlimited warrant was about to expire. He really hoped what they found on the other side of the door was going to be worth all the trouble he was causing.

The door clicked and swung open. Chief Bahadur was the first through it with his stun-stick held at the ready, then Theresa. Benson followed her through and into the…

Palace. Benson and Bahadur stood dumbstruck by the size of the penthouse, while Theresa stared at its lavish furnishings with palpable avarice.

The penthouse's ceilings stretched up six, maybe seven, meters. Brilliant red and gold Chinese columns carved with dragon reliefs ran from the vaulted ceilings down to the floor. The floor was covered with intricate rugs, under which lay genuine wood flooring laid in complex patterns. Even if the wood was just a thin veneer, it would still have taken an entire tree to cover an area so large.

The three of them swept through the home, checking each room in turn for any surprise guests. The first floor consisted of a full kitchen, dining room, living room, bathroom, and a small office. Artwork covered every wall. The second floor sported three bedrooms, and a second bathroom. What the hell did three people need a *second* bathroom for?

The home secured, Bahadur leaned over the second floor railing and called down to Devorah. "We're clear in here, Madame Curator. You may enter."

She trotted through the doorway and stopped dead on the textile rug under her feet. Her eyes took in the open plan room with awe, darting from rug, to vase, to each painting in turn. She knelt down and ran thin knotted fingers over the rug.

"This is real silk, woven on a hand loom. Almost certainly genuine Persian."

She shuffled over to a blue and white vase perched precariously on top of a three-legged wrought-iron table. She picked it up and ran a fingernail over the glazing, then flipped it over to inspect the base.

"Ming Dynasty."

"Is it valuable?" Theresa asked.

"Priceless," Devorah answered curtly.

"That's not going to go 'missing' from the evidence locker later, right?" Benson chided.

Theresa put a hand on her chest in an exasperated gesture. "I'm sure I don't know what you mean."

Devorah set the vase down gently, then hopped over to the closest wall hanging, a scroll of Chinese calligraphy.

"It's a stone rubbing, probably Wang Xizhi if I'm any judge."

Benson appeared behind her. "Are any of your missing items here?"

"I don't see any of them yet, but they'd have to be pretty daft to hang them in the living room, wouldn't they?"

"Point."

"What's upstairs?" Devorah asked.

"Bedrooms," Theresa said. "And another bathroom."

"And closets?"

"Walk-ins. Can you believe it?"

Devorah turned and looked up at Benson. "Follow me, detective."

Devorah had set foot on the first step when a voice exploded from the wall behind them.

"What the hell are you doing in my home?"

Benson spun around, stun-stick at the ready, only to come face to two-meter-tall face with a hologram of Chao Feng's enraged head.

"Detective Benson! I don't know what you *think* you're doing, but you have no authority in Shangri-La.

You are breaking and entering."

Benson felt more than a little bit like Dorothy being dressed down by the Wizard. Even knowing the little man behind the curtain didn't help.

"Ahh…"

"How did you get in? Explain yourself!"

"He didn't get in, Chao. I did." Devorah shoved Benson out of the line of fire. "Detective Benson is here at my request."

It sounded good, and had the advantage of being true, provided one didn't know the context of what had prompted Devorah to ask him to come along in the first place.

"And what, exactly, is Detective Benson helping you do in my home, Madame Curator?" Feng's giant floating head looked down his nose at her. If she was intimidated, it didn't show. Then again, *everyone* was bigger than Devorah, so she was in familiar territory.

"Answering some questions," she said. "Like why the museum has an entire Oriental wing no one told me about."

"Those are all either family heirlooms or property of the Qin Shi Huang Building LLC."

Then why aren't they in the lobby? Benson thought, but he kept it to himself.

"And I'm sure documentation can be provided for any of them," Feng continued. "So I'll have to ask you to leave, Madame Curator."

Devorah smirked. "You can ask anything you like. I have intelligence that puts stolen pieces from the museum in this house, and I'll leave once I've either found them, or I'm satisfied they're not here."

"You have no authority!"

"You know I do, Feng. Goodbye." She elbowed Benson in the ribs. "Turn off his head."

"As you wish, Madame." Benson's hand stretched out for the wall's holo projector controls.

"Benson, don't you da–" With a touch of an icon, Feng's giant head disappeared, leaving them in silence.

Devorah scoffed. "Thought he'd never leave. Go lock the door, he'll be here in fifteen minutes, with friends."

Benson jogged over to the door and turned the deadbolt. It wasn't connected to any servo, just a good, old-fashioned manual latch. It wasn't standard, in fact, it wasn't technically legal. Feng probably had it installed as insurance against anyone trying to hack their way into his penthouse. Probably never dreamed he'd be the person getting locked out.

In a fit of childishness, he set the keypad in the hallway to "Do Not Disturb."

"We're good, unless someone brings a battering ram."

Bahadur shouted down from one of the bedrooms. "I think I've found something, Madame Curator!"

Devorah took the spiral stairs two at a time. Benson followed, admiring her spirit. It wasn't that long ago that he'd thought her a dry and passionless academic. Most people did. They were wrong. Most people focused their fire on the here-and-now, fretting over mundane details of their daily grind that would be forgotten as soon as the lights came on in the morning. Devorah didn't trouble herself with the present. She lived in the past. Benson was only now getting a sense of just how much she lived.

The older woman reached the landing at the top of the stairs and grabbed the railing to keep from falling over, her chest heaving. Benson tried to hold her up, but was rebuffed. "I'm fine," she huffed.

"Are you sure? Seems you left your breath down in the living room."

"We're not all pro-athletes, Bryan."

Theresa's head popped out of the guest bedroom. "The whole closet's full. Come see."

Benson and Devorah glanced at each other. She held out an arm and let him balance her shaky legs down the hall.

Bahadur had already done a preliminary search of the room, mainly by throwing anything out of the closet that looked old or expensive.

"These are all printed repros. What did you find?"

"In here." The chief pulled out a pair of paintings. Neither fit with the Asian motif of the collection downstairs.

And one of them looked very familiar indeed.

"It's another of Monet's Haystacks!" Benson hopped from one foot to the other, unable to contain his excitement. He pulled up a search browser in his plant and snapped a picture. The report came back almost instantly.

Wheatstacks (Sunset, Snow Effect) 1890-91 ACE.
Reported missing from the Art Institute of Chicago 18,
April, 2135 ACE.

Behind him, Devorah was giddy. She'd already laid the other painting out on the guest bed.

"It's my missing de Kooning, all right."

"What about this one?" Benson grabbed her shoulder and pointed her at his find. "Is it authentic?"

She took a quick but careful look at it, running a finger over the side and sniffing the canvas. "It certainly feels and smells right. I can confirm later, but provisionally, I'd say it's genuine too."

Benson actually pumped a fist in the air. He'd never before thought art history could be so thoroughly satisfying.

"Does that help your case?" Bahadur asked.

"Oh yes. Immensely," Theresa answered for him.

Devorah ripped the thousand-count silk sheets off the bed with a flourish. "These two don't have any glass. Wrap them up until we get back to the museum. I don't want them getting any more contaminated than necessary." She whipped out her little knife and sliced the ruinously expensive sheet right down the middle.

Bahadur actually winced. "Feng isn't going to like that."

"He's going to like being charged with receiving stolen artifacts a whole lot less," Devorah said mirthlessly.

"You're awfully quick to whip that thing out," Benson observed.

Devorah poked him in the thigh.

"Ow!"

"It's amazing what you can do with a little prick."

"I'm sure I wouldn't know." Benson rubbed his leg while Bahadur laughed.

"I would," Theresa quipped. Devorah actually chuckled. First time for everything.

They secured the paintings, and after a last cursory glance through the rest of the house, returned to the living room. In the hallway, someone very earnestly pounded away on the door.

"Who is it?" Devorah called out sweetly.

"You know damned well who it is. Open my door!"

Theresa's eyebrows inched up. "Boy, he got down here in a hurry."

"Good, saves us the trouble of chasing him down." Benson turned the lock. The door snapped open, revealing Feng midway through an angry knock. Bahadur greeted him with a raised stun-stick.

"Are you mad? Put that down!" Feng demanded.

"First Officer Feng, it gives me no pleasure to do this, but I'm placing you under arrest on two charges of receiving stolen artifacts."

"Are those the sheets from my guest room?"

"Hands on your head, sir. I won't ask again." Bahadur pushed Feng down to the rug. It wasn't difficult. He pulled out a pair of handcuffs and secured Feng's wrists behind him.

Feng shot a withering glare up at Benson. "I know you're behind this. I tried to reason with you, but obviously that wasn't enough. I'll have your badge on my desk by morning."

Benson pulled the fabric back, exposing a snow-covered haystack.

"No, you won't. Don't worry, I'll make sure your sheets are returned to your wife."

CHAPTER FOURTEEN

Everyone was in high spirits as they escorted Devorah and the artwork back to the museum. Everyone but Feng, that was. After passing the first dozen onlookers, Feng asked Bahadur to pull off his jacket and hang it over his head to hide his face. Bahadur agreed, but the damage was already done. Plant recordings from the first handful of shocked citizens were already hitting the social net.

Benson's elation at busting Feng lasted right up to the moment the doors of Shangri-La's stationhouse slid open.

"Captain Mahama." Benson stopped dead in his tracks. The Ark's commanding officer locked eyes with him. Her face didn't look nearly as warm and friendly as the last time they'd talked.

"What are you doing here?" Benson rushed to add, "Sir?"

"One might ask the same of you, detective. You're in the wrong stationhouse, if I'm not mistaken."

Bahadur stepped up to answer. "I asked Chief Benson to assist in an investigation."

"May I ask why my first officer is in handcuffs?"

"He's been arrested on two counts of receiving stolen artifacts, sir."

168

"I see."

"And," Benson broke in, "he's the prime suspect in the murder of crewman Edmond Laraby and attempted murder of a constable, namely me."

"You see, captain?" Feng shouted. "He's mad!"

"Quiet, Chao. You're in deep enough, don't you think?" Captain Mahama ran a hand through her tightly-curled hair. "Those are serious accusations, detective."

"They're serious crimes, captain."

"Indeed." The captain stood. "Gentlemen, I think we should continue this conversation in Chief Bahadur's office. If you have no objections, chief?"

Bahadur wore the face of a man who knew when and where it was appropriate to have objections. "Be my guest, sir."

"Thank you. Lieutenant Alexopoulos, is it?"

Theresa straightened her shoulders. "Yes, sir."

"I'm sure you have other duties that require your attention?"

Theresa shot a conflicted glance at Benson. He answered with a tiny nod letting her know it was OK.

"Yes, sir. I'm needed at the stationhouse."

Mahama nodded her thanks as Theresa turned to leave, then the captain, Benson, Bahadur, and Feng all piled into the small room. It was a perfect copy of Benson's office in Avalon. Only the wall hangings and chairs were different. Barely two people could sit comfortably. Benson chose to stand, as did Bahadur who motioned for the captain to take his seat. Feng sat in the other chair, or more accurately, was pushed down into it. One of Benson's hands remained on his shoulder as a none-too-subtle reminder of the folly of trying to run.

Captain Mahama cleared her throat, then began. "You will find, constables, that your plant's recording features have been temporarily deactivated. The camera and audio pick-ups in this room have also been shut down. This is to be a private conversation. Is that clear?"

Alarm bells rang through Benson's mind like a cathedral at noon. He tried to start recording, but just as the captain had said, an error message floated across his field of vision.

Bahadur fidgeted with the steel band around his wrist. "This is highly irregular, captain."

"It's not just 'irregular', it's breaking protocol," Benson objected.

"I understand your concerns, constables, really I do. But this situation is 'highly irregular.' Let's just say for the next, oh, ten minutes or so, that protocol has been suspended. Temporarily, of course."

Benson had met the woman in person only once before their talk outside Sickbay, when she'd presented the Mustangs the 221 PE Season Zero Championship trophy, her first year of command. Benson had managed to shake the woman's hand and say "Thank you, captain," without making a mess of the presentation.

Police work had hardened him up a little since then.

"Fine by me," Benson said. "Because no protocol means we're all just people in this little closet, and that means there's nothing stopping me from telling you what a load of horseshit this is!"

Captain Mahama very carefully placed her elbows on Bahadur's desk and laced her long fingers together. "By all means, detective. But please, be quick about it so that we don't get bogged down."

The captain's response threw him off. Benson had expected to be shouted down, accused of insolence, or otherwise reminded of his position. He hadn't expected a green light for his brewing tirade.

"Well." He tried to reignite the fire in his belly. "We're supposed to be independent. At least, that's the line I was told when I took the job. Constables answer to the law, and to the people. But we bust a senior crewmember, and before we can even interrogate him, lo and behold, the captain of the whole goddamned ship shows up to personally interfere. What kind of message do you think that's going to send to the cattle? And don't pretend no one saw you come down here to the deck. I'm sure it's already all over the social net."

"There'll be rumors, of course, that's unavoidable, but we have systems in place to clean up the net."

"Yeah, I think I've run into one just recently," Benson said, the frustration of Laraby's personal files still fresh in his mind. "It's quite amazing what your people can clean up." Benson's fingers flexed on Feng's shoulder until the smaller man shifted uncomfortably. "But some stains are really hard to get out, like blood. Might take a couple of tries."

"Too true." Mahama held out an open hand. "Now, if you're quite finished abusing your prisoner?"

Benson looked down. He hadn't realized how hard he was squeezing Feng. His temper was getting the better of him. His grip relaxed.

"Thank you. Now, to your point, yes, I very much worry about what sort of message this sends, but I'm even more worried about the timing of the message. We're flipping the ship in just a week and a half. Many thousands of man-hours of preparations still remain before we can light off the first bomb. Distractions are the last thing we need right now, and the circus that will inevitably follow the trial of the ship's first officer is just such a distraction.

"That is why I'm here, detective. Not to impede your investigation or to prevent justice from being done, but to avoid a panic. So, keeping that in mind, I would like you to tell me exactly what First Officer Feng has gotten himself into."

Mahama listened quietly and intently while Bahadur relayed everything that had happened in Feng's home, pausing here and there to share important moments of video from his plant on the wall screen. The captain stopped him twice to ask questions, but otherwise let Bahadur complete his report.

"And that brought us here to you," Bahadur said in closing.

"Well, that all sounds very official. But it leaves me wondering where, after a three decade hiatus, our indomitable museum curator suddenly found a lead in the Heist case."

Bahadur flashed a glance over at Benson. It was a small gesture, but Mahama picked up on it and turned an expectant look at Benson.

"Well, detective?"

Benson shifted on his feet but met his gaze. "Devorah was given information by a confidential informant."

"And would this 'confidential' informant be Salvador Kite, by chance? I know you questioned him only two days ago."

"I beg your pardon, sir, but I do not have to reveal my witnesses until trial."

"Of course. But, for the sake of argument, wouldn't any information provided by a felon be more than a little suspect?"

"It would be very suspect if we hadn't found the first painting we were told to look for, where we were told to look for it. Being right kinda lends its own credibility."

"The first?" Mahama interrupted. "There are others?"

Benson nodded. "My informant has given us leads on all of the pieces still missing from the Heist."

"I see. I have only one issue with what you've told me so far. Provided my arithmetic is still any good, Commander Feng was only three when the Heist occurred. It would be the rare three year-old trafficking in stolen art."

"Well yes, obviously. The information pointed to his father being the original buyer. But Feng had it in his possession, and the charge is for Receiving Stolen Artifacts. Nothing in the code says he had to be the first one in line."

"No, but I read the code in question on the way down here. It says the accused must have *knowingly* taken receipt of stolen artifacts. So, how about it, Chao, did you know the paintings were stolen?"

"No!" Feng blurted out. "They were just part of my father's collection that I inherited when he died. He never told me they were from the Heist. Believe me, I'm as shocked as anyone that he dishonored his family this way."

"Oh, please," Benson moaned. "You had them buried behind a bunch of worthless reprints in a closet. You were hiding them."

"They were in the closet because I never bothered hanging them. Why would I? One was just paint slashes, and the other one was a boring landscape piece. I thought they were worthless like the rest."

"Right, you just missed the fact you had a Willem de Kooning in a closet your entire life."

"How well do you know twentieth century *Chinese* artists, detective?"

"About as well as anyone from Avalon," Benson snapped. He immediately regretted it. His temper had gotten the better of him and he'd walked right into the trap.

Feng smirked, damn him. "Exactly my point. I would have turned them both over to the museum if you'd just asked, if only to repair the damage my father did and restore my family's honor. You didn't need all these theatrics."

Captain Mahama leaned back in Bahadur's chair. "So you're willing to turn over the paintings without protest?"

"Yes, of course. I'm glad to be rid of them."

Mahama opened her palms. "Well, I've heard enough. Chief Bahadur, I'm taking Commander Feng back with me. Please release his handcuffs."

"I'm afraid I can't do that, sir. He's already been arrested and the complaint has been submitted to our magistrate. He must remain in custody until she decides whether or not to pursue the charges."

"And we haven't even gotten to his involvement in the Laraby murder," Benson added.

"Ah, yes, you'd mentioned that before. I assume you have stronger evidence for that accusation than for the other charges, yes?"

Benson bit off another impulsive reply that he would

have regretted. The truth was, everything he had linking Feng to Edmond's murder was circumstantial. The disappearing video records, picked over files, it was suspicious as all hell, but it wasn't hard evidence. It burned at Benson to see the little shit wriggling off the line after he'd come so close to landing him, but it would have to wait.

"I'm still building the case, sir."

"Good, keep at it. I won't detain you any longer." Captain Mahama stood. "Chief Bahadur, I understand your objections, but I'm afraid I must insist. I'm invoking emergency operational authority. The smooth operation of the ship requires Commander Feng to be in command until the Flip is done, at the earliest. This supersedes any claim you have on him until the crisis has passed."

"So am I to take it that protocol is back on, sir?" Benson asked testily.

"Yes, you are."

Bahadur stood at parade ground attention, his eyes fixed to the wall. "Captain, I must go on record as formally objecting to this. A complaint will be submitted to the citizen's council."

"That's your right, chief, and frankly I'd be disappointed if you didn't follow through. I recognize how unorthodox this whole situation is, but we're approaching the most critical moment in the history of this ship, perhaps in all of human history. We can't afford to rock the boat." She held out a hand. "Now, the handcuffs, if you please."

Reluctantly, Bahadur obliged. He really didn't have any choice. Tradition and case law had given Command wide-ranging powers over anything that could impact ship operations. Once an "emergency" was declared, the captain's powers were virtually limitless. Even if a Council inquiry eventually overturned her actions, the process would take many weeks, even months. The Ark would be in Tau Ceti G's orbit by then.

"You may go, Chao," Mahama said quietly.

Feng stood up and rubbed circulation back into his wrists and glared at Benson.

"Be seeing you, detective."

"Yes," Benson simmered. "You will."

Feng just sighed and shook his head as he walked back into the lobby and out the doors a free man. Benson glowered at the ceiling, but managed to keep his thoughts to himself. The captain came out from behind Bahadur's desk.

"I'm… sorry for the necessity of that, really I am. But we all know that the charges wouldn't have stuck in trial. There's no way you could have proven Feng knew the paintings were stolen."

"Oh, please, you didn't buy his little performance, did you?" Benson asked.

"It doesn't matter if I did or not, it's what you can prove. You know that."

Benson pushed off the back of the chair with a huff. Bahadur broke the awkward silence that followed. "May I speak openly, sir?" Mahama nodded curtly. "You aren't going to allow us to finish the rest of the raids, are you?"

"I wouldn't waste your time, detective. I think you'll find the rest of the missing artwork will be anonymously returned to the museum within the day. That will have to be the end of it, for now."

"For now?" Benson said. "You mean you're not just going to roadblock us again?"

Mahama shot him a scornful look. "I meant it when I said I was sorry about this, detective. I also meant it when I told you to keep building the Laraby case."

"I was trying to, sir. I'd be in the interrogation room sweating Feng about it right now if you hadn't shown up!"

"I understand, detective, but this had to be done." The captain picked up the framed picture of Bahadur's family from his desk and stared at it for a long moment.

"Our jobs aren't that different, you know. Between the two of you, you're tasked with the security of mankind. But I'm tasked with its *survival*. That has to take precedence, especially now. We're already riding on the knife's edge. Dissent is trending up. You may not see it, because we've managed to keep the provocateurs' net presence isolated, but there's more each week. The last thing we need right now is a scandal involving senior command staff throwing the whole chain of command into question.

"The next few months are critical to the success of this new colony. After that, I don't care how many crows come home to roost. Once we're dirt side and the first season's crops are being harvested, I'll help you set the traps. I promise you that. But for now, the only thing I need you to take away from this conversation boils down to this: don't rock the boat. Clear?"

It was clear all right, as clear as the imaginary glass partition that separated the crew from the cattle. Rules for the ruled, but none for the rulers. Benson thought back to the first conversation he'd had with Sal Kite. He'd thought then that the man was just a bitter old cynic. And he was, but that didn't make him wrong.

"Completely clear, sir," Bahadur said, once the silence

became unbearable. Benson answered with a nod and a grunt.

"Good. I'm glad we could come to an understanding. You can be proud of yourselves for laying a three-decade-long mystery to rest. I'm sure the news reports will flatter you both."

And there it was again. Not a threat, just a reminder that it was so much easier to follow the current. Don't struggle against it. Do as you're told and everything will be fine. But Benson was more worried about the young man thawing on a slab in Sickbay.

Captain Mahama saluted, then followed her first officer out the door.

"Well, it was fun while it lasted," Bahadur said after the door slid shut again.

"Are you quitting on me, old friend?"

"Not at all. But a good sailor has to gauge which way the wind is blowing. If I may say so, perhaps you were… impatient, going after Feng so soon."

"Yeah, I'm beginning to see that."

"Adjust your aim. Work on identifying the man who attacked you."

"Or woman," Benson corrected. "I don't even know *that* much."

"Still, work your way up the ladder."

"You're probably right."

Bahadur grabbed his shoulder. "I'll help you any way I can, but let's try to keep our coordination off the grid, yes?"

Benson squeezed his friend's wrist. "Agreed."

CHAPTER FIFTEEN

Benson and Theresa spent the evening in Laraby's apartment working through the frustration of their raid turning bust. It took a while. They were both very frustrated.

Basking in the afterglow of their second round, Theresa gently ran a finger through the valley between Benson's pectoral muscles. Like everyone aboard, his skin was smooth and hairless below his head and face. A small tweak of the genetic code as old as the Ark itself, speeding up evolution by a few hundred thousand years so precious protein wasn't wasted manufacturing useless hair.

Whatever gene-coder had mucked about in Benson's double-helix had somehow forgotten to turn off his goosebumps, however. Theresa's fingertip shot little arcs of electricity through his skin, leaving a minefield of tiny bumps in its wake, miniscule muscles tugging on hair follicles that had never existed. Benson intercepted the wandering finger before it ventured too much further south, then held it up and kissed it.

"I need a little more time to recharge than that, my dear."

"Hmm," she pouted. "Too bad you don't run on batteries I could swap out like my–"

"Little black market *novelty item*?"

"It's for my tennis elbow."

"You don't play tennis."

"No, but I plan to start any day now."

Benson sighed. "I'm going to make an honest woman out of you one of these days," he whispered.

Theresa laughed. "That's rich. I *was* an honest woman before you came along. Before all this fraternizing with my superior, midnight rendezvous, contaminating crime scenes." She waved a hand around Laraby's bedroom.

"Which was *your* idea, as I recall."

"More of a passing suggestion."

"Well, if it's bothering you, we could always go back to my apartment."

"And give up silk?" Theresa pumped her legs playfully against the nearly frictionless sheets. "Mmm, never."

"I thought not. Still, it won't be much longer before we can be… honest about everything."

"We're not the best kept secret as it stands, Bryan. You're too honest to be a good liar."

"Make it official, then."

She kissed his cheek. "I'd like that."

"We can build a little cabin on the surface and start filling it up with–"

Theresa put a finger on his lips. "Slow down, hotshot. One problem at a time. What are you going to do next?"

"Roll over and take a nap."

Theresa slapped him on the stomach. "Be serious. What's your next move?"

"Bahadur thinks I should go after my attacker and

work the links from there."

"I agree with him." Benson shot her a wounded face. "OK, fine. What do you think?"

"I think I don't even know where to start! I know they're about a hundred and eighty-five centimeters tall, light build, and probably fair-skinned. So average height, average weight, and Caucasian or Asian ancestry. That narrows the pool of suspects down to what, thirty thousand people? And I have no way to track them? It's like chasing a boogeyman."

Theresa ran a hand gently over the bandages on Benson's forearm. "Your wounds are real enough."

Benson found himself looking around the bedroom, getting lost in little details like the crown molding. "This place still doesn't make sense to me. How did Edmond find himself here? There's no way he could have afforded it. Who approved the transfer?"

"I looked into that and couldn't find anything. This apartment wasn't even on the register."

"What? Why didn't you tell me that?"

"I just did, you've been a little busy."

"Don't tell me you think it's an oversight."

Theresa shrugged. "It wouldn't be the first time an important record just happened to be incomplete, would it?"

"But look at this place, it's like a, a hotel suite. It doesn't look like *anyone's* lived here. It's too perfect."

"Maybe that's exactly what it was," Theresa said absently.

Benson looked at her, confused. "Explain."

"Well, look around. This place was appointed to impress, from the furniture, to the linen, to the artwork, and it's off the registry. Perfect."

"Perfect for what?"

"What we're using it for!"

"Are you saying Feng set this up as some sort of love nest? He's married and has a son."

Theresa made a funny face. "You mean to tell me you never fooled around on a girlfriend back in your Championship days?"

"No! Well, maybe. But it's different once you get married."

She let out a tired little sigh, then put a hand on his cheek. "Oh, honey, you're a keeper. But not everyone takes their vows that seriously, and Feng is a very powerful man. That means he has... opportunities."

Benson tried the idea on for size. It fit the facts, and it would explain the Monet that had hung downstairs until very recently. The silk sheets were also very familiar, now that he thought about it.

"But then why was Laraby in here?"

She shrugged. "Maybe Feng was stuffing Laraby's girlfriend. Maybe he found out about it and blackmailed Feng for a better place to live."

"He didn't have a registered girlfriend."

Theresa passed a hand over her naked body. "And what am I?"

"Yes, OK. But da Silva said she never saw him with girls, like he was scared of them."

Theresa shrugged off the objection. "One of his coworkers, then."

Benson shook his head. "We always have the best pillow talk."

"Eh, I've heard worse."

"Really?"

"Oh god, yes. My last boyfriend was in the spectrographic astronomy department. If I ever hear another word about the mineralogical composition of the Tau Ceti asteroid belt, I'll seriously kill someone."

"You dated a crewmember?"

"For like a month. He was sweet, but skinnier than I am."

"White, average height?"

"Yeah?"

"Good, I'll start with him, what's his name?"

"Don't you dare harass that poor boy," Theresa scolded. "He's harmless. I doubt he'd even know how to use a knife that didn't have apple-butter on it."

"I'm joking."

"You'd better be."

Benson rubbed his chin. "I'd still like to know how they blocked the plant signal."

"If they did," Theresa added wistfully.

"Well, who else would have done it?"

"That's not what I mean. You're assuming there was a signal to block."

"Of course there was, everybody has a plant signal."

Theresa put up a hand in defense. "Yes, I know, and I'm not saying you're wrong, just that it's an assumption. But our plants aren't like our hearts, are they? We don't actually *need* them, even if most of us couldn't imagine living without them. Maybe it's time to start thinking crazy."

Benson had to admit, it would solve an awful lot of problems in the case. Plants were tied into everything on the ship. They didn't just let you browse the net at will and keep track of where you were. They opened doors, turned on lights, tied into security protocols, medical information, everything. Someone without a plant would be virtually invisible to every system onboard, because every system onboard assumed everyone had one.

What had Salvador said in the museum? *You would be surprised what a ship this large can keep hidden.*

"Hold that thought," Benson flipped through his contact list and placed a call.

<Jeanine, it's Bryan.>

<Ugh. What?> the doctor thought groggily. <It's not even one o'clock.>

<I know, I'm sorry, but I have a question.>

<No, detective, I haven't done Laraby's autopsy yet. I told you he needs to thaw slowly.>

<It's not about that, Jeanine.>

<Well then, no, you have a girlfriend. Sorry, 'coworker.'>

<It's not about that, either. I wanted to ask about plants. Do you know anyone who doesn't have one?>

<Doesn't have a plant?> she asked, trying to focus. <What are you talking about?>

<I don't need you to break patient/doctor confidentiality. Just… hypothetically. Is there a reason someone might have their plant removed or deactivated?>

<You *can't* remove a plant. They fuse with the tissue of the frontal-cortex in the second trimester. You might as well stick an icepick up their nose and hit it with a hammer.>

Benson thought about this for a moment. <OK, what about a natural birth?>

<What does this have to do with crewman Laraby?>

<That's confidential.> The line went silent for a long

moment. Benson broke it. <Hello?>

Jeanine rejoined the conversation. <Hypothetically?>

<Yes, hypothetically. C'mon Jeanine, I need help here.>

<Your plant has a search feature, you know?>

<Not everything ends up on the net. Believe me.>

<Fine. Hypothetically, no method of birth control is one hundred percent effective, not even the sterilizing chems we use on everyone. Hypothetically, some people only pretend to take them. Hypothetically, this means abortions have to be performed a couple times a year, on average.>

Benson couldn't believe what he'd heard. Abortion was supposed to be one of those things that had been left behind with old Earth. Total government control over when one became a parent was the guiding principle behind the population control regime in place aboard the Ark for over two centuries. Conception didn't even happen internally anymore. Everyone was a test-tube baby.

<Hello?> Jeanine asked.

<Sorry, I was soaking in what you'd said.>

<There's a reason we don't talk about it.>

<I can see that. Is it possible babies have been born naturally without being detected, and never got a plant because of that?>

<I don't know how. Pregnancy trips off a dozen different medical alarms. The other doctors and I are informed automatically.>

<What if the mother doesn't want to have an abortion?>

<...I'd rather not talk about that. It's usually an even

bigger surprise to them. The monitoring software can catch hormone changes in the first week of pregnancy. I know before the mother does.>

<But if someone was trying to get pregnant off the grid, could they bring a baby to term without being discovered? Hypothetically?>

<It would be very difficult, but not impossible.>

Benson smiled. <Thanks, Jeanine. I owe you a drink. And I really don't want to rush you, but anything you could give me about Laraby's body would be helpful. Even if it's just fingernail scrapings, defensive bruises, anything that would suggest a physical struggle. His torso doesn't need to thaw out for that, does it?>

Jeanine let out a mental sigh that her plant actually managed to translate. <No, it wouldn't. I'll get started in the morning.>

<Thanks, Jeanine. I owe you one.>

<If memory serves, you owe me three, but I doubt Theresa would be very happy if I came to collect.>

<I'd sell tickets for that fight.>

<Who says there'd be a fight? I might just snatch her away from you.>

<I'd sell tickets to that, too. Goodnight.> Benson cut the link before the banter got any thicker, among other things.

"I have an idea," he declared to the room at large.

Theresa's eyes wandered down to his waist. "I bet I can guess what it is," she purred.

Benson glanced down. "Oh, um, not that. Not just now, anyway." He threw the silk sheets aside and jumped out of bed, then headed for the door. "I have to go. Something to check on."

Theresa shook her head. "You might want to think about putting pants on first."

Benson was surprised to find that Salvador Kite wasn't at work, at least not where he expected to find him working. Mindful that all of his searches and plant communications were probably being monitored, Benson opted to just go talk to the ex-con face to face again. But his old supervisor down in the reclamation ponds told him Kite had been transferred.

"To where?" Benson asked.

"The museum, believe it or not."

Benson stared at him. "Curator Feynman approved the transfer?"

"No, you don't understand. *I* approved the transfer just this morning. Curator Feynman was the one who requested it."

A week ago, Devorah would have been the first in line at Salvador's stoning. People kept finding ways to catch him off guard. For once, the surprise was a pleasant one. The odor in the machinery under the reclamation pond tanks was something you could never really get used to, and it had the unique ability to stick around inside one's nose long after it had worn out its welcome. Benson was only too happy to return to the surface.

He found Devorah in the museum's atrium, starting a tour for a group of eager, yet bleary-eyed students from Avalon on a fieldtrip. They were all staying up well past their bedtimes for the chance to see the wonders the immense building held. He sympathized; it had been nearly two Avalon Time when he'd left Theresa in bed to chase this hunch. His eyelids tried to pull themselves down like automated blinds.

The kids looked about eight to Benson's eyes, which meant they were probably closer to twelve. Everyone looked too young since he'd turned thirty-five. Devorah noticed him standing at the back of the group, which should have been easy considering he was a good head taller than even the largest child. Then again, Devorah was a good head shorter than them, too. She waved over one of the other museum staffers and handed off the tour temporarily. The kids all followed along as their new guide walked them towards *David*, where the little girls pointed and giggled at his marble manhood, while the little boys mentally sized themselves against it.

Devorah stepped up next to him. "A package was waiting for me when I got to work this morning."

"Really?"

"You're surprised?"

"Yes, surprised to hear you ever leave the museum."

"Hilarious. So you know what was inside?"

Benson shrugged. "If I had to guess, I'd say the eleven missing artifacts from the Heist."

Devorah nodded. "And nothing else. No names, no confessions. I suppose that means we're supposed to drop it and move on. Case closed, eh?"

"That's what we're supposed to do, yes."

"But you're not going to?"

"Nope. I can't get at Feng directly, he's too well protected. But I can try to figure out who attacked me."

"I see." Devorah picked a bit of lint off her jacket. "How can I help?"

"Actually, I went down to the reclamation ponds looking for Mr Kite, but I was told he'd been transferred here, at your request."

"Does that surprise you?"

"I wouldn't have bet on it, no."

"Mr Kite is more knowledgeable and passionate than any two of my staffers, and that's saying something. It would've been a waste of talent to leave him fixing leaky shit pipes. Besides, this way I can keep an eye on him if he gets any funny ideas about coming out of retirement."

"Keep your enemies closer, hey?"

"Something like that. Why do you want to see him, is he in more trouble?"

"Not at all," Benson said. "I just want to tap his expertise for a few minutes."

"Right. He's down in the archives. I'll let you in."

"You let him down into the vault by himself?"

Devorah smirked. "Yes, and I will let him back out again when I feel like it."

"You're evil."

"I'm efficient. C'mon, I want to catch up with the tour again."

"Don't tell me you have a soft spot for kids. That would wreck your whole image."

Devorah put a hand on her hip. "Well, someone has to instill some respect for history into them. Their parents certainly aren't doing it."

A minute later, Benson was back underneath the museum. Salvador heard his approaching footsteps and looked up from his workbench. "Oh lord, what do you want now?"

Benson put up his hands disarmingly. "It's fine, Sal, you're not in any trouble this time either. I just wanted to ask you something."

Salvador squinted. "Off the grid."

"As off the grid as anything gets around here, yes."

"You're a copper. Don't you have any other perps to harass?"

"Not of your... caliber, no."

It was true. In his ten years on the job, he'd slapped a lot of wrists, but by and large they had all been good people who had either forgotten the little rules, or had done well enough that they forgot the little rules still applied to them. The one really bad guy he'd busted had been led into a specially-modified hyperbaric chamber to be executed by nitrogen asphyxiation.

"Yeah, well," Sal finally said, "I guess that makes me a crooked unicorn." He pushed away from the bench and put his hands in his lap. "What can I do for you today?"

"I need to know about people without plants."

"Babies get a plant while they're still in the tanks. Everybody knows that."

"Of course, but what about babies that aren't born in the tanks?"

Sal's eyes narrowed. "Who told you about them?"

Bingo, Benson thought. "No one told me. Someone attacked me with a knife and my stun-stick didn't work, and they weren't wearing aluminum foil on their head. I figured the rest out from there."

"That's not their way."

"That's not *whose* way?"

Sal sighed long and hard. "I don't want to bring them any trouble."

Something about the way he'd said it gave Benson the impression that he wasn't talking about just one person.

"I'm only looking for the person who attacked me,

and probably helped to kill Edmond Laraby. They have brought trouble on themselves. Whoever else is out there doesn't have to worry about me."

Sal turned Benson's assurance over in his head, churning over what to do.

"C'mon Sal, you can trust me on this."

"You did right by me, sure enough. OK, here's the deal. There's a small community that lives down in the guts of the habitats, below the surface."

"How small a community?"

"No idea, but it can't be many. They call themselves 'the Unbound,' but the muckers just call them Geisha."

"They're all women?"

"I expect not, but the girls are all anyone sees, maybe all we were allowed to see. I only ever met one of them."

"What did they want?" Benson asked.

"Well, to trade for things, of course. Food mostly, but medicine too, and old clothes that were tagged for recycling."

"What would they trade for in return?"

"Services..." Sal shuffled in his chair.

"What kind of *services*?"

"Christ, man, it's the oldest profession in the world. Do I have to draw you a picture? Actually, I'm sure there's some racy lithographs in a box down here somewhere."

Normally, that would have presented a big problem. Prostitution was expressly illegal aboard the Ark. It didn't tend to promote social stability, for one thing, and sex was not recognized as a service that contributed to the functioning of the ship or the mission, so it was illegal to spend money on it, at least directly. Any other day and Benson would have to write him up for admitting to being a John, not to mention at least a dozen other violations of the Conservation Codes for wasting medicine, food, failing to recycle clothing…

But he wasn't in Avalon, so technically he couldn't charge Sal even if he'd wanted to. And if it should simply slip his mind to tell Chief Bahadur the next time they spoke, well, who could blame him for that?

Benson put up his hands. "OK, I get the picture. I didn't mean to embarrass you. How long have they been down there?"

"No idea, twenty years at least. Probably longer, though, judging by the age of the gir… young women."

"I have to conveniently forget an awful lot of this conversation after I leave here, you understand that, right?"

"Yeah, I know."

"Can you set up a meeting? I need to talk to them."

Sal snorted. "You don't go to see them. They come to see you, and only when they're ready. Besides, I'm out of the loop. I ain't been down to see her in years. I'm a little past my expiration date for that sort of thing."

"C'mon, how hard to find can they be?"

Sal looked at him with a raised eyebrow. "Have you even *been* in the sublevels? Never went down on a Halloween dare?"

"Yeah, of course I did." Everyone had. Sneaking down into the basement levels was a rite of passage among primary school kids. Most of them didn't make it much past the first sublevel. Benson had gone back and fixed the sticky hatch he and his friends had used as kids.

"The first thing you gotta understand is there's six levels," Sal went on. "Think of it as a six-story building wrapped all the way around Avalon."

"I know that," Benson said defensively, but, if he was honest, the full implications of it had never sunk in. He did the math in his head, ignoring the plant calculator that automatically popped up when he struggled momentarily. Each habitat was two kilometers long, times two wide, times pi. Just over twelve and a half square kilometers, times six. Right around seventy-five square kilometers of area to search, in *each* habitat.

Sal saw the light dawning on Benson's face. "That's right, now you get it."

"Holy crap. What's down there?"

"Plumbing mostly, and a shitload of electrical conduits and atmospheric ducting. But that's mostly in the top three levels. Below that are the ballast tanks–"

"Ballast tanks? This isn't a submarine."

Sal rolled his eyes. "You've been living on this barge your whole life and never wondered how it worked? The ballast tanks balance out people moving around and keep the habitats spinning straight. If you have ten thousand people collected by the lake for a beach party, that's a thousand tons all in one place that needs to be balanced out on the other side of the module. Otherwise you start getting stresses on the main bearings that'll burn them out if you let it go on too long. Those parts can't fail, we have no way to replace them, and they've had to run continuously for more than two centuries. So, whenever there's an imbalance, we pump water from one set of tanks to another to cancel it out."

"How do you know all this?"

Sal shrugged. "I've bounced around from one dirty job to the next for thirty years. You pick up things. Anyway, after that the last levels are mostly just structural matrix, insulation, and radiation shielding. Each level gets colder with more cosmic ray exposure the lower you go, so I'd take a jacket with you. If you get to the bottom, I wouldn't recommend staying for very long, not that you'll want to."

"So, how do I find one of these Geisha if you can't introduce me?"

"Go down there and wait. Hope one of them takes an interest in you."

"How will they know I'm there?"

"Believe me, nothing happens on their turf that the Unbound don't know about. They'll be watching you the second the lift doors open."

CHAPTER SIXTEEN

The doors slid open and a rush of cool air licked Benson's face. The space outside was dark and cramped with a maze of pipes in every size and color, providing countless opportunities to bash one's forehead or shins.

Sal had given him what meager intel he could. He knew which lift to take down, and he knew it would be dark. The Unbound preferred the dark, so they'd simply disabled the motion detectors that controlled the lights inside their territory.

Benson had run back to his apartment to throw on a turtleneck under his sport jacket and grab a hand torch to fight against the cold and shadows. On a whim, he also pocketed the tablet he'd broken in a fit of anger and a few protein bars so he had something to barter with. He felt ready for what he'd been told to expect.

What he wasn't ready for was the decay. He stepped out of the lift and flicked on the torch only to be met by two centuries of neglect. Paint flakes the size of potato chips curled off the thin, perforated metal frame members. Insulation foam yellowed by age disintegrated and accumulated on the deck in little piles that looked like muffin mix. Corrosion streaked any unprotected metal. Rust crept into his nostrils, smelling of dried blood.

Benson stopped a few steps outside the lift for a long, uncomfortable moment. His younger self didn't remember the decay, either because he hadn't noticed, or had been too young to understand its significance. It was the only place where the Ark revealed her true age. But seeing the rot down here made the pristine buildings and perfectly manicured parks only ten meters above his head seem all the more artificial. A façade.

It was an eerie feeling, to say the least, made all the more unsettling by the overpowering quiet. Even in the dead of night, the habitats bustled with activity. A constant din of machinery, conversations, even wind rustling through the trees filled the air. But down here, its absence was deafening. The only sound Benson's ears could pick up was the metronomic tap-tap-tap of water leaking from a loose pipe fitting somewhere in the distance.

The sound of the closing lift doors startled him. Already he regretted coming alone. It had made sense at the time; Theresa was busy holding down the Avalon unit and spare manpower was hard to come by. He'd thought about bringing Bahadur along again, but being the chief here in Shangri-La, he wouldn't have the luxury of overlooking any code violations he saw, which, if Sal's intel was right, would be numerous. That, and Benson didn't want it to look like he was leading a raiding party to round up these Unbound once and for all.

All of those considerations made Benson think it was best to fly alone for this one, but now a sick feeling trickling up his spine made him wonder how much of his old Zero captain's ego had pushed that decision.

He pushed forward regardless. The air was cool, damp, and stale. It felt utterly abandoned, like the ruins of a long forgotten city. People were always walking about in the habitats. You had to work to escape them and find any privacy. But here? No one came down here unless something broke, and they obviously limited their time to whatever it took to complete the work order and not a second more.

Benson couldn't help but think of the isolation he had felt inside the EVA pod. He had to remind himself people lived down here. They'd just grown very adept at being seen only when it suited them.

The piping and ductwork only got thicker as he ventured further away from the lift. Benson had, hesitantly, downloaded a schematic of the lower levels and synched it up to his plant. A ghostly white map floated in an overlay on the right side of his vision, but it quickly became clear the schematics were inaccurate, out of date, or both. Paths that should have been open were cluttered with pipes, square ducts, or large gauge electrical conduits. Signs of splices and bypasses were everywhere. Benson marveled at how patched up his home was just under the surface. It was obvious now why these levels were restricted. If the cattle understood just how fragile the bubbles they lived in really were, mass panic would follow.

What had Mahama said? *Appearances to maintain*, he thought sourly. Sweeping his torch around, Benson wondered if appearances were the *only* thing the crew maintained. He swiped a fingertip over the top of an ancient electrical box, leaving a shallow trench in the accumulated dust.

"I must remember to speak with the maid about this."

Someone giggled behind him. Benson span around on a heel and jabbed his torch at the sound like a spear, but saw no one. He took a deep breath, then let it leak back out nice and slow. Maybe his mind was playing tricks. The torch cast long, strange shadows through the maze of pipes and conduits. With a million places to hide, it only made sense that his brain stem would start to insert monsters into every nook and cranny.

A light sound of footsteps came from behind him. Again Benson span around and shone the light, and again he was met by empty air. He thought about turning the light off completely. It was messing with his night vision and made him far too easy to spot.

But he was trying to be found, wasn't he? Instead of chasing ghosts or shouting into the darkness, Benson decided it was best to just sit down and wait. He found a little clearing in the forest of conduits and laid out the items he'd brought for barter in front of him, then crossed his legs and leaned back against a large diameter air duct. Hopefully, it wouldn't take long before whoever was out there grew tired of playing hide and seek.

The duct was a return line from the surface and warmed his back. As he waited, Benson wondered just how many of the Unbound there could be. The space down here in the basement levels would be enough to fit the entire human population a dozen times over.

However, it was a question of resources, not room. The people living down here scraped by on whatever they could barter or steal from the surface. Margins up top for food, water, oxygen, and raw materials for clothing, furniture, and electronics were incredibly thin.

The total population never varied more than a tenth of a percent due to strict birth licensing. Any more than that threatened to collapse the whole life support infrastructure.

With every cup of water and calorie of food monitored, how many people could possibly survive on table scraps before the drag was noticed? Twenty? Fifty? Probably no more than that. Still, if things went badly, twenty people were more than enough to make sure Benson never made it back to the surface to tell the tale. Sal had said they were nonviolent and preferred to avoid confrontations. If trouble came looking, they just melted deeper into the lower levels and waited it out.

Benson hoped he was right. His stun-stick would be useless against these folks, and if the last time he fought without it was any indication, the outcome wouldn't be in his favor. Just as the first shiver of cold ran through his legs, Benson heard footsteps. Not echoes this time, but a slow, deliberate pace. With all the obstructions, he still couldn't place the exact direction. They stopped as abruptly as they'd started.

Goosebumps on the back of his neck stood at attention. The whole scene was starting to feel too much like a dozen different horror movies he'd watched with Theresa at the Golden Age Theater. He continued to sit, trying to look impassive and unthreatening.

A sharp *clang* of metal hitting the deck sent a tremor through Benson's body as if he'd been shocked. *That* had definitely come from behind him. He jumped to his feet and turned around to see past the air duct he'd been leaning against.

Nothing.

"Getting tired of this game, friends," he shouted into the shadows. He turned around to settle back in when he saw eyes staring at him.

A startled little yelp emerged from his mouth. A girl crouched on top of a junction box considered him with almond-shaped eyes. Just like with his attacker, Benson's plant had no information to offer about her.

She looked down at him curiously, then slowly unfolded like an origami crane until her feet touched the deck. She stood at her full height, which, at a meter and a half, wasn't much. A light blue, formfitting dress clung to her thin, elegant frame, swelling at her hips and ending just above her knees.

It wasn't hard to see why the workers down here called them Geisha. Her Asian ancestry was obvious from the shape of her eyes to her straight, raven-black hair. Her skin was smooth and milky, save for some dirt on her hands and knees, made all the more pale by the contrast against the darkness surrounding her. She almost looked painted. As she gazed down at him, Benson realized she wore no makeup, but her face was all the more striking because of it.

And young. So young.

Her attention turned from studying Benson to the items he'd set out for barter. Without saying a word, she knelt down and picked up one of the protein bars, tossed the wrapper aside, and sniffed it. Benson almost scolded her for littering, but fought back the reflex. She took a small nibble from a corner with her tiny mouth. Apparently satisfied, she set it down and moved on to the broken tablet. She pressed the power button and the screen lit up her face. In spite of the shattered glass, she looked up at Benson and smiled excitedly.

The smile turned into more of a smirk as she set the tablet down to stalk towards Benson on her hands and knees like a jungle cat. Despite the girl being half his size, he actually retreated from her until his back was flat against the air duct behind him.

"Um…"

She slinked up to him until her body hovered over his legs, then placed a delicate finger on his lips. When she pulled it away, her puckered lips replaced it and kissed him deeply. For just a moment, Benson forgot what he was doing and slipped back into old habits. She smelled like apple blossoms.

A wandering hand settled on his crotch and broke the spell. Benson broke free of the kiss and pushed her back gently, but firmly. Undeterred, she sat back and slipped one dress strap off her shoulder, then the other.

Fighting mightily against the base instinct to let her finish undressing, Benson moved up and put the straps back on her shoulders.

"That's not why I'm here. You can keep it on, please."

The girl looked at him uncomprehendingly, then withdrew to chew on a fingernail.

"You no like me?" she asked, in a heavy accent. Her eyes darted back and forth to the shadows.

"Oh, sweetie, no. You're lovely." Benson ran a hand down her arm, trying to comfort her. "But I didn't come down here for… love."

"I in trouble?" Her eyes went back to a particular patch of darkness, hunting for approval. Benson wasn't even sure she had addressed the question to him.

"No, no trouble," he said, as softly as he could. Then

he turned to face the shadow she kept looking at. "No trouble," he repeated more loudly.

Benson drew himself to his full height, then slid a foot back into a solid, defensive stance. His heart raced in his ears, more aware than ever of the danger he was in. He looked down at the girl. With her predatory confidence stripped away, she looked like the confused, vulnerable adolescent she really was. She shivered, ever so slightly. Despite the cold, Benson took off his jacket and draped it over her narrow shoulders.

At the edge of his vision, the darkness moved. He turned to face it head-on.

"May as well come out, I know you're there."

As an answer, not one, but four men stepped out of their hiding places and moved towards Benson with a slow, deliberate gait. Their hands were empty of weapons, fortunately. They were skinny, verging on malnourished, but looked no less menacing for it. The quartet closed around Benson like a pack of hungry wolves, but a raised hand from one of them halted their advance. The girl glanced up at him, but looked away just as quickly.

That's the leader, Benson thought. The man was scarcely taller than the girl trembling at his feet. He looked to be around twenty, maybe twenty-five, but the others were younger still. If Benson's size intimidated the younger man, his face showed no trace of it. Then again, why would he? He had Benson outnumbered five to one.

Benson *really* hoped Sal was right.

The ringleader held a hand down to the girl to help her up, then hugged her.

"You not here for love?" His tone was more accusatory than questioning.

Benson shook his head. "Not today, no."

"Then you not welcome." He snapped his fingers and they all turned around to fade back into the darkness.

No one touched the small pile of barter.

"Wait!" Benson knelt down and grabbed the protein bars and broken tablet before jogging after the retreating leader. "I want to trade with you."

"For?" the leader called back over his shoulder.

"Information. There's been a murder. I'm a... a constable."

"We know you, Benson-san."

That caught him off guard. He hadn't been down here since he was eight. "Wait, how can you know me?"

"We see in the dark," the leader said.

The implied meaning forced Benson to adjust his estimation of these people. On the surface, nearly everyone spoke English. It had long been the language of international science, business, aviation, exactly the sorts of disciplines so many of the original pilgrims had been drawn from. It was rare to come across someone who wasn't fluent. But these people didn't have the advantage of the formal education everyone on the surface took for granted. And uneducated wasn't the same thing as unintelligent.

Still, they were all too young to be the Unbound's founders if Sal's twenty year estimate was right. Not unless the man standing before him had been the world's most cynical and ambitious five year-old.

"Whoever did this, I don't think they had an implant. I would like to ask your, ah, elders, for help."

"No," the leader said flatly. So his guess had been right; others were down here, maybe even the movement's founders.

"You speak for them, do you?"

Whispers stirred between the others. The question had obviously struck a nerve.

"Look, I came down here alone to talk. But if I have to come back, I won't be alone, and it won't be to talk."

Speaking in an unfamiliar language, the leader raised his voice at one of the others, but they didn't back down. Benson decided to call him Lefty. Like most people from Avalon, Benson spoke Mandarin passably himself, but this wasn't it. The vowel sounds, syntax and structure was completely different. Japanese? He decided to let the private little argument play itself out.

Lefty threw up his hands in surrender and shouted something that probably translated to "Fine, be my guest!" He turned his back on the rest of them and disappeared into the shadows. One of the men who remained nudged the girl on the shoulder. She walked up to Benson with more caution than the first time. She bowed with her arms at her sides, then held out her hands and waved them to her chest in a "give me" gesture. Benson figured she meant his barter, so he turned it over.

"Wait here," she instructed.

"And you'll bring your elders?" he asked hopefully.

"And I will ask." Cradling the tablet and bars in her arms, the young girl bowed again, then left. The three other men stayed behind, but they retreated to a less threatening distance and simply watched to make sure he stayed put. Benson obliged and sat back down. He wondered just how long he'd be waiting for the elders' decision.

He looked around at the gaunt faces eying him with suspicion, and decided to make the best of it.

"Anybody got a deck of cards?"

CHAPTER SEVENTEEN

As it happened, they didn't, but one of them did have a bag of Mahjong tiles. After a brief struggle, they agreed to the Old Hong Kong rules to give Benson a fighting chance, then proceeded to embarrass him in successive games anyway. It was just as well the Ark didn't use hard currency, because they would have cleaned him out.

"I think you three are ganging up on me."

They all flashed their best "who, us?" looks and laughed. One of them even slapped Benson on the back.

"No, you just bad player."

"Maybe, but I'd wipe the floor with you at cribbage."

On cue, one of them reached into a backpack and pulled out a small cribbage board and a deck of cards.

"You know cribbage?"

The man shrugged. "Lot of time to kill."

"Wait, you said you didn't have any cards!"

This was met by another round of laughter. They were enjoying jerking the foreigner around.

"Yeah, yeah." Benson set up the board. "Which one of you jokers am I going to beat first?"

He'd just started to shuffle the cards when the phone rang in his head. It was Doctor Russell.

\<Jeanine, you have something for me?\>

\<Well, hello to you too, Bryan.\> She didn't bother hiding the sarcasm in her voice.

\<I'm sorry. How are you today? Lovely weather we're having. Is that better?\>

\<Loads. Where are you? Your voice is patchy.\>

Benson smirked as he dealt the cards. \<I'm about to run the board with some cribbage newbies over in Shangri-La.\>

\<Shouldn't you be sleeping?\>

\<Shouldn't you? Whadaya got for me?\>

\<Well, I stayed up late and ran the tests you asked for. Laraby's torso is still frozen solid, but his legs and… remaining arm are thawed, along with most of his dermal layer. I can already see some bruising and other signs of physical struggle.\>

\<And you're sure it's not from decompression?\>

\<No, vacuum and freezing leaves uniform damage to the capillaries across exposed flesh. These aren't uniform, and they're deeper in the tissue. They're consistent with handprints, like someone squeezing his wrist and shoulder. But there's more. I found skin cells and traces of dried blood under his fingernails.\>

The man who had volunteered to play slapped him on the hand, pulling him back to the scene in front of him. Benson glanced down and realized he'd misdealt the hand. \<Hang on, Jeanine. Really sorry.\> He picked up the cards and reshuffled, then dealt them properly.

\<OK, go ahead.\>

\<Sorry, am I interrupting your game?\>

\<No, it's… complicated. Anyway, fingernails?\>

\<Yes, Laraby had someone else's skin and blood under

his fingernails when he died.>

Benson's excitement almost boiled over. <Enough material to run a DNA match?>

<More than enough, and I already ran the test. The skin cells belong to–>

<Don't say it!> Benson mentally blurted out. <Not over an open com. Are the results accessible on the net anywhere?>

<Well, yeah, but they're firewalled behind medical privacy protocols.>

<That's not enough. Put a copy on a tablet, then pull the file from the central database and delete it. Power down the tablet, take its battery out, then hide it somewhere. Do you understand?>

<Yes, I think so.>

<Good. Don't tell anyone about the test results until you see me in person. I'll be down as soon as I can.>

It probably wouldn't be enough, Benson knew. Everything about the case was being monitored, he was sure of that. Whatever advantage surprise could have given him was gone. Still, saving a copy offline should keep it from being altered or deleted, provided Jeanine was quick enough. It would have to do.

<You mean as soon as you're done with your game?>

<I'm chasing a lead. I'm waiting to speak to someone.>

<Rough job.>

Benson looked around at the dust and decay surrounding him. <Rougher than you might think. I gotta go.>

<OK. I've already stayed up too late and I have another shift in five hours. I'll drop it off at your stationhouse on my way home.>

<Ten-four.> Benson cut the link and picked up his hand, and smiled. Four, six, jack of spades, a two, and a pair of fives. It was a good start. He picked out the jack and two to throw in his crib. He'd be giving up points no matter what he threw down, but the crib had nobs at the very least, and a good chance of–

"Agong will speak with you."

The girl's voice gave Benson a start. He'd been so focused on his conversation with Jeanine and dealing the cards right, he hadn't heard her approach.

Benson looked down at his hand and sighed at the lost chance for retribution. He stood up and turned it over to the man sitting next to him. "Here, play for me until I get back." The man looked at the cards, then gave him an enthusiastic thumbs up.

Benson followed the young lady as she led him deeper into the darkened basement level. The third man not playing cribbage fell into formation behind him, but kept a respectful distance.

"Agong." He knew the term. It meant "grandfather" in Mandarin in a generic sense, but it was more an informal title than a direct family association. They walked for a few minutes at least, weaving back and forth through the labyrinth of pipes that formed Shangri-La's circulatory system. Benson wasn't sure, but he got the feeling they'd circled back at least once, probably to confuse him and make it that much harder to find their hideout if he should ever try to return with ill intentions.

These people were as clever as they were cautious. Then again, you'd have to be to spend decades hiding right under the nose of what was probably the most invasive surveillance state in human history.

"What's your name?" Benson asked the young lady leading him.

She pointed to herself. "Mei."

"Yes, you."

She rolled her eyes. "No, Mei."

"Oh, right. Sorry. Have you always lived here, Mei?"

"Agong will talk to you."

"Yes, I know, but I want to talk to you as well."

"Agong says not to."

And that was the end of the conversation. Ahead, light shone through a bramble of pipes. The air took on the distinct odor of ammonia the closer they came to the... settlement. The smell came from stacks of trays from floor to ceiling, tended by young members. Benson stepped off to take a look. The trays slid out to reveal a layer of dirt and perfectly white, round–

"Mushrooms." Morel, shitake, and a half dozen other varieties poked up out of the rich, dark soil. He picked a small button mushroom from the bed and snapped off the stem, then popped it in his mouth. "Can't beat farm fresh."

The youth tending the stack of mushrooms looked up at him with a mix of terror and impotent rage. Mei came over and calmed the boy, then gently herded Benson back down the path. They passed more racks of mushroom beds, something that looked like a large, multi-stage still cobbled together from spares, and even small shacks and lean-tos complete with beds, reclaimed tables, and patchwork rugs made from carpet remnants.

It felt just like a refugee camp from the vids on old Earth. Except the people here didn't look desperate and hopeless. They seemed earnest, yet determined. The few children around pointed and laughed at the strange man passing through their village.

Then Mei stopped at the foot of what looked like a small chapel built into the pipes and bowed. A chill trickled down Benson's spine like a bead of ice water. Staring back through eyeless sockets, nine human skulls sat in three rows of three. Ever the detective, Benson reached out and scratched one of them with a fingernail to see if it was genuine bone, but Mei's hand shot out and slapped him as though he was a child reaching for the cookie jar.

"Don't. Touch. Anything." She poked him in the chest with each period to accentuate the point.

Benson held up his hands in surrender. "Sorry."

She mumbled something unflattering about his possible ancestry in Japanese, then continued walking. They came to the source of the lights; trellises of tomatoes, squash, and grapes glowed brightly under strips of grow lights, exactly the same sort he'd helped to maintain years ago working in the aeroponics farm, solving the mystery of why some of the units they'd sent in for refurbishment had never returned from the shop.

At the epicenter of the farms and shacks stood a... something or other. To call it a building would be an insult to many centuries of architects. Its walls were a patchwork of sheet metal and plastic laminate built in and around the pipes and ductwork. It looked like an angular beehive with tree branches sticking out of it at right angles.

A worn shower curtain served as a door. Mei pulled it aside and beckoned him to follow. Inside, an old man leaned over a bonsai tree. Several others in varying sizes sat in tiny pots on a shelf to the left of his small workspace. He wore thinning gray hair tied back in a ponytail. On the other side of the large room, Lefty regarded him with a scowl. Next to him, a young girl no more than eight or nine chatted excitedly while she worked on her own project. Before Benson could see what it was, the old man stood up and approached him.

"Thank you for coming, Chief Benson. I'm sorry to have kept you waiting."

Benson took his outstretched hand and shook it firmly. Something about the man's face cried out for attention. Benson studied his eyes, cheekbones and jawline, trying to look past the wrinkles and liver spots to the foundation of the man. A flash of recognition burst into Benson's mind as he realized he was shaking hands with a dead man.

"Ah, now you see me," David Kimura said.

Benson blinked twice, dumbstruck. It wasn't often he found himself at a loss for words, but shaking hands with a genuine ghost was enough to paralyze his tongue. David Kimura had been dead for thirty years. Longer. He was a legend, and his untimely death had been interpreted as a subtle warning to the cattle not to push too hard against their fences. But here he was, in the flesh, which didn't appear to be reanimated.

"You're David Kimura?" Benson asked. The older man nodded. "But you're dead."

Kimura raised an untrimmed eyebrow, then patted himself on the chest. "I don't feel particularly dead. I do hope your deductive skills are usually better than that, my son."

"I mean," Benson struggled to regain his mental

balance. "I mean, you're *supposed* to be dead."

The older man smiled. "And that is what you were, until this very moment, *supposed* to believe. Let's just say that reports of my death were deliberately exaggerated and leave it at that for now. You're a long way from home, detective. What brings you down here?"

"I'm investigating a murder."

"Yes, so I've heard. First one in years, thanks in no small part to your performance at the helm of the constables." He placed an odd inflection on "performance".

"Was that a slight, Mr Kimura?"

"No, not at all. You've proven well suited to the role." The inflection again, on "role" this time. "But it does beg the question of what you're doing here in Shangri-La's basement. Aren't you outside your jurisdiction?"

Benson shrugged. "Yes, but because of that, I can be more… selective in the sorts of things I remember to report when I get back." He glanced over his shoulder to where Mei stood at the doorway. "And it's a good thing, too."

Kimura saw the disapproval in Benson's eyes. He waved to Lefty and Mei, then asked them to leave them in private for a few minutes. Lefty, whose real name was apparently Huang, stared a couple of daggers at Benson as he passed, but said nothing. Mei bowed deeply and let the shower curtain fall closed.

Kimura put a hand on Benson's shoulder and gently turned him towards the work station where he'd been pruning the tiny tree. He picked it up, delicately, reverently.

"Are you familiar with the art of bonsai, detective?"

Benson nodded. "You starve trees to stunt their growth."

"Starve them?" Kimura turned and held the tree up for his inspection. "Tell me, detective, does this tree look like it's starving to you?"

Benson played along and regarded the tree with more than just a cursory glance. The leaves, though in miniature, were full and a vibrant green. They even sported the beginnings of flower buds. He had to admit, it looked perfectly healthy.

"No, I suppose it doesn't."

"Of course not. A starving tree withers and dies. But this one will blossom soon, and even produce apples. It is a tree, full and complete. The art is in finding the right balance." He set it back on the shelf among its fellows. "Do you see the lesson?"

"Enlighten me."

Kimura sighed. "The lesson is that beauty and fulfillment can be found even among great scarcity. Bonsai arose in Japan, and for good reason. With so many people crammed into such a small space, with such limited natural resources, it's no wonder that they could make an art out of using less. We find ourselves in a similar situation here."

Benson gritted his teeth. What was it with the tree metaphors lately?

"Yes, that's a beautiful sentiment, but let's be clear on one point here. Your little commune is adding to the scarcity. I'd be surprised if there was a single Code of Conservation you're *not* breaking down here. Everything you have is stolen from everyone else."

Kimura took the sudden assault in stride. "That's one view. But I prefer to think of it as borrowing. Every liter of water we use is purified and returned to the same pipe it was siphoned from. We grow most of our own food right here, fertilized by our own waste. What we can't grow or build for ourselves, we trade for. Things fall off the back of a truck even here on the Ark."

"I've seen what you 'trade' for, Kimura. It's not pretty."

The true leader of the Ark's lost tribe sat down heavily in his chair, old knees popping on the way down. "An unfortunate necessity, I'm afraid. But all of them are adults, and they volunteer for the duty."

Benson snorted. He'd been chief long enough to know all the little tricks to make someone "volunteer" for just about anything.

"You know, at your prime, you were an inspiration to a lot of people. A hero, even. What do you think they would see now?"

Kimura waved off the question. "They would see a man who stopped trying to change society and instead chose to live outside it. But the same could be asked of you, Zero Champion. How many people did you inspire with your innovative formations? How many new rules were written in response? Now you dutifully enforce the rules without question. I can't speak for everyone else, but I know I was a little disappointed by your metamorphosis."

"You follow Zero?"

"Of course. A beautiful game, all the grace of ballet mixed with the brutality of old American football. Sport has never seen a more perfect reflection of the human experience."

"But how? You've been down here since before I was even born."

Kimura held out his hands. "Just look around you.

Information flows through fiber-optic cables just as surely as water flows through pipes. It's only a matter of knowing how to tap it."

In the far corner, the young girl squealed with glee and ran over to where Kimura sat, chattering excitedly. She hopped up onto his waiting lap and handed him a tablet. The screen lit up at his touch, and an approving smile grew on his face. Kimura opened a small box on his table and pulled out a piece of candy. The girl opened her mouth and pointed at her tongue. Kimura popped it in her mouth obligingly. She beamed up at Benson with a grin missing a front tooth, then jumped down and ran out of the room.

"Cute kid," Benson said.

"Yes, and quite the little tinkerer." Kimura handed the tablet over. "Ah, you might want to change your passwords."

"What do you mean?" Benson looked down at the screen and realized it was his tablet, the broken one he'd brought for barter. Restored screen aside, the only difference was the wallpaper image had been changed to a picture of himself taken only moments ago, with the addition of a big orange mustache and a garish pink feather boa crudely drawn in with a crayon widget.

"How?"

"How did she fix it? Well, someone traded us for a tablet with a good screen but a burned out power core. As far as how she broke your password, I honestly don't know."

"Who is she?"

"My daughter," Kimura said flatly, almost challenging Benson to push the line of inquiry. He wanted to, badly.

He wanted to ask what gave Kimura the right to keep innocent children sequestered down here in the dark, cut off from the rest of humanity. He wanted to ask when they would get to choose if they wanted to live outside society, but decided to keep quiet. They were already drifting too far off track, and he wasn't the first idealist Benson had met recently who'd run afoul of common sense.

"She's beautiful," he said simply. Kimura studied his face for a moment, perhaps trying to tease out Benson's thoughts. "But that's not why I came. As you've already heard, I'm investigating the suspected murder of this man…" Benson tried to bring up Laraby's profile from the ship's records, but the query was met with an error message. "Um, I'm not sure she fixed this all the way."

"If you're trying to use wireless, it's not going to work in here." Kimura pointed up. A thin metal screen had been tacked to the ceiling. "It continues into the walls, and under the floor. It's a Faraday cage, you see."

"A what?"

"Forgive me. It blocks RF inside this building. No signals get in or out, signals from your tablet, or–"

"Or my plant." Understanding dawned. "You still have your plant. This is one giant foil hat. That's how you faked your death. That's how you've stayed hidden."

Kimura nodded. "Along with the help of a sympathetic reclamation tech who recycled my 'body', yes."

Benson couldn't conceal his shock. "You've been living in this hut for thirty-five years? Without leaving?"

"Not this one specifically. The camp has moved from time to time, and I have a helmet for the occasional excursion outside my home. But most of that time, yes, I've been here, or someplace very much like it. My gilded cage."

Benson's opinion of the man changed ever so slightly. The sacrifice he'd made to live his ideals were extreme. He turned off the wireless transceiver in his tablet to get rid of the error message, then dug around in the case notes he'd kept firewalled and picked out an image of Laraby.

"Do you know this man? Has he ever come down to... visit one of your women?"

Kimura took the table and inspected Laraby's portrait carefully, swiping it left to right to rotate the three-dimensional reconstruction.

"No, I do not know this young man. Is he the victim?"

"Yes. His name was Edmond. I fished him out of the vacuum a couple days ago." Benson switched the picture to Chao Feng. "And this man?"

Kimura again took the tablet, but he recognized the face immediately. "Ah, our illustrious first officer."

"You know him?"

"I knew his father, and I met him as a young boy. Is he your suspect, then?"

"He is suspected of involvement, yes."

Kimura whistled. "Playing with fire, my boy."

"Trust me, I don't need to be reminded of that. Has he ever been down here to take advantage of your women's services?"

The older man chuckled. "No, he has no need of our women. What does this have to do with my people?"

"Feng was in his quarters when Laraby disappeared, and we can account for all his movements for the day before and after. They were never in contact. Someone else put

Laraby in the airlock. Someone we couldn't track."

"What makes you think there was anyone else involved? Why not suicide?"

Benson rolled up the sleeve on his right forearm, revealing the angry red slice held together with stiches.

"Call it a hunch."

"I see." Kimura leaned back in his chair. "And it must be one of my people because they don't have plants."

"I'm just covering my bases. I'd like to interview them, starting with the men."

"I'm afraid that's not possible. They won't talk to you."

"Because you've instructed them not to."

Kimura tilted his head and shrugged his shoulders in a noncommittal gesture. "They honor my guidance, most of the time at least. Huang argued against talking to you at all. He believes your presence is a huge mistake."

"Then why did you?"

Kimura held his hands open. "We're coming to that. I speak for the Unbound, and I can assure you that none of us were responsible for these crimes."

"What about your people in Avalon?"

The older man sighed heavily. "We don't have any people in Avalon."

"That's not what I've heard," Benson said. "The same source that led me down here says there are people under Avalon just as there are here."

"There probably are, but they're not Unbound."

Benson rubbed his face in frustration. Another crazy cult to deal with?

"There was a schism two years ago," Kimura continued. "Between my followers and a young man with more, we'll say *progressive* ideas. At first, the split was amicable, and he started a new colony much like our own. We traded supplies and news for quite a while. Members migrated between the two groups freely. But that ended abruptly five months ago after he expelled three people for 'spying.' We haven't heard anything from them since. The people who returned said he'd taken to calling himself Mao and had grown paranoid and aggressive."

"Hold on. You mean to tell me that a revolutionary terrorist cell's been growing under my feet for the last five months?"

"That's a bit of an overstatement, I think. I don't know Mao's intentions, you would have to ask him. Although I wouldn't expect the same warm welcome you received here."

Benson felt a migraine coming on. This just kept getting better by the minute, although it fit the facts of the case better. They still didn't know which lock Laraby had been thrown out of, but his own attack had been in Avalon, and someone with intimate familiarity of the habitat's bowels would be perfectly positioned to disappear after the murder attempt failed.

Still, Benson had trouble seeing why a revolution minded malcontent would be willing to work for Feng, even if it was to knock off a crewmember and a cop.

"Can you give me an idea where their camp is?"

Kimura shook his head. "No. Mao's group is smaller and more mobile. They haven't set up a permanent camp as far as I know."

"How many?"

"Six, eight at the most."

Benson chewed on the number. Few enough to hide

easily, but enough to be in many places at once and cause all sorts of mayhem.

"All right. I can work with that. So, now's the part where we haggle over how much that information just cost me."

Kimura put up his hands. "No need to haggle. I have only one request."

Benson waved in a "go on" gesture.

"I promise that the Unbound will provide you with any intelligence and support we can in finding your killer, in exchange for clemency for any code violations and sanctuary leading up to the Flip."

Benson stared at him slack-jawed for a moment. But then, what else would he ask for? He'd been hiding here in the shadows for decades, but chose this moment to expose himself, his people. They were running out of time, and Kimura knew it. There was no way his little tribe would survive the month of hard deceleration coming in less than two weeks down in these quarters. He was desperate, but too proud to say it out loud. So, he'd found an opportunity to bargain.

"That's... a tall order," Benson said finally.

"Still, it is my price. Not for myself, you understand. I will take my chances down here. But the rest of my people are innocent and must be protected."

"How many?"

Kimura hesitated, but gave in to the inevitable. "We are forty-seven. Forty-eight, if you include Mei's baby."

"She's pregnant? How far along?"

"Two months, give or take."

"You know how irresponsible that was."

Kimura hung his head. "It was not foreseen."

"I should hope not! She's a child, for God's sake!" Benson shook his head in consternation. There had been a moratorium on child licenses for the last five years, and for good reason. The day fast approached when the ship would Flip and everyone would be locked into deceleration webs for twenty hours a day for weeks. Dealing with pregnant women or toddlers wouldn't make enduring the experience any easier.

"That's a lot of people to make space for, Kimura. I don't have the authority to make the call on my own."

"I'm sure you'll do your best." Kimura stood uneasily. Benson held out a hand to help steady him, but Kimura waved him off. He had to be in his early seventies. Benson knew what a month spent decelerating alone down here would mean for the man. He was choosing death.

"But now, you'll have to excuse me. It's just about time to hand out the day's rations. Mei will escort you back to the lift. We'll be in touch soon, detective."

Kimura put a hand on his shoulder and walked him back to the door. Mei waited just outside.

"Good luck catching your man."

"Mr Kimura, wait, I have to ask."

"Yes?"

"The skulls. Who do they belong to?"

The smile faded from Kimura's face. "The Clock still ticks in the museum, yes?" Benson nodded. "So our shrine maintains the count down here. Good day, detective."

CHAPTER EIGHTEEN

Riding the lift on the way back down to Avalon, Benson's thoughts raced to try to catch up with everything he'd learned. Prostitution, underground cults, crew conspiracies; it had been a rough few days for his preconceptions. He'd spent his entire life onboard the Ark, but it was becoming apparent that he knew virtually nothing about it, as though he'd been living on the surface of a soap bubble someone had just pricked with a needle.

As his weight grew against the soles of his feet, Theresa's name popped up to the side of his vision along with her customized ring. He answered.

<What's up, Esa?>

<Where have you been? I couldn't find your signal.>

<I'll tell you, but you won't believe me.>

<Whatever. You have to get down here, right now.>

<Where's the fire?>

<Burning in my hand. Your doctor friend stopped by–>

Benson tensed up involuntarily. Only a limited number of conversations existed that the two of them could have that wouldn't land him in trouble.

<–and dropped off a tablet. You need to see this straightaway.>

The test results.

<You looked?> Benson asked. <You've seen what's on it?>

<...maybe.>

<Don't say it over the com, and don't upload it into the police central files!>

<I figured that out for myself, thanks. It's not my first day.>

<Are the results who I think they are?>

<Just get down here, quick.> Even over the com, he could hear the apprehension in her voice. Whatever she'd seen had Theresa spooked.

<I'll be there as soon as I can. Out.>

Benson cut the link, wishing he could make the lift go faster. Still only halfway down to the surface, Benson flipped around in his foot-straps and peered out at Avalon. It was nighttime, yet even now he could make out the dots of tiny people strolling along under the network of streetlights. They branched off into smaller and smaller streams, like a circulatory system. Funny how he'd never made the comparison before. The Ark was one big organism, each individual acting as a single cell. And if that was true, he was the ship's immune system. But was he investigating a disease, or learning how the beast actually functioned?

Benson banished the thought. The darkened pillar above reminded him of the time, at least so far as his body was concerned. He'd been awake for thirty hours already. Jumping from the daytime in Avalon to the daytime in Shangri-La, it was easy to lose track of his circadian rhythm, but eventually sleep would come calling.

He slapped himself in the face a couple of times,

hoping the shock would wake him up until he could find a strong pot of tea.

The lightness in his arms disappeared as penthouses flew by in his peripheral vision. Soon, Benson's full weight was felt as the lift braked on approach to the deck. The sutures in his right shin protested under the strain, but he ignored the discomfort.

The doors slid open as Benson stepped out into the warm air and familiar smells of home. Yet even here, he was keenly aware of the dangers just a few meters under his feet. Mao's splinter cell would have to be dealt with sooner rather than later, in case his plans included disrupting the Flip or something equally grandiose.. He didn't have the manpower or time to search dozens of square kilometers of basement. And with what weapons? An image of his officers raiding the baseball field equipment locker for bats was less than appealing.

It would have to wait for the moment. He marched down the short pathway to the stationhouse, eyes scanning the bushes and corners for threats. If anyone was going to try to take another shot at him, now would be the time.

The walk passed without incident, however. Either his precautions really had kept news of the test results off the net, or whoever had ordered the first attack had lost some of their nerve.

Theresa was waiting in his office, the tablet sitting on his desk in front of her.

"Where were you?" she demanded.

Benson walked past her and poured himself a generous cup of tea. A little spilled over the side in his jittery grip.

"Visiting a new friend in Shangri-La."

"Does this friend have a name?"

Benson swallowed the tea in three big gulps, fully aware of how crazy his next sentence was going to sound.

"David Kimura."

The name didn't hit home for her right away. Theresa's eyes went a little unfocused as she consulted her plant for a match.

"*That* David Kimura?" she asked. "But he's dead."

"I know. I told him the same thing, but he wasn't convinced."

Theresa gave him a sideways glance. "You know how crazy that sounds, yeah?"

Benson gulped down the rest of his tea and poured another cup without answering.

"When was the last time you slept?" she asked.

"I'm fine."

"You're shaking."

"With excitement," he snapped. "What's on the tablet?"

Theresa's patience wore thin. "Fine, read it your damned self. I'm going home to get some sleep so one of us isn't a zombie in the morning!"

Benson grabbed her wrist as she passed, but she twisted out of his grip. "No, Bryan, you want to do this all on your own, and I'm going to let you."

"Esa, wait. I'm sorry. You're right, I'm tired and punchy."

"You're running yourself into the ground. I've never seen you like this before."

"I know, but I have to see it through."

"Why?" Theresa pleaded. "Why is Laraby so important to you?"

"Because…" The words didn't come right away. Benson's muddled mind tried to find a way to articulate what he'd been feeling for days. "Because I see myself in Edmond. He was an only kid with old parents and he had to work really hard to get where he was. Because the crew is supposed to be the best of us. They are the de facto government, and we're expected to follow their leadership, almost blindly. But I've gotta tell you, the shit I've seen the last few days, I'm starting to think that trust has been misplaced. Someone is literally trying to get away with murdering a good kid who never hurt anybody, and they expect us to just go along with it. I'm not the historian Devorah is, but it can't be too hard to find examples where that doesn't turn out well for the people being governed."

"We're about to Flip, is this really the right time to rock the boat?"

"I think it's our last chance to right its course."

Theresa crossed her arms. "Did you practice that line, Zero Hero?"

Benson shook his head. "No, totally spontaneous. Did you like it?"

"Yes, I did." She grabbed the tablet and turned it on. "You were right. About everything. The skin and blood cells under Laraby's fingernails belong to Chao Feng."

Benson grabbed the tablet and scrolled through the results for himself. It was strange; the results didn't surprise him at all, but he felt a surge of adrenaline all the same. This sealed it: the paintings established the link between the two men, Feng's skin cells established they'd fought, and his actions since amounted to attempts to cover up the crime and intimidate a constable. He was at the scene, had the opportunity, Benson could prove everything but the motive, and that would almost surely come out now that he'd have Feng in custody and could interrogate him, not to mention do a proper search of his files. And once reality set in, Feng was almost certain to roll over on his accomplice, whether it was Mao or another member of his cell.

Today was a good day.

Benson linked the tablet with his own and copied the results, then he tossed it back at Theresa. "Make a copy. Make a dozen copies."

"Where are you going?"

He slid his own tablet in a desk drawer and locked it with a thumb print. "To finish this."

Benson grabbed Constable Korolev out of bed on his way back to the lift. He stepped back out not five minutes later in a clean, pressed uniform and perfectly groomed hair, without a trace of the sleep he'd just shaken off.

Benson reached up and mussed Korolev's hair.

"Never look better than the boss, son."

"But you look like shit, sir."

Benson could only laugh. He was about to put the young man directly into the line of fire of the most powerful people alive, whether Korolev knew it or not. He could forgive a breach of decorum.

"Do you know why I've pulled you out of bed, constable?"

"I've heard the rumors, sir."

"And you're not afraid of them?"

Korolev set his jaw. "Not enough to refuse to do my job."

Benson put a hand on his shoulder and smiled at the younger man. "Good answer. Do you have your stun-stick and some cuffs?"

"Always."

"Good, let's roll."

Benson phoned Magistrate Boswell and had a warrant in his inbox before they'd reached the top of the lifts. Getting it was one thing, executing it would be another. Commander Feng was on the bridge, not in his quarters, so they were headed for the command module. In theory, the warrant gave Benson authority to run down a suspect anywhere onboard, but in practice he didn't have control of the lock into Command. If someone on the other side decided to play hardball, Benson and Korolev couldn't do much about it short of pinching a couple of cutting torches from engineering. They'd just have to see who was willing to make a bigger scene.

Benson was pretty sure it was him, but just in case, he set up an encrypted video link through his plant back to the stationhouse. If the crew tried to pull anything funny, Theresa would stream it straight to the social net. It wouldn't take them long to shut it down, but by then killing the stream would be the most damning thing they could do.

Ten seasons playing Zero had taught Benson a thing or two about playing dirty.

They drifted in silence through Shangri-La's axis corridor. They weren't challenged at the entry to the bio-lab module, or at the lock to the command module itself. Just as Benson felt sure news of the warrant had somehow fallen behind their progress, they hit a wall.

"What is the nature of your visit to the bridge,

detective?" asked a holo image of a squeaky clean bridge officer who scarcely looked older than the uniform hanging on his narrow shoulders.

"We're here to execute an arrest warrant. Please open the lock."

"May I see your warrant?"

Benson grunted with irritation, but uploaded the warrant file from his plant. The young man pulled it up on his console and audibly gasped as he read the name. The cat was definitely out of the bag now.

"I, um, I'm afraid I can't let you in just now, detective. We're running a very sensitive simulation related to the Flip, and the captain has ordered–"

Benson held up his hand to cut the young officer off mid-sentence. "I'm going to stop you right there. What's your name, son?"

"Ensign Barta, detective."

"Well, Barta, you drew the short straw when they saw me coming and told you to stall me, I understand that. You probably didn't even know what this was about until just this moment. I sympathize, really I do, but I'm in the middle of pursuing a suspect. I have a warrant signed by the civilian authority to collect that suspect, and right now the only thing between me and him is this door. So either you open it, right now, or in ten minutes I'll be issued another warrant. Except this one will have *your* name across the top of it, followed by 'Wanted for Obstruction of Justice.' Are we clear?"

Benson swore he could watch the young officer's brain working its way through the flowchart, but the outcome was never really in doubt. Barta decided to just get out of the way and let the big boys fight it out for themselves.

The light above the lock turned green and the door hissed open.

"Thank you," Benson said, as Barta's image faded into thin air.

Benson floated into the short antechamber and waited for the doors to cycle. Korolev bumped into him. The inner door scrolled open to reveal their welcoming committee. Three crew members floated in the opening, surrounding Captain Mahama like a flock of hawks.

"Detective Benson," Mahama said. "Forgive me, but I seem to be experiencing déjà vu. I could have sworn we'd already had this conversation."

"These are new charges, captain. You asked me to continue my investigation, and I have. New evidence has come to light and I cannot ignore it in good conscience. I should warn you that I have a secured video link streaming this conversation. Is it your intention to continue to interfere with my murder investigation?"

Mahama was taken aback by the implied threat, while the trio around her exchanged confused looks. Did they not know about the murder? If the official line was still that Laraby had offed himself, it was possible this was the first they'd heard of it.

"Are you trying to blackmail me, detective?"

Benson feigned surprise. "That's an awfully cynical way to look at it, ma'am."

"You know I can have any transmission shut down and wiped from the net in minutes."

"Of course you could, but people will be talking about it in *seconds*. Cutting it off after that, well, that wouldn't make anyone look good, would it?"

Mahama glared at him hard enough that Korolev

actually tensed up, anticipating action. Benson put a calming hand on his shoulder to try to settle the young constable.

"Bending the rules of a new game, hey, Zero champ?"

Benson's face remained implacable.

"OK," Mahama said at last. "There's obviously more than a little testosterone in the air here. Let's take a step back and work through this like the professionals we all are."

"Fine by me. I have new evidence that puts Commander Feng in a physical struggle with crewman Laraby in the hours before his death."

"May I see this evidence?"

"Sure, you can see it at the trial like everyone else."

"I seem to recall this part of the conversation, too," Mahama sighed. "Come inside, I will listen to this new evidence, and I will listen to Commander Feng's reply. If his explanation does not satisfy me, I'll rescind my emergency authority and turn him over to you right now. And I can personally guarantee that you will be satisfied with the outcome. Deal?"

"You know I don't have to take any deals. The command module isn't your personal fiefdom, the rules still apply up here."

"And you know that I can invoke emergency powers and we'll be tied up in court with counter-complaints until well after landing. I'm offering to accommodate you, detective. Take it or leave it."

Through a force of will, Benson tamped down on his immediate reaction and weighed his options. Long term, he knew he'd win a court challenge against the captain's actions, just as Bahadur's challenge would eventually.

But for now, the captain held all the cards, unless Benson was prepared to stun the entire bridge crew and drag Feng out by his hair.

While that plan held a certain undeniable caveman appeal, it wasn't very practical.

"Fine, deal. Where is he?"

"We can speak in the conference room. This way." She flipped over and pushed off against the wall. The other three officers waited for Benson and Korolev to push off before following.

Benson soared across the bridge's enormous open space, drifting through holographic displays and work stations as he flew. Korolev's micro-grav wings proved to be less accurate, and he drifted off course. He bumped into a holo-projector console, knocking a large image of the local comet population out of place. One of the crew shouted something about a "bull in a china shop", followed by a chorus of mooing. Korolev ignored them, but overcorrected and hit another display a few seconds later, leading to general laughter throughout the bridge.

Benson grabbed his spinning body and helped right his trajectory. "Don't worry about them," he whispered. "Just challenge them to run one lap around Avalon. See how quick they shut up."

Korolev snorted as they touched down on the far side of the bridge. Captain Mahama waited by an open portal and motioned them inside. It wasn't a conference room in the traditional sense. Built in between the command module's double hulls, the three of them drifted down through the ceiling and towards the floor, so much as those concepts applied in micro gravity. The room had no table, because anything set on it would just float away anyway. Instead, the walls had a dozen small alcoves each, with footloops and handholds to keep everyone in place, and refreshment tubes that had been hooked up for water, tea, or a variety of fruit juices and protein shakes to keep everyone from getting parched or hungry during long meetings.

Nestled nervously into one such alcove on the far wall floated Commander Feng.

"Ah, our resident witch-hunter has returned. Wasn't Salem hiring?"

"Hello again, commander. You may be less jovial in a minute or two," Benson taunted.

"That will do, gentlemen," Mahama said. "This is an official inquiry, and I expect you both to act like professionals."

"Professionals?" Feng shouted. "He broke into my home and arrested me. I can't believe you're allowing this harassment to continue, captain."

"Detective Benson is doing his job, as he understands it, and he assures me that new evidence has been uncovered."

"Don't you see what's happening here?" Feng bit off. "This is a vendetta. You know his family's history. That line's been holding a grudge for generations. Now one of them gets a whiff of authority and immediately makes a suicide run against the crew. We never should have promoted him."

"That's enough, Chao," Mahama snapped. "The civilian magistrate has heard the new evidence and believed it merited a warrant, and that's an end to it."

Feng's face twisted up in desperate rage, but he remained silent.

Mahama continued. "Good. Personally, I've grown very tired of this distraction, so it ends right now. Commander, I am ordering you to submit to a BILD scan."

Feng's face turned white, or at least whiter than normal. "You can't give me that order."

"My emergency powers go pretty far, Chao. And right now, I'm seriously questioning more than one promotion I've approved over the last few years. This ends in this room, right now."

"Wait, hold on," Benson said. "What's a 'Build' scan?"

Mahama looked back to Benson, then glanced over at Korolev. "I'm going to have to ask your constable to wait outside."

"Like hell I will," Korolev blurted out before remembering to add, "Sir."

Benson put a hand on Korolev's shoulder. "Pavel, I need you to cover the door. Please." He pitched his voice lower so only the two of them could hear. "Don't worry, I can handle these floaters if they get too rowdy."

Korolev relented. "OK, chief. I'll keep anyone from sneaking up behind you."

"Good man. See you shortly, and keep your stick handy." Korolev nodded understanding, then floated back up through the hatch in the ceiling. Once the door span shut, Benson turned back to the captain.

"Your subordinate is a loyal one," Mahama said. "A little rough around the edges."

"He'll polish up in time. Now, let's hear it."

Mahama nodded. "BILD stands for Brain Imaging Lie Detection. It's actually a very old technology, dating back to old Earth. It—"

"Scans the electrical activity of the brain, looking for

patterns that indicate recognition of pieces of physical evidence or the regions of the brain associated with creating and telling lies," Benson said for her. She looked at him in confusion.

"What?"

"Well, it's just that you have a reputation as a bit of a…" Mahama grimaced. "A Luddite."

"You think I've just been looking at sports almanacs for the last ten years? I read. I've just never heard that particular acronym before. I know about the tech, I also know it's been illegal for almost three hundred years. There was a damned UN treaty against it. It's one of the reasons I *am* a Luddite when it comes to stuff digging around inside our brains."

Captain Mahama shrugged. "The United Nations is a footnote. The software was preserved, we've even upgraded it here and there."

"But our laws are based on our original UN charter," Benson objected. "They still apply."

"To citizens, yes. In fact, the safety interlocks prevent it from being used on citizens at all," Mahama agreed. "But crewmembers are another matter entirely. The crew gives up quite a few of their civil rights, just as members of old Earth militaries were required to. And as I've already said, my emergency powers go pretty far. This is how we handle problems in the command module, detective. So, how about it?"

Benson looked back and forth between the two of them. Feng's defiance had melted away, replaced by a pleading expression that almost managed to generate a pang of sympathy from the pit of Benson's stomach.

Almost.

"Do it," he said at last.

Mahama nodded. Feng cowered, sinking into his alcove as if he hoped to become incorporeal and slide right through the hull. A jolt ran through his body as Mahama activated a holo-emitter in the center of the conference room. A moment later, a much-larger-than-life false-color image of a human brain coalesced in three dimensions in the middle of the room.

"What you're seeing right now is a live stream of Commander Feng's brain being fed directly from his plant. The pulsing blue netting represents electrical activity between neurons, while the red-through-green spectrum represents oxygen consumption. Green means more calories are being burned, red less."

The captain asked Feng a series of calibration questions, such as what day it was, what his name was, etc. Once that was finished, she turned back to Benson.

"The BILD software will match up truthful patterns and give you a result in nearly real time, but don't rush it. Ask specific questions, and give the system enough time in between to return to baseline. Do you understand, detective?"

"I think so." Benson pushed off and floated over to Feng's alcove. Little droplets of sweat drifted off the commander's forehead. He retreated even further as they came face to face, determined to find a place to hide.

But whatever empathy Benson felt was overridden by the ache in his forearm and shin. This man had sent someone to kill him, and it was time to collect on that debt.

"Does the scan hurt?"

"N... no."

True.

"Darn. Let's start with the little stuff, shall we? Did you give Edmond Laraby the Monet Haystacks painting from your collection?"

"No," Feng said unequivocally.

Benson glanced back up to the brain floating behind him. Even to his untrained eye, the patterns of activity changed noticeably. It was less than a second before multiples of the word "false" appeared in crimson, slowly orbiting the display like scarlet letter satellites.

"Really? You sure about that?"

"OK," Feng panted. "I gave him the painting as a gift."

"True" appeared in green a moment later. *Damn,* Benson thought to himself, *no wonder they banned this tech. This is too easy. I wouldn't be surprised if cops fought the hardest to get rid of it. Who would need them?*

"And did you arrange to get Edmond assigned to that palace he was living in when he died?"

"Yes."

True.

"Why?"

"That's too broad a question, detective," Mahama injected. "The results get less reliable the more nuance the subject can introduce. Narrow it down to simpler yes or no questions."

Benson nodded. "Did you alter Edmond's personal files before they reached my desk?"

"Yes."

True.

Benson's smile nearly reached around his head to shake hands with itself.

"Did you murder Edmond Laraby?"

"No!"

True.

Benson's smile shrank.

"Did you conspire to murder Edmond Laraby?"

"No, I did not."

True.

Benson leaned further into the alcove and closer to Feng's face. "Did you hire someone to kill Edmond Larby?"

"That's the same question," Feng protested. "And the answer is still no."

True.

"Did you send someone to attack me the night I returned with Edmond's body?"

"No."

True.

Benson's frustration threatened to boil over. "I think your machine needs recalibrating, captain."

Mahama shook her head. "It's within parameters. You're just not getting the answers you expected."

He looked back to Feng. "Did you alter the security video logs of the locks to mask whoever killed Laraby?"

"No! No one killed Edmond. He committed suicide."

True.

"He threw himself out of an airlock, then erased the video from the outside? That's a neat trick. How did he do that, commander?"

"Well, I..."

A chime sounded from the display behind him. Benson turned around to see an error alert flashing in orange.

"What does that mean?"

"I'm not sure, exactly." Mahama dug through the

menu, sifting through conflicting data and system messages. "He's experiencing cognitive dissonance. You're confusing him."

"That makes two of us." Benson turned back to Feng. "You really believed Laraby killed himself?"

"Of course. I called you in, remember? I wanted you to find him more than anything."

True.

"Then why did you alter his files before you gave them to me?"

Feng didn't answer.

"I know something was hiding in his files. Was he blackmailing you?"

"No."

True.

"Then why are your skin cells under his fingernails?"

That got Mahama's attention. The room went very quiet as they both waited to hear Feng's response.

"Well? Answer his question, commander."

Benson got back in his face. "Why the lavish presents? Why the huge apartment? He was hiding something for you, but the price got too high, didn't it? You confronted him and got into a fight. Things got out of hand, didn't they?"

"No! For the last time, no!"

True.

"Then how do you explain your skin under his fingernails?"

"Because we were lovers!"

Benson stopped cold. You could hear a pin drop, if indeed a pin could drop. Benson looked back over his shoulder at the BILD display.

True.

Feng's face twisted up in pain and shame. "Are you happy now, you bastard?"

"You're gay?" Benson asked, utterly confused.

"That would follow, wouldn't it?" Feng snapped sarcastically.

"But, you're married..."

Feng just shook his head. "You wouldn't understand."

"You're right, I wouldn't," Benson said. "It's nothing to be ashamed of. No one cares if you're gay. Hell, one of my teammates taught me how to dance at La Cage. The only people left who give a shit is that ultra-orthodox Shia sect, and there can't be more than a couple dozen of them on the entire ship."

"It's not that simple," Feng sobbed. "Oh, sure, you all congratulate yourselves on being so fucking enlightened, but if any of us want a family, the door gets slammed in our face."

"That's not true. You can get married just like everyone else. That's been true from the beginning."

"And then what?" Feng demanded. "When was the last time a homosexual couple was given a child license? Never, that's when. They always go to married, biological parents. And with every woman on birth control, there are no unwanted children. There are no adoptions, there are no orphans. So either we let our lines die to live openly, or we stay in the closet. I chose to have a future."

True.

Captain Mahama pushed off and floated to Feng's alcove. "Commander, why didn't you say something before now?"

"You think we haven't tried? Read the old court cases,

it was brought up a half dozen times over decades. We always lost. The civilian court always sides with biological parents. It's not like back on Earth. After a century of that, we just gave up and did what we had to."

Benson listened intently. It made a sad sort of sense. Any child that went to a gay couple would be a license that didn't go to a "normal" couple. It was easy to support someone else's rights when it didn't mean giving up anything in return.

"That's why you altered his personal files. You erased any mentions of your relationship to keep it secret after he died."

Feng nodded sadly.

True.

"Does your wife know?" Mahama asked.

"No, it would kill her inside. I love my wife, and our son. I just… needed more. Edmond was always pushing me to force changes, but I always told him to be patient, that it wouldn't matter once we reached Tau Ceti. 'Keep your head down,' I said. But he was braver than I was. I thought he finally gave in to the pressure. I've been blaming myself for days without even being able to grieve, with you breathing down my neck the whole time accusing me of killing him! Do you have any idea how hard it's been?"

"How hard it's been?" Benson tried to contain his temper, but it was difficult. "You've been interfering with my investigation from the start! Now I've wasted three days chasing you down. If you'd just told me the truth in the first place I'd be three days closer to catching the real killer."

"I tried to get you to look somewhere else, but you wouldn't listen."

Benson's eyes rolled. "Jesus man, I'm a cop, not a crewmember. If you tell me not to look in the box, I look in the box to see what you're hiding. Now Edmond's killer has had three days to cover their tracks. They might even get away with it now, doesn't that matter to you?"

"Of course it matters!"

True. Feng tried to continue, but emotion overwhelmed him as tears erupted from his eyes.

Mahama put himself between Benson and his first officer. "All right, you have your answer, detective. This debriefing is over."

"But he admitted to obstruction of justice."

"And he will answer for that, later. But right now, he's staying put at his post. I can't afford a major shakeup in the chain of command just days before we Flip. We'll deal with his punishments administratively once we're safely inserted into Tau Ceti G orbit. Not before. Now, you're going to turn around and get back to work. This is a dead end."

"Someone with command level network permissions either killed Laraby, or helped," Benson said gravely. "Your BILD system can find them by the end of the day."

Captain Mahama was incensed. "Are you quite mad?"

"Well, how else do you explain the altered security logs?"

"That's not the point!" Captain Mahama physically shoved Benson out of the alcove and into the middle of the room. "Ten minutes ago you were lecturing me that it was illegal. Now you expect me to run my crew through it looking for a needle in a haystack! I only agreed to use it now because you came with a warrant. I'm not about to run innocent people through that monstrosity without *some* sort of due process, and frankly I'm deeply concerned that you would even suggest it!"

Benson bumped up against the ceiling next to the door. The captain's words hit home. He could hardly believe how quickly the switch had flipped in his brain. It scared him.

"Of course you're right, captain. But if I can dig up enough evidence for another warrant?"

"I'll *think* about it. You're dismissed."

Benson saluted, and the lights went out.

Total darkness enveloped the conference room for several agonizing seconds, until amber emergency lights sprang into action, outlining the exit. Alarms screamed from the walls all around them.

Benson, Captain Mahama, and even Commander Feng stared at each other blankly for a long moment amid the pulsing yellow emergency lights and blaring alarms.

"What the hell was that?"

CHAPTER NINETEEN

"Main power's down," Mahama said.

"Down everywhere, or just this room? Wait... My plant's lost connection."

"Mine too," the captain said. Feng also nodded.

Benson's internal warning bells went off. The whole thing smelled of an ambush. Behind him, the manual handle of the door span ominously. Benson pushed off from the ceiling, trying to put a little distance between him and whatever was trying to come through. Was it an attack? Did they already get through Korolev?

"Stay behind me, sirs." He pulled out his stun-stick and leveled it at the hatch.

"Does that still work if the network is down?"

Benson shook his head. "No idea."

The three of them watched in mute horror as the handle squeaked and span before finally coming to rest. The door swung open ponderously and clanged against the bulkhead. Benson tensed as a darkened figure emerged, but the next flash of amber emergency lights revealed Korolev's chiseled features. His eyes quickly locked onto Benson's stun-stick as he reflexively threw up his hands.

"It's only me, chief!"

Benson's tension eased. "Dammit, man, announce yourself. You scared us half to death."

"Sorry, sir."

Benson tried to peek around the young constable and saw that the bridge beyond was just as dark as the conference room. The power outage had hit the whole module, maybe more.

"Status, constable?" Mahama asked politely.

"Main power's out, looks like it's shipwide. They're asking for you on the bridge, sir."

The captain nodded and pushed off from the wall. Feng followed like a scolded puppy a moment later.

"You let him go?" Korolev asked once they were alone.

"He's not our man."

"Are you sure? I thought you had him dead to rights."

"Trust me, I'm sure. C'mon, we'd better go see what's happening."

Benson followed Korolev out, then span the hatch shut. The dozens of holographic displays that had filled the air were gone, replaced by dim backup lighting and the rushed, confused conversations of the bridge crew. Captain Mahama had returned to her place in the eye of the storm.

"I need an engineering status report," Mahama said testily.

Like everyone else on the bridge, he was used to getting a constant stream of data on the ship's operation through his plant. But with the network down, everyone was busy digging through screens and trying to remember how to navigate the user interfaces. Everything was taking ages longer than it should.

The shaky answer came from an ensign who could do little to conceal the nervousness in her voice. "We've restored emergency power to secondary systems, but both main cores are down, sir."

"Both?" Mahama nearly shouted the question. "Get Director Hekekia on the line."

"Yes, sir." The ensign dug through the menus on her screen, trying to remember how to connect the call. It took a few moments as Hekekia had to be tracked down and brought to an intercom panel.

"Go ahead for Hekekia," he said, through the bridge's hidden speakers. The connection was audio only.

"Hekekia, it's Mahama. I just heard a nasty rumor that both our reactors are down."

"It's no rumor, captain. We're flat-lined."

"They're independent systems, that's not supposed to be possible."

"Tell it to the reactors. They've lost magnetic containment."

In the not-too-distant past, "lost containment" and "reactors" appearing together in the same sentence would have caused an immediate panic, followed several days later by a whole pile of people sick and dying from radiation poisoning.

Happily, the Ark used third-generation fusion reactors. Fortuitously enough, they'd been perfected in the decade before Nibiru showed up and started eating the Oort cloud. Without containment, the hundred million degree cloud of Helium-3 plasma simply cooled off and ceased to do anything dangerous.

"How long until we can restart?" Mahama asked.

"No idea. I need to figure out what the problem is first."

Mahama rubbed her eyes. "How's our capacitor charge?"

"Thirteen percent, sir."

"What?" Mahama's voice boomed across the bridge, sending shocks through the assembled crew. "Eighty percent is the safety limit. How are we below a *quarter* charge?"

"We discovered a cascading short in the recharging system this morning. It had been causing the capacitors to discharge. We just got done patching it up less than an hour ago."

How convenient, Benson thought, but he kept quiet. A shared glance with Korolev confirmed that the same thought had occurred to the younger man.

"How much time can we get out of what capacitor charge we do have?" Mahama asked.

"Well, none, sir."

"What do you mean, 'none'?"

"We need whatever's left to restart the reactors once they're fixed."

Mahama slapped herself on the face. The reactors needed a huge jolt of energy to get their magnetic constriction bottles squeezing down hard enough to convince the Helium-3 to fuse and start making power. On the few occasions they'd had to be shut down for maintenance, only one was taken offline at a time, leaving the other available to jumpstart its twin.

For the whole time the Ark had been in space, not one second had passed when one of them wasn't running. Until a few minutes ago.

"Options?" Mahama asked. The question was met with embarrassed silence as everyone came up empty of ideas. "C'mon people, give me something to work with. A stupid idea is better than no idea."

"What about the habitats?" a nervous ensign ventured.

"Explain," Mahama said.

"Well, they're spinning awfully fast to maintain artificial grav. There's a lot of energy locked up in their angular momentum."

"And? Keep going."

"Why don't we use it? Reverse the habitat's drive motors from spinning them to recharging the capacitors?"

Mahama's face brightened with the possibility. "Hekekia, can you do that?"

"Stand by." The entire bridge held its breath while he went through the calculations.

"Yes, but it'll require an EVA and four hours to make the conversion. I could do it in less, but we're still down the EVA pod that idiot broke."

Benson hoped no one remembered who "that idiot" had been. He was not so fortunate.

"Another victim of our detective's crusade," Commander Feng mumbled just loud enough for it to carry through the entire sphere. Accusing eyes glared back at him.

"Well, I didn't see any of you clamoring to do it," Benson shot back at them.

"Is Benson on the bridge with you?" Hekekia barked. "Don't let him touch a bloody thing!"

Mahama looked down, (or up, or over, depending on one's perspective) as if he had only just noticed Benson's presence.

"Detective, what are you still doing here?"

"Trying to figure out what's going on, same as you.

And before you grind the habitats to a halt, ask yourselves if you really want fifty thousand people floating around like panicking parade balloons."

"They'll have warning, chief, and if everyone has followed the preparation schedule, most everything in the habitats should be tied down by now anyway."

Benson thought about his own apartment, where the only things that were properly secured had been bolted down by the builders. Some quick exchanges between crewmembers showed he wasn't alone.

"I think you'll find a significant percentage of the population has procrastinated on that particular preparation, sir."

"Then that's on them!" Mahama fumed. "We're running on batteries up here, chief. Our superconducting magnets are down around command and engineering. We're all getting extra rads of cosmic background radiation as we speak. But more importantly, we don't have power for our Vasimir thrusters or navigational lasers. We're deep inside Tau Ceti's Oort Cloud doing fifteen thousand KPS, and if any rock or splinter of comet much bigger than a pebble hits us in the next four hours, it'll go right through our ablative shield and straight through half the ship. Bigger than a peapod and we could lose her entirely. Facts I would have assumed your recent experiences would have made you more sensitive to."

"Captain," Hekekia interrupted. "I've just got a revised estimate from one of my techs. We're going to need at least twenty percent capacitor charge to restart one of the fusion reactors. We're already too low, and we're going to be burning at least a percent for every hour of emergency power."

"Can we get enough recharge out of the habitats to get back up to twenty?"

"Maybe. I don't know where to begin making an estimate for that. And this whole thing assumes we don't burn out the drive motors or roast the bearings in the first place."

"But it's our only chance, yes?"

The line went quiet for an uncomfortably long time. "The only one I see."

"That settles it, then. Hekekia, pull the trigger." Mahama looked down between her feet. "As for you, detective, coordinate with Chief Bahadur. We'll make the announcement shortly. Get your constables ready to disperse any crowds and prepped for rescue operations for anyone who floats off when the gravity goes away. Understood?"

"Yes, sir." Benson saluted, then shoved a stunned Korolev towards the exit. The first door slid shut behind them, leaving them alone while the outer door cycled.

"Did you hear all that, chief?"

"Yes, Pavel, I did."

"What are we going to do?" Korolev was a ball of nervous energy mixed with indignant righteousness. Benson imagined it to be what small dogs looked like.

"You're going to follow the captain's orders and get Avalon ready for micro-grav."

"Weren't you listening, sir? We've been *sabotaged*! Somebody isn't happy just killing one person anymore, they tried to whack everybody! And they would have done it if these floaters hadn't gotten clever."

Benson reached out his legs to brace against the far end of the entry chamber, then pushed Korolev up against the side for a little bulkhead counseling. The impact stunned the younger man enough to jar him loose from the growing fury that was threatening to overtake him.

"I *know* that, Pavel. And if we don't get the power Hekekia needs to relight the reactors, they may still succeed. We need to help the crew right now to have any chance. It's all that matters right now. Are we on the same screen?"

Frightened, Korolev nodded. "Yes, chief. But… nobody said anything. They acted like damaged capacitors and the reactors failing at the same time was just a damned coincidence."

"Because they're not cops, son. They're crew. They live in a little bubble where they see all and control everything. They don't see the million little ways people figure out to cheat the system. We see it, because that's our job. We don't believe in coincidence because we're the cynical assholes who have been dragged through the muck long enough to know the truth: they don't control everything. Sometimes I wonder if they control anything."

"But…"

"But nothing." Benson let him go. "They'll figure out it wasn't an accident soon enough. Engineering will find some cables cut or a sensor blowtorched, whatever. Until then, you are going to follow the captain's orders and coordinate with Bahadur in Shangri-La. You're going to find Lieutenant Alexopoulos and tell her to deputize the lightbulb jockeys and their jet packs to grab any strays who float away. Got that?"

"Yes, sir. But… those were the captain's orders to you."

"Very astute, constable."

"Well, then what are you going to be doing?"

"Trying to see in the dark."

Korolev frowned. "That's the only answer I'm going to get, isn't it?"

"Yep. Is that a problem?"

Korolev's spine stiffened. "No, chief."

"Good." The light over the outer door turned green before it slid open. "Let's get to it."

Travel was immediately curtailed. Constables with biometric hand scanners were brought up to secure the locks to the command module, which had gone into automatic lockdown when the plant network failed. The doors had to be operated manually.

The lifts only went down, and only because they recaptured much-needed energy as they fell. Movement between the modules was effectively shut off, save for any hearty souls who felt like climbing the kilometer tall ladders from the deck to the hub.

Meanwhile, Benson requisitioned a case of hand torches from the lockup in Bahadur's stationhouse, (he'd fill out the actual requisition forms later) and took a little detour back down into Shangri-La's basement levels to search out the Unbound for another little chat with Mr Kimura.

Something Kimura had said in their first meeting jumped out at Benson during Feng's interrogation. When Benson asked if Feng had ever visited the Geisha, Kimura laughed and said Feng "has no need of our women." He'd assumed it just meant Feng was faithful to his wife, but now his real meaning was clear. Kimura knew about Commander Feng's romantic preferences.

What else did the man know that he hadn't been forthcoming about?

With the miserly trickle of emergency power engineering was allowing, Benson knew Kimura and his people would be running around in complete darkness. But more than that, they would be caught entirely flatfooted by the coming micro-grav.

The lift doors opened into the dark and quiet of Shangri-La's basement levels again, but somehow it managed to feel even darker and emptier than it had the first time. Maybe that was just a reflection of Benson's mood.

Right now, his mood was pretty dark.

For days, he'd been getting jerked around by his superiors, but worse still, his own instincts had led him straight into a dead end. Now instead of hauling in a killer, he'd given someone worse the time they needed to make a go at genocide. A fact that was sure to be pointed out once the sabotage was discovered, however long that took.

Benson held no doubts that it had been sabotage. He could almost believe either the capacitor damage, or the reactor failure individually, but both? Someone wanted to turn out the lights permanently. But why? If this Mao was the anti-establishment revolutionary Benson suspected he was, what was the motive for destroying the power grid? If Hekekia's jerry-rigged solution failed, everyone would be dead in a matter of days as the O_2 ran out.

Hardly a great plan for launching a revolt. Acts of terrorism needed someone left to terrorize into doing what you wanted. Unless they miscalculated? Maybe they didn't realize how much capacitor charge it took to restart a reactor.

Benson pondered the possibility as he moved deeper into the forest of pipes and ducts, holding the hand torch high over his head, trying to be as conspicuous as possible. It seemed improbable. Anyone with enough engineering knowledge, or access to said knowledge, to knock out both systems without being discovered would surely know to keep enough charge in reserve.

Unless that was the point? Maybe they'd gamed out the entire scenario and expected someone to come up with the habitat plan. Maybe someone had even been in place to help it along. Mao's people, if indeed that's who it was, were still being helped by someone among the crew, Benson was absolutely certain of that. He'd just been wrong about who. What about that ensign who had suggested the plan? Had she planted the idea purposefully? She certainly seemed nervous. Damn, what was her name?

But why stop the habitats? A show of force? No demands had been made, no threats. If anything, they'd played their hand. As soon as power was back up and the sabotage was confirmed, every man and woman who could be spared would be hunting for them. It might take from now until the Flip to search all the basement levels, but with enough manpower, they would be driven, cornered, and found.

Which brought Benson back to genocide. The attack only made complete sense if it had been a deliberate attempt to kill everyone aboard and turn the Ark into humanity's tomb. But why in the name of God would anyone want to do that? And if they had, how long before they tried again?

It was the question that had brought him back down here in search of Kimura, hoping the old kook would have new insights to share. But he'd been wandering around far longer already than he had the first time.

"Hello?" His voice echoed around a few times before dying away. No one answered.

"It's Benson!" he shouted. "I've come back to barter. I have hand torches and information to share."

Nothing.

"Lefty? Mei? Kimura? C'mon, it's important."

Silence. Benson headed off in the direction he thought their camp was located, but after a half hour he was on the verge of giving up and returning to the lift. Just as he turned to leave, a faint whiff of ammonia bit at his nose. He sniffed again and walked around, trying to get a bearing on the source of the smell. He followed the trail until he spotted one of the mushroom racks. It was completely empty. Someone had pulled up every last white head and shitake, leaving only disturbed soil behind.

The rest of the camp was similarly abandoned. Even the altar of skulls had been emptied. Benson's first thought was of betrayal. Kimura had fed him the line about this Mao to send him on a wild goose chase hours before the nutcase flipped the switch. He certainly had the resources.

Benson stormed to Kimura's shack and ripped the old shower curtain off the rings. Steam still curled up from a teapot sitting on his workstation. Benson growled at the near miss, then rummaged through the piles of old electronics. He didn't know what he was looking for, but he'd know it when he saw it, like a set of reactor schematics titled *My Senselessly Crazy and Evil Plan*.

Instead, he spotted a genuine paper note hanging off one of the Bonsai. He pulled it off the delicate branch, careful not to break it in spite of his anger. In carefully handwritten ink, it read:

> *Detective Benson,*
>
> *I apologize for our hasty departure, but my people voted to go into deeper hiding. We are aware the habitats will be stopped and are taking precautions. Our arrangement is still in place. We will be in touch soon.*
>
> *Sincerely,*
>
> *David Kimura*

Frustrated, Benson twisted up the note and threw it back on the table, then turned around and stalked off towards the lifts.

CHAPTER TWENTY

Benson reached the lift, but as soon as he got command on the intercom to approve an override, he met resistance.

"Aren't you supposed to be in Avalon, Chief Benson?" It was Commander Feng's voice. "Why are you still in Shangri-La?"

"I was coordinating with Chief Bahadur, as ordered. I'm trying to get home presently, commander."

"From sub-level three?"

"Hit the wrong button."

"I see." Feng's voice sounded suspicious. "I'm sorry, chief, but our power margins are just too thin. We can't afford to waste another watt. You'll just have to stay put, unless you feel like huffing it, of course."

He's enjoying this, Benson thought. *Fair enough, let him get some of his own back.*

"I wouldn't mind a climb. What's the door code for the maintenance shaft?"

"Ah..." Feng consulted someone off the line. "Seven, four, two, zero, five."

"OK. Good luck with the repairs. Benson out."

Annoyed, he walked to the side of the lift tube and found the hatch that read "Maintenance Access." He punched in the door code, and was a little surprised when the light turned green and popped the seal. He stepped inside and looked up. Illuminated by only the faint amber glow of emergency lights placed every ten meters, the rungs of the ladder seemed to stretch up to infinity.

He sighed, and put his foot on the first rung. Theresa would be furious if he decided just to sit this one out.

Every little emergency light was attached to a small platform, not much larger than a barstool, which gave climbers a spot to rest and recover before continuing. The paint had worn off, and the metal underneath was polished smooth by generations of athletic-minded people challenging themselves, or young lovers searching for privacy. Indeed, some graffiti had been drawn near one platform, displaying exactly the sort of artistic rigor one would expect of swooning teenagers. It declared "Charlie & Kendra 4EVER." It had been worn down by a lot of sweaty palms. Charlie and Kendra had likely been dead for a century or more.

He wished them well and resumed climbing. Fortunately, each rung shaved a few grams off his effective weight. As he climbed, he grew lighter at nearly the same rate as his muscles tired, downgrading the kilometer-long climb from "completely fucking impossible," to merely, "really goddamned exhausting."

The climb gave Benson time to think. At first, he thought about what a petty asshole Feng was for not authorizing a lift. But could he really blame him? Benson had publicly accused him of murdering his lover. Even if the little shit had been acting suspicious as hell, that had to hurt deeply. Couldn't really fault him for carrying a little vendetta.

Vendetta. Feng had used that word to describe his investigation. Benson had dismissed it as an ugly smear. A transparent attack on his sullied ancestry, a last second effort to discredit his case.

But was that all it was? Benson *knew* Feng was guilty before the BILD test, he could smell it. Looking back, though, how much of that had been built on the meager evidence, and how much of it had come from his own prejudice? He'd wanted Feng to be guilty. Had Feng become a stand-in for all of the frustrations Benson had been feeling since the polite veneer of society had started to peel off with Laraby's death?

Even worse, what clues had he *missed* by focusing all his attention on Feng?

Benson was a good two-thirds of the way up the ladder by then, breathing almost as heavily as he was sweating. He paused to catch his breath and take a moment to look down, and immediately regretted it. Somehow, heights always managed to look higher when one looked down from them. The tunnel lacked the sense of infinity he'd felt out in space, but that was part of the problem; a fall from here would most definitely have an ending.

Benson decided it was a sign to stop looking back and focus on the task ahead. Up here, he weighed scarcely thirty kilos. He sprinted up the ladder two, then three rungs at a time. Near the top, he bounded like a scorched monkey up a tree, until he was effectively weightless. He covered the last thirty meters in a single exuberant leap.

In fact, it took Hekekia's teams almost seven hours to finish their work. With the plant network down, his engineers were flying blind for the first time in their lives.

They'd discovered the hard way that no one aboard had any experience multitasking. Their plants had always carried the extra load and coordinated activities for them.

This was enough of a problem for the team deep in the Ark's stern racing to repair the reactor damage. It was doubly so for those on the EVA assignment to reverse the habitat's drive motors, who discovered flying their pods while making delicate repairs was like performing thoracic surgery while dangling from a blimp.

However, the delay had a silver lining in that it gave Benson and Bahadur's constables enough time to secure the habitats for microgravity. Everyone had known for their entire lives that the Flip was coming. Countdown clocks had been running on billboards in most public areas starting at T-minus one year. But just like in-laws visiting for the holidays, nearly everyone was waiting until the last minute to get their houses in order. The attack managed to goad the population into doing more preparation for the Flip in those seven hours than they had in the previous seven months.

Benson grabbed the last lift down to Avalon's deck, saving him another arduous climb down the maintenance ladder. As he walked up to the stationhouse, Benson had never seen Avalon so empty, not even late at night. But the most jarring omission wasn't the people, it was the hum. Vibrations from air exchangers, water pumps, waste disposals, and even the habitat drive motors themselves carried through the air, rose up through the decks, and permeated every cubic centimeter of the Ark. You could never escape the low hum of machinery. It was the heartbeat of the Ark. The silence was a sponge, soaking up any sound that did escape into the air.

A siren blared through the seldom-used public address speakers, signaling that command was about to flip the switch. Theresa had everything in hand by the time he arrived. Nearly everyone was locked behind their doors. No one wanted to be caught out in the open when the gravity went away. The stationhouse was packed with constables waiting for the aftermath. Benson took a spot next to Theresa and braced against the wall.

"Here we go," she whispered.

"How long will this take?" Korolev asked.

"They said it could take an hour or more to stop completely."

"Could they really need that much energy? I mean, we're spinning a million tons at three hundred and fifty KPH. Do you have any idea how many mega-joules of potential energy that is?"

Hernandez shrugged from the corner. "OK, rookie, I'll bite. How many?"

Korolev's mouth opened, then closed again. "Um… a lot."

"Pssh," Hernandez snorted. "Great answer. We got us a regular Einstein here, boys and girls."

Korolev's cheeks flushed as a round of nervous laughter traveled through the ranks.

"That's enough of that shit," Benson said.

Theresa patted Korolev on the shoulder. "I think they're probably just covering all their bases, constable."

A tremor rumbled through the deck like an earthquake as the modified drive motors engaged and stole the module's kinetic energy. It was subtle at first, but gre in intensity as the habitat's structure twisted und strain like a beer can.

For all their immensity, the habitats were incredibly fragile. Without any internal bracing running through their two kilometer length, they were little more than glorified aluminum and composite balloons. The pressure differential between the inside and the vacuum outside kept them rigid like old Earth zeppelins.

Without looking at him, Theresa reached out and grabbed Benson's hand, squeezing it until he wanted to flinch. He squeezed her back, although not as hard. Everyone shared nervous glances as the habitat groaned like a mythical beast waking from a centuries-long slumber. Benson couldn't remember feeling so powerless in his life.

No one could do anything except put their heads down and wait it out. The deceleration was slow at first, but as Avalon's structure absorbed more of the stress without breaking, Hekekia's people ramped it up. The resulting force pulled everything spinward as the effective gravity pulling down on their feet weakened. Everyone leaned to keep their balance. Several failed, unable to resolve the disconnect between their inner ears and what their eyes told them should be true.

Hernandez threw up with gusto, sending vomit flying diagonally before splattering across the floor.

"Jesus, Hernandez, don't tell me you ate a big breakfast before this," Benson taunted.

"Yes, chief," he answered weakly.

"Should have stuck with bananas."

"They're good for nausea?"

"No, but they taste about the same coming up as they do going down."

This was met with a round of anxious laughter from the entire room.

"I'll remember that, chief."

Hernandez wasn't the last to pop over the next twenty minutes as the Coriolis effect they'd lived in their entire lives weakened and threw their sense of equilibrium into chaos. Even Benson felt it after a while, despite thousands of hours spent in micro. Then, as suddenly as it began, the deceleration stopped, sending everyone lurching to one side. The habitat's structure let out the same deep, tortured groans as it settled back into its proper shape. Cautious hands grabbed anything bolted down in case it started all over again.

"What happened?" Benson asked no one in particular after the noise subsided.

"Maybe they got all the charge they needed."

"Let's hope. How long does it take to restart a fusion reactor?"

The question was met with shrugs and blank stares, confirming that everyone else in the room had just as much physics and engineering background as he did. As the seconds ticked by into minutes, people started milling about again. The good news was Avalon hadn't lost all of its rotation, but everything was at least a third lighter than it had been only minutes before, so everyone had to recalibrate their legs.

Benson felt like he was high-stepping everywhere. He could handle micro just fine, but this fractional gravity was really throwing him off his stride.

"Well, that's the easiest weight I've ever lost. C'mon lads, we'd better get outside and check on the civvies."

The daytime lights were still dark overhead, leaving the sickly yellow emergency lights to cast deep shadows onto the buildings and trees. Yet even among this eerie landscape, people emerged. Children and adolescents had already taken to the footpaths to see how high they could jump in the new gravity. One intrepid girl was already eight or ten meters up an apple tree when Benson spotted her.

"Come back down here, young lady."

"But I'm higher than I've ever got!" she announced enthusiastically.

"I can see that. But you could get hurt really badly if you–"

As if to finish his sentence, a thin limb gave way with a *snap*, sending the girl tumbling towards the ground at two-thirds speed through a cloud of white flower petals. Benson ran to catch her, but she met another branch, altering her trajectory. He pivoted to get beneath the shrieking girl and managed to get a shoulder under her. The impact took both of them to the ground and knocked the wind out of the girl, but a few moments later she was up and running back towards her home.

"You're welcome," Benson shouted to her back.

Kids were a resilient lot, you had to hand it to them. Benson felt the pang of an opportunity lost.

Not lost, he reminded himself. Delayed. Would the test tube births resume once they made landing, or would people revert to the more traditional method? Theresa was a couple of years younger than he, and had plenty of time left on her biological clock, if that's what she wanted for them.

He'd never asked and she'd never said. Partly because Theresa thought their relationship was always one anonymous complaint away from a forced end, but that wasn't the whole reason. If he was to be honest with himself, Benson felt guilty at the idea of bringing children into the world with a cloud hanging over their heads. Chao Feng wasn't the only one to remember the crimes of his ancestors. He remembered the taunts of other school kids before he'd grown big enough to silence them with his fists.

Benson shook the thought from his mind when, far above, a million clicking sounds rained down as the pillar's bulbs began to cycle. The power was back on. This development was met with a round of cheers that seemed to roll through the enormous space like thunder. Benson had never heard anything like it. Not even five thousand shouting Zero fans could match it. The celebration took on a life of its own, growing still more as more people ventured outside and onto their balconies to see what the fuss was about.

"They did it, chief." Korolev came up and slapped him on the back. "Now what?"

"Now, we go find the people who tried to kill us and crack skulls."

"While respecting all of their civil rights?"

"Naturally."

CHAPTER TWENTY-ONE

The first order of business was to form a posse, Old West style. After Mahama publicly confirmed the reactor damage had been sabotage, the crew declared a state of emergency and took immediate steps to curtail movement between modules and ramp up security. Benson and Bahadur were put in charge of the response in the habitats. Benson had no shortage of volunteers for his response.

Just under seven hundred people showed up outside of Lift Spoke Number One within twenty minutes of Benson putting out the call. He deputized the lot of them in a mass ceremony. Theresa had misgivings about using civilians in the search, but they needed lots of eyeballs to search an area as large as the basement levels. Even with this, keeping Mao's people from slipping through the net and doubling back was going to be difficult.

More than anything, Benson was hoping to rile them, throw them off balance enough that they made a mistake. Maybe he'd get really lucky and one of them would crack under pressure and turn state's evidence. Although he wasn't at all sure what kind of deal the prosecutors would be willing to cut on fifty thousand counts of attempted murder.

The plan they patched together was simple enough: divide into four groups and line up on each deck from one bulkhead to the other, then walk around the entire circumference of the habitat in unison, a four-story wall of searchers.

Based on what he'd learned of the Unbound over in Shangri-La, Benson ignored the first two levels. He arranged the search groups so that the larger, younger people would search levels five and six, while the smaller and older volunteers stuck to three and four. If Mao's group followed Kimura's pattern, they could be expected to retreat to the lower levels once they saw the search party coming, right down into the path of his strongest people.

As plans went, it had about as many holes as a lemon zester, but it was the best he could do on short notice. He'd assigned three constables to play shepherd over each group, and everyone was plant-linked back to the central computer grid where their visual feeds could be assembled into a single landscaped image of the entire search in real time. Any sightings would be passed out to all four groups instantly, along with a replay of the encounter and location information through their plant interface.

Theresa was back in the stationhouse where she could stay on top of the mountain of data streaming in and do her best to keep the four teams coordinated. She wasn't particularly happy about that, either.

Benson keyed up his plant and opened a call to the entire party. <OK, can everyone hear me?>

A tidal wave of *yes, yeah, yup, sure, uh-huh, mmm,* and a half dozen other affirmatives in hundreds of individual voices crashed into his consciousness so hard he actually took a step back as if he'd been struck. He wasn't alone; quite a few people in the crowd covered their ears against the noise.

<Really should have seen that coming. I'll talk. The rest of you lot stick with nodding for the moment, OK?>

The crowd chuckled back and nodded understanding.

<Excellent. Here's the deal, folks. The people we're after are dangerous in a way none of us have seen before. They are armed, not afraid of attacking police, unaffected by our stun-sticks, and they have home field advantage. If you see one of them, *you are not to chase or engage them*, I can't stress that enough. Your plants have already been programmed to identify, record, and report automatically. You're just cameras, but cameras we can't afford to lose. If we spot one of these suspects, we will coordinate and isolate them. If they refuse to surrender or put up resistance, the constables in your team will deal with them. Nod if you understand.>

They did.

<Good. I'm cutting this call now, but you're all still going to be linked up to the people on either side of you in line to keep the chain connected. If one of your buddies runs into trouble, help them, but only in self-defense and only as a last resort. Now let's roll.>

The first people in line headed for the far bulkhead. Once they were ten meters out, the next deputy followed, and so on until two kilometers and almost half an hour later the lead man reached the other side of the module. With the lines fixed in place, everybody faced spinward and marched ahead. Benson keyed a command that turned on all the lights. As far apart and dim as the bulbs were, it wasn't much, but it beat the hell out of total darkness.

Benson led the party on the sixth and last level, and it was cold. He thought the command module was cold, but he'd never seen his breath up there. The volunteers down here were almost exclusively men, several of whom had been on the Mustangs in years past and were only too eager to help their old captain. Korolev was there too, several hundred meters further down the line. He was shaping up to be a very good constable, but still needed supervision.

The scenery this far down was sparse, to say the least. Stretching out in every direction was an uninterrupted grid of catwalks set on top of a honeycomb matrix of insulation cells. Each was a meter wide, two deep, and made of aerogel, so light and translucent that it looked like frozen smoke.

It was also the best insulation mankind had ever devised. While the air down here was only a few degrees above zero, only two meters of aerogel and a thin composite/aluminum weave outer hull separated him from a degree above *absolute* zero, so named because the temperature had nowhere else to go. The habitat's aerogel blankets here and in the level above were so efficient, they needed no heaters. The rate of heat lost to space was actually less than the heat given off by the fifty thousand human bodies and waste heat from the machines that kept them alive.

Unlike the levels above, no tangle of pipes cluttered the space down here, no conduits, no fiber optic bundles, and no air ducts. The air was dry and stale, yet had a sharp, metallic edge to it like ozone. The mold and decay

Benson had seen visiting the Unbound in their lair on level three was totally absent. This far down, only a single layer of radiation-reflecting meta-materials lay between them and the torrent of high energy cosmic ray particles assaulting the ship from all directions. They very effectively sterilized any mold spores or bacterial colonies that wandered down here and tried to take root.

A bright light flashed in Benson's right eye as one of these particles crashed headlong into one of the cone cells at the back of his retina at the speed of light, reminding him that spores weren't the only things they would sterilize given enough time. It's what made the lowest levels the perfect hiding place; no one wanted to be here in the first place.

Still, the utter lack of scenery had one benefit. Benson's people could see hundreds of meters fore or aft without any obstructions, and the only thing blocking their views to spinward or anti-spinward was the upward curvature of the floor and ceiling, which would also prevent their quarry from spotting them until it was too late.

They had six point three kilometers to walk. Benson maintained a brisk pace; indeed, he found it difficult not to break into a jog. Still, the other three teams had far more cluttered spaces to navigate. Theresa had to tell him to slow down and keep his team in line every few minutes. After the first two kilometers, the inflection and cadence of her reminders sounded suspiciously consistent.

<Theresa?>

<Yes, dear?>

<Did you record that warning to slow down and put it on a timer?>

<I can recognize a pattern when I see one, sweetie.

Now, Mommy's busy.> She cut the call.

Good old Esa. Never afraid to knock him down a peg. It was probably for his own good, in the long run. She ordered stops several times while volunteers on other levels either had a false-positive sighting, or came across remnants of temporary camps and supply stashes, but Mao's group was thorough. The most interesting thing the searchers found was a fifty liter bucket with DRINK ME painted on it in blocky letters. Upon closer inspection, it was filled with piss and shit.

This is pointless, Benson thought. *They saw us coming, how couldn't they? Seven hundred people don't exactly move around as quiet as church mice. But then where did they go to?*

<Esa, has there been any activity on the locks between Avalon and Shangri-La? Anything at all?>

<No, they're locked down tight, just like you asked.>

Benson growled loud enough for the man to his right to hear him.

"Everything all right, sir?"

"Fine, fine… Just keep your eyes open."

"OK, but another thousand insulation cells and I'm going to go cross-eyed permanently."

Benson snorted. The endless pattern of hexagons really was starting to strain his eyes. He had no point of reference for them to get a fix on the distance, like getting lost in floor tiles.

"I know what you mean."

Someone had tipped Mao off, probably whichever floater had been helping him all along. Feng was the only one he could safely cross off the list, which left hundreds of possible…

A thought jumped out at Benson. He'd given up on

Laraby's files because Feng had altered them. But Feng had altered them to conceal their relationship, not to cover up whatever had actually caused someone to shove Edmond out of the lock. Those clues might still be in there, waiting to be read. Benson had given up on his best possible lead for entirely the wrong reason.

He opened his plant and tried to retrieve the files. Maybe he could run a few more searches while they completed the sweep. But his exhilaration hit a wall when the query for the files came back with an error message.

[File Not Found]

Bullshit. He tried again, but the files were completely missing from his plant memory. Benson pulled up his download history and backtracked the file address and network transfer paths to a single holographic data node. He tried again from the source.

[File Not Found]

Benson queried the node's network ID and tried to open its entire directory. He'd go through the files one at a time if necessary. But the effort was cut short by the next error message.

[Data Node Inaccessible.]

Oh, for fuck's sake. Benson opened a call to command. <Hey, I'm trying to access a data file, but the system is telling me the node can't be accessed. I just sent you the address. I have clearance, so what's the hold up?>

<Please hold.> The line went silent while the tech at the other end ran through their diagnostics. <I'm sorry, detective, but we've lost that node.>

Benson blinked several times before he answered.

<You *lost* it?>

<Yes. I'm very sorry.>

<Where was the last place you remember seeing it?>

<No, detective, you don't understand. We haven't lost it, per se–>

<It was a joke, crewman. You do have jokes in the command module, yes?>

<Oh, yes, of course. Good one, detective.>

Benson pinched the bridge of his nose. Just once, he wished his stun-stick didn't require a line of sight to work.

<What's wrong with the node?> he asked patiently.

<Burned out. Probably a power surge from the blackout or when power was restored.>

<Were any other nodes affected?>

<No. We were lucky and only lost that one.>

Benson savored the man's naiveté, a trait apparently shared by the entire crew. A single data node blows out that just happens to contain files critical to the only murder case in the last decade, and nobody smells anything suspicious about it.

<Can any of the data be recovered?>

<We won't know until someone physically pulls the node, but it doesn't look good. The holographic matrix looks like it's been completely flash-burned.>

<Naturally. Thank you, command.>

The gears kept on turning as Benson cut the call. Someone really didn't want Laraby's files read, and now they'd succeeded. But the million dollar question remained. Had they simply taken advantage of the power outage to wipe the node, or had the entire blackout been a window to delete the files once and for all?

And what were the odds the plan ended there?

A new call rang through Benson's mind. It was Jeanine. He accepted the call.

<Hello, doctor. What can I do for you?>

<Is this line secure?>

<They're all secure, Jeanine.>

<Oh, well, why would I know that?>

<You've been watching spy movies, haven't you?>

<...maybe. But you're sure no one's listening?>

<No more than usual. What's up?>

<I think you should come and hear this for yourself, Bryan.>

<That bad?>

<Let's just say that interesting. I'm in exam room two. See you shortly.>

The connection dropped. Benson looked down the line of volunteers as the futility of their task set in. He phoned Theresa.

<Call it off, lieutenant.>

<What?>

<Shut down the search and recall the volunteers. We're not going to find anything down here.>

<You do remember we're looking for terrorists, yes?>

<They're not here.> He looked around the empty level and its endless honeycomb. <Nothing's here. Besides, something's come up.>

<What, you got a hot date?>

<No.> Benson sighed. <A cold one.>

Benson shivered away the last clinging remnants of cold. He was glad to be out of the sub-basement, with its pervasive chill and subversive radiation. A short, invigorating walk later and he passed through Sickbay's doors. An orderly directed him to exam room two. Inside, he found Jeanine standing over Edmond Laraby's body.

He'd had some work done since the last time Benson had seen him in the form of a large "Y" incision down his chest. It was still open.

Benson looked up at her, confused. "You've done the autopsy already?"

Jeanine nodded grimly.

"But I thought you said he had to thaw for another day at least."

"That was just an estimate I found in the database. Turns out the cadaver thaw tables were from mid-twenty-first century America. The average person was rather substantially larger and ah... better insulated than our man here."

"I don't doubt it. What have you got?"

"Bad news first?"

"He's dead," Benson said. "I don't think the news gets much worse than that."

"You may change your mind. Mr Laraby was alive when he was pushed out of the airlock, and probably conscious."

He had to admit that *was* worse.

"Are you sure?"

"As sure as I can be. This is my first murder investigation. I'm learning as I go. But the bruising on his forearms and wrists are definitely consistent with defensive wounds."

"Could they be from... ah, rough sexual activity?"

She went silent for a moment to consider the question, or perhaps consider how to answer it tactfully. Was that a small streak of red flushing her cheeks?

"I don't think so, unless this 'activity' was happening inside the lock just before the outer door was opened. The bruises are nascent, less than a half hour old at time of death."

Benson had to look away from the corpse. Thrown into the black, arms pinwheeling through the vacuum, trying to swim back to the lock while the air was ripped from your lungs and your eyes bulged out of your head, spending your last few moments of life gasping for oxygen that wasn't there.

The thought of it made Benson sick. Killing him was bad enough, but this? By all accounts, he'd been a good kid, well-liked and a hard worker. What could he have done, what could he have known, to justify *this* death?

"That's... unsettling. But it doesn't actually help identify the killer."

She looked confused. "Don't we already know that? I mean, the fingernail results–"

"Wasn't him." Benson shook his head. "We were wrong."

"Oh," she said. Followed by "ooohh," as the relevance of the sex question hit home. "Well, that explains the claw marks on his back."

"You got it. But that's privileged information. We're not to share it with anyone."

"I understand."

"Believe me, I wish it wasn't true. We're back to square one."

"Not exactly." Jeanine handed him a tablet with several files already open on the desktop. "This might help us."

Benson tried to skim through them, but they were, to all intents and purposes, indecipherable. "I'm sorry, but what am I looking at?"

"Mr Laraby's toxicology report."

"He was drunk?"

"No." Jeanine shook her head. "He was drugged."

That got his attention. Every pill and injectable drug

synthesized onboard, legally at least, had nanotube tags that acted as serial numbers.

"With what? Did you find the tags? Who prescribed it?"

Jeanine waved her hands in a "slowdown" motion. "It wasn't a prescription, or anything manufactured, so there're no tags to find. It's a biological poison, as it turns out, but I have no idea where anyone could have gotten it from."

"What kind of poison, then?"

"Well, it was at least partially metabolized, and the freeze/thaw cycle didn't do the protein strains any favors, still I'm ninety percent sure it's TTX. It's a neurotoxin that attacks the nervous system's sodium channels."

"Dumb it down for me, doc."

Jeanine huffed, but continued. "It's a paralytic. It kills when the patient ingests enough to actually stop the diaphragm. That didn't happen here."

"But he was incapacitated?"

"Oh, surely. His muscle control would have been very weak and uncoordinated. He probably had spasms too."

"So, wait, you mean somebody poisoned him just enough that he couldn't fight back, but not enough to knock him unconscious so he could be alive when they threw him into the black? That's horrible."

She shrugged. "Maybe. Or maybe they meant for him to die, but he didn't ingest enough. Maybe they got the dosing wrong. There's no way to know that."

Benson nodded. It would make more sense if the suspect had tried to kill him with poison. They'd be able to get rid of the body at their leisure, then. But if it didn't work and Edmond had felt the symptoms and went looking for help, they would have to improvise quickly. That would explain the ensuing fight, even the airlock. That was one thing about plans; you could always count on them to go wrong.

"OK, it fits. You said this TXX–"

"TTX."

"TTX, thank you, was biological?"

Jeanine nodded and pulled up another file on the tablet. "It was found in a family of fish on Earth called *Tetraodontidae*, the most common example being–"

It was Benson's turn to interrupt her. "Pufferfish."

Jeanine didn't bother hiding her surprise. "How did you know that?"

"I watch a lot of nature documentaries."

"I didn't take you for the get-back-to-nature sort. Anyway, what I can't figure out is where they got the poison in the first place. Pufferfish went extinct with the Earth. And even if someone snuck onboard with a vial, the poison would have broken down within a few years, even refrigerated. It shouldn't exist."

Benson handed the tablet back to her and turned for the exit. "Send over everything you've found, and make extra offline copies just like you did for the fingernail results. OK?"

"Sure, but… where are you going?"

Benson looked back over his shoulder as he walked out the door.

"I'm suddenly in the mood for sushi."

CHAPTER TWENTY-TWO

You had to hand it to Chef Takahashi. Looking around the Koi Pond, you'd have never known the whole habitat had been in lockdown only ten hours earlier. Then again, the prices his food commanded meant he could afford to hire the best help in Avalon.

Theresa squeezed Benson's wrist from across the table. "Do you think we'll get chicken again?"

"Actually, I'm hoping for something more exotic."

"More exotic than *chicken*?" Her face was incredulous.

"Oh, quite a bit more."

Theresa eyed him suspiciously. "Are you going to tell me what this 'surprise dinner' is actually about?"

"Eventually." Benson poured Theresa a cup of sake. It was a cloudy Nigori this time, chilled. She did the same for him. They clinked the little porcelain cups and let the milky sweetness drain down their throats.

Their waiter reappeared. "Have you had enough time to look over the menu?"

"Yes," Theresa said. "I'll have a perch roll, fried rice, and a side of vegetable tempura."

"Very good, madam. And for the gentleman?"

Benson looked up at the young man, studying his face

carefully for reactions. "Actually, I was hoping to go off the menu tonight."

"Of course, I forgot to mention our specials. Tonight, we have–"

"Fugu?"

They locked eyes for an uncomfortable moment. Benson saw his demeanor falter for a split second. He recognized the word, and the veiled accusation behind it. Benson knew from years interviewing code violators that the next thing the man said would be a lie.

"I'm afraid I'm not familiar with that dish, sir."

"No? It's quite famous. Some might even call it infamous. I'm sure Chef Takahashi knows about it. Let's go ask him, together."

"He's quite busy preparing orders."

"Oh, nonsense." Benson stood up and set his napkin on the table. "It'll only take a minute."

"This is quite irregular, sir."

"I *insist*." Benson put enough stress on the last word to make sure the waiter understood it was Detective Benson talking. The waiter surrendered with a nod and turned for the kitchen. Benson followed. Theresa shot up from the table and jogged a few steps to catch them up while confused murmurs rose up from the surrounding tables.

"What's going on?" she whispered in Benson's ear.

"Do you have your stun-stick in your purse?"

"Yes, but–"

"Keep it handy."

"I'm not going to get to eat that perch roll, am I?"

"Probably not," Benson admitted. "I'll grab us takeout on the way back."

She sighed as she pulled her stun-stick out of her purse

and hid it in her palm. "Not falafel again, please."

Benson smirked as they followed the waiter around the bar and through the double doors that led into the kitchen. A cyclone of sounds assaulted them on the other side. Pots clanged, knives chopped, cooks shouted out orders, all while aromas of fry oil, fresh vegetables, soy sauce, and fish swirled and mixed in the air.

At the center of it all, the tallest Asian Benson had ever known guided the chaos of incoming orders, food prep, and plating, while lithely decimating a pile of onions with a ceramic chef's knife. Chef Takahashi was a full head taller than Benson. If the NBA had survived the death of Earth, he'd have played in it. Instead, he towered over waiters, bartenders, and assistant chefs.

He spotted the intruders in his kitchen and pointed for the door, shouting over the din in a strange collision of Korean and Japanese. He wanted them out, but Benson wasn't in the mood.

"Aw, c'mon *Frank*, I know you speak English," Benson chided. "Your mom was a school teacher from Avalon, for crying out loud."

Takahashi stopped yelling just long enough to let his goatee twist up around his mouth into a very disapproving scowl.

"Not in the kitchen."

"Fine, can we talk somewhere private, then?"

"I'm busy."

"You'll be busier if I have to come back when I'm on duty."

The background noise of the kitchen dropped as a circuit of nervous glances passed between the other workers. Takahashi shouted at them. Benson didn't need translation software running to know he'd said "get back to work!"

Takahashi motioned for them to follow. He pulled open a slab door at the back of the kitchen that he had to bend over double to walk through. Racks of fish fillets and plastic bins filled with off-season veggies filled the small space almost to the point of bursting. They were in the restaurant's deep freezer. The biting cold hit him immediately, worse than even the sixth-level subbasement had been. Their breath transformed instantly into large, billowing clouds before vanishing.

"Isn't there someplace warmer?" Theresa's teeth were already beginning to chatter.

Takahashi shrugged. "You want to talk in private, and I want this conversation to be short. The freezer ensures both."

"Fine." Benson put his hands in his armpits. "I'll get right to the point. I know you've been making fugu. I want to know which crewmember grew the pufferfish for you."

Takahashi was calm as he answered. "Fugu? I'm not familiar with that dish."

"Funny, your waiter said the exact same thing. I thought you were the best sushi chef on the ship. Why does a lowly gaijin know more about traditional Japanese cuisine than you?"

Whatever nerve Benson touched caused Takahashi's eye to twitch and his shoulder muscles to tense. It was only then that Benson's eyes registered the fact the walking totem pole of a man was still holding a chef's knife.

"Careful, Benson-san. It is not polite to insult your host."

"Could you put down the knife, please? It's making me twitchy."

Takahashi glanced down at the razor-sharp wedge of ceramic in his hand as if he only just remembered it was still there. Delicately, he set it on the shelf midway between himself and Benson.

"I apologize. When you hold it all day, you can forget it's not attached."

Benson waved it off. "It's fine. But I have to level with you, I came here off duty and had some sake out of respect. Nothing I see or hear right now is admissible. I just need to talk, off the record. I know it wasn't even your idea. Some bloody idiot probably read about fugu or saw it on some old Samurai movie. You're the only person with the skills and experience to prepare such a dangerous dish, so they threw a bunch of money at you to make it happen."

Takahashi crossed his arms. "I can't bring animals back from extinction."

"No, but you have friends who can. We ate your chicken, remember?"

"Which was excellent, by the way," Theresa added helpfully.

Takahashi acknowledged the compliment with a small bow. "But if what you say is true, Benson-san, it would not be illegal, as long as the Codes were respected."

"No, it wouldn't," Benson agreed. "But poisoning someone with TTX is."

That, Takahashi wasn't ready for. His head almost hit the low ceiling. "Who? Who was poisoned?"

"You heard about the Laraby boy, yeah? The doc's just found TTX in his bloodstream, same stuff as in pufferfish."

"I would never serve tainted fish!"

"C'mon Frank, I'm not saying *you* poisoned him. I'm sure your preparation was perfect. But somebody got their hands on the stuff and gave it to Laraby. I just need to know about the fish. Who supplies them? Who eats them?"

Takahashi looked around the freezer as if he'd lost something. "What you ask is... difficult."

"I'm sure it is, Frank. I'm not any happier about it than you are. We love this place and would hate to get blacklisted."

The big man sighed, and pushed past the two of them and opened the freezer door, then motioned for them to follow. They wound back through the kitchen and into a larger pantry filled with the rich smells of spices, fresh vegetables, and the starchy aroma of dried rice. Tucked back in a corner an old tablecloth betrayed the outlines of a rectangular box. A low hum drifted out from underneath it.

Takahashi pulled off the tablecloth with a quick jerk, revealing two perfect little bubbling aquariums, maybe a hundred liters each. In the left tank, two plump, prickly-looking fish bobbed along contentedly like potatoes in a sink. In the other, a dozen smaller fish darted one way, then the other in a school of pea-sized copies of the larger fish.

"There you are, the freshest fish anywhere on the Ark."

Theresa leaned in to look more closely and smiled as the little school of fry bunched up against the glass to do the same to her.

"You farm them right here in the restaurant? No one supplies them to you?"

"Yes, after a couple of false starts. Keeping the salinity and pH levels right is a pain in the ass. The two adults spawn, and we put the fry in the other tank to keep them from getting eaten."

"From getting eaten too soon, you mean."

"Yes, I suppose so."

Benson was impressed. He'd never seen a saltwater fish before, not outside of his nature documentaries.

"And it's worth all the trouble?" he asked.

Takahashi nodded. "The tanks and pumping equipment cost me almost four months of 3D printing rations, and a couple of favors. But with what I charge for them, I made it all back on the first two plates."

"Who grew the first fish for you?"

Takahashi shrugged. "It wasn't for me, not right away. You were almost right, Benson-san. It wasn't my idea at first. The first batch was grown in the bio-labs for some research project. An... interested party brought me a fish and asked if I could prepare a plate of fugu for a party they were throwing. I was afraid to at first, so I threw an outrageous number at him. When he didn't back down, I made the plate, on the condition that he get me a male and female too. That's what you see here."

Benson didn't much like what he was hearing. It was just more of the same behavior he was coming to expect out of the floaters. The rules and regulations that kept everyone else in line were just suggestions for them to dance around in the dark.

"How entrepreneurial of you," Benson said at last.

Takahashi crossed his arms. "You don't get to build on the roof of the Alexander Building without taking some risks and greasing some wheels."

"I suppose not. What happens to the remains when you're done making a dish?"

"The guts? They go in the reclamation bin just like all the other scales and bones."

"And that doesn't strike you as dangerous? Putting a deadly neurotoxin into our compost supply?"

"I don't see how it could be. As chewed up and processed as everything gets down in the emulsion tanks? Besides, it would be so diluted by the time it goes back out, how could it be harmful?"

"It was harmful enough to Edmond Laraby."

"You don't know it came from my end," Takahashi protested. "Why don't you go talk to the people in the lab?"

"Trust me, I will, but I'm sorry Frank, I can't have this here in my habitat. You're breaking half a dozen food safety regs, and at least as many Conservation Codes. I'm choosing not to remember seeing this for now, but if I come back tomorrow, there had better not be anything lying around to jog my memory. Agreed?"

Takahashi balked. "They are unique, and not easily replaced. May I take the adults to my quarters and keep them there until landing if I promise not to serve anymore fugu until the new colony is running?"

"Of course," Theresa answered for him. "I'm sure Bryan can forget a little thing like that."

They both looked at him expectantly. "All right, fine, on two conditions. First, you go through proper channels, adhere to health and safety, and no more of this crew only, off the menu nonsense. You'll post them and whatever price you're going to charge right out in the open where everyone can see them."

The chef was decidedly unhappy with the arrangement, but he bowed nonetheless.

Benson leaned in and pitched his voice lower. "I'm sure I don't have to tell you that if I find out someone else has been poisoned, yours is the first door I'm beating down, yes?"

The color faded from the big man's cheeks. "I understand."

"Good. One final thing, we'd like to make reservations for dinner before Game Seven. For two."

Takahashi looked as though he was about to erupt like one of the onion volcanoes on his hibachi tables, but quickly tamped it down as his inner businessman asserted itself.

"We would be honored to have you, Benson-san, provided your Mustangs win tomorrow and force Game Seven. Six o'clock?"

"Perfect. We'll see ourselves out." Benson turned around and winked at Theresa as he pushed towards the door. A small groan let him know she was apparently unimpressed by his interrogation and negotiation skills. They were almost to the door with Takahashi following behind irritably when Benson spotted a plastic container filled with mushrooms. He would have gone right on walking if it weren't for the faintest whiff of ammonia that clung to them.

On impulse, he grabbed one out of the bin and inspected the stem. "What's this?"

"Shiitake mushroom. For soup," Takahashi said, clearly losing patience.

"Where did you get it?"

"From the market, of course. I send a buyer down twice a week."

"I would like to talk to this buyer. Pass his name along to me, would you?"

"Of course, Benson-san. Will that be all?"

Benson set the shiitake back in the bin with its brothers. "Yes, sorry to trouble you with all this. Enjoy the rest of your day."

Theresa grabbed him under the arm and dragged him out of the restaurant. As soon as they were back in the elevator, she pushed him up against the doors. Benson's first impression told him she was in the mood for a risky tryst, but a glance down at her face corrected that assumption.

"What the hell was that?" she barked.

"Look, I'm sorry about dinner–"

"I'm not talking about *dinner*, you twit. Why are we wasting time on the Laraby case when there's a saboteur on the loose? Unless you've forgotten the lights going out already and how the human race almost died?"

"They're connected, Esa. It's the same people, I know it."

"You can't know that."

"Can't I? While the power was down, somebody took the liberty of frying the memory node that had all of Laraby's files in it. Not just erased them, I mean physically burned out the node. You think that's just a coincidence?"

Theresa shrugged. "An opportunistic killer with a guilty conscience could have done the same thing."

"And know where the specific node was? C'mon. And how did these terrorists get into engineering in the first place? They had help from a crewmember."

"We don't know that for sure."

"There's more. That mushroom I was just holding?"

"Yeah..." Theresa regarded him with look that said he'd better come up with something good pretty quick.

"It had traces of dirt on its stem."

"So what, they hadn't been washed yet."

"They're all grown in aeroponic shelves, Esa. I worked a farm for years, remember. There shouldn't be any dirt."

The elevator chime dinged for the ground floor, but Theresa reached around him and pressed the door hold button.

"OK, so they shouldn't have dirt on them. So what? Start making sense."

Benson took a deep breath. "Remember when I said I'd met David Kimura down in the basement over in Shangri-La?"

"How could I forget?"

"It's true, and they were farming mushrooms in trays of compost. Mushrooms don't need light, so it makes perfect sense down there. I'd bet this Mao's group here in Avalon adopted the same farming strategy."

"We didn't find any farms."

"We didn't finish the search, either."

"No, *you* didn't finish the search. How do you think that looked to everyone?"

He didn't have an answer for her. Theresa rolled her hand for him to continue.

"I think that this buyer was trading with Mao's people for mushrooms for Takahashi's kitchen, and in exchange some of the poisonous bits of one of the pufferfish found their way into the bad guy's hands. From there, they poisoned Laraby and then killed him when it didn't take."

Theresa scowled. "That's the most convoluted, crackpot conspiracy theory I've ever heard."

"So... you're on the fence?"

"You sound like a mad-hatter in the making."

"It fits the facts," Benson protested.

"Mushroom smuggling? Really? We have to refocus, Bryan, on the terrorists. Laraby's killer will just have to wait."

Benson shook his head. "I'm telling you, they're the same people. It's all part of the same story."

"Then it won't matter if you come at it from the other direction," Theresa said, her voice straining just below a scream. She took a moment to calm herself before continuing. "Sweetie, you need to hear me on this. People are starting to talk."

That caught Benson off guard. "Talk about what? What people?"

"About the job you're doing. You already upset a lot of important people with the way you handled Feng–"

"He was acting guilty as shit, you know that!"

Theresa put a hand up to stop him. "I'm not saying you were wrong to, but it ruffled feathers. It's not just the crew; even some of our own people want to know why you called off the search early. They think you just gave up."

"You know I didn't."

"*I* know, but it doesn't look that way from the outside. I fielded calls from two Council members while you were down in Sickbay, including Chief Councilman Valmassoi."

"What? Why didn't you forward them to me?"

"Because they didn't want to talk *to* you, Bryan. They were gathering info *on* you."

"What did you tell them?"

"That you were a narcissistic man-child and could stand to be a better tipper."

"That hurts, Esa. I tip just fine."

The doors chimed again as someone on the other side grew tired of waiting.

"Just think about what I said, please? I mean it, Bryan." Theresa reached over and released the hold button, ending the conversation.

Benson had a sinking feeling in the pit of his stomach that didn't have anything to do with skipping dinner.

CHAPTER TWENTY-THREE

Benson was back inside the wildly spinning EVA pod. The cracks in the canopy grew, slowly at first, but then faster until they touched and spread into spiderwebs. The entire bubble shattered into a constellation of debris as Benson was blown free of the cockpit, impotently pumping his arms as he drifted away next to Laraby's body.

He awoke with a shot, dripping in sweat. It was the third time he'd had that nightmare.

"Lights!"

He looked around his bedroom, trying to get his bearings. It was 02.37. He'd finally gotten into bed at 23.45.

Dammit.

The falafel he'd scarfed down on the way back to his apartment didn't sit right either. Something about the cucumber sauce was... off. So far, the nightmare only came on nights he was alone. He'd held out hope that he might spend tonight in the love nest, but Theresa wasn't particularly amenable to the idea after their tense conversation in the lift.

He couldn't blame her, really, and the uncomfortable truth was she made more sense than he wanted to admit.

He knew he was under the microscope, but having council members talking to his subordinates behind his back couldn't be a prelude to good news.

Maybe he was obsessing over Edmond. And if he really believed his own story that Laraby's killer and the saboteurs were the same people, then what was the harm turning around and burning the candle from the other end?

Game Six would start at 09.00, in just over six hours. It was a morning game by Avalon Time, but late evening for the players from Shangri-La. The stadium held almost ten thousand people at full capacity, which it certainly would be in the morning. Twenty percent of the population would be there to cheer on their team, versus no more than two dozen constables vying to keep the peace.

As far as venues were concerned, it was hard to imagine a more tempting target to make a statement. Security would be tight, but the large crowd would confer a certain amount of anonymity. A mad-hatter or two might be able to slip through security if they timed it right and didn't draw undue attention to themselves. His officers would need to check under every cap that came through.

But then, Mao's people wouldn't have to wear aluminum-lined hats, would they? No plant meant they could sneak in with a large group with every lift car that came up. They'd have to scan everyone individually as they came out of the doors.

Benson threw the covers off his body and got a pot of tea going. He was too wound up now to fall back to sleep, and the prospect of repeating the nightmare was less than appealing anyway. He'd head down to the stationhouse and start coordinating security for the game with Chief Bahadur, then get his own people up to speed.

He took just enough time to rinse his mouth and throw on clothes. He didn't bother freshening the creases in his pants. He saw little point, only one or two people would be in the stationhouse at this time of night anyway.

The kettle whistled just as he slipped on his shoes. Benson poured himself a generous cup and jogged down the path to the stationhouse. The restored gravity and background hum gave the illusion that everything had returned to normal. But, now more than ever, Benson understood the thin blue line of his constables was all that preserved that normalcy.

Korolev sat in the duty officer's chair as Benson crossed through the doors, the stress of the last few days etched in his face as well.

"You look awful, Pavel. Have you slept?"

"I could ask you the same thing, chief."

Benson shrugged. "As much as I'm going to today, it seems. I didn't know you were on night watch tonight."

"Switched with Feingold. She had a… thing."

"This thing have a name?"

"She didn't mention it."

"I see." Benson put an elbow on the high desk and leaned over. "All quiet?"

Korolev nodded. "Surprisingly so, actually. I think everyone had enough excitement for one day."

"Good. If anyone needs me, I'll be in my office organizing security for the game."

"Ten-four, chief."

Benson closed the door behind him, then collapsed into his desk chair. The tea wouldn't kick in for a few minutes yet. He sat, staring at nothing, thinking that leaving his bed hadn't been the most prudent course, when his eyes fell on his desk drawer.

Holy crap, he thought, *I'm an idiot*. He reached out a thumb and the drawer slid open, revealing the tablet he'd stashed yesterday. It had gone offline when he threw it in frustration and broke the screen two days earlier. He'd never thought to reconnect it to the network.

Now fully awake, he powered it up and searched through the document history looking for a pot of gold. When he found it, he almost jumped out of his chair and danced around the room. Glowing in front of him were the only surviving copies of Edmond Laraby's personal and work files.

Benson's hope swelled. It was the first genuine break he'd gotten since the whole situation had blown up. The answers he needed were there, he knew it now more than ever. Feng had already done his damage to Laraby's personal files, but it had been to cover his own tracks, not the real killer's. They might still prove useful. On a whim, Benson ran a search of all the images in the file. More than seven thousand images popped up, contained in hundreds of folders. Someone liked to take pictures.

Overwhelmed, Benson ran a simple sorting program to differentiate between portraits, action shots, selfies, art, and so on. He spent the next half hour scrolling through the endless stream of pictures of Edmond, his coworkers, his amateur photography of apple blossoms and force-perspective shots taken from... interesting positions inside the habitats. It seemed Edmond had been a bit of a daredevil in his off hours.

One of them was a really interesting shot of row after

row of daytime lights taken from the point of view of someone floating just outside the hub itself, like a field of bulbs stretching out to infinity. Lord only knew who he'd talked into letting him get in position to take it.

Not that Benson was an expert, but the kid had a real eye for composition and lighting. He flipped through other folders at random, hoping something jumped out.

Something did. One folder was a couple orders of magnitude larger than the others. Benson opened it and was floored by the torrent of images of Tau Ceti G. The collection itself was impressive for its size, but it was hardly unusual. The images were public record. Benson even spotted a couple that Edmond had picked for the slideshow on the wall in his apartment.

What was unusual was the cache of orbital images Laraby had labeled "Atlantis." Benson went through them one at a time. What he found was an endless stream of pictures of, appropriately enough, the Dark Continent cloaked in a permanent cyclone covering a land mass nearly the size of North America.

Meteorologists had struggled with the enduring enigma of the storm since Pathfinder had arrived in the system two years earlier, a job further complicated by the fact the reentry shuttle that was supposed to disperse drones and rovers throughout the continent had fallen victim to the storm itself. But judging from the barometric pressure charts, wind records, false-color infrared, and radar mapping, it looked like Edmond was taking a stab at solving it.

It seemed like a harmless enough hobby, but as Benson dug deeper into the stack of pictures, he became alarmed. Somewhere along the way, Edmond started marking the images with bright red circles and slashes, becoming angrier and more frustrated as time passed.

He'd scrawled *DUPLICATION!!!* connected by arrows to two red circles on one image, and again on a picture time stamped from several days later. Benson brought up both pictures and put them side by side on the tablet. The cloud patterns did indeed look very similar, although they were in different locations and were different sizes. He set one to transparent and laid it over top of the other, moving and scaling the top layer to see if the bits in the circles really did match.

It took some fidgeting, but blown up to two hundred and fifty percent, then mirrored and rotated ninety degrees, the cloud patterns overlapped precisely.

Benson stared at the screen for a long time, aware that he'd found something important, but at a loss for what it meant. It was more tampering, that much was obvious, but to what end? If the clouds weren't real, what was hiding under them?

Benson skipped to the end of the images, like peeking at the last page of a book. What he found was a series of increasingly intricate composite images of Atlantis using all of the different data sets. It looked like Edmond had been trying to reconstruct whatever was hidden under the clouds, to undo the tampering. He couldn't be sure how much of what he was seeing was accurate, how much was conjecture, and how much was pure artistic license, but it all certainly looked convincing.

Benson glanced down at the clock in the corner of the tablet. 05.59.

"Shit," he mumbled. Two and a half hours spent tumbling down the rabbit hole. It was exactly what he'd promised himself not to do. Benson glanced at the picture of Atlantis one more time and paused to consider the excited green circles Laraby had drawn near the continent's eastern coastline. Whatever he'd seen inside them, Benson couldn't pick it out. He pulled up the image's edit history to see when Edmond had been there last. Less than three days before his murder.

Here, Benson finally felt like he was on the right path, even if he didn't understand where it led. But he'd have to make time for it later. Still, one other thread that needed tugging, and hopefully it wouldn't take two hours.

He checked his clock against the time in the command module. The floaters insisted on running their clocks smack in between Shangri-La and Avalon Time. They claimed it was to prevent the appearance of playing favorites between the two modules, but Benson was fairly sure its real purpose was yet another layer of separation between the crew and the cattle.

As the crew flew, it was just before lunch. The perfect time for the conversation he hoped to have. Benson pulled up Director da Silva's contact and made the call.

<Good morning, director. Can you spare a few minutes?>

<A very few. I was about to heat up a burrito. What's up, detective?>

<I want to talk to you about pufferfish.>

<A strange topic at this hour. *Tetraodontidae*,> she said as if reading out an encyclopedia entry. <Saltwater fish with an incredibly potent poison. Why do you want to talk about them?>

<Because I just saw a handful of them swimming in a tank.>

<Outside the lab? Where?>

<I can't say, but it's been dealt with. Still, I need to know where they came from, who had them grown, who had access, that sort of thing.>

<We did, specifically Edmond. He was studying their neurotoxin as a base for more effective pain medications. So we put in a request with the genome archive, and they grew him a small batch of fingerlings, for all the good it did.>

<What do you mean by that?>

<Well, he's not exactly here to finish the project, is he? And now that all of his notes are gone, we don't have the time or manpower to restart from square one. So much work lost. Really, if you find whoever burned up his files, I'll be happy to shove *them* out a lock.>

Benson was about to correct her, to tell her that a copy of Laraby's work notes had survived, but something told him not to play that card. <I'm sure you're not alone. But I thought he was working on those, what did you call them, slider plants?>

<We all have multiple projects running. There's actually quite a bit of downtime between experiments as we wait for plants to mature, genes to sequence, so we bounce back and forth. Pain medication was a side project of Edmond's. Why, did something happen with the fish?>

Benson paused. <What I'm about to tell you isn't public information yet, but with Laraby's files erased, you're the only source of information I've got. Can you keep this between us?>

<Of course.>

<OK. Edmond died with TTX in his blood, the very

same stuff that makes pufferfish so deadly.>

The plant interface didn't carry gasps, but Benson could almost hear one in the silence anyway.

<That's what killed him?>

<No, the vacuum did that. Whoever poisoned him didn't use enough. He was still alive when they pushed him out.>

<That's... horrible. Suddenly the joke about shoving whoever deleted his work files out a lock doesn't seem as funny.>

<It's OK, you're hardly the first. But now you understand why I need to know about the puffers. Could anyone in your department have leaked either the fish or their poison? Anyone at all?>

<I'm sorry, detective, but it was Edmond's project. He had all the materials. None of my people would tamper with someone else's experiments without permission. The entire thing might have to be scrapped and started again.>

<Well, then I'm at a dead end. Er, sorry, that wasn't the best choice of words.>

Avelina chuckled softly. <It's OK, you're hardly the first. Is there anything else I can do for you?>

<No.> Benson paused. <Actually, yes. Did Edmond ever talk to you about 'Atlantis'?>

<Like the continent? Not that I remember. Why?>

Benson took a moment to consider how much of his hand he wanted to reveal. He had no illusions about the security of the plant network at this point. Even if he could trust da Silva, anything he revealed here was going out to Lord only knew how many other ears. Still, maybe it was time to stir the pot.

<It was a name he used for the Dark Continent, apparently. He seemed very interested in it, obsessed even.>

The line went quiet for a long moment.

<Avelina, are you still there?>

<Hmm? Sorry. Yes, I'm not surprised that Edmond might fall into something like that. A big part of his job was to reconstruct Tau Ceti G's biosphere. He spent years trying to extrapolate how everything on the ground works with incomplete data. The Dark Continent must've been an irresistible challenge.>

<Do you think his little hobby could have something to do with his murder?>

<I don't see how. There's a million wild theories about what's under the clouds. I haven't heard about people killing each other over them.>

Benson sighed. <Yeah, me either. Thank you for your time, Avelina. Enjoy your burrito.>

<That's going to be a little harder now.>

<Been there. I'll let you get back to work.>

Benson cut the link and leaned back in his chair. Well, that went nowhere. The snake that ate its tail. The tablet taunted him to dig deeper, but he put it back in the drawer. Its secrets would have to wait until after he and Chief Bahadur had hammered out a plan to make sure the only exciting thing about Game Six was the Mustangs trouncing the Yaoguai.

CHAPTER TWENTY-FOUR

They agreed on final security arrangements with only ninety minutes to spare before push-off. This didn't leave Benson much time to get his constables up to speed, but they took to the new protocols without much complaint.

The Mustang fans, for their part, were as predictable as ever. Despite the fact it was not even 09.00 Avalon Time, fans arrived well-lubricated after pre-gaming in one park or another. One unfortunate young man didn't make it through the security line before he popped, sending a cascade of tofu-chicken wings, tortilla chips, guacamole, and a fountain of cherry-infused vodka spreading throughout the compartment. He was sent home while men with vacuum packs attended to the mess. Vomiting in micrograv was a quick way to lose friends.

The Yaoguai fans streaming in from the other entrance had the twin disadvantages of getting off work several hours ago, and being of predominantly Asian and Middle Eastern lineage, meaning they had even more time to drink, yet less natural ability to process it. It wasn't long before the line from Shangri-La bogged down under the new and unfamiliar set of rules.

Benson waved at Korolev. "Hey, Pavel. Float over and

help Bahadur clear his backlog, will you?"

"Sure thing, chief."

Benson grabbed a handhold and surveyed the scene with satisfaction. His constables were handling things well with little help. The fans, for their part, were being patient about the additional layers of security. After the sabotage, everyone understood the need.

The fact the series had been allowed to continue had been a minor miracle in and of itself. The crew had pitched a fit. Many members of the council agreed with them, arguing it was too risky in light of the threat to assemble so many people in one place. Others felt it was a waste of manpower to assign so many constables to police the crowd when they should have been looking for the terrorists. But in the end, it was generally agreed that the threat of cancelling the last Zero Championship and the thousands of irate fans that would result was at least equal to the threat of the saboteurs. The status quo was upheld.

Players began filtering into the stadium from the locker rooms to the cheers of spectators already in the stands. "Stands" was something of a misnomer, considering the entire volume was in micrograv and everyone had to strap their feet to the walls to keep from floating away. Then again back on Earth, people used to sit in the stands.

<Ah, chief?> It was Korolev.

<Go ahead, Pavel. What's up?>

<There's a young woman over here asking for you.>

<What's her name?>

<She won't say.>

<What do you mean she won't *say*? Scan her plant. You're supposed to be doing that anyway.>

<Yes, sir, I did. It's just that... she hasn't got one.>

Benson's eyes snapped up to the far entrance, but he couldn't spot them. Korolev and the girl were a good two hundred meters away and surrounded by other spectators. Still, the list of people it could be was awfully short.

<I'm coming. Don't let her leave.>

<Wasn't planning on it, chief.>

Benson set his feet against the bulkhead, adjusted his body, then pushed off hard. Flying a straight line in micro was easy. Flying the *right* straight line was a skill, especially over such a long distance. He wasn't quite as fast off the push as he'd been back in his playing days, but he was still moving fast enough that he could hear the air rushing over his ears. A knot of spectators recognized him as he passed and started chanting.

Benson waved to them and smiled, trying to look nonchalant. The far side of the compartment quickly became the near side. Air resistance had cut a fraction of his momentum, but he was still moving at a good clip. He timed his flip just right so that his feet clanged against the bulkhead instead of his face.

"Over here, chief!" Korolev shouted up to him. Benson spotted him, Chief Bahadur, and a slim, raven-haired Asian girl floating to the side of the line of spectators. It was Mei, just as he'd assumed.

Benson pushed off more gently and floated down to meet them.

"What are you doing up here?" He pitched his voice low so only the four of them could hear.

"You know her, Bryan?" Bahadur pointed a finger at the young mystery woman.

Benson nodded. "We've met. Her name is Mei. She's from the basement levels."

Bahadur's face hardened. "She's one of the terrorists?"

Benson put up his hands. "No, a different group. They're from Shangri-La."

"My module?" Bahadur's voice took on a steel edge. "How did you know this?"

"Because I visited their camp. They're harmless, Vikram."

"And when were you going to tell me this, Bryan?"

"I'm sorry, but if I'd told you, you would've had to go after them. They helped me, so I had to help them."

Bahadur was incensed. "We're supposed to work together, Bryan! How would you feel if I went poking around in Avalon and didn't tell you about it?"

"It's not Mei and the other Unbound we have to worry about. It's Mao and his group, they're the threat."

Mei perked up. "Who Mao?"

Everyone looked at her, but Benson was the first to answer. "Mao, the leader over in Avalon. The one who sabotaged the reactors two days ago."

Mei shook her head. "No Mao."

"No Mao?" Benson repeated.

"No. Kimura-san. We broke the ship. I say no more, he try to kill me but I escape." Mei pulled up her shirt, revealing three deep slashes on her flank. They were untreated and fresh enough to still ooze blood. Benson winced, gripping his forearm in sympathetic pain.

"Huang attacked you, didn't he?"

Mei nodded.

Benson held up his sutured arm. "And me, yes?"

Mei nodded again.

Bahadur strained to keep his voice down. "Harmless, are they?"

Korolev broke in. "She needs stitches."

"He lied to me, Vikram. I was trying to protect them."

"Protect them from what, the Codes? You're supposed to be a detective!"

"Listen to me!" Mei stopped the growing fight in its tracks and even drew some looks from the line of spectators queued up for the game. Benson reached out and gently squeezed her shoulder, hoping to calm her down, but Mei threw it off and pointed an accusatory finger at Benson and Bahadur. "You argue like old couple. Something bad happening."

"What's happening, Mei?"

She took a deep breath. "Kimura do something under the lake. Told me to be lookout, but I run. Huang almost catch me twice, but I hide. Always win hide and seek."

"The lake in Shangri-La?" Bahadur asked. She nodded.

"What's he doing to the lake?" Benson asked.

Mei shrugged. "He not tell me, but bad. Worse than turning the lights out."

Benson's mind raced. What could Kimura want with the lake? Poison the water supply? That didn't make any sense. Any poison could just be processed and filtered out again. Unless he was going to sabotage the water reprocessing facilities while he was at it?

"Great. We have to get down there."

"She needs medical attention," Korolev said.

"Fine, Pavel, take her down to Sickbay over in Avalon. Take her to Doctor Russell, no one else. Do you understand?"

"Yes, chief."

"Good. Tell nobody about her. She's under protective custody as of right now, so stay with her. I may need to ask her questions, and you'll be the only connection I have."

Korolev nodded and turned back to Mei. "Miss, if you'll come with me, please, we'll get those cuts looked at."

Mei looked up nervously at Benson and put a hand on her belly.

"It's OK, Mei. You can trust Pavel. He's a good man and will protect you until I get back." Benson grabbed Korolev's collar and pulled him close to whisper in his ear. "Make sure Doctor Russell knows that she's pregnant."

Korolev's eyes went wide with shock. He looked at the young girl, then back to Benson.

"But she's just a kid."

"I know."

"It's not, you know, yours?"

"What? No! Why would you even ask?"

"Well, she asked for you, I just thought maybe… never mind, it was a dumb question."

"You got that part right, at least. Go now, quickly, but try not to attract attention."

Korolev shrugged. "A pregnant teenager with no implant, who would find that interesting?" He gathered up Mei, who was having a difficult time orienting herself in micro, and headed for the lifts on the far side of the compartment.

Benson turned his attention to a fuming Chief Bahadur. "We've got to stop him."

"No, *I* need to stop him. I think you've done quite enough already."

Benson put up his hands. "Look, I was tricked, that's obvious now. And I should have come to you in private about what I found."

"You should have trusted me."

"It wasn't about trust, Vikram. I didn't want to put you in a hard spot."

Chief Bahadur pointed towards Korolev and the girl as they floated away. "And where am I now?"

"I said I'm sorry, OK? We have to figure this out, fast. I've actually met the man, and I've been down in the basement levels recently. Can you say the same?"

Bahadur frowned, but shook his head.

"You need my help, Vikram. We can fight over the other stuff later, yes?"

"Oh, we will." Bahadur looked around at the thousands of spectators already packed into the stadium. "We need to cancel the game and get everyone out of here."

"No!" Benson brought his voice back under control. "No. You'll incite a panic. They're safe here. Sending everyone back down the lifts will just clog them up and make them vulnerable to whatever Kimura has planned. The fewer people in Shangri-La right now, the better."

Understanding spread across Bahadur's face like the dawn. "So, open the flood gates and go get the bad guys? It has the advantage of simplicity."

"That's me in a nutshell. Can we get on with it?"

After an argument that lasted exactly as long as a lift trip from the Zero stadium down to the deck of Shangri-La, Benson and Bahadur decided to split their efforts. Bahadur would take a lift full of constables to the lake, while Benson would take a handful of his own men to the waste water reclamation facility in case Kimura had something else waiting for them.

The lift doors opened. A small queue of spectators milled about, waiting for their turn to get in the car. They walked a short distance away to wait for the rest of their team. Benson looked over at his friend. "Nervous?"

"You'd be a fool not to be."

Benson nodded. "I didn't have enough time to be nervous. Kimura's man Huang jumped me from the shadows. He was tough, but I wasn't armed. Is it safe to assume that you know how to use that kirpan of yours?"

Bahadur pulled the ceremonial Sikh dagger free of its sheath and ran a careful finger down the blade, checking its edge. It wasn't much of a stabbing knife, but the blade ended in a wicked curve that would make short, brutal work of any exposed flesh it came across. Bahadur's hands went through a series of well-practiced movements, one kata flowing smoothly into the next before the tip of the knife slid quickly and effortlessly back into its sheath with a *snick*.

"Very safe."

Benson nodded, glad it was one knife he wasn't going to be on the wrong side of. He only wished it was sharp enough to cut the tension that had built up between the two of them.

"He's going to try to ambush you. Don't let him. Watch the shadows and check your corners. Keep your distance, make him come to you."

"And this Huang is his only fighter?"

Benson shrugged. "He's the one Kimura sent after me, and I'd bet my left nut that he's the one who pushed Laraby out the lock. Kimura probably has others, but

Huang is his most dangerous."

"I understand." The lift doors slid open again and disgorged a dozen hopped-up constables ready for a fight. Benson was afraid they were going to get more than they could handle.

The inescapable fact was, their men and women weren't trained fighters. For as long as humanity had been living on the Ark, the gravest threat any constable had faced was the occasional crazy person armed with nothing more deadly than clubs or carving knifes. The 3D printers had an enormous catalogue of firearms schematics that they were locked out from producing, and advanced algorithms scanned incoming requests for patterns that suggested someone was trying to get around the lockouts.

Cadets were drilled in hand-to-hand combat with a focus on Krav Maga for its brutal efficiency, but once they were issued their stun-sticks, most constables seldom set foot on the mats again. They didn't see the need.

Recent events had taught Benson better. He took a few moments to drive the point home to anyone who would listen and hoped it wasn't falling on deaf ears. Then they split up into their assigned teams.

Chief Bahadur reached out his hand. "Good hunting, my friend."

Benson took it and shook it firmly. "Watch your back."

Bahadur nodded, then marched off in the direction of the lake with his men trailing close behind.

Benson turned to his own men. "OK everyone, plant links only from here on out." His small unit of three constables nodded understanding and opened a temporary link network.

<Is everyone online?> Benson asked. They sounded off. <Good, keep the cross-talk down. Let's move.>

He and Bahadur had agreed on the ride down that it would be best to move overland and get as close to their targets as possible before entering the basement levels. They'd also decided not to inform command of their movements in case whichever floater had been helping Kimura's group caught wind of the operation and blew the whole thing. Bahadur had required some convincing on that last point, but the threat of ambush had brought him around.

The water treatment machinery was two levels down and two kilometers away from the lake, which seemed like foolish placement until one remembered the need to keep the whole spinning mass of the habitat modules in proper balance. The lake sat at one point of a triangle, the immense reservoirs waiting to be reclaimed sat at another, and the museum campus made up the third.

Benson led his men through the fading light with purpose. The odds were good that Bahadur's force would see the bulk of the action, but Benson's gut kept focusing on the poison threat, and that would mean sabotaging the filters. It wouldn't be hard to do, really. The water reclamation system had several stages, but the final stage consisted of banks of reverse-osmosis tubes hundreds upon hundreds of meters long that forced the water through nano-mesh screens under immense pressure. Poking a few holes in those screens would render the entire system useless and take days to find and repair.

By the time they neared the closest entrance to the water treatment plant, the lights above had gone dim. Somewhere in the back of Benson's brain, a little voice reminded him that they'd be floating the ball in preparation for push-off right about now. Maybe the last game of Zero ever played, and he was down here chasing terrorists. Trying to wipe out all human life was bad enough, but did they really have to be so inconsiderate of everyone else's schedules?

He brushed the thought aside as he opened the facility door. The four of them swept into the building and headed for a stairwell leading to the lower levels. So far, they had seen no one, but that wasn't terribly surprising. Nearly the entire facility was automated. The process at this stage wasn't nearly as labor intensive as some of the other upstream jobs.

Benson caught sight of the first workman from behind as they reached the first sub-floor landing. At first glance, he didn't look like one of Kimura's people, but it was hard to tell from the back. Carefully, he snuck up behind the shorter man, threw one arm around his neck, then cupped his free hand over his mouth to muffle the startled yelp.

"Relax, friend, I'm a constable," Benson whispered. "I'm going to let you go now, but you have to be quiet. Nod if you understand."

He did. Benson released his grip and quickly scanned the man for a plant. Gerald Lee, age forty-nine, supervisor of maintenance for the facility. Height, weight, and facial recognition all matched.

"You're in charge here?" Benson asked in a hushed voice.

"Yes." Lee glanced at the other three constables coming down the stairs, their stun-sticks drawn. "What's all this about?"

"We think someone might be trying to tamper with the water system."

"You mean like those bastards what knocked out the reactors?"

"Exactly like those bastards, yes. When did your shift start today?"

"17.00."

Benson nodded. "Have you seen or heard anything strange? People here who weren't supposed to be?"

Lee shook his head. "No, sir. Just me and young Wilson. We only call in extra help when something breaks."

"Which nothing has today?"

"Nope, running smooth as silk."

"And where is 'young Wilson'?"

"I... ah, I let him head off early to watch the match, sir. He's a big Mustang fan."

Benson smirked. "No crime in that. Can you lead us down to the filters? We need to clear and secure the entire facility before we move on."

"Sure, you're halfway there already. This way."

They cleared the first level, finding nothing, then moved on to the second sub-level. Racks of filter tubes three meters tall filled the space and stretched out past the curve of the hull.

<Damn,> Benson said.

<We have to clear this whole room?> Hernandez asked in a half-whine. <That'll take forever.>

<Yes, Hernandez, the whole thing. Unless you have something better to do?>

<No, sir.>

<Good.> Hernandez could be an insufferable jerk, but that didn't mean he was wrong. It really was a big

space for four people to search.

<Split up. Hernandez, with me. Do not take your eyes off your partner. If you see anything, and I mean anything, call it out and we'll regroup before moving on them.> He looked over at the workman. "Mr Lee, can you get out of here on your own?"

"Sure."

"OK, call it an early day. Grab a beer and watch the match somewhere."

Lee gave Benson a small bow. "Don't have to tell me twice." The last Benson heard of him was the sound of his feet scurrying up the stairs.

They split into two-man units and methodically cleared the racks of filters, one row at a time. After five minutes, Benson was already wishing he'd followed Lee out of the building. He opened a link to Bahadur to check up on his team's progress.

<Go ahead for Bahadur.>

<How's it looking?>

<Negative so far, but we only just reached the bottom level. What about your team?>

<Goose-egg, we've found nothing.> Benson rubbed a bead of sweat from his forehead. Unsurprisingly, it was pretty humid in the water treatment plant. <I'm starting to think my hunches aren't very good.>

<Don't be too hard on yourself. I'll do that for you when this is...>

<When this is what? Bahadur? What's wrong?>

<Standby.>

Benson waited, nervous with concern for his comrade.

<C'mon, Vikram, talk to me. What do you see?>

<Movement. No one is showing up on the plant grid,

so it's probably one of your ghosts. Can you ID them if I feed you an uplink?>

<Maybe, patch me through.>

Benson held up a fist, signaling Hernandez to stop. "Cover me," he whispered. Benson closed his eyes to avoid the disorientating double vision that came with a plant video overlay.

A moment later, he was looking out through Bahadur's eyes. Benson took a knee to fight the growing sense of vertigo caused by his eyes and his sense of balance being in completely different places.

<Are you onboard, Bryan?>

<Yes, I'm in.> He tried to look around, but of course it didn't work. Bahadur controlled the view. Benson was just a passenger.

Bahadur moved forward, his kirpan held tightly in his right hand. His team was pretty far below the surface already. The lake was ten meters deep at its lowest point, which meant it took up the first three sub-levels all by itself. The whole thing sat inside an enormous carbon-composite container, like a bathtub built for a Titan. The level below it was a tangle of pumps and pipes, as well as a forest of structural bracing much thicker than nearly anywhere else in the module, there to support and distribute the weight of tens of millions of liters of water.

<There are a thousand places to hide in that maze, Vikram. Keep your people close.>

Bahadur nodded and motioned for his team to tighten up their formation. He was careful to check his angles and corners, and to shine a light in the deeper shadows. Cautious, but relentless.

Bahadur's vision swept past something that Benson

thought looked out of place.

<Hey, stop. Look back at that pillar to your right.>

The view swiveled back at a particularly thick support truss, obviously a primary loadbearing part of the system. Something round protruded from the base.

<There, look down.> Bahadur did so and spotted the object. He bent down to get a closer look. It was a roughly cylindrical bag with a small grey box haphazardly stuck to the outside. The whole thing was fixed to the pillar with what looked like gaffer tape.

<That doesn't look like it belongs here, does it?> Benson asked.

<No, it most certainly does not.>

<Well, don't touch it until we know what it is.>

<Are you sure that's wise?>

<Sure? No, but I have a hunch.>

Bahadur ran the fingers of his free hand through his beard. <You have a strange sense of humor, Bryan, but I think you're right.>

Bahadur motioned his men to continue deeper into the maze. Something caught Bahadur's attention. He sprinted forward, kirpan at the ready.

<I heard movement. Moving to engage.>

The image became chaotic and rushed. Benson couldn't make sense of the rapidly flickering lights and deep shadows. Then everything stopped. Dead ahead, a hooded figure clad in the same black pullover as Benson's attacker hunched over a tablet. The man looked up and locked eyes with Bahadur. Illuminated by the soft light of the tablet's screen, Benson recognized Huang's face instantly.

<That's him!> he shouted into the link. <Take him down!>

The image blurred as Bahadur lunged at Huang, but he anticipated the move and span off to the side. It wasn't without cost, however, as the tip of Bahadur's kirpan bit deeply into the back of Huang's left calf. Benson felt a predatory surge of excitement as Huang yelped and limped behind another pylon. Bahadur juked to the other side, trying to flank him as the rest of his men converged on the scuffle.

They chased each other around the pillar twice before Bahadur finally got a hand on Huang's ankle and brought them both crashing down to the deck in a pile of tangled limbs. The impact knocked the tablet from Huang's hand and sent it skittering across the floor. Huang wasted no time jumping to his feet before pulling a familiar knife.

Bahadur took a long step back and pulled his knife hand tight against his side, then brought his free hand up to his throat, protecting his heart, neck, and face. The ready stance gave Huang pause; he'd probably never faced down a trained knife fighter before. Favoring his left leg heavily, Huang lunged at Bahadur's stomach, but found only air. Instead, Bahadur deftly pivoted right, letting the point of Huang's blade slide by harmlessly while his off hand dropped down and grabbed his attacker's wrist. His kirpan glinted as it came forward and sank deeply into Huang's forearm.

Huang's face contorted in pain as he yanked his arm free of Bahadur's grip, causing even more damage as the kirpan tore skin and muscle as he struggled. Somehow, he managed not to drop his knife in the process and flipped it to his off hand. Bahadur calmly reset his stance and awaited the next attack. By then, the rest of Bahadur's team had set up a perimeter around the two men, cutting off all avenues of retreat or escape.

Bleeding freely from his arm, Huang took stock of his situation. After a moment's reflection, he flipped the knife around in his hand and grabbed it by the blade. But to the surprise of everyone, instead of surrendering, Huang flung the knife at Bahadur for all he was worth. Benson watched through his friend's eyes as the blade came tumbling through the air towards his face. The image in Benson's mind's eye was so realistic and immediate, he actually flinched.

Bahadur, by comparison, simply moved his head a few centimeters to the left and let the deadly blade pass before clanging harmlessly against a pillar some distance behind him. But by the time Bahadur looked back to Huang, the real damage was done. He'd used the distraction to grab his tablet. Huang looked up with a deranged, vicious smile as his finger hovered over a flashing red icon. With unbridled terror, Benson realized what was coming next.

"Stop him!" Benson screamed both into the link and out loud, but it was too late. Huang's finger came down, and the whole world went white. The flash overwhelmed Benson's visual cortex for a moment before an error message floated into view.

— *Error: User Bahadur, Vikram J. cannot be located at this time. Please try your call again later.* —

The shockwave raced through the habitat's structure and up through Benson's feet. He opened his eyes and grabbed Hernandez by the arm. <We have to move!> he shouted into his team's shared link. <Everyone upstairs, now!>

They sprinted back towards the stairs and met up with his other unit. Benson took the steps three at a time in the race to get back to the surface. He tried to reestablish the link with Bahadur's plant in the slim hope that it needed to reset, but it was futile.

Four flights of stairs flew by as Benson reached the top and threw open the door to the outside. He looked to the lake. Smoke billowed from a half dozen wounds in Shangri-La's deck. Fire alarms screamed into the night from all directions. Alerts popped up through Benson's plant like billboards inside his eyeballs. He blocked them. He blocked everything and ran for the lake, dimly aware of his men trailing behind him.

But then, a shriek of tortured metal stopped him dead in his tracks. A third of the way around the module, the lake... sank, then disappeared entirely. A cloud of splashing water and debris rose in its wake. A heartbeat later, the cloud itself blew out, replaced by a field of stars in the shape of the missing lake and the howl of an approaching hurricane.

CHAPTER TWENTY-FIVE

A fog thick as cream formed around the breach as hundreds of thousands of cubic meters of atmosphere blew out into space. For several seconds, Benson froze up as he stared blankly at the all-consuming horror unfolding before him.

It took Hernandez to shake him back into the present.

"Chief, we can't stay here!"

He couldn't argue the point. Benson's other men were already running full tilt for the lifts at the far end, but no matter which way they ran, the closest exit was a kilometer away. Even with the stadium filling up, north of twenty thousand people were still in Shangri-La, with only a few dozen lifts, that could only carry twenty people at a time.

<Everybody stop,> Benson said into their mutual link. <The lifts will be swarmed by the time we reach them. We need another way out.>

<What about the civilians?> Hernandez asked.

<There's too many of them and too few lifts. They can't be evacuated in time. We'll just get trampled if we try.>

<What's your play, chief?>

Benson looked back at the water plant when the solution struck him.

<Follow me.>

He led his team back down the stairs until they were three levels down. From there, the team ran as straight and fast as they could towards the aft bulkhead. It was the longest kilometer of Benson's life. The breach left from the lake tearing its way out of Shangri-La was over a hundred meters across, and nearly as many wide, but over six *billion* cubic meters of atmosphere were trying to force their way out of it. Benson didn't know the equations to figure the rate of escaping gasses. He hoped there was enough time for what he'd planned before they all suffocated.

The air around them cooled as the pressure dropped, but no one noticed. Their legs burned from the strain of sustained sprinting. Benson thanked his past self for refusing to skimp on his morning run around the habitat. Still, if they got out alive, he promised to do more interval training.

Finally, they reached the aft end of the module. As he'd hoped, they were completely alone. Sweating and huffing for air both from exertion and dwindling oxygen, Benson jogged the last few steps up to the lift. The queue for a lift car already stretched over an hour from everyone above trying to flee, but that wasn't his plan. Instead, Benson moved around to the maintenance hatch. For a terrifying moment, he couldn't remember the override code. He punched in numbers, trying to remember the pattern. The panel turned red.

"Dammit." He tried again.

Red.

"C'mon!" Benson frantically jabbed his fingers at the keypad. On the third try, the panel turned green.

"Oh, thank God."

Benson looked up the shaft's infinity with relief. It was clear. Either out of panic or lack of access, no one else had managed to get inside. They still had a fighting chance for survival. *And*, Benson thought darkly, *to avenge Vikram*. He wasn't sure how a Sikh would feel about revenge, but he knew they were big on justice. That would do.

He waved his men inside. "Everybody up the ladder. Double time."

Hernandez looked up the shaft and turned about as white as he could. "You've got to be kidding."

Benson's patience worn thin. "Then stay here."

"But it's a kilometer straight up!"

"And? I climbed it a couple days ago. Unless the old man is in better shape than you?"

Hernandez scoffed, but took hold of a rung and started the long climb. Benson let the other two go next. He'd take up the rear. With the hatch sealed behind them, he used his security clearance to put a permanent lockout on the hatch that could only be overridden from Command. The hatch was airtight, and with it locked down, they didn't have to worry about somebody opening it in desperation and getting sucked back down hundreds of meters of shaft. That would be a bad day.

Another hatch gleamed three floors above. Ground level. The desperate screams of thousands of people blended together and echoed through the shaft. Fists on the other side pounded frantically against hatch. Benson's men glanced down at him, deep lines of guilt etched into their faces.

"We can save a few of them, at least," his lead man said. It was said almost in a whisper. Benson understood the sentiment, he felt a powerful pull to do just that, a pull his rational mind had to fight against with all its might.

"Twenty thousand people are on the other side of that hatch. If we open it to let even one person through, we'll never get it closed again. And there's no way anyone will make it to the top before the air escapes."

Everyone nodded understanding, but it was obvious none of them were happy about the grim reality. Benson wasn't a big fan of it either. As he locked out the hatch and continued up the ladder, he knew he'd be hearing the sounds of fists banging and people screaming for the rest of his life.

The climb was dramatically worse than he remembered. Then again, starting off with burned out legs and reduced oxygen levels didn't help. Three different times on the way up, Benson tried to get command on the link and update them of the situation, but each time he was met with error messages. The network was either down from the explosion and decompression, or the network's bandwidth had been overwhelmed in the aftermath.

When Benson and his exhausted team finally reemerged from the top of the maintenance shaft almost a full hour after the explosion, they were walking blind into the chaos inside the hub. The hatch swung open and Benson floated out into the micrograv. The lift terminal was to his right, but it was locked down. The hub itself was crammed with refugees from the decompression with nowhere else to go.

The match had been cancelled, obviously, and Benson picked out several players from both the Mustangs and the Yuoguai floating about, trying to help what was left of Shangri-La's constables keep order.

Someone in the crowd spotted Benson and pointed.

"That's him!" she shouted. "That's Bryan Benson, he's still alive!"

Every head in the corridor turned and shot daggers right at him. If looks could kill, Benson would have been lit on fire.

<What's going on, chief?> one of his constables asked tentatively.

<No idea.> The crowd floated menacingly close to his team. <Stun-sticks out, hold your ground. But don't zap unless you're sure of the threat.>

"Sorry, chief," Hernandez said from behind him. "But you're the threat."

Benson turned his head around only to see all three of the men he'd just led to safety pointing their stun-sticks at his head.

He threw out his hands to calm down the brewing situation. "Whoa, everybody, what's the deal?"

"Orders just came in through our plants. You've been suspended by the Council. We were just sent the warrant for your arrest."

"On what fucking charge?"

"Aiding and abetting the terrorist David Kimura."

Benson didn't bother to hide his rage at the betrayal. "You'd all be bright blue right now if not for me!"

Hernandez shrugged. "And maybe a lot of other people wouldn't be. Now, are you going to comply, or do you intend to resist?"

Benson felt his leg and arm muscles tensing involuntarily. His lower brain was itching for a fight, but he forced himself to remain calm and assess. Hernandez had already floated too close in a sophomoric attempt to intimidate. Benson could get a hand on the overconfident young man and break his arm before he could hope to react. Worse, he was stupidly blocking a clean shot line for his partner behind him.

But that still left one stun-stick pointing at him, along with several hundred refugees who had also heard the news already. *And who told them that, I wonder?*

He could *probably* take out Hernandez, could *probably* get a shot off at Flowers before she hit him, and could *probably* stay behind Hernandez long enough to hit the last man before he could get a decent angle. Aside from the other Zero players in the tube, nobody had his hours flying in micro, and few had his size and strength. He could probably stun thirty or forty refugees before they overwhelmed him, maybe even enough to get them to back off.

But even if everything went right, there was nowhere to go. Command was surely monitoring and would lock down the exits at the first hint of trouble. Then he'd just be the guy who attacked his own people while resisting arrest.

Benson was no lawyer, but he suspected that wouldn't look good at trial.

All of those thoughts passed between his ears in less than two seconds. By then, two of the late Chief Bahadur's people had floated in behind him and trained their stun-sticks on his back, cutting off any chance of even short term victory.

Growling like a cornered bear, Benson flicked his stick at Hernandez's face hard enough to make him flinch, then put his hands on his head.

•••

Like hunters returning from safari, Benson's captors paraded him down the boulevard on the way to formal booking at the stationhouse. Word spread fast as hundreds, if not thousands, of people lined the street to jeer and harass Benson as he sulked by in humiliation. Soon, the assembled rabble grew bolder, throwing the traditional lettuce and occasional tomato.

Some of them had good arms.

"Ow!" Benson said as a tuber struck him in the calf. "That was a potato!"

"Quiet," Hernandez said.

"I'm a suspect under your protection, *constable*. You're not doing much protecting."

"You're lucky I don't turn you over to them right here."

"Forgetting your oaths now? You're sure not doing anything to enforce the Codes. I've never seen so much food wasted."

Hernandez shoved him, hard enough that Benson had to take two big steps to keep from stumbling. The crowd roared in approval.

"Well, we have twenty thousand fewer mouths to feed, don't we, *chief*? Another word out of you and I'll stun your ass and drag you the rest of the way by your feet, face down. Now, walk."

Benson strained against the plastic cuffs zipped too tightly against his wrists, itching for the chance to even up with the hothead, but this wasn't the time. Instead, he locked eyes straight ahead and did his best to dodge the occasional ballistic onion until they reached the end of the path.

The inside of the stationhouse offered a measure of

calm compared to the mob outside, at least. But the price
was seeing the angry, devastated faces of the men and
women he'd led for the last five years. Theresa sat at the
duty officer's desk, weeping softly into her hands. He
frowned sympathetically at her as he was roughly led
past. She didn't look up.

Hernandez shoved Benson into his office, where a
familiar face sat behind his desk.

Chao Feng looked up and nodded to Hernandez. "Wait
outside."

Hernandez obeyed and shut the door behind him.

"Feng," Benson muttered. "You're in my chair."

"Not anymore. Sit, detective." Feng motioned for the
guest chair behind him. Benson caught a glimpse of an
evidence bag in Feng's lap as he sat down, but he couldn't
see what was in it.

"Should I be surprised you're behind this little witch-
hunt? Because I'm not."

"Witch-hunt?" Feng snorted. "That's an ironic charge,
coming from you, detective."

"We don't have time for your vendetta, commander."

"Vendetta?" Feng leapt up from the chair and punched
Benson in the gut as hard as he could, which admittedly,
wasn't very hard. Benson anticipated the blow and tensed
his abs. When he failed to double over, Feng stepped
back, rubbing his wrist.

"So you brought me down here to work me over a
little, is that it? You might want to bring Hernandez back
in here. At least he can throw a punch."

"This is funny to you? Two-fifths of the human race is
dead. Including my wife, you bastard!" The fury returned
to Feng's face, fueled by the anguish of another fresh loss.

The admission hit Benson harder than Feng's fists ever could have.

"What about your boy? Is he safe?"

"Why do you care, butcher? You had Edmond killed, too, then set me up. Don't deny it!"

"I do deny it, categorically," Benson said flatly.

"Oh really? Then explain this." Feng reached back and grabbed the small evidence bag from the floor where it had fallen, then held it up to Benson's face. Through the clear plastic, Benson saw a crumpled slip of paper that had been smoothed out, with a handwritten note on it. Benson's heart sank as he recognized it:

Detective Benson,

I apologize for our hasty departure, but my people voted to go into deeper hiding. We are aware the habitats will be stopped and are taking precautions. Our arrangement is still in place. We will be in touch soon.

Sincerely,

David Kimura

"We found this down in the sub-basement not long after the power failure. I wanted to have you arrested right then, but the Council disagreed. They chose to put you under surveillance instead. I couldn't believe it. It was bad enough you and your little harlot had spent almost every night of the last week contaminating a crime scene, but this?" He shook the letter furiously. "You're a disgrace, even to your own sullied name!"

Benson locked eyes with Feng. "Chao, I know how this must look, but it's not what you think."

"Save it for the jury. I just want to know where he is. What's his plan?"

Benson shook his head. "I don't know."

"Bullshit. We sent men down to the lake in Avalon and found the same stolen mining explosives that caused the breach in Shangri-La. But we got there before the terrorists finished rigging them up. Guess where that was? Less than a hundred yards past the point where you called off the search. You *knew* they were making preparations and stopped the search to protect them."

"That's absurd!" Benson shouted.

"Is it really?" Feng slammed his hands down on the desk. "You led Chief Bahadur's people into an ambush, knowing they'd be blown to hell, while you were safely several clicks away. You even had an escape route planned out."

"You think that was a plan? Vikram was my friend, Feng. And we almost died too. The only reason we got out was the maintenance hatch code *you* gave me."

Feng ignored him. "Less than a thousand people got out in time, but here you are. You didn't even bother to save anyone but yourself."

"Don't you think I wanted to? There wasn't any way. Don't you see? Kimura lied to me. He set me up. I know it looks bad, but everything you have is just circumstantial."

Feng shook his head. "Bravo, detective, you're a hell of an actor. I might almost believe it if you hadn't tried the same thing on me."

Benson tried to deflect Feng's growing anger. "Look, I'm sorry. I was wrong about you and Edmond. Totally wrong. But you have to see it from my perspective. You were acting very suspiciously. I understand why, now, but none of that would have happened if you'd just been honest with me from the start. I'm being honest with you now. Kimura used me. We have to stop him."

"*We* will. Without your 'help'. I don't know what caused you to turn on your own people, but I'm giving you one chance at some sliver of redemption. Where is Kimura?"

Benson recognized a lost cause when he saw one. Slowly, he stood up from the guest chair and looked down at Feng.

"I invoke my right to remain silent. I'm formally requesting legal counsel to be appointed to represent my interests in this case."

Feng leaned back in Benson's chair. "You're really not going to give him up?"

"I can't give you what I don't have, Chao."

"Fine, we'll do it your way. Constable!" The door opened and Hernandez reappeared. "The prisoner has decided not to comply. Please escort him to his apartment, where he is to remain under house arrest until he is arraigned for trial."

Hernandez grabbed Benson by the upper arm and dragged him for the door, but Benson twisted sharply out of his grip and shoved him back with a chest bump.

"I know the way, constable."

CHAPTER TWENTY-SIX

His apartment was a little more... Spartan than he'd left it, yet somehow quite a bit messier. Men had swept through to prepare it for his house arrest, and they hadn't come with an eye for cleanliness.

Benson spent the first hour of his confinement just tidying up, trying to push the echoes of the people lost in Shangri-La out of his head. That task completed, he sat down to watch a movie, a documentary, anything to occupy his mind. But he found all of his permissions had been blocked.

The only thing they'd left him access to on his display screen was the news channel, which, needless to say, was providing 24/7 coverage of the aftermath of the disaster, updated casualty lists, harrowing interviews from the handful of people who had managed to survive, and the endless speculation surrounding Kimura's fate.

Did he and his followers die in the explosion and decompression with the rest of Shangri-La? Did he escape? Was he plotting another attack? Why hadn't he made any demands? How had he faked his death and stayed in hiding for so long? Why had the people's champion turned mass murderer? And of course, the question on everyone's lips, why wasn't former Chief Benson being tortured for information about his "co-conspirator"?

It seemed the court of public opinion hadn't heard that his trial hadn't actually taken place yet. Still, he could hardly blame them. The circumstantial evidence connecting him was damning, and his family's... notoriety sealed the deal for most everyone else. He had to admit, if it had been someone else, he'd have probably been first in line to throw the switch that opened the lock.

After a few hours, not even Benson's guilt for all of the lives lost on his watch could make him continue wallowing in the self-abuse. He shut the display off and looked in his small refrigerator for the dozenth time, hoping a case of sake had magically appeared so he could numb out the next few hours in peace. His wish hadn't been granted.

Benson's ears perked up at the sound of commotion coming from outside his front door. Probably more protestors come to harass the guards. A small part of him wished the guards would let them in and be done with it. Still, better see what was stirring, just in case.

He shuffled over and keyed for the hallway camera. No point trying to open the door, it was locked from the outside. A small image appeared on the door itself where a peephole would traditionally be. But instead of another mini-mob of angry citizens bent on vengeance, all Benson saw outside his door were his two guards, and a tiny woman, holding a book almost as big as she was.

"Devorah?" His heart raced. He'd never thought to check the casualty list for her name because she was *always* in the museum. He reached up and keyed for audio, which streamed in through the imbedded sound system.

"I already told you, ma'am, he's not to have any visitors." It was Hernandez, Benson was sure from the voice. Little shit probably volunteered for a shift watching over his former boss.

Devorah stamped a tiny pointed shoe. "That's baloney, young man, malarkey even. I've probably interviewed and interrogated more people in my day than you've ever arrested. I know the rules about house arrest, and he's allowed one visitor at a time between 15.00 and 17.00. And unless my plant's clock is broken, it's just after 16.00 right now. So unless he's entertaining some fan, you're going to let me through."

"Ma'am, this is a special case, Commander Feng's orders."

"Oh, you're a crewmember now, son?"

"Well, no…" Hernandez looked around, suddenly on uneven footing.

"No, you're a civilian constable, who takes his orders from his civilian superiors, who take their orders from the Codes. Do I need to recite the code in question to you?"

Benson almost felt bad for him. Almost. He knew how hot Devorah could get. Her self-righteousness generated its own electromagnetic field if you got her spun up enough.

"Now are you going to let me through, or do I have to call up Acting-Chief Swenson to straighten this out?"

Even though Benson could only see the back of Hernandez's head, he knew the expression he had to be wearing. The two guards took a moment to converse, and apparently decided it was just easier to step out of the way of a speeding train than to try to stop it, even if it was only a hundred and sixty centimeters tall.

"We'll have to search you for contraband, ma'am," the other guard said earnestly.

Devorah set down the book and held out her arms. "Be my guest. It'll be the most action I've seen since college."

The guards blushed as they performed the quickest, most perfunctory pat down Benson had ever seen. It was the first time he'd laughed in days.

"And the book," Hernandez said.

"What, this?" Devorah leaned down and opened the cover, then flipped through a handful of pages. "Not much you can hide between the pages, boys. Besides, it's the stuff *inside* a book that's really dangerous."

Hernandez let out a sigh and waved her in. "Fine. Ten minutes. Then you're leaving. Understood?"

"That will be just fine, young man."

Hernandez shook his head and turned around to speak into the audio pickup. "Mr Benson," his voice boomed through the speakers like the God of the Old Testament.

"I can hear you, Hernandez, you don't have to swallow the microphone."

Hernandez rolled his eyes before continuing. "Step back from the door and sit on your couch with your hands on your head."

Benson took his time moseying over to the couch, but complied. The door slid open as Hernandez and the other guard who Benson didn't recognize spun into the room, stun-sticks leveled squarely at his head.

Unfazed, Devorah pushed past them clutching the gigantic book to her chest and sat on the love seat adjacent to the couch.

"That'll be all, boys."

"Are you sure you don't want one of us to stay, ma'am?"

She glared up at him. "Son, if Bryan here wanted to do me harm, neither of you little twits would make much difference. Besides, I think I'm far safer with him than either of you are."

Hernandez glowered at her. "Ten minutes." They left, and the door locked shut behind them. Benson nearly jumped out of his chair in the rush to embrace Devorah.

"You're alive!" He swept her up out of the chair and into a bear hug.

"Not if you keep squeezing me so hard." She emphasized the point by kicking him gently, but firmly, in the shin with one of her dangling legs.

Benson set her back down. "You never leave the museum. I assumed the worst."

"And you would have been right if it wasn't for Salvador. He remembered the vault was airtight while the rest of us ran around flapping our gums arguing over what to do."

"Sal made it out, too?"

Devorah's face darkened. "He made three trips down to the vault and back up, grabbing these panicking idiots banging on the front doors and dragging them down to safety. I was one of them, I'm ashamed to say. He went back up to grab one of the summer interns, but she was just frozen, couldn't move a muscle. Best we can tell, he was carrying her down the stairs like a fireman when he missed a step and broke his ankle. They found them both at the bottom of the steps. He was hugging her when the air ran out."

Tears ran down her cheeks. Benson got up to grab her

a napkin, but she waved him off.

"Forget it. He deserves to have someone crying over him. Never in thirty years thought it'd be me, but here we are."

Benson rested a hand on her boney knee. "It's not your fault. People can surprise us."

"Sure can. Which brings me to you. Did you do it?"

"You mean did I conspire with a lunatic to kill twenty thousand people and two-fifths of what's left of humanity? No. No, I did not."

Devorah grabbed his chin and looked him square in the eye. Her gaze was so deep, so penetrating, he could have sworn he felt it coming out the back of his skull.

"No, I expected you didn't." She let her hand drop back down to the book in her lap with a sigh. "But there're not many people on the other side of that door who would agree. You're going to have the devil's own time finding competent counsel willing to represent you."

Benson shrugged. "I don't care anymore. Truth is, I'm just as responsible as anyone. Kimura played me like a harp. I believed him when he told me his people were innocent. I bought his line about a terrorist that never existed, and I led Vikram and all his people straight into an ambush. My incompetence killed those people just as sure as Kimura's bombs did."

Devorah slapped him hard across the cheek.

"Bullshit. You kept on the case when the most powerful men in the universe were telling you to drop it. You ran after Kimura just as soon as you figured it out and stopped him from doing the same to Avalon. You are the only reason anyone's left at all. Now, pardon my French, but I didn't come down here for a fucking pity party. So, if you're quite finished pining for the executioner?"

Benson rubbed his cheek where she'd struck him. It was already hot to the touch.

"Oh, what, are you going to whine about that, too?"

Still in shock and unsure of what else to do, Benson simply shook his head.

"Good. Now, since you're probably going to have to prove your own innocence–"

"I am?"

"Yes, you are."

"But I'm not at all qualified to represent myself in court."

"You'll get no argument from me. Which is why you're going to need this…" Devorah spun the book around so that Benson could get a look at the cover for the first time. *The History of Jurisprudence*. To call the book thick was an understatement. In a pinch, it could serve as a decent coffee table all by itself.

Devorah opened the cover and turned to the introduction page. "Here. Start at the beginning."

"Where's the beginning?"

"The Code of Hammurabi, I think. Anyway, by the time you reach the end, you'll be ready to get out of here."

Apparently lacking any more to say, Devorah stood up from the chair and walked back over to the door, then summoned the guards.

"Wait, that's it?" Benson called after her.

"That's it. You should probably assume the position, detective."

Benson plopped back down on the couch and put his hands on his head. The doors slid open again as

Hernandez and his partner took up positions on each side. Devorah turned to leave, but paused just as she reached the hallway and looked back.

"Oh, and Bryan, I trust you're not one of those naughty boys who peeks at the last page, are you?"

"No, ma'am," he said, more confused than ever.

"Good, I hate it when people skip ahead to the end and spoil the surprise. Good day, detective."

Hernandez gave Benson a contemptuous little sneer before pulling back into the hallway. The door shut behind him, leaving Benson alone with the book. He stared down at it and had to repress a sudden urge to kick it for fear of breaking his foot in the process. Instead, he shrugged and flipped through it. May as well do some light reading before his trial and summary execution.

Benson hefted the book and sat down on his couch. He skimmed through the first chapter and the significance of all two hundred and eighty-two of Hammurabi's edicts, but his mind kept wandering back to the last five minutes and the bizarre conversation with Devorah.

The whole thing had felt strange, almost scripted. Was she speaking in code? Devorah hardly seemed the type to dance around. She was, without a doubt, the most direct person he'd ever met. And what was that line about spoiling the surprise? It was a history book, not a novel. There was no surprise twist in the plot, it just… ended.

Benson found himself eyeing the book very suspiciously. It *did* seem too heavy, after all. He shifted his position so that the camera in his living room couldn't get a good angle on the book. Odds were good they were monitoring his plant's visual output without his knowledge, but it was a risk he had to take.

Swallowing hard, Benson turned to the last third of the book. Starring back up at him, nestled inside a small cavity laser-cut into the pages themselves, lay an FN Model 1910 handgun in 9mm Kurz. The last gun in the world. A small note had been rolled up and stuffed inside the trigger guard:

So you peeked after all. It's loaded and the safety is off.
Just point it at anyone annoying you and pull the trigger.
Seven shots is all you get. And don't get blood on the
book. It's bad enough I have to tape all the pages back
together later.

Sincerely,
Devorah.

Benson shut the book and smiled.
"You crazy, beautiful old bitch."

CHAPTER TWENTY-SEVEN

When the men outside hadn't burst down his door after the first five minutes, Benson felt confident Devorah's gift had not been discovered by anyone prying remotely through the cameras in the apartment. He could hardly believe it worked at all. It was, quite literally, the oldest trick in the book.

But that left him with the small issue of what exactly to do with it. His dinner would be delivered in the next twenty minutes, if they kept to the schedule. Slowly, trying not to raise suspicion, Benson took inventory of his apartment. Men had been through to sweep it clean of potential weapons or suicide methods before his house arrest had begun.

They hadn't left much. His kitchen knives were all gone, although for some inexplicable reason they'd left the block behind. Silverware and other utensils, all of his food, cleaning products, bedding, pillows (how exactly he could kill himself with a pillow escaped his imagination), most of his clothes, glassware... they'd left a set of plastic cups behind, but the water had been shut off to his sink, presumably to keep him from trying to drown himself in it.

The water to his shower still ran, however. Surveying their work, Benson couldn't help but feel as though his captors were just winging it. Maybe that shouldn't have been such a surprise. Still, *he* would have done a more thorough job of it.

Then Benson opened his pantry door and knew for certain he would have. Sitting in its place on the shelf, untouched for at least the last two years, was his roll of aluminum foil. He suppressed a manic cackle as his plan fell into place. He would get only once chance, and every second would count, but he'd get his shot at freedom.

And one last chance to stop Kimura.

Wearing an appropriately dour face, Benson sat down on his couch and waited for dinner to arrive. It wasn't long before the door slid open and his meal was set on the floor. A peanut and apple butter sandwich with a side of green beans and a glass of water with a plastic fork. Somewhere along the line, his sushi order must have gotten misplaced.

Still, it would suffice. Benson grabbed it up and sulked back to his spot on the couch. He moved his food around the plate, feigning disinterest like someone struggling to find their appetite. Eventually, he nibbled around the edges of the sandwich and ate a string bean or two, then finished it off.

He waited a half hour until the lights outside spooled down into night before starting the really tricky part. He paced around his living room, holding his stomach and panting. Benson had to get himself worked up without obvious exertion, to fool anyone monitoring his plant data that he was having a health emergency. Thinking about Kimura and the twenty thousand people his madness killed certainly managed to get his blood pressure up, but he needed to push it further.

Benson staggered around a bit for the cameras before falling onto the couch. He took shallow, rapid gasps until he saw stars streaking through his vision. Wiping his brow, Benson realized he was actually sweating.

Sensing it was time for the *coup de grace*, Benson struggled to get up from the couch, still hyperventilating. He collapsed to the floor in a heap while waves of spasms coursed through his muscles, playing it up for the cameras. If his acting was any good, whichever floater was stuck monitoring his vitals would think he'd been poisoned just as Edmond had been.

The ruse worked. The door slid open as Hernandez and the other guard rushed in to check on him. Someone reached down and grabbed Benson's neck, fumbling around for a pulse. It was the opening he'd been waiting for. His eyes snapped open and looked up on a startled Hernandez. Benson couldn't suppress a smirk of satisfaction as his hands clamped down on Hernandez's wrist.

With a violent twist and a shriek, Hernandez's wrist snapped like a twig wrapped in a wet towel. The other guard lined up a shot with their stun-stick, but Benson grabbed Hernandez's shoulder and pulled his head down into the line of fire, forcing them to hesitate. The tiny delay was all Benson needed to pull the gun from his waist and train it on the guard's chest.

"Drop it!" he commanded. The constable looked back and forth between the gun and the small slice of Benson's head that they could see.

"Do you know what this is?" Benson twisted a little

harder on Hernandez's wrist to get a moan out of him for effect.

"A gun?" the guard said in disbelief.

"Very good, you've seen a movie. Yes, this is a gun, the last gun. The last time some idiot fired it, sixteen million people died," Benson said, parroting the line Devoralı had used when she'd first shown him the weapon. "So unless you want to be sixteen million and one, you're going to toss me your stick and get on the ground."

"You wouldn't," the guard said, without much conviction.

"Haven't you been watching the news? Drop it and kick it over here."

He obeyed and put up his hands.

"Thank you. Hernandez, if you would stun him, please."

"Drop dead!"

Benson ground the muzzle of the handgun flush against his temple. "I'm running low on patience, my friend. Now, please."

Growling, Hernandez raised his stun-stick and dropped his partner to the floor in a quivering heap.

Benson adjusted his stance and sat up. "Thank you for your cooperation." He raised his arm, then brought the butt of his gun down hard onto Hernandez's temple.

"OW!" Hernandez's hand shot up to cover the wound to his face. "That really fucking hurt, you bastard!"

"Sorry, that was supposed to knock you out."

"Well, it didn't!"

Feeling discouraged, Benson tried again.

"OW! Goddammit!"

"I'm not sure what I'm doing wrong." Benson hit him

again, with the same result.

"Oh, for fuck's sake, I'll do it myself!" Hernandez put his own stun-stick to his bloodied head and hit the stud.

Benson didn't have time to reflect on the absurdity of what had just happened. Instead, he grabbed an end table and dove for the doorway, wedging it in place even as the door slid shut. He hit the lights, hoping to confuse whoever was on camera duty. He ran for his pantry and wrapped three layers of aluminum foil around his head, then secured it with the only thing he could find: a bright pink towel Theresa had left the last time she'd spent the night.

Benson wished Vikram was still around to show him how to secure a proper turban, but he managed to tie it off. He figured thirty seconds before the stunned guards woke from their seizures, and maybe a minute before reinforcements came pouring out of the lifts.

He snuck a peek into the hallway, relieved to see his retinue of protestors had gone home for the night. Gun in hand, he sprinted for the emergency staircase at the end of the hall and kicked it open, sounding the fire alarm. For the first time, Benson was glad for his apartment being on "only" the third floor.

Emerging into the night, Benson kept low and off the footpaths. Countless nights lost watching the camera feeds finally paid off. He knew right where all the blind spots in the surveillance net were, which cameras had malfunctioned or couldn't track properly anymore. Between the dark, trees, and gaps, Benson found it unsettlingly easy to move around unseen. He even managed to dodge a pair of his own constables out looking for him.

Despite the fact they had to know who they were looking for, they didn't break from their normal patrol route. Benson was dismayed by their lack of imagination, even as he was grateful for it. He was starting to understand how the Unbound had managed to hide for so long and move about with such apparent impunity.

His constables would be getting some retraining, provided by some miracle he lived through all this. Benson's destination lay directly ahead, Edmond's apartment. The crime scene tape covering the door still fluttered in the breeze, although with the Shangri-La refugee crisis mounting, it couldn't be long before someone remembered it was open.

Benson breathed a small sigh of relief when he spotted the guard standing watch outside the door: Pavel Korolev. The boy was stubborn and duty bound, but he was also loyal and independent thinking. He just had to trust that those traits won out over whatever ambition for promotion Korolev had. *Only one way to find out*, he thought.

Slowly, so as not to startle the young constable more than necessary, Benson stepped out of the shadows and onto the walkway.

Korolev's stun-stick snapped to attention immediately.

"That's far enou… Chief?"

Benson put up his hands to show he was unarmed, which he wasn't, but some things could wait. "Yes, Pavel, it's me."

"You're supposed to be under house arrest."

"I got bored and slipped out for an evening walk."

"Slipped out, eh? And Hernandez just saluted and let you out the door, I suppose?"

Benson smirked at the image of Hernandez pointing his own stun-stick at his head. It did bear a passing resemblance to a salute, in a cruel sort of way.

"Something like that."

"Is he alive?" Korolev asked in earnest.

"Of course he is. You know me, Pavel. Am I a killer?"

"Floaters say you are. One of the worst to ever live, in fact."

Benson put his hands down flat to his sides. "And what do you say?"

Korolev stared at him down the shaft of his stun-stick. For an uncomfortably long moment, Benson thought he was going to press the stud. With a sigh, Korolev relented.

"I think you're an honorable man. I think you've been set up. And I think that's aluminum foil under that stupid pink towel on your head and it doesn't actually matter what I think because my stick is useless and you're a lot bigger than me."

"It's not my towel. And you've already decided not to turn me in anyway."

"What makes you think that?"

Benson pointed at the doorway behind Korolev. "Because as soon as I stepped out, you moved in front of the door camera to keep the floaters from seeing I'm here."

Korolev lowered his stun-stick. "So I did."

Benson stepped up and waited patiently for Korolev to key open the door, then walked through into the darkened kitchen and dining room beyond. With Korolev following close behind, he moved into the living room, pausing to review the artwork that remained. He turned on the vid screen on the far wall and watched as it scrolled through the latest batch of Pathfinder images from Tao Ceti G.

The image took on new weight now that Benson had discovered Edmond's Atlantis obsession. In a few short years, the new colony could be up and running, and people would turn from growing crops to growing fortunes. Greed had always been a powerful motive for murder. Something about Atlantis was integral to long term plans already being laid out. Edmond's curiosity threatened those plans. But what any of it had to do with Kimura's attacks, Benson didn't have the first clue.

He stopped in front of the empty space where the Monet had hung before all this started. A light still shone. Standing in his own footsteps, Benson felt as though he was coming full circle. If only he could peek at the ending.

Another light caught his eye, streaming through the wrought-iron of the spiral staircase leading up to the bedroom.

"Is that you, Korolev?" a familiar voice called down from the room above.

"Yes, ma'am. And I've brought a… guest."

Theresa's head poked down through the portal and locked eyes with Benson.

"What the hell are you doing here?" she scolded.

"I'm relieved to see you too, Esa."

Theresa ran down the steps, stopping just centimeters away from his face. "They let you out on bail, did they?"

"Not exactly."

"Of course not! They say you killed half the human race. How did you escape?"

"I had a little help." Benson pulled the FN out of his pocket.

"What is that, a gun?"

"Yep."

Korolev whistled behind him, impressed.

Theresa was less enthusiastic. She slapped him on the chest. "A real gun? Where the fuck did you get a gun, Bryan?"

"A friend."

"A friend with a museum, you mean?"

Benson shrugged innocently.

"So Devorah busts you out, and you come here with one of my damned towels on your head? What are you going to do, take a bath?"

Benson smiled and pulled up a corner of the towel, revealing the aluminum foil underneath. Theresa took a step back as if stunned.

"My God. You've finally gone off the deep end."

"It was the only way to block my plant. Otherwise they would have found me in the first minute."

"So you come here? You idiot, they know we've been using it as a love nest. It's the first place they'll think to look."

Benson shrugged. "Which is why they haven't. They knew I was loose the second I took out Hernandez. I passed two patrols already. No one thinks I'd be dumb enough to come here."

Theresa looked at him suspiciously. "You didn't... shoot Hernandez, did you?"

Benson's shoulders sagged. "Why is everyone asking me that? No, I didn't want to waste the bullet. He's got a broken wrist and probably a concussion, but he'll be fine."

"Well, they're going to come around eventually. You can't hide here forever."

"I'm not here to hide. I need some answers."

Theresa blinked. "What answers? I know everything you know. I've been reading your reports, remember?"

"Yes, but as much as I want to, I didn't actually come here to talk to you."

"Then who?"

Benson looked up to the stairwell and called out. "Mei, it's OK sweetie, you can come out now."

"But…" Theresa looked back and forth between him and the barefoot girl gingerly walking down the stairs. "How did you know she was here?"

"Call it a hunch."

"But your hunches suck!"

"Maybe they're getting better. It made sense. The last thing I told Korolev to do was put her in protective custody. I figured he'd trust you with it, or you'd find out through Jeanine, and this was the obvious place to hide her." Benson took Mei's delicate hands in his and led her over to the sumptuous antique chair.

"Mei, honey, I need you to tell me everything. About Kimura's plans, about what he's going to do next, all of it."

"I… I shouldn't."

"Mei." Theresa knelt down and put a hand on the young woman's knee. "It's OK, you can trust us."

"You were so brave yesterday, Mei," Benson smiled, warmly and authentically. "You saved thousands of people yesterday, did you know that?"

"But almost everyone died!"

"In Shangri-La, yes, but that was my fault, not yours. I couldn't get there fast enough to stop them. But Mei, Kimura tried to do the same thing here in Avalon. They didn't have the chance to finish, because of you."

Theresa nodded her head in agreement. "It's true, Mei. Mankind still has a fighting chance, thanks to you."

Mei sank deeper into the chair, mirroring her attitude. "We were the last chance."

Benson cocked an eyebrow. "What do you mean?"

"Agong teach us that Unbound would be the first men."

"Agong?" Theresa asked.

"It means grandfather. It's what they call Kimura."

Theresa nodded and urged Mei to continue.

"The Unbound chosen to fill Tao Ceti G. Agong was picked by God to lead us after the rest of man fall."

For a long moment, everyone was silent as the full weight of Mei's words sunk in.

Korolev was the first to continue. "So, you were taught that your people would rebuild everything? Like *every* everything?"

Mei nodded. "We were chosen, like Noah and his Ark."

"How many of you are there?"

"Forty-six now." Mei's hand shot to her gently swelling belly. "Forty-seven," she corrected.

Theresa exhaled slowly. "Mei, forty-seven people isn't enough to start a colony. It's not even enough to get off the ship."

"Yes, it is!"

"Can you pilot a shuttle?"

Mei hesitated, but shook her head.

"Can any of you pilot a shuttle?"

"We not stupid! We learn."

Theresa put up her hands in a conciliatory gesture. "I don't think you're stupid. But piloting a shuttle isn't something you can learn in a day, or a month. It takes years of training and drills and simulations. I couldn't learn it in a year, much less the month we have left."

Mei crossed her arms. "You are not chosen."

Benson crossed his arms, mirroring Mei's body language. "Mei, do you think I'm a cheater?"

Mei shook her head, afraid she'd somehow offended her hosts. "No, Benson-san."

Benson pressed on. "My ancestors were. They lied to get on this ship, lied about who they were. Do you blame me for that?"

Mei tried to hide her discomfort at the question, poorly.

"No one is chosen by birth, Mei. We choose for ourselves what kind of people we grow up to be. I did. You did when you betrayed Kimura and came to me. And so will your baby, if we all live long enough to give it the chance."

Benson backed off to let his words sink in with her. He motioned for the others to come over by the dinner table.

"Well, that explains the attacks," he said.

"What do you mean?" Korolev asked.

Theresa jumped in. "We couldn't figure out what the terrorists wanted. They never gave any demands, never took hostages. It didn't make sense because we were looking at the attacks as a political statement. But they're not terrorists, they're a cult."

"But he almost killed everyone, twice now!"

Benson shrugged. "Kimura wouldn't be the first cult leader to decide doomsday was taking too long and try to give it a nudge. History is littered with charismatic leaders who turned incredibly violent to keep their flock loyal." Benson thought back through the series of events over the last few days, trying to put together a timeline.

"So, he took down the reactors, but not to destroy the ship. Instead, he bought time while all the security nets were down to hit deep storage and steal enough mining explosives to rig up the habitats. Then he waited until most of our constables were at the game to set them up, but he didn't expect Mei to turn, so he had to improvise."

"He still got twenty thousand people. That's hardly a failed attack," Korolev said.

"It is if your goal is to wipe out everyone but yourselves."

"Well, then why didn't he make any move against the command module?" Theresa asked. "Hundreds of crew are in there."

"Because he needs it intact. With command knocked out, he has no way to control the ship. Remember, he wants the Unbound to take over when the Ark reaches Tao Ceti G."

Korolev rubbed his chin. "How many people do you think he lost in Shangri-La?"

Benson shook his head. "I can't be sure, but if it was me, I'd have pulled everyone back as soon as I knew Mei had escaped. Huang either volunteered or was picked to stay behind while the rest of the group escaped, to take out a whole bunch of constables and the module at the same time."

"So what happens now?"

"He's going to make another play on Avalon, but it's going to be fast and dirty. There's not enough time left for another complex operation."

Korolev piped up. "And we're watching for him now. Avalon is locked down tight as a drum."

Benson looked at him quizzically. "Is it now? I'm here, not in my apartment. Still, he's not going to be able to do a repeat on the lake. It's being drained anyway."

"So he needs to make a hole. What if he has some extra mining explosives lying around?"

"Wouldn't matter. Those explosives aren't powerful enough to cut through six sub-levels. That's why he had to rig them to the lake and let its mass do most of the work. No, he needs a *big* hole, something engineering can't patch in time."

"Well, where's he going to get explosives big enough before we Flip the ship and the nukes start..."

Everyone froze in place as the same icy thought clawed its way out of their brains and down their spines.

"A nuke," Benson sighed heavily. "That'd certainly do the trick."

"Oh, no." Theresa put a hand over her mouth. "He wouldn't."

"He most certainly would," Benson said.

"But that would destroy the entire ship, wouldn't it?" Theresa asked.

"I doubt it. The propellant bombs aren't the city-killers we used to build. They're much lower yield, and the Ark is huge. You don't really understand how huge until you've seen it from the outside."

"But he can't reach them, we've had a security contingent guarding the only lock to engineering since right after the reactors were sabotaged."

"We go around it," Mei said.

Everyone looked at the antique chair where Mei sat, her legs drawn up to her chest and her arms crossed around them.

"What do you mean, Mei?" Theresa asked.

"We not use lock. Go around it with a secret way to break reactors, then come back. No one see."

The doorbell chimed. Then chimed again. Whoever was outside wasn't exhibiting an abundance of patience.

"Check it," Theresa said to Korolev.

The young man nodded curtly and jogged over to the small screen by the door.

"It's Hernandez," he said. "He has three other constables with him, and he looks mighty pissed."

"Well, that didn't take as long as I'd hoped," Benson muttered.

"Stall him." Theresa grabbed Benson under the chin to ensure she had his full attention. "You're not thinking about digging in your heels for some testosterone-filled last stand, are you?"

"No, ma'am."

"Good. I hate that macho bullshit."

"Sure you do." Benson grabbed the back of her head and pulled her in for a deep, penetrating kiss. Korolev looked away out of respect. For just a moment, they both forgot about all the tragedy and uncertainty that had plagued their lives since the call about Laraby's disappearance came in a week ago. The world shrank down until it was just big enough to fit two lovers sharing a passionate embrace before the winds blew them apart again.

In the blink of an eye, the moment passed and Benson was on the move again.

"Wait, I want to come with you," Theresa said, pleading in her moist eyes, but Benson could only shake his head.

"They're only guessing that I'm in here. But if your plant suddenly goes dark, they'll know for sure."

She gave a small, resigned nod. "Go."

Benson steeled himself. He'd been nervously anticipating this moment for months, putting it off for selfish, silly reasons. But circumstances forced his hand now. This was the last chance he was going to get. He took a deep breath, then said the words.

"I love you."

Theresa stepped in and punched him in the gut.

"Jesus, Esa." Benson bent over and tried to catch his breath.

"No, you selfish shit," she said. "You don't get to say that. Not here, not like this. Not until you come back to me."

"Right, sorry." Benson jogged over to Mei's chair, holding his stomach. "Mei, I need you to show me the secret way into engineering."

"OK," she said. "But you not like it."

CHAPTER TWENTY-EIGHT

Mei was right. Benson did not like it.

"What is this, duct-tape?" Benson poked a finger at the gray strip covering one of the elbow joints of the ancient spacesuit.

"Yes. Duck tape work like lucky charms."

Benson decided it was a language barrier issue and moved on. "Where the hell did you dig these things up from?"

"People throw them out, we fix them up." Mei turned around and pointed at a zipper at the bottom of her suit's back flap. Benson obliged her.

"Are you sure about this? You're pregnant, after all. Can't you just tell me where to go?"

Mei shook her head. "You get lost. Turn around." She tugged at his zipper, but couldn't get it to close. "You too fat."

"I'm not fat," Benson said defensively. "I'm just a little bigger than average."

"Breathe out."

"But we wear these things *to* breathe."

Unimpressed by the line of logic, Mei slapped him in the stomach. Begrudgingly, Benson exhaled and she managed to finish zipping him up. The suit was indeed a bit snug. He wiggled around in it trying to find any extra room. But instead he found that the left shoulder joint was sticky and didn't want to go higher than forty-five degrees.

"Hey, my arm can't move all the way."

"It just need oil."

"Great, do you have some?"

"No."

"Of course not. It was a silly question."

Mei slung on her backpack life-support unit and cinched down the straps before hooking up the trio of hoses that connected to the front of the suit. Benson followed suit, and immediately felt cool air circulating inside the tight confines.

"How many times have you gone outside?" Benson asked.

Mei shrugged. "Many. Whenever we need to move between the modules. Sometimes we go outside just to watch the stars."

It explained how they'd gotten around security. Only a smattering of external cameras studded the hull for maintenance inspections. They were equipped with floodlights, which would make them easy to avoid for anyone walking around in the dark.

Benson had realized his gun wouldn't do much good zipped up inside his suit, so he fashioned a lanyard and tied one end to the trigger guard and the other to the suit's belt. Not that he could actually fit a gloved finger inside the trigger guard to fire the gun, but if push came to shove, he could jam a stylus inside the guard to pull the trigger.

The helmet was the last piece of Benson's suit to put in place. The top of his scalp pushed up against the inside of the helmet, matting his hair flat against his skull.

"This was built for somebody ten centimeters shorter than me."

"You complain too much."

She turned away and ambled towards the small maintenance lock, her usual feline grace lost inside the cumbersome suit. Benson followed in his bouncy, halting way. Someone had long ago spliced through the lock's control panel to avoid tripping any alarms. Mei spun open the inner door, and before Benson had the chance to talk himself out of it, pumps had pulled out all of the air. His suit popped and crinkled like an inflating balloon as it swelled in the vacuum, sending little waves of fear through him. But the suit's integrity held, even the duct-taped elbow, although Benson intended to flex the joint as little as humanly possible.

The outer door opened and Mei signaled for him to step out. The suit had short-range radio coms built in, but using them could give away their presence, so Mei had given him a short run down of hand signals the Unbound used during their jaunts.

With a deep breath, Benson stepped out onto the small platform and back into infinity. It had enough space for one person, barely. Mei was already climbing towards the hub.

Benson, meanwhile, was busy beating back panic. From his perspective standing on a tiny metal grate bolted to the outside of Avalon's rear bulkhead, the entire universe was busy spinning along at three hundred and fifty kilometers an hour. The effects this had on his sense of balance and stomach were all too predictable.

With sweat already forming on his forehead, Benson shut his eyes and took deep, calming breaths. The sensation of spinning wildly through open space brought the memory of the EVA pod accident bubbling right back up to the surface. He turned around to face the outer hull, suddenly very interested in reading the serial numbers of each honeycomb composite tile.

Something tapped the top of his head. It was Mei's foot. Her face looked more impatient than concerned, but he couldn't blame her for that. The spacewalk to the secret entrance would already push the safety margins on their suit's endurance without time wasting freak outs.

Get it together, Bryan, he admonished himself. The ladder had no cage around it, but it did have a saw-tooth arresting rail running up the right hand side for a tether to hook to. Still, he'd prefer the claustrophobic maintenance tube on the inside to this.

Benson hooked one of his tethers to the safety rail, then followed Mei, keeping his eyes straight ahead. Every twenty meters, he had to stop to swap over his tether to the next length of rail. He very quickly came to look forward to these little breaks. Making the climb had been hard enough without almost forty extra kilos of equipment to lift up each rung. All the while, the aluminum foil still wrapped around his head shifted and chafed.

Mei scampered up the ladder with little apparent effort, pausing with annoyance to wait for Benson to catch up. Youth alone couldn't account for the difference. Maybe he really was getting fat.

It wasn't long before he fell into a rhythm as the
distance shed the kilos. He reached the top without
throwing an aneurism. Of course, the "top" was actually
the middle, which is where things got complicated. The
hub sat directly above their heads, spinning away at just
over one revolution per minute.

Mei made a "V" with her fingers and pointed at
her eyes, signaling him to watch her carefully. She'd
explained the procedure earlier as best she could, but
some things only made sense when you saw them.

Like Avalon's hull, every panel on the outside of the
Ark's spine was studded with at least one loop. They'd
been welded in place to serve as anchor points for the
men and drones building the Ark back in Earth orbit.

With one tether still attached to the safety rail, Mei
reached out ahead and snagged one of the approaching
loops, then deftly unhooked her other tether from the
safety rail an instant before the rotation took out the slack.

Benson swallowed hard as his turn came up. Even
though the hub wasn't moving by at the breakneck pace
of the outer hull, it still *seemed* plenty fast, and although
his effective weight up here was only a kilo or two, it still
wasn't zero. If he missed his mark, he could fall off into
empty space, albeit very slowly. By the time the Ark's
gravity pulled him back in again, he'd have been out of
air for quite a while. Mei had made sure to reinforce this
point in her little safety briefing. She'd watched a man
killed exactly that way less than a year ago.

Soon, Mei rotated out of sight, leaving Benson alone
with his fear. He picked a loop to shoot for and reached
out a tentative arm, but his sticky left shoulder kept him
from stretching to his full arm span.

"Figures." He forced the hobbled joint into position. He spotted another loop and tried again, and failed again. By now, Mei was cresting on the horizon, holding a finger to her wrist in the sign for, "Hurry up, you incompetent jerk."

Assuming third time lucky, Benson lunged at a loop, willing his arms longer to cover the last few centimeters. To his surprise, the carabiner hooked in as if he'd just caught the universe's largest fish.

"Yes!" he shouted in a moment of triumph, while completely forgetting to unhook the other tether from the safety rail. Benson could only watch in muted horror as the tethers snapped taut, until one of them inevitably failed with a tear he could hear through his suit.

Still connected to the module, he watched as the tether attached to the hub sped out of reach. The look on Mei's face as she passed was... clinically unimpressed.

"Of course the wrong one broke," Benson said to himself. "At least my luck remains consistent." Heart pounding, Benson unhooked his remaining tether from the safety rail and switched it to his good hand.

Before he had the chance to change his mind, Benson leapt clear of the ladder and crashed into the hub. His teeth snapped together from the jolt, and as soon as he hit the deck, he bounced and fell away again. His arms pinwheeling wildly, Benson screamed as if trying to propel himself back on sound waves alone before floating off into total silence forever.

With a last desperate flail, the carabiner clinked against a loop and hit home. Already at its full reach, the tether yanked Benson hard, stopping him dead.

"Fuck," was all he could think to say. Yet it felt

perfectly appropriate. Benson pulled himself back down along the tether and grabbed one of the anchors, then slowly worked his way hand over hand back around to Mei. Reunited, she led him further down the Ark's spine, methodically swapping tethers from one anchor point to the next.

Mei still had the two she'd started with, but Benson was down to one. Every time he unhooked his carabiner, a small electric shock of panic went through his body until it was firmly connected to the next loop.

Their progress was slow, to put it mildly, but eventually they reached the part of the engineering module commonly referred to as the Aviary. Surrounding them, a flock of enormous atmospheric shuttles, each a hundred meters long, laid belly-up to the stars where their ablative ceramic composite tiles had protected them from centuries of micro-meteor impacts and would soon protect them from the hellish heat of reentry through the atmosphere of Tao Ceti G. *Well, just entry*, Benson corrected himself.

The shuttles gave him something to focus on instead of just the deck. He could look at them without getting lost in the sea of stars beyond. They totaled a dozen, two of which hadn't weathered the long journey very well and would be used for spare parts. Enough redundancy had been built into the plan that the loss of two shuttles wasn't going to be catastrophic; indeed the twin habitats themselves had been a form of redundancy. If some disaster crippled one, humanity didn't have all of its eggs in one basket. A contingency plan existed to start the colony in the event half the population was lost to a meteor, plague, or mechanical failure.

That plan had been officially activated yesterday. No one, not the Ark's builders, or the eleven generations that followed, ever thought the calamity would come from one of their own.

"When did we become so naïve?" Benson asked. No one else could hear him. He didn't expect an answer.

Their pace quickened. The individual anchor points had been replaced by long, straight rails that they could hook their tethers to and slide from one to the next. Apparently, the people building the Ark had gotten just as fed up with the stupid loops as he had and came up with something more practical. They left the Aviary behind, crossed the maintenance hangars and the handful of EVA pods, and soon reached the bulbous compartment that housed the ship's twin fusion reactors and massive Helium-3 tanks.

The reactors were, thankfully, still there, but of the forty-eight tanks the journey had started with, only six remained. The rest had been jettisoned as they ran empty along the way with enough force to send them off on new headings. Every kilogram of unnecessary mass the ship shed along the way was a kilogram that didn't have to be decelerated at the other end, which meant more velocity could be built up back at the beginning of the trip. The enormous ablative cone that had protected the bow of the ship for so long would meet the same fate during the Flip.

Provided Benson could stop a lunatic from nuking what was left of humanity. No pressure.

By then, he was starting to feel the heat, literally. They were passing through an alley between two of the reactor's titanic radiator fins. Pressurized steam passed through thousands of meters of tubing, slowly radiating excess heat from the fusion process back out into space before condensing back into liquid to cycle through the system all over again. It was funny to think, but save for the donut-shaped stars at the heart of the reactors, the actual mechanics of the system would be familiar to any nineteenth-century train conductor.

Benson checked a small data monitor on his wrist and realized his cooling unit was working overtime to try to keep up. But even more worryingly, the monitor very casually mentioned that he had ten minutes of oxygen reserves left.

"A fucking alarm would have been nice!" he shouted into his helmet hard enough to hurt his ears. Benson took a deep breath to calm himself, then realized that was probably even worse. With a hard tug on the rail, he closed the gap between himself and Mei and grabbed her foot to get her attention, then pointed at his wrist screen.

She shook her head and pointed at her own wrist, then made an "OK" sign with her fingers. She raised her hand, then flipped the palm over and lowered it again, repeating this gesture slowly several times. It took Benson a moment to realize she was telling him to slow his breathing. Apparently, she thought they were close enough for his supply to last, if he was cautious.

Breathing shallow, Benson followed Mei as they left the reactor compartment behind. Ahead of them, the immense disk of the ship's pusher plate eclipsed all of the stars behind it. Benson felt like he was running out of superlatives, but nothing about any component of the Ark was small. Ahead of them, and much deeper than Benson had ever ventured into the ship's bowels, was their destination.

Behind the reactor module, deep storage loomed, but no one called it that. The few techs who ever had cause to come back here had dubbed it the Bomb Shelter. The space served as a repository for most of the hardware and construction materials being carried to seed the new colony, but its most important cargo was a repository of tens of thousands of nuclear bombs.

Mei unhooked from her rail and pushed off in a new direction. Benson's fingertips tingled from the diminishing oxygen, making it hard to unhook. Hopefully, they didn't have far to go.

Just off the main street of rails sat an odd, lumpy-looking structure about three meters tall and as many across, a sun-faded yellow that clashed against the uniform white of the hull. It looked out of place, almost parasitic sitting against the hull. It wasn't until Mei climbed on top of it and disappeared inside that Benson realized what it was: a lock, but not like any of the standard locks he'd ever seen. It looked like an afterthought, and maybe that's exactly what it was. A temporary lock set up by the builders to make their work easier, then forgotten as they moved on or ran out of time. That would explain why it wasn't on the security grid or any blueprints. The Ark was the most complex object mankind had ever built by a wide margin. Alterations and oversights along the way from paper to reality were inevitable.

Little shooting stars flew across Benson's field of vision, sending a fresh jolt of dread through him. For a fleeting, paranoid moment, he realized that if Mei had been playing some elaborate double cross, now would be a perfect time to just lock the door and leave him out in the cold, gasping like a freshly-landed fish.

Benson scrambled up the side of the temporary lock to get at the hatch. With a sigh of relief, he pulled the loose hatch open and slipped inside head first. It had enough room inside for himself, Mei, and maybe half a sandwich, so cramped that she had trouble spinning the hatch shut behind him.

His suit finally sent out a warning bell when his reserves had been completely depleted, but by then, Mei was already cycling the lock. Even as grey crept into the edges of his vision, Benson could feel the air rushing into the tiny compartment, deflating the shell of his suit as the pressure equalized. Benson wasted no time getting his helmet off and sucking down a big lungful of air the moment the light turned green. It was dry, stale, and tasted like an unsealed tomb, but he didn't care one bit. Mei tapped him with her foot and pointed at the inner hatch.

Benson spun it open and floated into the darkened space beyond. Weapon in hand, ready to face down a monster.

CHAPTER TWENTY-NINE

Benson didn't even know where to start. He'd never studied the schematics of the Bomb Shelter in any detail and had no idea where he was or where he should go.

He pulled off his suit's gloves and tossed them back in the lock with his helmet. Normally, he'd just pull up a map with his plant, but connecting to the network would give away his position to the floaters before he was ready.

"Mei, can you show me where they are?"

She shook her head. "I not go so far before."

Benson sighed. *Figures, no map and a blind guide.* "OK, you stay by the lock. If anyone comes by, hide. Agong probably isn't going to be happy to see you, and I don't want you to get hurt."

She didn't offer up a fight. He'd hoped she wouldn't. Benson reached out for her wrist and brought the young woman into a bulky hug, like two people wearing sumo suits.

"Thank you, Mei. You've been so brave already. I'll take it from here, OK?"

He let her go and pushed off down the small corridor nestled between the double-hulls.

"Benson-san!" Mei called out. He flinched and put a

finger to his lips, pleading with her to lower her voice.

She held a hand over her belly and gently rubbed at the tiny life growing inside her, completely unaware of the drama playing out that would decide its fate.

"Stop him," she whispered. "Please."

Benson pulled the FN free of its lanyard and slipped the handle into his palm.

"Count on it."

He decided that without a map any old hatch was as good as another. Benson had a basic understanding of the Bomb Shelter's layout. Very basic. Essentially, the vault was nothing more than a giant magazine designed to feed bombs through barrels at the center of each of the Ark's three dozen shock absorbers, themselves each fifteen hundred meters long, and out the back of the pusher plate.

Magnetic conveyor belts cycled the nukes into electromagnetic railguns at the top of each shock absorber, which then fired the bomb through a small aperture in the plate itself. Only three bombs detonated with each cycle, giving each railgun a full twelve cycles to cool down, recharge, and reload before firing again. This way, ablative wear on the pusher plate remained evenly distributed.

But as far as the actual internal layout of the mechanisms went, Benson was in the dark. Quite literally, since none of the lights were on. Here and there, a small display or status light cast a red or amber glow across the thin corridors, reminding Benson of every low-budget sci-fi horror movie he'd ever seen, leaving his lizard-brain to fill every dark corner with scaly alien monsters and decomposing zombies. It wasn't helping his heart rate.

Neither was the heat. Despite the bone dry air, the temperature was stifling. Heat bleeding through from both the reactor compartment and the radiator fins outside kept the bomb shelter cooking, but since few people ever came here, little point existed to spend energy cooling the air down.

Benson soon felt like a plump carrot trapped in a vegetable steamer. He wished he'd just taken the entire suit off and left it back at the lock with Mei. Fortunately, one of the suit's few positives was an LED spotlight built into the chest piece. Turning it on risked giving away his position to Kimura and his men, but short of evolving night vision in the next handful of minutes, he didn't see an alternative.

Still unsure of exactly what he was looking for, Benson switched on the light and illuminated the hallway. At the far end, just before the curve cut of his line of sight, he saw the body floating limply in the corridor dressed in the gray and blue uniform of the maintenance crew. A bright slash of blood clung to the dead man's chest due to the surface tension.

"Well," Benson said to himself. "This is the place." Quietly, he floated up to the hatch adjacent to where the body floated. He span the hatch unlocked and, very gently, pushed it open, trying not to let a squeaky hinge announce his presence in the deathly silence. Peering into the compartment beyond, he had to muffle a gasp.

Hundreds, no, thousands of perfectly spherical nuclear bombs, each little bigger than a beach ball, sat in a stacked queue waiting for their turn. It was like looking inside the gumball machine of the apocalypse, and this section was only one of thirty-six identical compartments.

However, it was the first one down the hall from the temporary lock he'd arrived through, and as it happened, was also the first one Kimura and his two henchmen had found. They hovered around a single nuke, dislodged from the queue and wired up to a tablet. Alerted by the noise of the hatch spinning open, the same three people stared up at Benson with looks that were, in order of appearance, surprise, admiration, and rage.

Quickly, Benson flicked on his plant's video capture feature to start recording, set it to stream onto an open, unencrypted public channel, then pulled off the aluminum foil hat from his head.

"Detective!" Kimura called out with genuine enthusiasm. "Welcome."

"It's just Bryan, now, *David*."

<Benson!> The voice exploded through his mind as if one of the nukes had suddenly gone off. Benson actually winced as Commander Feng continued to shout through his plant. <What the hell do you think you're doing?>

<My fucking job, Chao!>

<But this is streaming on a public feed. There'll be mass panic!>

<If you don't get some of my constables down here fast, there won't *be* anything, period.>

<Fine, but don't touch anyth–> Benson cut the link.

"Trouble, Bryan?"

"Just a little headache. You're not going to be so happy when you hear what I have to say."

"Oh, I expect I know already. You're here to stop the madman from stealing a nuke and bringing his evil plan to fruition."

Benson shrugged. "Something like that. I had a talk

with Mei, I know the lies you've been telling these people."

Kimura, still wearing a full suit complete with custom helmet, waved his hand dismissively. "There's nothing more subjective than the Truth, my son. My people have done very well following their own."

"*Your* own, Kimura. You've been filling them with hot air about their destiny as the chosen, or whatever. Maybe you've kept them isolated and naïve enough for them to believe it, but you know damned well that a few dozen people don't stand a chance of starting a new colony. You don't have the labor force, or the genetic diversity to make it work. You're only leading them to extinction."

Kimura glared at him for a long moment, then shook the tablet in his hand at him. "Good show, my lad, trying to turn these two against me at the eleventh hour. But the trouble is, they already know."

"What?" Benson was genuinely shocked. He looked at the faces of the others and saw only determination. In a flicker of recognition, he realized they were the same two men he'd played cribbage with before his first meeting with Kimura. They knew they were going to die, but were helping him anyway?

Kimura evidently decided the conversation had gone on long enough and barked something at his goons in Japanese. Each man drew a knife from their waistbands and pointed the tips at the intruder. On command, they turned on Benson like a pair of angry pitbulls and pushed off hard.

Working off instincts honed on the Zero field, Benson sized up their speed and trajectories in an instant and pushed off at an oblique angle to their flight path that would leave him just out of arm's reach. But then they surprised him. The closer man rotated ninety degrees until he was perpendicular to his partner, then pushed off him and straight into Benson's new flight path.

Without access to the stadium, Benson had assumed that the Unbound would wallow around in micro like children learning to swim, but the clever move proved he had severely underestimated them. These men flew well, they knew how to work as a team, and both of them were free of their bulky suits.

Caught off guard and with almost no time to react, Benson pointed the muzzle of his gun at the man barreling at him with an outstretched knife and a face twisted with adrenaline and hate.

With a jerky pull of the trigger and a flash, Benson fired the shot heard around the Ark. The sharp *snap* of the gun's report was instantly replaced by a ringing in his ears, while the recoil sent him spinning as though someone had punched him in the chest.

Benson's arms and legs flailed as he tried to halt the unexpected spin until he struck the far wall like a sack of potatoes. The suit's layers absorbed most of the shock of impact, but the ringing in his ears remained. A metallic, almost sweet smell filled his nostrils as he scanned the compartment for the different threats.

The second goon had been pushed to the far side of the compartment by the midair maneuver, while the man Benson had shot had drifted into the ceiling. He floated near a corner, whimpering softly, curled up in a ball with his hands pressed tightly to his shoulder while droplets of crimson hovered around him. His knife hung in the air, out of reach.

Just above the threshold of the ringing in his ears, Benson heard a *tink* as the spent brass cartridge reached a wall and bounced off.

For a moment, nobody said or did anything, as if the gunshot had cast a sort of spell. Kimura was the first to break free of it.

"Where did you get that?"

"From a friend." Benson decided the other man was too far away to pose a legitimate threat and trained the gun on Kimura. "It's a loaner."

Kimura only chuckled and held up his tablet. "I'm afraid you've brought a gun to a nuclear bomb fight."

<Chief!> Feng's voice broke through again. <We can't hack his pad. It's entirely offline, and so is the nuke!>

<Oh, so now it's chief again?>

<Just stop him!>

Benson returned his attention to the crisis in front of him. "I wouldn't underestimate this gun. The last time some idiot fired this thing, sixteen million people died," he said, echoing Devorah's words again. They had a nice ring to them. Weighty. "David Kimura, you are under arrest for sabotage, the terrorist attack on Shangri-La, the death of Chief Constable Vikram Bahadur, the murder of Edmond Laraby, and a shit-ton of other things. Let go of the tablet and push away from the bomb, or I'll be forced to shoot."

Kimura glanced at the tablet, then folded his hands behind his back. "Do your duty, constable."

This time, Benson was ready for the shot. With his off hand, he grabbed a frame member to steady himself from the recoil and took extra time to line up the simple sights. He aimed for Kimura's center mass, and pulled the trigger.

The tiny copper and lead slug tore through the air at hundreds of kilometers an hour, covering the handful of meters between the two men in the blink of an eye. It struck Kimura in the abdomen, lower than Benson had aimed for, but he crumpled around the hit regardless.

But then, to Benson's horror, Kimura straightened out, pulled the flattened bullet out of the fabric of his suit… and smiled.

"An excellent shot, Bryan, but you forget that these suits are rated for micrometeorites up to a millimeter." He let the squashed bullet float in front of him, then pulled out the tablet and let his finger hover over the button. "Your pebbles aren't going to cut it."

"David, just stop. You're going to end everything."

"Everything?" Kimura shook his head. "What an egocentric statement. Everything will be just fine. A single, insignificant mote of dust will be destroyed, and the universe won't even notice."

"I'll notice! Everyone I know will notice. Everyone I love will notice. And the memories of everyone you've already killed will notice. Not to mention the half million people we've lost along the way, and the souls of the ten billion we left behind." Benson pointed at his head. "We're *all* watching you right now."

Kimura smirked. "Streaming this, are you? You're more clever than I gave you credit for."

"You're not the first."

"No, but I'll be the last. Here you are, vilified and derided by your betters, yet still you do their bidding. It's sad, really."

"I'm doing no one's bidding. I'm doing my job."

"Yes? Did you know your job is to maintain a lie?

Maybe you deserve to know, maybe everyone does."

An error message appeared in Benson's vision. His plant's live stream had just been cut. Benson's heart sank. Someone knew what Kimura was about to say, and despite the impending Armageddon, still wanted to keep the cattle in the dark.

"I'm not killing anyone, Officer Benson, because we're all ghosts. This grand project, this final rage against the dying of the light, was the last gasp of human folly. We were destined to die with our home."

Benson adjusted the grip on his gun. "Start making sense or I'll shoot you just for the satisfaction of it."

Kimura gave a curt bow. "Nibiru, the black hole that swallowed our home, wasn't some cosmic accident. It was sent by God."

If anyone had still been watching his live stream, they would have seen Benson's eyes roll like stones trying to shrug off a moss infestation. "That's all you have? Really? The same crackpot nonsense spouted by every pseudo-messiah for the last three centuries?"

"They didn't know what I do, they merely guessed. Nibiru changed course to hit Earth. Twice."

Despite the heat, Benson's veins filled with ice as the full implications of what Kimura said set in. A black hole couldn't alter course, unless something was acting on it. Controlling it? But that meant Earth died, billions died, as part of someone's plan. A deliberate act of genocide.

"That's impossible," Benson said.

"For mere mortals, yes. But God?" Kimura turned up his palms and shrugged. "It's been known that Nibiru couldn't have occurred naturally for centuries. It was created artificially, to be a weapon."

"You're lying."

"I can assure you, I'm not. The course changes were known even before the Ark launched, but were classified top secret and buried as deep as anything could be. "

"Even if that's true, it doesn't prove that some god, or *the* God was responsible. It could have been, I don't know, aliens."

"Is the distinction important? All we have to know is an intelligence with powers beyond our comprehension decreed that our time was over. Put whatever label on it you like, it won't change the facts." Kimura lifted the tablet. "Now that you know, there's no more reason to delay the inevitable."

Benson's hand clamped down on the gun so hard it was starting to cramp. "But you're going to murder an entire race!"

Kimura shook his head. "No, Bryan. I'm saving one."

"What do you mean?"

"I'm sorry."

With nothing left to lose, Benson aimed for the tablet itself and emptied the magazine with five shots in rapid succession. The first shot struck Kimura low in the torso, again. The second hit the shell of the nuke itself, while the last three missed entirely. But the tablet was safe. As Benson let out a battle cry and launched towards the older man with all of his strength, Kimura composed himself and pushed the icon.

Benson saw a blinding flash. Then the world went black.

CHAPTER THIRTY

The first thing he noticed was the smell. Antiseptics mixed with burnt hair, and worse. Slowly, other sensations pierced the fog surrounding Benson's consciousness. Pain, for one, in his hands, neck, and face. And the ringing all around him, like standing between the tines of a giant tuning fork.

He opened his eyes, but only the right field of vision responded, and blurry at that. He tried to raise an arm to wave a hand in front of his left eye, but it felt like an anchor held it down to the bed. A bed! He was in Sickbay... again.

A shadow fell over his face. Benson tried to turn and see who it was, but his neck wouldn't respond. Frightened, he tried to call out, but he couldn't hear his own words. Just an intense ringing that seemed to come from every direction at once.

<It's all right, Bryan. It's Jeanine. I'm right here.> Her voice in his head was like a calming lullaby. <We really need to stop meeting like this. People might start getting suspicious.>

<I'm not dead?> Benson asked incredulously.

<No, but looking at the state you're in, you get an 'A' for effort.>

<The ship?>

<It's fine, Bryan. We're all fine, thanks to you.>

<I can't move.>

<That's the anesthetics doing their job. You're being prepped for surgery. I'm surprised you woke up at all. You're swimming in enough tranquilizers to drop a horse.>

His vision cleared up enough that he could recognize the general outline of Jeanine's face. She was smiling, but it masked deep worry. Benson steeled himself for the next question.

<How bad is it?>

She rubbed her mouth before answering.

<The good news is your suit protected you from the worst of the explosion. It absorbed most of the shrapnel and radiation. Both of your eardrums were punctured from the overpressure, which is why you can't hear. Your left eye took a shard and will need to be replaced, and you have first and second degree burns on your hands and most of your face. You also won't be in need of a haircut for a few months. There are... deeper injuries, especially to your lungs. The shockwave ruptured a lot of alveoli, so their capacity is way down and you have a lot of fluid build-up. For the moment, we're oxygenating your blood to make up the difference until they heal, but we're going to have to watch you for blood clots for quite a while. You also inhaled more than your recommended daily allowance of plutonium, so we're getting a batch of nanites ready to scrub it out.>

<But, how am I alive at all? It was a damned *nuke*, and I wasn't even twenty meters from it.>

<It didn't go nuclear. Somebody said it was a dud.

You'll have to ask one of the tech geeks about that. It's not really my field. But we really have to get you into surgery now.>

<No, wait! I need you to do two things first.>

<OK,> she said expectantly.

<First, tell Lieutenant Alexopoulos there's a tablet in my desk drawer. Have her bring it down here for when I wake up. And second...>

This time, Benson awoke to the smell of apple blossoms.

Vases filled with flowers and other gifts from throngs of grateful fans and admirers filled every available surface of the recovery room. Two days had passed since his showdown with Kimura, and it was another day before the good doctor would allow any visitors through the door. He spent the extra day reviewing the tablet that Theresa had liberated from his desk and getting caught up on the fallout of his confrontation with Kimura, or at least the version of events approved for public consumption.

Kimura was *very* dead. He was less than a meter away from the center of the explosion. His suit had protected him from bullets, but against a dozen kilos of high explosives and an open visor, it only managed to keep most of his odds and ends in one place. His henchmen had fared better in the short term, but they were going to survive just long enough to be put on trial for the deaths of twenty thousand people and promptly executed anyway.

Apparently, quite a queue had formed to rub elbows with the hero of the day. Fortunately, Benson got to assign priority to the list. The door opened gently, and the moment Benson had both longed for and dreaded for three days had come.

"Hello, Esa."

Theresa walked slowly into the room. She swallowed hard as she took in the extent of Benson's injuries. She didn't gasp or cry, but it was obvious the sight shook her to the core. Shame welled up in Benson's gut. He regretted asking her to come before he'd recovered more fully. Not that she couldn't handle seeing his condition, but she shouldn't have to.

Very gently, Theresa took his bandaged hand in hers and gave it a little squeeze. The pain was immediate, but Benson suppressed a grimace. It was worth a little discomfort to feel her touch.

"You look good, Bryan." Her voice sounded tinny to Benson's ears, mostly because he wasn't hearing with his ears. For now, a pair of temporary implants were dumping an audio feed directly into his plant until his ruptured eardrums had time to heal properly.

Benson gave a dry little cough. "I look like a Friday night fish fry."

"The doctor says it's mostly superficial."

Benson chuckled. "Just like me, huh?"

"That's just the Zero Hero talking. But I know your secret."

"Oh yeah, what's that?"

She touched the side of his face. "You go a lot deeper."

"Believe me, no one was more surprised than me," Benson smiled, and promptly cracked his lower lip open.

"Oh God. Here, let me get that." Theresa dabbed the blood away with a piece of gauze from the tray next to his bed. "Actually, I lied. You're a mess."

"Lucky you, huh?"

"Yeah," she said softly. "Very."

"Well, you won't have to worry about competition. They're not going to be lining up for me for a while."

"I wouldn't count on that. You're a hero, Bryan. Maybe the biggest ever."

Benson changed the subject. "How's Korolev? He didn't get in trouble for letting me in, did he?"

Theresa leaned back. "Hasn't anyone told you? Pavel pulled you out of the room. He ignored Director Hekekia's direct order to do it, too. He got a lungful of radiation for his trouble."

Benson's blood went cold. "Is he OK?"

"He's resting in his apartment. They pumped him full of the same nanobots clearing out your lungs."

"Tough kid. I owe him one."

"We both do." Theresa put her hand on his bandaged cheek, then kissed him, careful not to aggravate his injuries, but not repulsed by them either. Benson felt himself get lost in it.

"I love you," she whispered.

"Because I came back?"

"Because you do what you say you're going to do." She smiled. "Even when you say you're going to do something stupid."

"I love you too. Now, get ready for one more stupid thing."

Theresa eyed him suspiciously. "What are you up to?"

"I need you to call the captain and tell her to get down here. There's something she's going to want to see in about fifteen minutes. You should stick around, too."

Theresa shook her head and smiled. "You're going to make all of this up to me."

"Count on it."

Theresa kissed him on the cheek. "Don't take too long to recover, hero." She winked, then walked back out the way she came, her hips gently swaying as she left. As he waited for his next visitor, Benson took a small measure of pride that not even getting blown up could dent his sex drive.

Commander Chao Feng passed through the door and gazed around the small recovery room, as if looking for an explanation for why he'd been summoned.

"Commander," Benson said, in a raspy voice. His mouth was dry from some of the medications, and he was still getting his fluids intravenously. "Thank you for coming."

"Thank you for inviting me, detective. Honestly, I was surprised to get the invite, considering everything that's happened over the last couple weeks."

"Don't mention it. We both jumped to some faulty conclusions, wouldn't you say?"

Feng snorted. "Yes, I guess you could say that. Mistakes we've both paid for."

"I'm sorry about your wife."

A sad sigh escaped his mouth. "She's at peace now, and our son is safe. I have you to thank, but I'd rather not talk about her right now."

"I understand." Benson coughed a dry little cough. "Actually, I'm not sure you can thank me for it. From what I hear, the bomb was a dud anyway. I only managed to land myself in the burn ward."

Feng shook his head. "Not exactly, chief. We recovered your plant's recording of everything that happened after the feed was cut. One of your shots hit the device's casing and left a dent in the shell of high-explosives around the plutonium core. It wasn't much, but the techs tell me the deformation was enough to make the implosion trigger fail, which is why the bomb didn't go critical."

"I was aiming for his tablet. You mean I *accidentally* saved the human race?"

"So it would appear. Although you might want to leave that part out of the official record."

"Appearances to maintain?"

Feng shrugged. "It makes a more… satisfying narrative. A falsely accused man and an infamous gun both find redemption in a defining moment of heroism."

The FN. Benson had almost forgotten about it. "I assume the handgun found its way back, ah, home?"

"It's back in Curator Feynman's hands, yes. Although she wanted me to ask 'Did he really need to use *all* the bullets?'"

Benson smirked through cracked lips. There really was no pleasing some people.

"She's not in trouble for springing me, is she?"

"It's hard to argue with results. The public would not be pleased."

"I imagine not. How's the ship? I haven't seen anything official in the news feeds."

"Surprisingly good, actually. The feed belt in the compartment you were in was wrecked, and a few dozen bombs were too damaged to use, but the shock absorber assembly is intact. Hekekia has already written a new firing pattern to account for the lost railgun. And as sad as it is to say, all the mass we shed from losing Shangri-La's atmosphere and lake means we actually have spare bomb capacity, even considering the ones we lost in the explosion."

Benson's face darkened as he remembered Bahadur.

"Small favors, huh?"

"Indeed. Detective, may I ask, how did you know Kimura's plan?"

Benson shrugged his shoulders. "I didn't, really. It just made sense, so I played a hunch and got lucky."

"We all did, it seems."

"What happens to the rest of Kimura's people?"

"That's... a difficult question. Your young friend Mei led us to their hiding spot. She's already received a full pardon for her cooperation, you'll be happy to know. But the rest of them..." Feng shook his head. "Without plant data, we're going to have a devil of a time sorting out who's responsible for what, and to what degree. It's going to be a while before we have any closure. The trials will probably have to wait until after we make landing."

"I understand. Also, I want amnesty for my people. Alexopoulos and Korolev were working under my orders."

Feng nodded. "Of course. You've also been reinstated as Avalon's chief constable. When you're back on your feet, naturally."

"Might have to be sooner than you think."

Feng cocked an eyebrow. "Oh?"

"I have one more hunch to test. Is my next visitor outside?"

"I think so."

Benson sat up in his bed as much as he could manage. "Good, send them in. Oh, and I'm leaving my plant feed open for anyone who wants to eavesdrop."

Feng nodded a silent understanding and headed for the door.

"Chao, wait," Benson called after him as the doors slid open. "Edmond was the hero in all this. He figured it all out by himself. I just picked up where he left off. I couldn't have done it without him."

Feng's mouth quivered. "That hadn't occurred to me. Thank you."

"You're welcome. Are we cool?"

Feng nodded. "Yes, Bryan, we're cool. I'll send her in." The door clicked shut behind him.

Benson took as deep a breath as he could considering the state of his lungs, then exhaled slowly. Oddly, he felt no thrill or satisfaction about the coming confrontation, but it had to be done.

Director Avelina Pereira da Silva swept into the room, carried by an easy grace that had only been enhanced by her age.

"Bryan!" She fell to his chest and hugged him tightly.

"Careful on the lungs, please."

"Of course, I'm sorry." She stood back up. "Forgive me, but everyone's been more than a little emotional lately."

"Oh, I understand, believe me."

She tucked a lock of silver-streaked hair back behind her ear. "I'm surprised I was so high on your list of visitors."

"You shouldn't be. We have a conversation to finish."

"We do?" Her voice wavered so slightly, Benson wasn't sure he'd heard it at all.

"Yes, about Edmond." Benson held up his tablet. "I've been going back over his work logs, trying to figure out why Kimura wanted him killed."

The air in the room dropped a degree. "You have his work files? I thought they were all destroyed in the sabotage."

Benson nodded. "So did I, but then I remembered this tablet. It wasn't connected to the net when the attack happened, so one copy survived."

"Well…" Her face changed from apprehension to excitement. "That's great news. I'd thought we were going to have to rerun all of his experiments. This will save us months of work." She reached out to grab the tablet, but Benson pulled it back.

"I'm sorry, but it's evidence, and the investigation is still active until all of Kimura's people have stood trial."

Da Silva pulled her hand back. "I see. Of course you're right. But if I could have a copy, at least?"

Benson nodded. "Yes, naturally. I'll upload a copy to the lab's server as soon as we're done here."

"That won't be necessary," she reassured him. "I prefer to compartmentalize my team, otherwise some of the younger techs get ambitious and we end up duplicating efforts. Just send it to my personal address. I'm sure you understand."

Benson smiled. "Of course I do. I've read a lot of his personal files, too. He really looked up to you, did you know that?"

"I–" She choked up for a moment and swallowed hard. "I didn't know that."

"Oh yes, almost like a mother figure, it seems. He loved working for you."

She nodded. "He was one of my best techs."

"In fact, the only thing he seemed to think about more was this 'Atlantis' obsession."

"Yes, you mentioned that before." A trace of impatience crept into da Silva's tone, but Benson plowed on as if he hadn't noticed.

"I wouldn't have thought anymore of it if it wasn't for something David Kimura said right before he blew himself up."

Her posture straightened. "What did he say?"

"Well, I was begging him not to kill an entire race when he said the strangest thing. He said, 'I'm saving one.'" Benson threw up his bandaged hands in exasperation. "Can you imagine? At first I thought he was spouting some crap about atoning for our sins, or whatever. But then I started thinking about Atlantis. I'd assumed it was just another word for a lost continent, but then it hit me. Atlantis wasn't just a continent, it was home to an advanced race. A race that disappeared."

"Yes, I suppose that's true." She walked over to the small rollaway table next to his bed that he ate off and picked up a water pitcher. "Your lips look dry, Bryan. Can I get you a glass of water?"

"Yes, please," he said.

Avelina smiled down at him and turned her back to pour the water. "You were saying, Bryan? About Atlantis?"

"Right, yes. So, I wondered if Edmond had found something on Tau Ceti G, or more to the point, someone."

She turned back around clutching a glass and held it out to him. "Here, take a sip."

Benson held up his mummified hands and shrugged. "Skin grafts. Do you mind?"

Avelina smiled warmly. "Of course not. Here, sit up." She reached around to cradle the back of his head and held the glass up to his parched lips. The cool water reached his tongue and he gulped it down greedily.

"Whoa, not so fast," she said maternally. "You'll make yourself sick."

Benson's expression hardened. "That's the idea, isn't it?"

"What do you mean?" Avelina held out the glass, encouraging him to take another sip.

With his one good eye, Benson locked onto her face like a missile. "The water tastes strange."

She shrugged off the comment. "Well, you know what they say about hospital food."

"That it's laced with puffer fish poison?"

Avelina froze, then stood and poured the rest of the glass down the sink. "What do you mean?" she asked over her shoulder.

"I know it was you," Benson said flatly.

Avelina crossed her arms. "I don't like what you're insinuating, Mr Benson."

"I'm not insinuating anything. I know the truth."

Her face softened and she laid a gentle hand on his shoulder. "I think the stress of the last few days has left you confused, Bryan. You should rest. We can talk more about this later."

"Oh, trust me, we'll have the chance," Benson said. "Because I had Dr Russell whip up a dose of TTX antidote before you came in. It's busy neutralizing the poison you just fed me as we speak. Did you hope they'd think I'd just succumbed to my injuries? You don't know Dr Russell very well if you think she'd skip an autopsy." Benson coughed from the strain of speaking. "The game is over, Avelina, unless you're prepared to smother me with a pillow, but I don't think getting your hands dirty is your style."

All of the built up tension released from Avelina's body as she collapsed into the chair next to Benson's bed.

"It's not. Never could find the stomach for it. I spend a lifetime ripping organisms apart and putting them back together at the molecular level, but I can't stand the sight of blood. Isn't that funny?" She chuckled, fighting against the tears welling up in her eyes. "How did you figure it out?"

"I had a couple days to read Edmond's work log. He never worked on the puffer fish toxin. That was your project. You tried to pawn it off on him after you thought his work files were erased to throw off suspicion. Files you destroyed while the power was down after Kimura sabotaged the reactors and all the security nets were down. But you didn't know about my copy, no one did."

Benson leaned back on his bed. "From there, it wasn't hard to guess you were coordinating with Kimura. We already knew a high-ranking crew member was helping him. Someone with a lot of network permissions and coding expertise. The only thing I can't figure out is *why*? That boy loved you, Avelina. Like a mother. Why kill him?"

Tears ran down Avelina's cheeks. "Because he said no."

"To what, Avelina?"

"To saving Atlantis." She shook her head and wiped away tears. "I tried to get him to stop, but he just wouldn't let it go. He was like a little pitbull. Maybe that's why he was so good at his job."

"What's Atlantis?" Benson asked harshly.

Avelina sniffled. "You said it. There's already a sentient race on Tau Ceti G, and we're about to kick down their door."

Benson swallowed hard, committing himself to the next question.

"Who else knows?"

She laughed through the tears. "The senior command crew, most of the division heads. Everyone who's anyone. We've known since Pathfinder made orbit. As soon as we had scopes in the high orbitals, we could see the grids of their villages, plain as day."

Loose strands connected in Benson's mind. "All of them on the Dark Continent. Which is where the unexplained storm came from, and why the landing shuttle crashed mysteriously."

Avelina nodded affirmation. "The storm doesn't exist, it's a cover up. There was never anything wrong with the shuttle or the drones. We've been watching the Atlantians for months. They live in unfired mud-brick buildings, but they're a beautiful, artistic, spiritual people. Do you know they built a temple around one of our rovers? The poor fools have been bringing it offerings and making little animal sacrifices."

The final connection fell into place. "And you conspired with Kimura to protect them from us, by destroying the Ark," Benson said. "As soon as you realized Edmond had figured it out, you tried to recruit him into your circle, but he refused, didn't he? He was going to blow the lid off everything and the only way to silence him was to kill him."

Avelina was sobbing freely by then. "He was too young to understand the truth."

"What truth?" Benson shouted. Fresh blood trickled down his cracked lips. "What truth could justify genocide?"

"Preventing genocide!" She screamed hard enough that even Benson wanted to sink into his bed and disappear.

"Don't you get it? Humans are fallen monsters. Are there any Neanderthals on this ship? Every single time we faced off against a weaker hominid, we eradicated it. When we ran out of other hominids, we turned on our own tribes. And when we were powerful enough, we turned on the whole of Earth." She stood and dug an angry finger into her chest.

"*We* were the Sixth Extinction, Bryan. Not a supervolcano, or an asteroid, or a plague. Just one shortsighted, greedy, selfish species. We killed the Earth decades before God sent Nibiru to erase His mistake." She made the old sign of the cross on her chest, then paced around the small room like a stalking predator.

"For the longest time, I thought this journey was supposed to be our atonement. A second voyage aboard the Ark. But we weren't meant to survive at all. God already started a Second Genesis on a world that should have been beyond our ability to corrupt."

"We're not dead yet, Avelina."

"That's the problem!" she howled. "Don't you see? We're destroyers. We'd use our technology to eradicate the Atlantians. Just like the American Indians and the Australian Aborigines. How many examples do you need, Bryan? And you almost ruined it. Don't you see? This has to be done."

"I'm afraid I've already ruined it." Benson pointed at the door. On cue, it slid open and Captain Mahama stepped through, flanked by two constables, including Theresa.

Understanding dawned as Avelina saw the constables. "You were streaming the whole time."

"Yes, I was."

Theresa stepped forward and grabbed Avelina by the elbow. "Director da Silva, I'm placing you under arrest for conspiring with the terrorist David Kimura, as an accomplice to the murder of Edmond Laraby, the death of Chief Bahadur, the attempted murder of Chief Constable Benson, twice, sabotage, and…" She consulted her tablet. "A whole bunch of other charges. Your rights will be uploaded to your plant before questioning begins."

Avelina offered her wrists to be placed in the cuffs without resistance.

"You've damned us all," she said quietly.

Benson only shrugged. "We've spent the last two centuries learning how to live within our means. I think we might be ready to stand on our own, without the help of gods."

She drew herself to her full height. "And who will stand up for the Atlantians?" she asked.

"I will," Benson answered. "And the humans, and anyone who stands on the right side of the law. Because that's my job, and I'm good at my job. I'm sorry you won't be around to help, I really am." He jerked his head to let Theresa know he'd finished.

"Goodbye, Avelina."

Theresa beamed down at him, then led da Silva out and the doors slid shut, leaving Benson and Captain Mahama alone.

Mahama was the first to break the silence.

"Thank you."

"I didn't do it for you," Benson said gloomily.

"Of course not. Still, you have honored your line. No one suspected da Silva, not even me. You seem to have a unique insight into the workings of the criminal mind.

Maybe that's an important trait we overlooked in our... zeal for perfection."

Benson snorted. "Takes a thief to catch a thief, is that it?"

"Or the grandson of a thief, at least. Take the compliment as it was intended."

"Captain, I have to know. Is what she said about the Atlantians true? Is there a sentient race already living on Tau Ceti G?"

"Yes."

Her blunt, unequivocal affirmation caught Benson off guard. He'd expected yet another wall of obfuscation.

"And what Kimura said about Nibiru? Was it sent after us by some... supreme being?"

"I can't speak to the supreme part, but yes. It was guided to Earth by someone."

A very bad feeling passed through Benson, like something walking over his grave.

"Why are you telling me this now?"

Mahama pulled out the small guest chair in the corner and sat down before collecting herself to answer.

"Because I, and the rest of the senior command staff, have decided it's time to stop keeping secrets. For a very long time, well before I was born, we thought we had everything under control. But the shouting of twenty thousand dead is enough to wake even the deepest sleeper. Our secrets nearly destroyed everything. Which is why your entire conversation with Avelina, and our conversation right now, has been allowed to stream freely, unedited and uncensored, to the entire ship. We're also going to declassify all of the data Pathfinder has collected on Atlantis."

Benson tried to whistle, but his lips weren't quite up to the task.

"That's a bold move," he said instead.

"An overdue one, it seems."

Benson pushed himself up onto his elbows. "And what about these people who sent the Hole after us?"

"Well, as you've already pointed out, we've learned to live… more quietly these last ten generations."

"And if they find our forwarding address?"

Captain Mahama stood and inspected one of the vases of apple blossoms.

"Progress hasn't stopped these last two centuries. Circumstances put a ceiling on what we can implement, but that hasn't prevented us from making plans. Inventions and devices that were merely theoretical when we left have run through many generations of testing and refinement in virtual space. An entire navy of ships already exist digitally that make the Ark look like a steamboat by comparison. They're only waiting for us to build up the industrial capacity to construct them. Within a century, we'll jump off from Tau Ceti G and spread across the galaxy like wildfire."

Benson snorted. "Ready to go toe to toe with aliens who throw singularities around like billiard balls?"

"Maybe, maybe not. But we'll never let ourselves be limited to one planet, one point of failure again. We've been awoken to that risk."

"Who's going to wake the Atlantians? They didn't ask to be put in God's crosshairs, you know."

Mahama held out her palms. "We're taking applications."

Benson fell back on his pillow and shook his head.

"Don't look at me. I'm taking five years' worth of unused leave."

Mahama turned and strode towards the door. "And well deserved it is. I won't keep you from it any longer. Rest well, chief. I have a feeling you're going to need it."

ACKNOWLEDGMENTS

Writing a novel often feels like a solitary endeavor, but that is an illusion. Every author builds around them a group of like-minded, supportive friends and family to help them manage the expectations, excitement, wild moods swings, bouts of alcoholism, and existential crises.

More than once over the last few years, I've had those "What the hell am I doing," moments. Without the patience and support of my girlfriend, Niki, I may have given into them. *The Ark* is as much a product of her stubbornness as it is mine.

I'd also like to thank my good friends and beta readers, Michael Todd Gallowglas and Bradley P Beaulieu, for their insights and confidence in the project as well as myself. I'd also like to thank my amazing agent, Russell Galen, for taking the chance on a debut writer, his tireless work finding it a place to call home, and his patience helping me navigate the turbulent and unfamiliar waters of the publishing industry.

Speaking of publishers, I'd be remiss if I didn't thank my crack team at Angry Robot, including Penny Reeve, Michael R Underwood, Phil Jourdan, and Marc Gascoigne for their boundless enthusiasm for the book, and Larry

Rostant for his pitch-perfect cover art.

And finally, I want to thank each and every person, both online and IRL, who have liked, commented, retweeted, or followed along over the last couple years as *The Ark* came together. You all kept me going and determined to see it through to the end. I sincerely hope you enjoy the finished product, and everything yet to come.

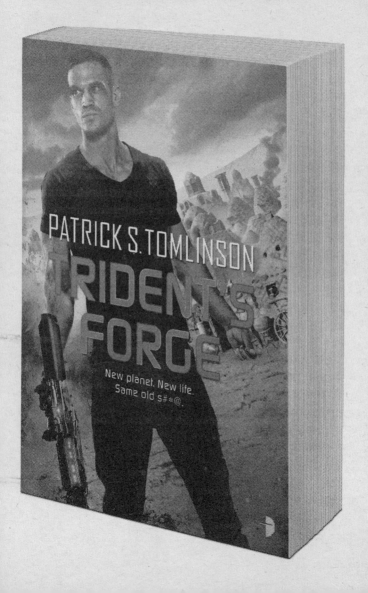